The Pride Unvanquished

Prideland Series: Book 4

Theo Mann

Invisible Publishing Company

Prideland Series

Contents

Chapter 1

Dina Dyer relaxed in the back of the wagon as the ox plodded down the road pulling her closer to the city in the distance. She would become Renfroe's helper once again as soon as this wagon entered the city streets.

She leaned against the boards to enjoy her last few minutes of freedom, but all too soon, a thunderous noise escalated in front of her. She, Sonya, and Alger Wainwright sat up and then stood up in the wagon bed to see what was causing the commotion.

Alger's father Porter reined the ox to a halt and all four passengers watched an explosive battle erupt on the road ahead.

A large group of forty cats advanced up the road leaving the city. Dina didn't see them at first. They made no noise, but as soon as they passed the last buildings, a mob of Children shot out of the bushes from either side of the road and attacked the cats.

Dina only saw twenty Children, but they attacked so fast and with such bloodthirsty fury that they caught the cats off guard.

The Children pounced on one cat each, killed or crippled them, sprang away, and attacked the rest just as fast.

The Children attacked the smallest cats first. This party of cats must have been on its way out to fight Children because it consisted mostly of panthers, jaguars, and pumas.

The Children went after the panthers first. The Children's sudden appearance and speed reduced the number of cats that could fight and that move leveled the playing field.

The Children tumbled over and over with the cats, slashed and tore with brutal venom, and scattered the cats. Dina didn't recognize any of the Children. None of them belonged to the group she'd spent the last three years raising in the jungle.

The battle spread out to cover the whole road. Multiple pairs of cats and Children locked together in deadly combat and tumbled off the road into the fields. A few cats fought their way free and tried to race back to the shelter of the city.

Out of nowhere, another group of Children broke cover behind the battle. It was an exact replay of the scenario Link suggested to Adrian when Adrian first asked Link to train the Children to fight.

The Children waited until the cats tried to retreat and then sprang their trap when the cats least expected it. The retreating cats ran into a fresh pack of Children blocking the only route to safety.

The Children barricaded the cats on the road. The cats tried one more time to retreat, but that only brought them back into the battle.

The Children stalked them down and then attacked with frightening brutality. They overwhelmed the cats in seconds and the same din of tearing, screaming, howling, and snarling drifted on the breeze.

"We can't go this way," Porter murmured. "We'll have to take a different route."

"We're as likely to run into the Children on another road as we are here," Alger remarked.

"That's true, but we can't get through on this one." Porter gathered the reins, slapped them across the ox's back, and turned the wagon around. "We'll have to go to the city another way."

He turned back and the ox started plodding up the road toward the village the passengers had just left. Dina, Sonya, and Alger watched the end of the battle as it got farther and farther away.

"The Children aren't messing around, are they?" Sonya breathed.

"No, they aren't," Dina agreed. "I didn't think they would escalate this war so fast, but I suppose I should have expected it."

"Do you know what they plan to do?" Sonya asked. "Do they plan to take the whole city?"

"I don't know their plans," Dina replied. "Except that they plan to win. They'll do whatever it takes to win."

"What does that mean?" Alger asked. "What does it mean that the Children would win?"

"I don't know," Dina replied. "I don't think any of us knows, not even the Children. I only know they don't plan to back off until......well, I don't know what the Children's victory would look like, but that's what they're going for—total victory."

Sonya sank back down to sit on the wagon bed's rough boards. There was nothing to see, now that the wagon was moving too far away. "Wow. It's incredible. I never thought anything like this would happen."

"None of us did," Dina replied.

"The cats did," Alger pointed out. "The cats knew the Children were a threat. That's why the cats tried to kill them all before this happened."

"The cats didn't decide to kill the Children because the cats thought the Children would rise up and go to war against the Pride," Dina countered. "No one could have foreseen that. The cats decided to eliminate the Children because the cats couldn't find a place for the Children in the Pride. The cats thought the Children undermined the structure between cats and helpers. The cats couldn't understand how to integrate the Children into the Pride, so they decided to get rid of the Children instead."

"Well, it's too late for that now, isn't it," Sonya pointed out. "The Children will never integrate into the Pride now. They don't want to. They wouldn't integrate into the Pride even if the Senate offered them the chance. Would they?"

"No, the Children will never join the Pride," Dina agreed. "Both sides have spilled too much of each other's blood for them to ever trust each other again."

"What if the Pride agrees to leave the Children alone and just let them live out in the jungle by themselves?" Alger asked. "That could work."

Dina made a face. "The Children would be stupid to trust any promise the Pride made about that. The Pride has ruled this planet by being the uncontested dominant species all these centuries. The Children's very existence threatens that. If the Pride agreed to let the Children live out in the jungle by themselves, the Pride would have to admit that the Children won the war, which would undermine the Pride's authority to rule all these people. If an agreement like that held at all, it would break down pretty soon and the Pride would attack again to reestablish the cats' dominance. These are cats we're talking about. They'll always have to establish their dominance no matter who they're dominant over."

The two young people fell silent and Porter didn't interrupt. He steered the wagon halfway back to the village and then turned onto a different road. He drove a long way around his original route before the wagon creaked eastward to head back toward the city.

The passengers rode in silence for another hour, but in a little while, another skirmish broke out in the fields north of the road.

This one started differently. A small group of ten Children happened to be crossing that field. They didn't follow any road and Dina didn't see what they were doing in the open like that.

These Children were just walking along minding their own business. They walked upright and anyone might have mistaken them for people from a distance.

Another party of fifty cats burst out of the city racing for the Children. Dina cringed and prepared herself to watch these cats tear the Children to shreds, but again, the Children attacked with unimaginable, almost sadistic intensity.

Tales of the Children's recent victories may have spread and made these cats more reserved, but Dina didn't see that. From what she saw, the cats simply lacked the Children's savagery. The cats went into the fight more carefully than the Children.

That one fraction of hesitation played against them. The Children launched at the cats in a frenzy of ripping, tearing, and destroying. Their merciless, relentless attitude made the cats even more conservative, which swung the tide farther in the Children's favor.

One large orange-coated man catapulted through the cats' ranks biting, slashing, and killing with no restraint at all. Cats shrank from him and wound up falling victim to other Children moving in from the sides.

Only half the cats tried to engage the Children on their own terms. Even then, any cat standing up to the Children in battle seemed to drive them to new heights of rage and violence.

Three jaguars teamed up on a slight, wispy woman with short, silver-white fur flecked with dark, silver-grey patches. They must have thought they could overpower her with their strength.

They all lunged for her at the same time and she went down underneath them. Dina lost sight of the woman for a second and the jaguars closed together on top of her.

An instant later, the woman erupted in a tornado of counterattacks. The jaguars' close quarters proved their undoing.

She attacked their legs and undersides. She squirmed under one of them, slashed open his belly with her fangs, and brought him to the ground by snapping one of his forelegs.

The second jaguar tried to use her position to clamp down on her throat. She kicked out her foot and sliced him open along the flank.

He spun that way with a fearful roar of pain. In the instant when he turned his head, she cut him deep down the side of the neck and hit the jugular.

That left one jaguar still fighting. He tried to use his weight, tackled on top of her, pinned her arms and legs to the side, and actually succeeded in getting his jaws around her throat.

He might have won, but as usual, her sheer mindless, maniacal energy overcame him. She kicked and slashed her claws so viciously that she cut his side. In the end, she caught one toenail into the muscle of his hind leg and ripped it down deep enough to hit the artery.

He collapsed on top of her, but he still didn't let go of her throat. She kept fighting and struggling until his own weight towed him off her.

The other Children overcame overwhelming numbers the same way—by unrelenting grit, tenacity, and balls-out determination to take any risk to win.

Porter sighed and turned his ox away. "I guess we don't need to see any more of that."

He got the ox moving. The fight remained far enough out in the fields that none of the cats or Children put the road in danger.

He drove past them. The cats and Children remained locked in a battle to the death even by the time he entered the city streets and Dina lost sight of them.

Chapter 2

The city Porter drove his wagon into was nothing like the city Dina had lived in for so long. The helpers' usual buzz of contented subservience and the cats' complacent superiority had evaporated.

Tension throbbed in the air and conflict broke out on all sides. Dina spotted cats driving their helpers out of buildings, helpers getting into fights against each other, and other helpers standing in clusters holding whispered conversations.

"What's wrong?" Dina asked. "Why is everyone so on edge?"

"They're all worried about the Children, of course," Porter replied. "No one knows who to trust anymore. The cats can't keep what the Children are doing completely quiet anymore. Everyone is worried the Children will invade the city and wipe out everyone... .and then there are relations between cats and helpers."

"What do you mean?" Dina asked. "Don't the cats want human helpers anymore?"

"Oh, they want them. They want them a little too much. That's the problem."

He shot her a significant look over his shoulder, but she still didn't completely get what he meant. "Are you saying.....?"

"No one wants to give birth to any more Children," he explained. "Relations are strained—relations that might result in more Children."

He left it at that and didn't explain any further in front of the two young people. He didn't have to.

So the cats and people weren't having sex with each other anymore. None of them wanted to produce any more Children. The situation with the Children who'd already been born was escalating so rapidly anyway.

That was bound to put a crimp in any relationship.....and then she remembered. She was going back to Renfroe's house. She wouldn't have a sexual relationship with him anymore, either.

She hadn't thought of that when she made the decision to come back here to be with him. How would their relationship work without that?

She kept seeing signs of conflict, hostility, and more outright violence between cats and helpers, helpers and helpers, and anxiety and strain on all sides.

Porter drove his wagon through the market, but he didn't stop there. The behavior of cats and people didn't look that much different than all the other times Dina had been here, but a subtle undercurrent of tension threatened to blow the place apart at any moment.

Plenty of people stood around talking here. They didn't talk with the casual certainty she'd seen before.

They waved their hands in agitation, pointed toward different parts of the city, and they stood too close together and talked too fast. They all either talked too loudly or kept their voices low and hushed.

"We won't stop here," Porter decided. "I'll drop you all off. I don't want to leave you here to wait for your benefactors to come and get you."

He drove off into the city's leafy western neighborhoods where manicured gardens and towering shade trees lined the avenues.

He stopped at a stately house a dozen blocks from Renfroe's house. "This is where Alger gets off," Porter announced.

"Whose house is this?" Dina asked.

"It's Hector's and Victor's house," Porter replied. "They share it."

"But......Hector's dead, isn't he?"

"He is, but Victor still lives here." Porter climbed down and Alger scrambled out of the wagon bed.

Porter gripped both of his son's shoulders and looked deep into his eyes. "Remember what we talked about. Do your work and don't give Victor any cause to find fault with you."

Alger nodded, but he looked back into his father's eyes just as deeply. "I will. Don't worry."

Porter pulled his son into a crushing hug. It was one of the very few signs of genuine affection Dina had ever seen from anyone in Prideland.

Even after Porter pushed his son back, he still held Alger at arm's length and gazed into his eyes with unusual intensity. "I'll come see you soon. I'll let you know about anything that happens."

Alger nodded, but his eyes didn't soften nor did he relax. He kept staring into his father's eyes until the last minute. "I'll see you soon, Father."

Porter gripped Alger's shoulders even tighter. He didn't seem to be able to let go, but just then, a grey-haired man strode through the garden gate next to Victor's house.

He wore nice clothes, but he hobbled as though the cuts from the House of Man hurt as much now as they did when he first received them.

"You're the new boy, then?" he snapped when he saw Alger and Porter together. "Well, get inside. There'll be no slacking off here."

Alger gave his father one last look and followed the man into the house without a backward glance.

Porter gazed after him long after Alger disappeared. Dina didn't make a sound and Sonya didn't say anything, either.

How much did Porter understand about the life his son would be subjected to as a helper in this city? At least Porter admitted that the cats had sexual relationships with their human helpers.

Then again, no one could really deny it any longer. The Children offered all the proof anyone needed that it really did happen and had been happening for a long, long time.

Neither Sonya nor Dina did anything to distract Porter. He finally shook himself and turned back to the wagon, but he didn't make eye contact with either of them. He climbed into his seat without saying anything and got the ox moving again.

He drove for a long time in silence until he stopped in front of Fallon's house—Amaryllis's house.

Just for a second when Porter stopped the wagon, Dina spotted someone leaping through the treetops behind the house. The branches swayed and the foliage crashed in a torrent of movement.

She froze when she thought Children might be up there, but it turned out to be cats instead. Five powerful, compact Manx cats raced back and forth through the branches, jumped from tree to tree, and swirled around each other in waves.

They reminded Dina so much of Children that she couldn't take her eyes off them. They vanished into the canopy above the house next door.

Sonya woke Dina from her trance by climbing down from the wagon Dina got down with her. "Are you sure you're going to be okay?" Dina asked.

"I'm sure I'll be fine," Sonya replied. "You don't have to worry about me."

"Do what Porter told Alger," Dina told her. "Keep your head down, do your work, and don't give Amaryllis any reason to find fault with you. She can be a harsh benefactor....."

"How do you know?" Sonya asked.

"She's a Manx," Dina explained. "All the Manx are hard, exacting, and they demand a lot of their helpers. They can also be unforgiving and brutal if anyone disobeys. Just take care of yourself. Renfroe's house is a few blocks from here. I'll try to check on you when I can. If you get into trouble, you can come there and I'll do what I can to help you."

Sonya brightened up and smiled. "Thank you."

That smile didn't put Dina's mind at rest at all. She saw already that Sonya had no idea of the dangers waiting for her here.

Porter might have filled Alger in on what to expect, but no way would Darcy and Alexander do it. They would have painted Sonya a rosy picture of perfect harmony between cats and helpers.

Dina found herself placing both hands on Sonya's shoulders the same way Porter did. Dina didn't want to let the girl go in there—not knowing what Sonya would face.

The time eventually came, though. "I better go," Sonya murmured.

Dina nodded. "Be careful. I'll see you soon."

Sonya walked away and Dina stood on the sidewalk long after Sonya disappeared inside.

Dina had come back from the *Savannah* to prevent this from ever happening again, but she couldn't prevent it. It just kept happening again and again and again.

What did Dina really think she was going to be able to do to stop it? Only the Children could stop it. Sonya was right about that.

Dina tore herself away with a heavy sigh, only to discover Porter watching her from the wagon seat.

She climbed back into the wagon bed, sat down, and he started driving. She knew the streets now. She recognized all the houses around her.

A heavy feeling of inevitability hung over everything. She was going back to Renfroe's house for good or bad.

Porter stopped the wagon by the path leading to the kitchen door. Everything about this place breathed familiarity. The simmering tension and hostility of the city didn't spill over here, but it still clouded the place with an air of something dangerous about to happen.

Dina climbed out of the wagon bed and Porter stepped down, too. He stopped in front of her and stared deep into her eyes, but he didn't grip her shoulders. That would have been too familiar, but his gaze accomplished the same thing.

"I appreciate what you're trying to do," he began. "Thank you."

"I don't know if I can do anything," she replied. "I'll try to see Alger when I can, but I can't promise anything."

"Thank you," he repeated, "for everything."

"I haven't done anything. I don't know if I've ever done anything besides make a giant mess of everything."

"It will work out," he told her. "You'll see."

She sighed again. "I hope you're right. I hope I can find a way to put right what I did wrong. I don't even know *what* I did wrong."

"You'll figure it out. I come into the city pretty often. I'll do what I can to see you and help you. I might be able to bring you information."

She nodded. "I'll try to do the same thing. If I hear anything, I'll tell you."

"Thank you—really. You're doing the right thing."

She looked away and wound up looking at the house. "I'm glad someone thinks so."

"You better go....and I better go." He put out his hand and touched her elbow just once. "Good luck."

"Thanks."

He turned away, got into the wagon seat, and slapped the reins on his ox's back. The wagon wheels creaked and he drove out of sight.

She watched him go with a sinking feeling in her heart. Those three people were the last allies she was likely to see for a while—maybe even a long while—maybe forever. She was going back into the lion's den—or the tiger's den.

The trees along the avenue cast the neighborhood in perpetual shade. She couldn't tell anymore what time it was. It might be twilight or early dawn. It might be any time of the day.

In the silence after the wagon rounded a distant corner, she heard another sound—the creaking of wheels.

She glanced over and spotted the Elite Battalion going into a different garden. They pushed their wheelbarrow in front of them and vanished behind the wall.

That squeaky sound of their wheelbarrow wheel sent a shiver up her spine and she turned away. She was in as much danger now as she had been when she lived at Renfroe's house before.

The factors would keep an eye on her. They would threaten and probably attack her if she set foot out of the house. How did she think she would visit or help anyone?

Chapter 3

Dina pushed open the door to Belinda's kitchen. It looked and smelled exactly the same, but Belinda wasn't in it.

A fire blazed in the fireplace with a cauldron of soup on the hook over the flames. A collection of kitchen knives stuck out of the heavy wooden table.

Cheeses, haunches of meat, bundles of herbs, and nets of root vegetables hung from the ceiling.

Dina crossed the swept flagstone floor and pulled open the door leading from the kitchen to the rest of the house. The whole house sounded empty and silent.

She inched out into the long corridor stretching to the far end of the house. The bedroom she once shared with Renfroe was down there. Did he still sleep in it? She would have been very surprised if he did.

The portico stood open to the garden outside. The fountain played its soft music in the calm silence, but Renfroe wasn't out there, either. He was probably out hunting or conducting Senate business.

She considered where to go and what to do. She couldn't move back into this house without facing him and explaining herself.

She took one more step toward the garden. She would sit by the fountain the way she used to. He was bound to find her there. Then she could talk to him—about everything.

She advanced another yard and heard another fire crackling in the parlor to one side. She didn't think to check there, and when she did, she spotted him stretched out on the carpet in front of the blaze.

He faced the flames, so he had his back to her. He didn't see her. The flames framed his coat and made his body look extra long, big, and powerful.

She tiptoed a few inches closer and one of his ears swiveled backward. She continued to the threshold and he rotated his head around to pierce her with those eyes.

She trembled at the sight of him—not because she was afraid of him.

Her mind reeled when she realized for the thousandth time how much Adrian resembled Renfroe. The eyes were the same. No wonder Adrian had become the Children's leader. He could look straight through anyone exactly the same way his father did.

She stopped in the doorway and looked down at him. It didn't seem possible that he didn't know about Adrian and Iona.

They'd encompassed Dina's whole life for three years. She found it next to impossible to believe there could be anyone anywhere who didn't know about them, especially not someone as intimately involved with them as their own father.

"So you've come back to me, Dina," he rumbled in that deep, chesty undertone of his. "I didn't think you would."

"I made you a promise," she replied. "I'm here to keep it."

He swiveled one of his ears away. "And our Children? Are they still alive out there in the jungle? Are they living independently now?"

Dina nodded. "They're fully mature now. They have their own lives."

He cocked his head to one side to study her. "Are they involved in this Children's rebellion?"

"Yes, they are."

"Come in and tell me about them." He turned back to gaze into the fire. "I want to know everything about them."

She advanced into the room and walked around to one side. She saw herself keeping a safe distance from him. She couldn't understand why. Coming back here would lead them to all kinds of intimacies. Why should she avoid him?

She squatted down next to him and finally gave in and sat down crosslegged on the carpet.

"Start by telling me their names," he began without looking away from the flames.

"Their names are Adrian and Iona," she replied. "Adrian is older....and he resembles you. He has your eyes....and your voice.....and most of your coloring."

Renfroe looked over at her and inclined his head to one side when he examined her. "That is interesting. And yet he walks upright like a human. Is that right? The Children have human features and human stature....but they have fur and pointed ears."

"They have the teeth and claws of cats," Dina replied. "They run on all fours when they want to move fast....and they move through the trees like cats. I stopped by Amaryllis's house just now on the way here. There were cats racing through the treetops there. The Children do that. They travel that way."

"Why did you go to Amaryllis's house? She harbors a particular hatred for you. Did you know that?"

Dina looked away and gazed into the flames to avoid his eyes. "Yes, I know. I didn't see her. I just stopped outside on the street. The wagon that brought me here delivered a different helper to her house. That's the only reason I went there."

"Ah, I see," he growled and sprawled back on the carpet. He rested his cheek on it so he could see the fire and her at the same time. "Tell me more about our Children. What is Iona like?"

"She's tall—statuesque, you might say. She has very pale, gold-white fur with white stripes. She's extremely beautiful—and very warlike. All the Children are."

"So I hear," he growled. "I haven't gone out to meet them yet."

"Count your blessings," she muttered. "You don't want to go out to meet them."

"You're right. I don't, but I'm not likely to. The other cats won't let me."

She spun around. "They won't? Why not?"

"They don't trust me due to my long-standing position of sympathy for the Children."

"Is that still a problem? So the Senate still won't listen to you?"

"I am no longer a senator, Dina. The Senate drove me out a long time ago."

Her jaw dropped and she stared at the side of his face. Why did this come as such a surprise?

She thought he'd always be a senator. She thought the other cats respected him enough to give him that position of honor even when he took a stand they didn't like.

Their tolerance must have passed its limit. He'd been pushing it for years and not just with his position on the Children. The other cats had already forced him to comply with their wishes even when Dina lived here before.

He glanced over, saw her gawking at him, and twitched one ear. "Go on, Dina. Tell me more about the Children."

She tore her eyes away. "There isn't a lot more to tell. They grew up, they became independent, and then they naturally started fighting back against the cats. The Children started hunting any random cats they found in their territory...."

"Their territory!" he interrupted. "The Children established territory?"

"They started out by establishing a buffer zone around our canton. They would hunt down any cat that trespassed inside this zone....and then Adrian......"

She realized a second too late that she probably shouldn't have told Renfroe that much, but it was too late.

She threw caution aside. What difference did it make if he found out that his son was the leader of the Children's war? Renfroe was bound to find out sooner or later. Keeping the information from him would only cause problems between him and her in the future.

"Then Adrian did what?" he growled. "What did Adrian do then?"

She took a deep breath. "He decided to take it to the next level and go after the hunting parties the Pride sent to kill Children. He decided to go on the offensive and attack the cats *before* they entered his territory."

"*His* territory!" Renfroe husked. "Are you saying....?"

"He's their leader. He's the leader of the Children. I guess it was about a year ago when he decided to go to all-out war against the Pride. He realized that he basically already was in a war since the Pride was trying to annihilate all the Children anyway. He realized that he only had two options—either the cats win or the Children win. Now he's determined to win at any cost."

Renfroe turned back to the fire and Dina let the silence linger. How surreal it felt to be sitting in this parlor and talking to him like no time had passed at all—but it had passed. So much had changed in the last three years.

It must have only changed for her, though. He seemed the same in every way she could imagine.

"Did you do anything to dissuade our Children from going to war against the Pride?" he finally growled. "Did you try to stop our Children from attacking cats—and from launching this war?"

"No, I didn't try to dissuade them. The other parents did, but we supported them."

"Who is we?" he demanded.

She opened her mouth to answer and stopped herself. Telling Renfroe about Adrian was one thing.

She didn't really plan in advance what she would tell Renfroe about Link. If anything, she planned to keep Link to herself. Renfroe didn't need to know about that.

Now she realized she had to come clean about Link, too. Keeping any secret from Renfroe would only lead to disaster. Maybe coming back here in the first place would lead to disaster, but she had to tell him.

"There was a man out there—at the canton," she began. "We loved each other....and we raised our Children together. He raised five of his nieces and nephews—his sister's Children—and he helped me raise......our Children."

She didn't tell him about all the other Children she raised—Tania's Children, Tom's Children, Osiris's Children, Aurora Hellion's Children, and even Fallon's Children. Renfroe definitely didn't need to know about that.

"So you loved this man.....?" Renfroe rumbled. "And he raised my Children with you? So our Children consider this man their father?"

Dina squirmed in her seat. "Yes, they do."

"Where is this man now? Is he out there fighting the Children's war with them? What does this man think of you coming back here to me?"

"He doesn't know. He's dead."

Renfroe didn't answer for a long time. So this was the tension that permeated the whole city—this right here.

The peace and understanding between cats and helpers had been irrevocably shattered—not by the Children's war but by the Children themselves. Their very existence destroyed the understanding.

They would have destroyed the Pride and its understanding with their helpers even if the Children never raised a claw against the Pride.

"I suppose what you really mean to say is that you never would have come back to me at all if this man was still alive," Renfroe growled even lower.

"The Children didn't want me to come back. They wanted me to stay out there and fight the war with them."

"Why did you come back, then?" he demanded. "Why are you really here?"

"I'm here because I made a promise to come back......." She trailed off. She could have said more, but the words got stuck in her throat.

She could have said that she didn't feel she belonged anywhere without Link, but that would have been saying to same thing Renfroe just said. She never would have come back to this city if Link had lived.

She also didn't remind Renfroe of his threat to kill her Children and keep her as a prisoner for the rest of her life if she didn't give her promise.

She could have ignored that promise and seen it for what it was—a sign that he was her captor instead of the lover he pretended to be.

She didn't remind him of that, though.

He kept staring into the flames. "It is curious how things have changed. Nothing can ever go back to the way things were. I'm not even sure anymore why I asked you to make that promise. It seems so pointless now—with the way things are going."

"Do you mean the part about the cats and helpers not being able to share sexual relationships? Is that what you mean?"

"It goes deeper than that. The sexual relationship was just a symptom of something much deeper. We cats used the sexual relationship to bind our helpers to us and to make them more fit for service. I don't think anyone anticipated that it would bind them as tightly as it did. Now we find ourselves bound in a relationship we can't get out of."

"I noticed that on the way into town," she replied. "Everything about the understanding seems to be gone."

"Indeed," he growled. "That is precisely what it is. The understanding is gone. I suppose we always thought we could rule this planet with impunity. Now we find that our own dominance is our undoing."

"So what is the Pride going to do about it?" she asked.

"It is as I told you before. No one can decide what to do about it. Some want to hysterically continue slaughtering Children even in the face of evidence that they can't anymore. Some want to negotiate peace with the Children on condition that they stay in their own territory in the jungle....."

"That won't work," she interrupted.

"I know it won't work. Anyone with a brain can see it won't work. The Children have gone too far...."

"How can you say that? The cats started this war. The cats were the ones who sent hunting parties into the jungle to track the Children down. The cats would have wiped out every living Child on the planet if the Pride had its way."

His head snapped around. "What are they planning to do? What do the Children plan to do with this war? How far are they prepared to go?"

She stiffened. "How should I know what they plan to do? I'm here and they're out there."

"You've been with them for three years. You must know something about what they plan to do."

"I already told you. They plan to wage war against the Pride and win. Adrian will do anything to win. He has to. The Pride has put him in a position where he has no choice."

"I mean specifically," Renfroe insisted. "Does he plan to invade the city and put every helper to the sword? Does he plan to invade the city and put every cat to the sword? What are his plans?"

Dina gaped at him with her jaw on the carpet. "I am not going to give you information on Adrian's plans! I didn't come back here to betray him."

"I'm not asking you to betray him," Renfroe countered. "I might be his only ally in this whole city—or maybe in the whole Pride."

Dina shut her mouth and turned away with an effort. "You aren't."

"If you know something, you could be saving millions of lives by telling me."

"I'm not going to tell you anything about Adrian's plans—and I don't know anything about his plans, anyway. He and Iona are furious that I came back here. They think I betrayed their cause and that I'm more loyal to the Pride than I am to them. They say I'm a slave and they'll never believe another word I saw as long as I live."

He sighed and stretched out again. "That is unfortunate."

She opened her mouth to say something else, but at that moment, Belinda strode down the corridor carrying a leg of some dead animal on a wooden plank.

She turned to enter the parlor and stopped dead on the threshold when she saw Dina sitting there. Belinda's features went through a rapid series of confused expressions from fury to terror to disgust to sneering triumph.

"You can bring the food in, Belinda," Renfroe rumbled. "You can see that Dina is back, so you can continue to prepare meals for her and tend to her needs the way you did before she left—and you'll need to bring her another set of clothes. Those will never do."

He wrinkled his nose at her clothes and she realized she was still wearing the same handmade clothes from the canton. She looked like the slag she was.

Belinda still took at least a minute to work up the courage to enter the parlor. When she did, she set the plank in front of Renfroe and left without a word.

"I imagine you'll have the same problems as before," he grumbled. "Nothing has changed in that respect."

"Does anyone know you let me leave?" she murmured.

"No, they don't know, but then again, no one asked about why you suddenly disappeared. I understand one of your companions from the *Savannah* disappeared at the same time—one of Khalid's helpers."

Dina looked away. "Yes, she did. She's out there living at one of the other cantons."

"Khalid assumes she was pregnant and ran away to save her own life. He swears that he'll kill his own Children if he ever finds them."

"I wish him all the best with that," she muttered. "He's going to get a rude surprise if he ever tries to threaten them."

He cocked his head again. "Do you know his Children?"

"I more than know them. I raised them. He has three sons who are as deadly and ruthless as he is—maybe more so. He wouldn't be able to land a scratch on one of them, much less all three."

Renfroe looked back into the fire with a deep sigh. "I suppose it will be like that for all of us. I suppose Adrian is bigger and stronger than I am now, too."

"He isn't bigger. He's just extremely ferocious and determined. The Children aren't governed by anything—and I mean nothing. They don't understand restraint and caution. They do what they have to do and nothing stops them. They're stubborn, determined, and tenacious. What they lack in size and strength, they make up for in raw lunatic, merciless aggression. They're far more aggressive than any cat."

"I have heard that much as well," he growled. "It takes a lot to convince any cat to go out against them."

"Really? Wow," she breathed.

"I doubt any cat would go out against them if we hadn't worked ourselves into a situation where we have to. Our backs are against the wall and now we have no choice. There are some whom I'm sure would come around to my way of thinking and try to make peace with the Children...."

"The Children will never make peace," she interrupted. "Never."

"I realize that." He twisted his head around to scrutinize her. "Tell me. Is Adrian as aggressive as you say? Is he as merciless and tenacious as you say all the Children are?"

She nodded. "Absolutely. He's the one....." She stopped herself again from telling him that Adrian was the one who killed Kaido Hellion—and the one who killed Hector.

Renfroe chuckled under his breath. "That's good. I'm proud of him. I would like to meet him."

"Something tells me that wouldn't be such a good idea."

He chuckled even more. "Perhaps you're right."

Chapter 4

Renfroe twisted his head sideways and gnawed the bone between his back teeth. He'd already finished all the meat.

He gave it up, pushed the bone away with his nose, and licked his chops with exaggerated satisfaction before he flopped back down on the carpet.

Dina finished sipping the soup Belinda had given her and then Dina set the bowl aside. "Thank you for your hospitality," she told him. "I wasn't sure what kind of reception I would get when I came back."

"Why wouldn't I welcome you?" he asked. "I asked you to come back. This is your home. It always will be."

"You said you didn't expect me to come back."

"I expected you to come back after the first year when the Children became mature. When you didn't, I assumed you had broken your promise and decided to stay in the cantons."

"The Children didn't mature until this year—at least not fully mature."

"No?" He cocked his head to study her. "That is interesting. I didn't expect that."

"I suppose none of us really knew what to expect when it came to how long it would take for them to grow up. I gauged their development against human development. By the end of the first year, they looked like ten-year-old human children, but the Children acted differently than human Children."

"In what way?"

"Apart from their ability to climb, run, jump, and their appetite for raw meat? They were more intelligent—more advanced mentally. Their thinking was much more mature, but their bodies didn't catch up until later. By the end of the second year, they looked like they were about fifteen or sixteen in equivalent human years. It wasn't until this year that I definitely felt like they were fully adult—but I didn't see them in between."

"How do you mean? Why didn't you see them?"

"They left for most of the second year. They went out on their own and established their own society. Link......" She had to check herself before she summoned the courage to talk about him. "That was the man who helped me raise them. He started to train them to fight.....and then they left for a long time and developed what he taught them into their own unique fighting style—which is what they're using now. They combined it all together into something completely different—something none of us could have anticipated. That's basically the lesson I've taken away from all of this—that none of us can anticipate anything the Children do. They're going to come up with something none of us will see coming."

He continued to stare into the flames. "Interesting. The entire Children phenomenon is so interesting. I would love to study it in more depth, but I don't suppose any of us will have any chance of that."

"I've probably made more of a study of it than anyone else and I still don't understand it. They're completely unique. That's all I can say about them."

"I would like to talk to them and get to know them. It's one of my great regrets that I'll never have a chance to."

"You did what you could to direct the Pride onto a different course."

He sighed. "Indeed I did."

He sat staring into the flames in silence. She didn't break that silence. Whatever might happen between them, she couldn't anticipate that, either. Their relationship had morphed into something she didn't recognize.

Without warning, he stood up, took three long paces toward her, and rubbed his face against the side of her head. He rubbed hard enough almost to knock her over.

He ran his cheek and then his neck across the side of her head and down the length of his body. He growled at her the way he used to and flicked his tail.

That sound and the feeling of his body rubbing against her brought back so many memories—not all of them good ones.

Her stomach tightened when she realized what he was trying to tell her. "Come to our bedroom with me, Dina," he rumbled. "You've been away too long. I've missed you."

"We can't.....do that," she told him. "You know that."

"You can still come with me to our room," he growled. "You are my companion more than anything else. We can still spend the night together."

He strutted around to her other side, shoved his forehead against her ear, and then slid his face, head, and neck down the side of her face to her neck.

Her hand flew to his head, but he'd always been too strong for her to stop him from doing anything.

He growled again. That growl communicated so much buried sexual desire that her nerves tightened.

She felt herself getting drawn into something she couldn't get out of. "Promise me... ..we won't do it....."

He gave an exasperated groan and turned away. "You have an uncanny ability to ruin my mood, Dina," he snarled.

"You know we can't do it," she countered. "We can't risk me getting pregnant again."

He stopped five feet away, sat down, and turned around to glare at her. "I am aware of that, Dina. You don't need to throw it in my face just when I'm trying to get close to you."

"It sure sounded like you were trying to do more than that."

He gasped again, got to his feet, and stalked over to the door. "Come along. It's getting late and I'm tired. We're going to bed."

He walked out and vanished into the dark house. She didn't realize how late it had gotten until she passed the portico. The fountain tinkled in the moonlight. It looked peaceful and inviting out there in the darkness, but it didn't solve any of Prideland's most pressing problems.

She didn't see Renfroe anywhere. He'd already evaporated into the shadows.

She tiptoed down the corridor to her old room—the bedroom she and Renfroe used to share. Someone had lit the lamp on the table. Golden, glowing light flooded the room.

A thick layer of dust covered everything including the bedding on the majestic four-poster canopy bed. As she suspected, no one had set foot in here since she left.

Renfroe sat in the doorway waiting for her. "I'm sure Belinda will clean the room tomorrow," he purred.

"It's fine the way it is," she replied. "I'll just shake the dust out of the bedspread and it will be good enough."

She advanced into the room, pulled the bedspread off the bed, took it out into the garden patio outside this room, and shook all the dust out of the bedspread. It took a long time before she got it clean enough to take it back inside.

She spread it on the bed and sat down on the mattress to take her shoes off. Renfroe jumped onto the bed behind her and started rubbing his face and head against any part of her body he could reach.

He distracted her and then shoved his head, neck, and shoulders between her chest and her arms. He made it impossible for her to do anything.

She laughed and tried to push him away, but he took that as a sign of encouragement and rubbed her even harder. He rubbed his face and cheeks all over her face and got his fur in her eyes.

He eventually pushed so hard that he really did knock her over. He pushed her down on the mattress, and before she even realized what he was doing, he seized her with his teeth.

He clamped onto her neck, but not in a killing bite. He bit down on the crease where her neck met her shoulder—just enough to make her freeze and to hold her down on the bed.

He rotated his body on top of her so fast that she didn't understand until he was already on top of her. He flexed his body to arch his pelvis forward and he let out a very different kind of growl—a threatening growl to warn her to keep still.

She couldn't mistake that he was trying to do it with her because she still had all her clothes on. She could never misunderstand what he was doing, either. He was staking his dominance over her the way he used to. He might not be able to go through with the act itself, but he used this to make it mean as much as if he did.

That growl came from deep inside his chest. It vibrated through her bones and his whole body shuddered with unstoppable tension. He angled his pelvis into her again and again and then spasmed once before he flopped onto the mattress next to her with a groan.

"It isn't the same," he grumbled and shut his eyes on the pillow with a broken sigh. "It will never be the same."

She rolled onto her side and draped her arm over his shoulders. "We can still spend the night together—as companions."

"I don't want you as a companion," he snarled.

She studied his face at close range. Lying like this with her arm around him—it woke her old affection for him. She ran her fingers through the thick fur on the side of his face and then on the back of his neck.

That motion brought back memories of the Children running their fingers through each other's fur, Iona rubbing and scratching the back of Karim's neck, and Naia running her fingers over Adrian's head when he rested it in her lap.

"You would be amazed how much you look like Adrian," she murmured, "or how much Adrian looks like you. It's a little scary."

"Tell me more about them," he growled without opening his eyes. "Tell me everything."

"Well.....they're married."

He stiffened and his eyes snapped open, but he didn't look at her. "They're what?"

"They're married. The Children have all pair-bonded with each other. They're all coupled off into pairs."

"Are Adrian and Iona both married?"

"Yes."

He growled again and shut his eyes. "If they develop the ability to reproduce, we're all in trouble."

"I hate to be the one to tell you this, but we're already in trouble."

He snorted and then chuckled. "That's putting it mildly. I've considered this at length and there doesn't seem to be any solution."

"I know," she murmured.

"Then I suppose we just have to wait and see what the Children do. If they decide to invade the city and mop the floor with us, no one will be able to stop them."

"What about just stopping all hostilities? What if the cats just stop sending anyone out to fight the Children? What if the cats just back off completely? I'm sure the Children would do the same thing. They don't want to fight anyone who doesn't at least defend themselves."

"The Pride will never agree to that. It's as I've told you so many times. No one can tell any cat what to do. If some cat wants to go out and fight the Children, he does it regardless of whether anyone else thinks it's a good idea."

"So who's in the Senate, now that you're gone? Who's the new Chairman?"

"Kaido Hellion took over after me, but he's dead now. I haven't gone back to the Senate since they removed me, so I don't know who they elected to replace Kaido."

"Are Elyse and Osiris still senators?"

"As far as I know. I don't keep up with Senate business anymore. It means I have a lot more time to hunt by myself—which is quite nice."

"You said you planned to back off from politics," she reminded him. "I guess now you're doing it."

"I planned to back off from politics so I could spend more time with you," he countered. "You've been gone for so long and I've been alone."

She almost told him she was sorry for not coming back sooner, but she decided not to say that. She wasn't sorry. Saying so would come across as disingenuous because it was. She didn't want to restart her life with him by lying to him.

She waited for him to say something else, but he didn't. He remained silent for a long time and then his breathing started to lengthen. He fell asleep.

She lay next to him without moving while she studied his face. She kept seeing Adrian in Renfroe and Renfroe in Adrian. They merged and became two sides of the same person.

Renfroe had always been kind to her, but that underlayer of danger and pure killing power always lurked beneath the surface.

It was the other way around with Adrian. He wore the danger and killing power on the outside where everyone could see it. He never made any effort to hide it.

The kindness, softness, and the need for a female to run her fingers through his fur—he hid that side of himself hidden underneath.

He only showed it to one person in the world—the female he chose to be his wife. No one else could get anywhere near him.

Chapter 5

Dina woke up when Renfroe shifted on the mattress. He growled under his breath, sneezed the dust out of his nostrils, and sat up with a grumble. "I must tell Belinda to clean this room. It's disgusting."

Dina took her arm off his shoulders and sat up, too. "Do you have plans for the day?"

"Osiris has asked to see me," he growled. "Heaven only knows why."

"Do you see the other senators much—now that you're out of it?"

"On occasion. I suppose word must have spread all over town by now that you're back—ever since Belinda saw you in the parlor last night. No one can keep a secret in this city—not that your presence is a secret."

She would have liked to question him further—mainly about Osiris. She'd never been certain of his loyalties, but she had spent the last three years raising his Children. Maybe he was more of an ally than she thought—or a potential ally.

She wouldn't know until she talked to him and she wouldn't be able to do that with Renfroe around.

She couldn't ask Renfroe to take her to Osiris's house anyway—and she wouldn't want to broach the subject with Osiris. He might not be an ally. Talking to him about anything would tip her hand unnecessarily.

Renfroe sprang off the bed and strode toward the door. "Come along, Dina. We'll have breakfast in the garden. We can't eat in here until Belinda cleans the room."

She followed him outside. The house looked different in daylight—and yet not different. All the statues, vases of flowers, windows and doors—everything was in the same places. Even the garden smelled the same.

She sat down on the edge of the fountain in her old place. Renfroe sat on the ground next to her and started licking his paw with elaborate care.

She found herself grinning at him and all his little ways. Everything about him seemed so familiar.

"It is good to have you back, Dina," he growled. "Life was so boring without you."

She snorted. "That could be a compliment or an insult."

He looked up. "I meant it as a compliment."

"I know. I'm just fooling around."

She shut her mouth when Belinda came out of the house. She carried a small table with Dina's breakfast on it and Belinda set the table next to Dina's seat.

Then Belinda went back inside and came back with a young fell deer fawn. It was still alive and bleated pitifully in Belinda's arms.

She set it down on its feet in front of Renfroe and let go. The fawn shot away into the garden and Renfroe sprang after it to run it down.

The fawn dodged a few times. Renfroe's claws scored deep grooves in the lawn before he finally pounced on it, pinned it down with his paws, and crunched his massive jaws across its back.

The fawn gave one last screech of pain and then wilted in his mouth. He crouched there on his stomach adjusting his grip on it before he got to his feet and strutted back to the fountain with the fawn's body flapping in his jaws.

He put it down, gave Dina one pointed look, and started eating. She turned to the table. Getting used to all this was going to be interesting.

He ripped the fawn's body open, tore off a section of the meat, and talked with his mouth full. "What are *your* plans for the day, Dina?"

"I don't have any plans for the day. I didn't make any plans until after I saw you and knew where we stood."

"Perhaps it would be best if you simply relax here and settle in—take a bath—change your clothes—all of that," he went on. "It may also hold some value to understand what we can expect from Buck and Belinda. Whatever they plan to do, I'm sure they'll show their hands today."

Dina froze with her mouthful. Buck and Belinda. Dina had forgotten about them.

She started eating again with an effort. She would have to deal with them one way or the other.

Renfroe was right. They would show their hands as soon as Renfroe turned his back on her.

She hadn't been safe outside the house before she left. The situation was likely to get even worse now.

She didn't say anything else while they finished eating. Renfroe left the fawn's bones and entrails lying on the pavement when he stood up, snorted a few tufts of fur out of his nose, and licked his lips. "I must be going, Dina dear. I will see you later."

He stalked over to her, put his head in her lap just long enough for her to rub his neck, and then he walked off into the garden and vanished behind the bushes.

She finished eating, but his last words wouldn't stop ringing in her ears. Buck and Belinda.

Belinda had helped Dina hide the Auroras in this house. That didn't make Belinda any less dangerous and that was saying nothing about Buck. He and his fellow factors would try everything to kill Dina the way they tried before.

Dina might be able to blackmail Belinda into keeping her distance. Maybe Belinda already planned to do that.

Then again, Belinda might be the one to try to kill Dina. That would earn Belinda some credit with the factors. Belinda might want to strike a blow for the Pride.

Dina glanced around the garden with new eyes. It had always been a source of tranquility and refuge for her, but not anymore.

She would have to be ready to defend herself at any moment no matter where she went, even in this house.

She didn't see anything out here that she could use as a weapon. She would have to change that. As usual, she couldn't just barge into Belinda's kitchen, take one of the butcher knives, and start carrying it around on her person.

Dina stayed sitting where she was and deliberately took her time finishing her meal. The factors could be watching her right now.

She would have to assume from now on that they were watching her every move. They would keep her under constant surveillance for any opportunity to attack her when Renfroe wasn't looking.

She left the table sitting by the fountain and strolled through the garden. She admired its beauty and vibrant growth.

The tree lizards looked especially brilliant here. They never looked this stunning in the jungle. The sunshine didn't catch the iridescent colors of their scales. The jungle canopy always cast the tree lizards in shadow and made them look dull and ugly.

She meandered between the rows of shrubs and trees until she spotted Buck's tool shed. It sat in the garden's back corner opposite Renfroe's sandbox.

Dina stopped at a distance from the shed and stared at it. Buck kept shovels, rakes, machetes, and other tools in there. She would be able to use any of them as weapons.

The problem would be to position them in places where she would be able to get to them at the right time. She couldn't just walk over there, take out a machete, and stash it near the fountain. Buck would notice that.

She continued her walk through the garden and subtly made her way back to the house. Belinda had removed the table from the courtyard and scrubbed the fawn's blood off the paving stones.

Once Dina got inside, she wandered through all its rooms and evaluated each one the same way.

The parlor was easy. The poker by the fireplace offered a perfect weapon she could grab whenever she needed it, but that was the only one.

She would have to be careful and work methodically to acquire weapons and plant them in strategic places. Belinda's thorough housekeeping would present another problem—an even bigger problem. Belinda knew this whole house and went over it with a fine-toothed comb every day.

Dina headed for the bedroom, but she backed off when she discovered Belinda in there cleaning it.

Dina returned to the fountain and sat there waiting for Belinda to finish. Would it always be like this—the two of them avoiding each other at all costs?

Dina should be the one to cross that divide, but she decided not to do it today. She spent the time thinking of ways to get her hands on some weapons without anyone finding out.

She couldn't ask any other helper to get them for her. She didn't want to put anyone else in danger—any more danger than they were all already in.

She even considered sneaking into the neighboring houses and stealing some knives out of the kitchen or tools out of their garden sheds. She wouldn't be able to do that if the factors were watching her.

She stayed where she was until she heard Belinda go back to the kitchen. Then Dina went down the corridor to the bedroom.

Belinda had dusted the room, cleaned the carpets, and changed all the bedding. She'd also laid out one of the drab knee-length tunics that all helpers wore.

Dina was still standing there staring at those clothes when Belinda walked in. She must not have realized Dina was back in here because Belinda reared back in alarm when she saw Dina standing by the bed.

Belinda gave a little cry of surprise and then, inevitably, the two women came face to face with each other.

Dina didn't know what to say and Belinda didn't say anything, either. They regarded each other and Dina read all her own mixed emotions on Belinda's face.

Dina finally found her voice enough to say, "Hello, Belinda."

Belinda jolted that Dina actually had the nerve to speak to her. Belinda went through multiple facial contortions and finally waved her hand at nothing. "Renfroe....said he... ..wants you to take a bath."

Dina grimaced. "I know. He told me."

"You can....." Belinda made a few different hand gestures that Dina didn't understand. "I usually.....take baths in the kitchen. You can.....come down there......You can do it there."

"Oh. Okay. Thank you."

Belinda darted past Dina and snatched the clothes off the bed, but Belinda made sure to keep clear of Dina so there was no chance the two women might accidentally bump into each other.

Belinda cast a wary glance in Dina's direction when Belinda got too close. Belinda's eyes sliced in Dina's direction as if Belinda actually expected Dina to attack her or something.

Belinda raced out of the bedroom and Dina followed her back to the kitchen. Belinda had pushed the wooden table aside and set up an enormous wooden tub in the middle of the room.

She'd already half-filled it with hot water, and when Dina walked in, Belinda laid the clothes on the table, lifted the cauldron of boiling water off the fire, and tipped it into the tub, too.

Then she went back and forth adding buckets of cold water to make the tub the right temperature, testing the water with her fingertips, and rushing here and there.

She brought out a towel and a bar of soap, put them on the table, too, and then hurried away without a word.

Dina watched the procedure from a safe distance. She would have liked to help Belinda, but too much water had passed under the bridge for that. She and Belinda would never be friends—which was a shame because they were the only two people in this house.

Dina suffered the same pang of regret that she couldn't establish some kind of rapport with Belinda. It would have been nice if they could have connected and given each other something, even if it was just company and conversation. That would have been nicer than avoiding each other like this.

Dina would never be able to overcome that barrier now. She tried to put it out of her mind while she took off her old clothes from the canton and stepped into the tub.

She couldn't put it out of her mind entirely, though. Belinda was more than just a piece of furniture in this house that Dina could ignore and pretend didn't exist.

Belinda was an enemy.....or was she? That was the problem. Dina didn't know what Belinda was. Not knowing made her harder to deal with than an outright enemy like Buck.

Dina took her bath, washed her hair, and changed into the helper's attire that Belinda laid out for her.

Dina faced another challenge when it came time to do something with her old clothes from the canton. She should have gotten rid of them, but she couldn't do that.

She stood by the table fingering the leather and homespun fabric. She didn't want to get rid of them. She wanted to keep them for when the time came to put them back on and go out to the jungle.

She didn't realize until right now that she intended to go out to the jungle again—and not just to visit. She intended to go back there for good—someday.

Had she been harboring that plan in her mind all along? Did she really plan to come back to the city on a temporary basis—until when?

She hadn't been thinking about that at all, but it all became clear to her when she touched and looked at her clothes.

This helper's outfit was something like a disguise. It wasn't her. It was a façade to cover up the real her—which was these jungle clothes. Her real self—her real life—lay out in the jungle.

The Children had been right about that, but she did have to come to the city. She just didn't know why yet.

Was it Renfroe? Was Adrian right about her coming back for Renfroe?

If that was true, she would have discarded these clothes without a thought. She would have been happy to stay with him forever, but she wouldn't do that.

These clothes—she would put them on again, and when she did, she wouldn't take them off. She would take off this helper's disguise, resume her real identity as a slag from the jungle—one of the Children's people—and she would reveal her true nature to the world without hiding or regretting it at all.

She had to work fast to stop Belinda from realizing that Dina was keeping these clothes. Belinda would want to dispose of them as quickly as possible. She'd want to eliminate any evidence that Dina ever had been a slag from the jungle.

Dina got busy, folded the clothes, and carried them out of the kitchen before Belinda came back. Dina took the clothes back to her own bedroom, checked once, and then pushed the pile of clothes under the mattress.

She was just standing up with her heart pounding in her chest when she spotted Buck out in the garden. He walked with his old stooped, shuffling step. He kept his eyes on the ground and crossed the garden beyond the courtyard.

He didn't see her stash her old clothes under the mattress, but his hunched posture and lifeless gaze didn't fool her anymore.

She lost sight of him, but seeing him drove home the point. The factors weren't just lurking beyond the walls and waiting for a chance to catch her unprotected. They were right here inside this house.

Chapter 6

Renfroe returned by mid-morning. He strutted out of the garden and found Dina sitting at the fountain.

He took one look at her clothes and sighed. "So you're a helper again. That's good."

"How did your meeting with Osiris go?" she asked. "What did he want to see you about?"

"About you, as it happens. He asked me a million questions about you, what you've been doing, where you've been, and why you came back here."

"What did you tell him?"

"I told him everything you told me last night. He's still in the Senate, so I assume he wants to know for that reason. He and the Senate want any information they can get about the Children's origins and activities."

"Did you tell him that Adrian is your son? So the Pride knows now that I got pregnant from you and ran away to have our Children in the jungle?"

"They don't know I let you go on purpose," he replied. "I let Osiris believe that you ran away on your own."

"Don't they think it's odd that you're taking me back and not reducing me as a punishment?"

"I don't have a clue what they think and I don't really care. If I had to guess, I'd say they probably think I'm so soft on you that I plan to let it slide because I'm so delighted to have you back. They think I'm so foolishly sentimental that I can't enforce order in my own house."

She laughed. "Thank you. That's really sweet."

"I won't say it isn't true." He put his head in her lap again. "Even being away from you for a few hours is a torture."

"I'm sorry to say this, but I was wondering if you'd be willing to do it again."

"Do what again?"

"Let me go again—not to the jungle, but just around the city. I was wondering if you'd let me go out by myself."

"You shouldn't do that, Dina. You know it isn't safe."

"I didn't come back here to make myself a prisoner in this house. There are people in this city that I want to visit and I want to start living a normal life—as normal as I can. I want to go visit them—if you'll let me."

"I can go with you if you want to visit people. I can protect you from anyone who tries to attack you."

"That won't work. You escorting me everywhere will only reinforce that I'm too protected to travel on my own. If I move around the city by myself, everyone will eventually get used to it and they'll accept me back into normal society."

"Don't be so sure about that," he growled. "They'll never forget. They'll visit you at the least and possibly reduce you at the worst. I couldn't let that happen."

She fell silent for a minute and then asked, "So you won't let me go?"

He sighed, took his head out of her lap, and turned his head away. "I must be a sentimental old fool. I could never deny you anything and you're as headstrong as you ever were. You'll keep pining over it until I let you go, so you might as well go. Just be careful."

"I will." She slipped her arms around his neck. "Thank you. This means a lot to me."

"I know it does," he growled. "So when do you plan to go? I suppose you plan to go today when we've only just reunited."

"I don't have to go today. I can wait until you have something else to do. That way, you aren't waiting here alone for me to come back."

"I shouldn't let you go at all," he grumbled. "I enjoy coming home when I know you'll be waiting for me. If you go, you may never come back."

"I will come back. I promise."

"Wait a little while, at least. Don't go now."

"I wasn't planning to."

He got to his feet. "Take a walk with me."

He stalked out into the garden and she strolled by his side, but she couldn't stop evaluating every corner of the garden for threats, possible weapons, and every angle of potential attack and defense.

"Who is it you want to visit in the city?" he asked after a few minutes of silence. "Is it Tom? He's the only one of your old teammates left."

"No, I wasn't planning to see him. There's another woman here that I know. She's a helper at Hellion House."

"Who is she?" he asked. "I wasn't aware that you knew any helpers at Hellion House."

"Her name is Fan Tiko. She's a helper to Aurora Hellion."

"Ah, I know the one. She's very loyal. I didn't expect a helper as loyal as that to associate with a slag like you."

Dina chuckled. "I know a few people in this town."

"What is it you want to see her about?"

"I just want to catch up with her. I haven't seen her since I left."

"She may be your friend, but other helpers at Hellion House won't be happy to see you and neither will the Hellions."

"So does everyone in the city know about me?"

"I would be surprised if they didn't."

"They can't all know about Adrian, though," she pointed out. "I don't see Osiris and the other senators spreading that around. Relations between the cats and their helpers are already strained enough."

"That is true."

"So what was Osiris's reaction when you told him?"

"He was circumspect about it, but he's circumspect about everything. He's one of the more rational cats in the Senate. Nothing rattles him, so he took this in his stride, too. I didn't expect him to be so curious about you, though."

She didn't answer. She might have felt tempted to blackmail Belinda into good behavior, but Dina would never do something like that to Osiris. She respected him too much for saving his Children's lives by taking them to the jungle and giving them to her for safekeeping.

She would never tell a living soul about that. He must have questioned Renfroe about her to get information on his own Children.

"I know some of the helpers who came to the city with me yesterday, too," she went on. "They're young people I know from the village. I want to keep an eye on them and make sure they're all right."

"You should avoid them," he told her. "If anyone found out they were associating with you, your young friends could get into trouble and get visited for subversive activity."

"Something tells me these people are already in danger of that. Besides, I promised I would help them as much as possible. They're new to being helpers. I want to give them as much support as I can."

"If they're smart, they'll stay out of it and do their work without getting involved with anyone," he growled. "That's the problem nowadays. No one seems to be able to stay out of politics at all. Everyone falls on one side or the other."

Dina spun around. "Do other helpers sympathize with the Children? Are other helpers trying to undermine the Pride?"

"I don't know for sure, but I assume they are. Whatever subversive elements may have lurked beneath the surface in the past will come to light now. The Children's war will embolden anyone who wants to overthrow the Pride. These subversive helpers will get bolder about recruiting more people to their cause—and they'll start with the young people."

She stared at him in wide-eyed shock. "Are they doing that now? Is there a rising movement of helpers who want to overthrow the Pride?"

"I don't associate with anyone in this city well enough to know that," he rumbled. "I assume it's true when I see helpers whispering in corners and fighting amongst themselves. They wouldn't do that if they were all peacefully satisfied to serve their benefactors and protect the understanding with the Pride. What do they have to fight about unless at least some of them are actively subverting the understanding? They wouldn't need to whisper if they were talking in the Pride's favor. They would be as likely to whisper against the Pride as they would be to whisper about what the Children are doing."

"Wow," she breathed. "I didn't realize it had gone as far as that."

He cocked his head to one side. "You are as subversive as you ever were—possibly more so. If I didn't know better, I would say that you came back here to use me and my house to undermine the Pride. I don't know why I even mention this. You have worked tirelessly to undermine the Pride since your first days on this planet."

"That isn't why I came back," she murmured.

"But you're thinking about it now, aren't you? You plan to encourage these helpers to rebel just as you encouraged our Children to rebel."

"So you would have preferred if I encouraged our Children to turn themselves over to the Pride for execution? Is that what you're saying?" she countered. "Adrian is right. There are only two possible outcomes here. If the cats win, they'll annihilate every Child on the planet. Why in God's name would the Children give in to that?"

"I can see we won't come to any resolution on this, Dina," he growled. "We are both so firmly entrenched in our own positions that there is no possible resolution."

"You're the one who's been speaking in the Children's favor all this time. You're the one who let me leave so your Children could survive. You're the one who said you were proud of Adrian for fighting back. If you support the Children that much, you should be happy that I want to support them, too. I didn't come here to betray them by giving my support to the Pride—although the Children certainly seem to think I did."

He sighed and turned away to sniff the breeze. "You are right, Dina. I don't know which side I'm on....and that isn't even true. I do know which side I'm on. I simply lack the courage to act on my convictions."

She gasped again. "You....you would support the Children?"

He snorted. "I've supported them as much as any cat can and I don't suppose it would work for a cat to go out to the jungle and join their army to fight the Pride. I'm not prepared to go that far, but yes, I have done all I can from here. I don't suppose you told our Children that."

Now it was her turn to look away. "I tried. They don't listen."

"Did you tell them that I let you go?"

"Yes, I told them."

"And they don't believe you?"

"They believe it happened. They just don't believe it happened the way I say it did. They interpret your actions differently. They assign different motives to what you did."

"I don't understand you. How could they?"

"I don't want to talk about it," she muttered.

He let the subject drop and they headed back to the house. "I have a mind to follow you through the city, Dina," he rumbled when they made it back to the fountain.

"You don't need to do that. I already told you I'm going to Hellion House."

"I wouldn't follow you to find out where you're going. I don't care where you go. I have a mind to watch you from afar to make sure you're safe."

She shrugged. "I guess that wouldn't hurt, but don't you have anything better to do?"

"I might. I must be as foolishly smitten with you as they say because this is more important to me."

She slipped her arms around his neck again and nuzzled into his fur. "Thank you. I'm grateful for your protection."

"If we're going to do this, I suppose it doesn't make any difference when you go. Would you like to go now?"

"I guess so." She glanced over her shoulder toward the house. "I guess we don't have any more reason to stay here."

Chapter 7

Dina opened the garden gate and paused there to look back into the garden. Renfroe trotted away from her down one of the paths, sprang onto the wall at the very back of the garden, and paused there to look back at her.

He perched on top of the wall and his drilling eyes stabbed her in the guts for one instant. Then he turned away and dropped down behind the wall where she couldn't see him.

She didn't realize until now how much safer she felt with him around. The danger surrounding her on all sides weighed more heavily without him nearby.

She felt it even in his garden and now she was going out into the city alone. Any loyal helper out there could take a shot at her and get away with it. Cats and helpers alive would probably praise or even reward anyone who attacked or killed her.

She shivered, but she couldn't turn down the opportunity to see and connect with anyone in this city who might help her.....do whatever it was she was going to do.

She slipped out of the garden, pulled the gate shut behind her, and hurried away through the neighborhood. If the factors were watching her, they would know now that she was out of Renfroe's house by herself without him around to protect her.

She glanced at the gardens of other houses on both sides, but she didn't see him. Where was he? If he was watching from that far away, he wouldn't be able to get to her in time to save her if something went wrong.

She would just have to handle it on her own. She really needed a weapon—one she could carry everywhere. Maybe Fan could help her with that.

She left the leafy outer neighborhoods and entered the city streets. She sensed people watching her as she passed, but she didn't recognize anyone. Were they looking at her because she was new and they'd never seen her before? Did anyone here know who she was and how she fit into all of this?

She got within half a mile of Hellion House and picked up the pace. She cast sidelong glances into the side streets, but she still didn't see anyone she recognized or anyone threatening.

She stopped herself from looking up to see if Renfroe was on top of the buildings. How could he keep an eye on her here? He wasn't exactly inconspicuous himself. Everyone knew and recognized him.

She spotted Hellion House in front of her, but when she happened to check down another side street, she spotted Harmon Farley and three other city factors.

Her heart stopped, but she refused to let herself hesitate. She kept walking....and then she caught a fleeting glimpse of movement out of her peripheral vision.

Two men stepped out of the same side street, moved into the street behind her, and started following her. She didn't dare to turn around to see if Farley and his friends were coming after her.

She picked up her pace and strode a little faster only for two more factors to step out of a different side street in front of her. They walked toward her to box her in behind and in front.

She made a snap decision and dodged into an alley. It emerged on a different street.

She couldn't walk any faster without bursting into a run. She turned the corner and headed toward Hellion House again. It was less than three blocks away, but right then, two of the factors who'd been following her came out of the same alley behind her.

She veered in a different direction, but the other two factors came around a corner in front of her to head her off.

She swerved into one last side street, and when she emerged on the third street, she threw caution to the wind and bolted the last few blocks to Hellion House.

She walked into the gymnasium-sized room packed from wall to wall with lions and people. Cats of every age and size filled the hall while dozens of helpers walked back and forth tending to the cats' every whim.

The helpers cut up meat to feed the cats, picked the cats' teeth and trimmed their claws, scratched their ears and necks, and lounged with them on blankets on the floor.

Dina sensed right away that something was wrong here, too. She didn't see any cats or people engaged in sexual activity and the tension and simmering hostility threatened to boil over any second now.

The cubs played, wrestled, and attacked each other as usual, but the lack of sexual activity translated into aggression. Adult cats showed more hostility toward each other and their helpers.

The cats snarled and bit at each other much more frequently than they did before. In fact, Dina couldn't remember the Hellions ever biting or snarling at each other during her last visit to Hellion House. They'd all seemed docile, satisfied, and contented. They had no reason not to be.

The minute she walked in the door, one young male attacked a young female, knocked her over, and bit a huge, bloody gash in her shoulder.

She retaliated and the two tumbled over each other on the floor. This was nothing like the cubs' playful bouts. Both cats bellowed, thundered, and threw their weight against each other. They actually looked like they might destroy each other.

No one intervened and Dina glanced around for Lord Hellion. Then she remembered. He was dead and so was his chosen successor.

She didn't see any male lion old enough or mature enough to take over as the family patriarch. That might be as big a problem as the lack of sexual activity. These lions didn't have a patriarch to maintain order.

She didn't see Fan anywhere, either. Just then, a young woman helper passed her heading somewhere else. Dina stopped her. "Excuse me. I'm looking for Fan Tiko. She's Aurora's helper. Do you know where I can find her?"

"She's in the back," the other helper replied. "I'm going there. I can show you where to go. Follow me."

The young woman led the way down a hallway to a different part of Hellion House that Dina didn't know was here.

They passed a dozen other rooms with helpers cooking in kitchens, attending young human children in another room, and a group of helpers playing with a bunch of very young lion cubs in another.

The young woman eventually turned off into the last room on the left side of the hall. Dina followed her into a room full of people washing laundry in wooden tubs, folding clothes and blankets, and talking while they worked.

Dina spotted Fan folding towels at one of the tables. Fan's eyes popped when she recognized Dina, but Fan didn't move out of place. She kept working while Dina thanked her guide and crossed the room to Fan's side.

Before Dina could say a word of greeting, a burst of animated talk broke out in the room. "We should mount our own campaign against the Children," one man exclaimed. "We should take up arms to defend the Pride."

"You know we couldn't do that, Penja," a woman countered. "We aren't allowed to carry weapons and our benefactors would never give us permission to leave the city."

"We could get permission and weapons," Penja replied. "The cats have already recruited helpers to fight the Children. We would be doing the same thing."

"Then we should wait for the cats to recruit us," the same woman told him. "We shouldn't go out against the Children until our benefactors tell us to. We might be working against their strategy."

"Whose side are you on, Rosa?" Penja fired back. "We should prove our loyalty to the Pride by taking the initiative. We shouldn't wait for our benefactors to tell us before we prove our loyalty by defending the Pride and killing its enemies."

"We wouldn't be able to fight the Children anyway," another man pointed out. "If they can kill cats, we don't stand a chance against them."

"That's just cowardice, Mako," Penja snapped. "Better helpers than you have already died fighting the Children."

"They didn't die fighting the Children," Mako murmured. "They died fighting the Children's human supporters. The Children's human supporters kill any helpers that go into battle. The helpers never get near enough even to raise a weapon against the Children, much less kill one. If the Children's human supporters can do that much damage, we wouldn't have a prayer of killing any Children. Only the cats can fight the Children—and even then the Children always win."

"I can't believe I'm hearing this!" Penja sneered. "Are you loyal helpers or not? Do you want to do everything possible to help the Pride defeat the Children or not?"

"Of course we're loyal helpers," Rosa replied. "You're talking about arming ourselves and leaving the city without our benefactors' permission, which by itself is an act of betrayal and subversion. We could get reduced for that alone."

Penja threw up his hands. "That's ridiculous. What better way to demonstrate our understanding with the Pride than to fight the Pride's enemies? The Children threaten us as much as the cats. We have no choice but to fight them."

The debate continued to rage. Dina turned to Fan to ask how she was doing, but before Dina could say a word, Penja noticed her. "You! Who are you? You support the Pride against the Children, don't you?"

Dina glanced around. "Who—me?"

"Yes, you," he snapped. "Who are you? Which house do you belong to? I don't recognize you."

"I'm Renfroe's helper," Dina replied. "I just got here yesterday."

"What do you say? Join us in taking up arms against the Children."

Dina raised both hands. "I couldn't. My benefactor wouldn't like it."

"Don't you have an understanding with the Pride?" Penja demanded. "You can at least tell us if anyone in your household is subversive."

Dina froze. "What do you mean? Are you saying helpers in this city are acting subversive—as in, they're helping the Children?"

"I don't know if they're helping the Children, but they want to. The subversives say we should mount an internal rebellion from inside the city to distract the cats from the war. The subversives think we should weaken the Pride from the inside to make it easier for the Children to win." He waved at Rosa. "We've put the word out to all the helpers in the city. If you see anyone acting subversive or working against the Pride, you report it to us and we'll take care of the person."

"Have you.....taken care of people before?" she stammered.

Fan seized her arm. "Let's not talk about that. You come with me, Dina. Come this way."

She towed Dina out of the room and into the room next door. It had been converted into a giant laundry supply storeroom. Shelves filled every inch of the room. Towels, blankets, sheets, clothes, and everything else lined all the shelves as well as tools and food supplies.

Fan pulled Dina between the shelves. "You're back here?!" Fan hissed under her breath. "What happened?! Why did you leave the jungle?"

Dina shrugged. "It was time to come back. The Children are all grown up. They have their own lives now and mine went in a different direction."

"Are the Children all right—the Auroras...and the others?"

"They're fine. They're all grown up like I said and now they're out there fighting the war. How are you? You look like you're doing well."

Fan grimaced. "This place never changes—except when it does."

"Is it like this all the time—with everyone talking about taking sides in the war?"

Fan nodded. "All the time. No one ever stops talking about it."

"Are you.......?" Dina broke off. She'd been about to ask if Fan was involved in any of the subversive activity, but asking that here would be too dangerous.

It turned out to be a good thing that Dina didn't ask because, just then, the same young woman walked into the supply room. "Aurora's asking for you again, Mother. She says to bring the bandages again to clean up Kuma's shoulder."

"I'm coming," Fan replied over her shoulder and turned back to Dina.

Dina stared at her and then glanced at the young woman. That......that was Fan's daughter?

The young woman started taking a stack of towels off the shelf when a teenage boy of sixteen strolled in at the same time. "Rigel is taking some of us out to patrol the city limits again, Mother," he told Fan. "We need weapons."

"You know where they are," Fan replied. "Just inventory of what you take and make sure everything you inventory everything when you come back so nothing gets lost."

"I know," the boy replied and crossed the room to a different shelf.

The shelf contained gardening equipment including shovels, pitchforks, knives, machetes, and axes.

Dina stared through a gap in the stacks of towels while he loaded his arms with everything and then left with it. Fan remained silent until both her children left.

"Are they.....they're your children, aren't they?" Dina whispered.

"The oldest two. I have three younger ones. Penja is my husband."

Dina spun around so fast she saw stars. "Seriously?"

"He's very loyal, so watch what you say around him." Fan's eyes softened. "I missed you. It's really good to see you."

"Is it true what he said about subversives? Are there really people in the city who are talking about helping the Children by attacking the Pride?"

Fan dropped her voice to a whisper. "They're doing more than just talking about it. They're actually doing it. I'm not sure how organized they are, but subversive elements have already killed a few high-ranking cats and senators. The subversives target anyone who organizes the Pride to attack the Children—or who does anything else to carry out this war."

Dina stared at her with huge eyes. "I had no idea!"

"Be careful," Fan whispered. "The cats and loyal helpers are retaliating even more harshly now than they did before if anyone shows any sign of sympathizing with the Children. The factors have already reduced thirty people just because someone accused them of subversive activity. The factors don't waste time investigating to find out if it's true. They just act."

"My God!" Dina whispered back.

"So be very careful what you say and to whom." Some other helpers passed in the hallway outside. "I better go. I'll see you soon....and be careful."

Fan hurried out of the room and left Dina standing there, stunned. She never dreamed the situation in the city could have evolved this far this fast. No wonder the city felt so tense.

She already knew that she was treading a dangerous path by even thinking about helping the Children. Now a whole new world of possibilities opened up for her.

She hadn't known what to expect when she came back to the city. She'd been prepared to find the whole society organized against the Children.

So helpers inside the city wanted to fight for the Children. These helpers were carrying out assassinations against senators to weaken the Pride. The Pride was as worried about the subversive helpers as the Pride was worried about the Children themselves.

Dina never imagined the city would become such a powder keg. One wrong move on either side could blow the whole place part.

She had to get out of here. She had to....do something—but what? Part of her wanted to set a match to the powder keg and blow Prideland sky high.

Doing that could cost millions of lives the way Renfroe said.

She shook herself and was just about to leave when she spotted the shelf where Fan's son got all the tools he and his comrades would use as weapons against the Children.

Dina stood rooted to the spot staring at all those tools. She wanted a weapon. Now here they were right in front of her. Did she dare to take one? Would these helpers get into trouble when they discovered something missing?

She would never get another chance. She raced over to the shelf and grabbed the first two things she could lay her hands on. One was a short gardening knife with a thick, stout blade. The other was a small sickle used for cutting weeds.

She shoved them under her tunic, tucked them into the waistband of her pants, and hustled out of Hellion House as fast as she could.

Chapter 8

Dina paused on the sidewalk outside Hellion House and glanced around again, but she didn't see Farley or the other factors anywhere. She didn't see Renfroe, either. Was he still here? Did he get tired of waiting for her to come out?

She set off walking back toward his house. She planned to stop by Amaryllis's house on the way to see Sonya. Dina would need to work out a way to do that without any Manx spotting her—or noticing her talking to Sonya. Dina didn't want to get Sonya into trouble.

Dina passed five blocks and slipped into the alley to get back to the main street heading for the outer neighborhoods. She got so preoccupied thinking about Sonya that she didn't notice another two men enter the alley behind her.

She stopped dead in her tracks when two more men advanced from the far end in front of her. Her hand flew to her waist, but she couldn't get to either of her weapons.

She realized her mistake too late. Her tunic hid the weapons, but it also stopped her from grabbing them when she needed them. She would have to change that.

She jumped when she heard the men behind her stop....and then the men in front of her stopped. She didn't recognize any of them.

"You're Renfroe's helper, aren't you—the one who ran away to the jungle to save the Children," one of the men in front of her began.

She frowned at him. "Who are you? How do you know about me?"

"We all know who you are. You escaped from the Pride before and you did it again to save your Children. You know where the Children are. You can help us get a message to them. You can tell them we want to help them—that we're ready to strike from inside the city whenever they need us to. They only have to give us the word and we'll kill anyone who tries to stop them."

Dina's heart stopped all over again when she realized what he was saying. This man wanted her to communicate....between the Children and their subversive supporters.

She had to gulp to get her voice working. "Who are you?"

"My name is Kubri James....and this is Angulo Duala." He indicated the man next to him.

Kubri James was a burly, thick-shouldered man of at least six-feet-one inch. He had a very blocky, almost square head and hard, brutal features, but some hidden light in his eyes reminded Dina of Link.

Angulo was five inches shorter with a wiry, energetic, whiplike quality and sharp, quick eyes. He looked much smarter than Kubri James, but Angulo didn't speak. He let Kubri James do all the talking—which meant Kubri James must be their leader.

Dina took a split second to register that she was actually having a conversation with subversives in this city. They wanted to attack cats to help the Children.

No, that was wrong. These subversive helpers already had attacked cats. The subversive helpers had already killed cats to support the Children.

She cleared her throat with difficulty. "I would help you if I could. I mean—I want to help you, but I don't know where the Children are. They move around a lot and I don't know their plans since I came back here."

"But you'll help us," Angulo finally interrupted.

"I will if I can," she replied. "I'm just not sure how. I have to be careful. I'm already in danger from the factors and the Pride. If I leave the city again, I probably won't be able to come back—if I get out of here alive."

"You wouldn't have to come back," one of the men behind her pointed out. "You could deliver our message and stay out there. The Children will attack the city and we'll do the rest."

Dina didn't turn around. "I don't know if the Children plan to attack the city," she replied over her shoulder. "The last time I talked to them, they were trying to avoid attacking the city so they wouldn't end up in a situation where they might kill innocent helpers. They wanted to keep all their conflicts outside the city limits where they could be sure to only attack cats and any helpers who specifically went out to support the Pride."

Kubri James's eyes widened. "So you talked to them. You know their leadership. You could talk to them again."

Dina tried to shrug that away. "Yes, I know their leadership. I could talk to them, but I don't know if they'll listen to me. The Children have minds of their own. They don't take direction from anyone. If you told them your plan, they would take it as a suggestion. They wouldn't necessarily do it the way you want them to—in which case you would need someone who could come back and deliver their message about what they actually wanted you to do."

Kubri James's features hardened even more than before. "Then we'll just have to keep arming. We'll prepare to support them if they do invade the city. We can't do anything else."

Dina opened her mouth and hesitated again. She was definitely taking a stand in this war by participating in this conversation. She couldn't claim she wasn't part of it or that she didn't want to fight anymore. She was as actively involved as if she'd stayed in the jungle to fight on the Children's side.

"Can we count on you?" one of the men behind her asked. "If we need someone, can we count on you to help us?"

She took another heartbeat to make up her mind. "Yes, of course. I'll help the Children in any way I can. Just be careful...and don't do anything that might put others in danger. The Children have more supporters in this city than we realize. Don't do anything that could expose someone or give someone away—including me."

Kubri James nodded. "I understand—and we will. Thank you."

He and Angulo turned away and walked off. She heard the other two men retreating behind her. They left her standing there alone in the alley.

Her hand flew to her waist again and she touched the knife handle. The weapon was still there, but she didn't need it anymore—not against them, at least.

She glanced behind her and up at the rooftops. Did anyone see those men confront her? Did anyone realize what it meant?

She set off walking. She was back in the middle of this upheaval again without even trying. She should have known she wouldn't be able to stay out of it.

Maybe she did know. Maybe some part of her knew before she left Riverbend canton and this was the reason she felt so compelled to come back to this city.

If that was true, then Renfroe was right and she was just using him and his house to undermine the Pride. Would it really be so bad if she did? Not according to Iona.

If Adrian and Iona were right, then Renfroe was as much the enemy as any other cat. Undermining, using, and subverting him would be the right thing to do.

She couldn't think of him that way. She couldn't think of him as the enemy—not after all he'd done for her and the risks he'd taken to defend the Children.

She continued on her way, but almost in the same thought when she made up her mind not to think of Renfroe as an enemy, she spotted another man on the street ahead of her.

He rounded a different corner heading off to the left. He was much taller than Kubri James with a thatch of curly brown hair that had grown longer around his ears.

Tom Sharples looked three years older and his hair was a few inches longer, but other than that, he looked exactly the same way she remembered him.

A whirlwind of memories and emotions overcame her at the sight of him. He had no idea where she'd been or what she'd been doing since the last time she saw him.

She had to remind herself that he didn't know about his own Children. He didn't know about Elyse slipping away into the jungle to give birth to Naia, Nova, Duke, and Darius. Tom didn't know about Elyse leaving his four Children with Dina to raise.

He happened to glance in her direction and his features went blank when he saw her. He stared at her with absolutely no emotion at all. Did he feel anything for her anymore?

He turned and strode down the sidewalk to halt in front of her. "Hello. How are you doing?" he asked.

She nodded. "I'm good."

"Are you still with Renfroe?" he asked in a flat monotone.

She nodded again. "Are you still with Elyse?"

"Yes. It's a good place."

He said it with no inflection or subtext at all. Did he even realize he was using the Prideland term for it?

He didn't say anything about her running away, either. She wouldn't have been in the least surprised if Elyse hid that from him, too.

She might have kept Tom in the dark about everything—including the fact that Dina had been out of the city for three whole years until just yesterday.

"If you need anything," he went on, "don't hesitate to come and see me. You know where I live."

He added no tonality to this, either. He might have been talking to a total stranger instead of the woman he'd been engaged to marry before all this started.

"Thank you. You, too," she replied in exactly the same meaningless undertone. What could she possibly offer him when Elyse was taking such good care of him?

He nodded again, muttered, "I'll see you around," and walked off in the direction he'd been going when he first saw her.

She watched him go feeling a bizarre mixture of emotions about him. She knew absolutely nothing about him anymore. He could have changed into someone completely different since he became Elyse's helper.

In fact, he *had* become someone completely different. Dina didn't know who he was, what he thought about, or what he might be capable of. She didn't even know what he might be able to do for her if she ever went to him for help.

One thing she did know with iron-clad certainty. She would never, ever, under any circumstances, EVER go to him for help.

She would never, ever, under any circumstances, EVER tell him that she wanted to help the Children's war against the Pride.

She would never trust Tom Sharples ever again—with anything—especially not something as dangerous and important as that.

She couldn't even bring herself to regret that she didn't trust him. She'd been ready to marry him and spend the rest of her life with him. Now that was over.

She might even think of him as an enemy—much more of an enemy than Renfroe was. Renfroe put his neck on the line to help the Children. It didn't do any good, but at least he tried.

Tom never did anything to help the Children and he never did anything to help Dina, either. He'd never done a single thing to help her since they first arrived in Prideland.

He'd done worse than not help her. He'd actually betrayed her, sold her out to Elyse, and gotten Dina caught and punished. He had been partially responsible for getting Frank, his family, and everyone else at Moonlight canton killed. Dina would never be able to forget that.

Chapter 9

Dina hurried down the avenue back to Renfroe's house. She rushed faster when she spotted cats moving through the trees. They were coming after her or at least following her.

She still didn't see Renfroe. Was he watching over her anymore? She hadn't seen him all day. Maybe something went wrong.

She changed her mind about seeing Sonya. Dina couldn't take the risk of the cats catching up with her.

She dashed through the kitchen, ignored Belinda, and shut herself up in her bedroom to catch her breath. Her pulse surged in her ears. She couldn't go back outside without being better prepared to cope with the dangers.

Today's events cemented in her mind what she had to do. She didn't know it before she came here, but now she understood.

She could act as a go-between to carry information and communication between the Children and their allies in the city. The subversive helpers could give Dina information and she could pass it to the Children. Then the Children could give these people instructions on how to undermine the Pride to help the Children's war.

Adrian might not believe so many helpers would want to help the Children. She would just have to remind him of Link's words.

Plenty of people wanted to break the Pride's dominance. The Children couldn't afford to turn away any ally, no matter what species a person belonged to.

She knew now that she was the Children's ally, too. She hadn't been sure before. They'd been right to accuse her of that. She might have come back to this city to see Renfroe, but she knew now which side she was on.

She pulled the two weapons from her waistband. She couldn't get caught anywhere ever again without ready access to them.

She had to keep them concealed but somewhere she could grab them when she needed them. She examined her tunic and made up her mind.

She tore out the side seams to make slits. Then she darted down the hall to her old room—the one where she'd hidden Tania and the Auroras before their escape.

Dina located some old sheets that Belinda used to make up the divan into a bed. Dina took them back to her own room and cobbled together two side pockets in the underside of her tunic.

These would hold her weapons where she could lay her hands on them at an instant's notice. No one could see them. It wasn't a perfect solution, but it would have to work for now.

She could also keep the pocketed weapons tucked into her waistband to stop them from flapping around. This would make them even less noticeable to the outside observer.

She didn't have a mirror to check how it all looked, but anything was better than walking around unarmed.

She strode out into the corridor feeling much better. She didn't have to wait for Buck to attack her. She was ready—as ready as she ever would be.

She went out into the courtyard and sat by the fountain, but Renfroe didn't come back.

Dina paced the garden in agitation and then searched the house. Did she miss something? Did he return while she wasn't looking?

He wasn't in the parlor or any of his other usual spots. She even checked his sandbox.

The sun started to go down and he still didn't come home. Now she knew something was wrong, but she couldn't go out to search for him, could she?

She made another tour of the garden. Nothing.

She went inside to find the fire blazing in the parlor. The place didn't look right without Renfroe there, but she sat down in her old place anyway.

Belinda had left a tray with a bowl of soup there for Dina's dinner. Belinda did not leave anything for Renfroe. Did Belinda know something Dina didn't?

She drank her soup, ate the meat and vegetables at the bottom, and put the bowl aside. What would she do if Renfroe didn't come back at all?

Thinking that made her stand up to go search for him again. She didn't know where she would go, but she had to look somewhere.

She turned toward the door and skidded to a stop when she saw him coming through the doorway from the dark corridor.

He stepped into the light and she gasped when she saw his face and coat torn to shreds. He bled from multiple wounds.

"Oh, my God!" she gasped and rushed to his side. "What happened?"

"You can see what happened," he snarled. "Leave me alone! Don't touch me!"

"I have to get you cleaned up." She hesitated for a second. "Stay here. I'll get some water."

She raced off to the kitchen and Belinda yelled out in surprise when Dina burst in. Dina completely ignored her, snatched a wooden bucked from the corner, and dumped a bunch of hot water into it from the cauldron over the flames.

Dina didn't ask permission. She ransacked the kitchen, put enough cold water into the bucket to make the water a decent temperature, grabbed a bunch of towels, and took everything back to the parlor.

Renfroe sat fuming in front of the flames and snarled at her again when she tried to dab the blood off his face.

"Who did this?" she asked. "What happened?"

"What difference does it make who did it?" he snapped and gave a ground-shaking snarl when she touched a nasty gash on his ribs. "Watch it!"

"I'm sorry," she breathed. "I'm just trying to help you."

"No one can help me," he growled. "They'll kill me next time."

"Why?" she exclaimed. "Why did they attack you? Was it cats?"

"Of course it was cats!" he roared. "Who else would it be?"

"I heard at Hellion House that there are subversive helpers going around killing cats to help the Children's cause."

"Oh, them," he muttered. He winced when she pushed too hard on his shoulder.

He grumbled a lot while she wiped down his many wounds, but he didn't snarl or snap at her again. She bandaged the cuts she could bandage, but she couldn't do anything about his face.

He finally flopped on the floor with a broken sigh. She tossed the bloody water into the garden and took everything back to the kitchen.

Belinda glared at her, but Dina didn't care anymore. She put everything away where she'd found it, threw the bloody towels into the laundry basket, and went back to the parlor.

She sat down on the floor and didn't move or speak for a long time. She waited for him to say something, but when he didn't, she finally let her hand fall on the scruff of his neck. At least he wasn't hurt there.

"So you see how it is, Dina," he growled under his breath. "I'm in more danger than you are if that's even possible."

"Do you want to tell me what happened?" she murmured.

"You already know what happened," he countered. "They attacked me."

"Why?" she asked again. "You said you weren't involved in the Senate."

"I don't need to be involved in the Senate to speak my mind."

"Who were you talking to?"

"This time? No one. I've said it all before, so everyone knows where I stand. I was following you through the city like I said I would and ten cats came out and jumped me. That's all you need to know."

She rubbed his neck a little harder. He'd told her enough times that the Pride pushed him out. They turned against him for speaking on the Children's behalf.

He never let her know that they outright attacked him. She couldn't believe this was the first time.

She would have liked to put her arms around him and make a fuss over him for being such a hero, but he wouldn't want that. He hated getting hurt. Touching him at all would only make him surlier.

She made up her mind, stretched out on the floor, and curled up with her back pressed against his side. He sighed heavily and leaned his weight against her. That was enough for now.

She woke up in the middle of the night. The fire had burned down to embers and neither she nor Renfroe had moved since he came in.

She sat up. "Do you want to go to bed?" she asked in a whisper.

"I don't care," he grumbled.

"Let's go. We'll be more comfortable there."

She got to her feet and he did, too. He padded down the corridor at her side. The faint light from outside stood out on the stark white of his bandages.

She opened the door for him and he slipped past her, hopped on the bed, and collapsed on the pillow.

She shut the door and lay down next to him with her clothes still on. This was turning into a regular routine. She would probably sleep in her clothes for the rest of her time in this house.

She scooted over next to him and stroked the side of his face on the one spot where he didn't sustain any cuts. He kept his eyes closed and pretended not to notice her attentions.

She experienced a rush of her old feelings for him. He got hurt like this for defending the Children. He'd been doing it for years.

He was the only cat to publicly suggest that the Pride not only let the Children live but integrate them into their society and make them an asset to the Pride instead of a liability. Not even Osiris had gone as far as that.

In that moment of dark silence, she thanked her lucky stars that she wound up with Renfroe as a benefactor instead of some other cat. She hardly believed her good fortune.

He wasn't perfect. He was a cat of the Pride. He couldn't change what he was, but he was the best of them. She knew that now.

She leaned in and kissed the side of his face. He pretended not to notice that, too, but even his silence and unresponsive resentment charmed her. It made her admire him more.

Adrian and Iona should have known him the way she did. She would have liked to do something to bring them around somehow or at least explain to them what he was really like.

Their destinies crossed in different directions. Too many opposing forces tore them apart.

They would never reconcile, but it would have been nice for them to know that their father was more than some monster out to exploit the world for his own power and domination.

Chapter 10

Dina woke up alone the next morning. Renfroe wasn't in their bedroom, and when she searched the house again, she didn't find him inside or on the grounds.

He must be sulking somewhere by himself. She only hoped he was safe wherever that was.

She ate breakfast alone and left the house. She no longer cared much about the danger. She'd fought cats and people alike before. She could do it again.

If she was going to help the Children, she better do it now. She'd squandered their goodwill by coming to this city. She better make it count for something.

She turned the opposite way and strode through the neighborhood heading for Amaryllis's house. Dina double- and triple-checked her weapons more than once to make sure they were still there.

Cats appeared in the branches overhead the instant Dina set foot outside Renfroe's garden. They streaked from branch to branch getting lower all the time, but they didn't drop down to attack her.

She didn't dare to go near Amaryllis's house with the cats there. She didn't want them to see her meeting with Sonya—if Dina could even get close to Sonya.

The cats followed her for fifteen minutes before they took off and vanished. She walked far out of her way to avoid Amaryllis's house, but the cats didn't come back.

Dina finally dared to approach the garden wall, ducked under the vines, and eased open the gate leading into Amaryllis's garden. Dina hid behind the bushes and peeked out to check the garden's layout.

She'd never been here before, but she spotted Sonya right away. The girl sat on the ground weeding a flowerbed twenty feet from Dina's hiding place.

Dina cringed when she saw bruises all over Sonya's face. One eye had swollen shut and her lower lip sagged with deep, dark, purple-black bruises. She must have already gotten in trouble.

Dina didn't see any scratches on Sonya's face or arms. She must have gotten visited by the factors—or maybe her fellow helpers. At least the Manx hadn't attacked her—not yet.

Dina snuck a little closer, but she couldn't get any nearer to Sonya without going out into the open.

Dina picked up a pebble and lobbed it into the bushes near Sonya. It rustled the leaves and Sonya looked up. Dina threw another one and Sonya glanced in her direction to see where the disturbance was coming from.

Sonya stiffened when she saw Dina waving at her. Sonya had the presence of mind not to glance over her shoulder or to look anywhere else.

She got up and walked through the bushes to a different part of the garden. From there, she could slip behind the hedges.

Dina met up with her, pushed open the garden door, and they darted out to hide under the vines behind the wall. "What happened to you?" Dina whispered.

Sonya shrugged. "One of the helpers caught me asking another girl about the subversives."

Dina gasped. "You have to be more careful! I tried to warn you about that. You can't just go asking anybody about it."

"This girl is subversive. Everybody knows it. She's gotten visited before for subversive activity."

"That doesn't mean anything!" Dina insisted. "The factors will visit anyone who even gets accused of being a subversive. Just because someone gets visited for that doesn't mean they're a subversive. They could be as loyal as they come and the accuser just wants to get them back for something else."

"No, she really is subversive. She got caught stashing weapons in a basement with a bunch of other subversives. The factors even heard them talking about assassinating Senator Osiris."

Dina stared at her in horror. The subversives were planning to assassinate Osiris.

Sonya studied her more closely. "Did *you* make contact with the subversives yet? Do you know what they're planning? You can tell me. You can put me in contact with them."

Dina shut her mouth with difficulty. "I don't think that's a good idea."

"If you don't, I'll just contact them another way. I don't care how many times I get visited."

"You could get reduced," Dina countered. "Do you realize that? If the factors think they can't convince you to reform, they'll get rid of you. Everyone in this city is much less tolerant of anyone on the other side."

"I don't care," Sonya snapped. "They can't stop me from doing the right thing."

"They can stop you by killing you."

"What did you find out?" Sonya asked again. "What are the subversives doing? You can tell me."

Dina hesitated. Should she? She didn't want to put Sonya in danger, but if she really insisted on getting involved in helping the Children, just telling her what was going on might be the best way to stop Sonya from talking to the wrong person.

"The subversive helpers are arming themselves in case the Children invade the city," Dina blurted out. "If the Children do invade, the subversive helpers plan to strike and help the Children or at least stop the Pride and the loyal helpers from putting up an effective defense. That's their plan. If you really want to help the Children, you could do something like that. You could get access to some weapons—without getting caught, Sonya. Do it carefully so no one notices anything missing. Then, if the Children do invade, you can help by stopping any cats or loyal helpers from interfering with the Children."

Sonya's face lit up as much as it could considering what bad shape she was in. "That's great! When are they planning to invade?"

"We don't know if they're planning to invade at all. No one can communicate with them."

"You could do that!" Sonya exclaimed.

"Keep your voice down!" Dina hissed.

"You could contact the Children!" Sonya murmured in a rush. "You could contact your son and find out when they're coming so we can be ready."

"I can't contact anyone without risking my life. I risked my life just by coming to see you today."

"But the Children....you have to help them! You can't just turn your back on them!"

"Will you listen to reason? If you don't pull your head in real quick, I won't come to see you again. You're putting all of us in more danger than the Pride itself with this reckless attitude."

That shut Sonya up. "Sorry," she breathed. "I just want to do something."

"We all do, but like I said, none of us can do anything if we get ourselves killed first and that includes me. I won't do anything unless I know I can do it without getting killed.

Renfroe got attacked last night for speaking out in the Children's favor. No one is safe, not even the cats themselves. They're turning against each other even for speaking in favor of making peace with the Children."

Sonya's one good eye widened even more. "Wow. I didn't know it was as bad as that."

"It is. It's worse than any of us realizes. If this keeps up, the Children won't have to do anything because the Pride will implode from the inside. Don't stick your neck out again, Sonya. Keep your head down and do your job—nothing else. I'll let you know if you can do anything to help the Children—or anyone else. Until then, the most useful thing you can do is to stay alive. Make the factors think you changed your ways and saw the light. If you act like you're loyal and be a good helper, someone might trust you enough to confide some important information to you that would really help the Children. It would help the Children more than you getting visited all the time."

"I didn't think of that," Sonya mused. "I should have thought of that first."

"Never mind. I have to go now. I just wanted to make sure you were okay." Dina turned away. "I'll take you back inside and then go home."

"Dina—wait!" Sonya caught her arm. "I....I think I know something.....something that could help the Children."

"What is it?" Dina asked.

"Amaryllis.......she's planning something."

Dina stiffened. "What is she planning?"

"Some kind of defense. She thinks she can work out a way to set up some kind of explosives along the roads coming into and out of the city. Don't ask me how she plans to do it because I don't understand it. I just overheard her talking to some other cats last night. They think they can work it out so that, if the Children use the roads to get into the city, the cats will blow the roads up and kill the Children before they get here. Do you think that will help?"

"It will definitely help," Dina replied. "I'll just need to figure out a way to get the information to the Children before it happens."

"How will you do that?"

"I don't know. I'll have to think about it. Now we both better go before anyone realizes we're gone. Come on."

Dina ducked out from under the vines, opened the garden gate, and took Sonya back inside. She returned to the same flowerbed, picked up the tool she'd just been using to dig out the weeds, and then Sonya went very still and quiet when she looked at the tool.

It was a short, broad, thick knife like the one Dina had taken from Hellion House. It had a sharp point and one sharp blade.

Sonya turned it over in her hand studying it as the truth sank in. She could use this as a weapon.

Her eyes darted up to meet Dina's and Dina nodded. Sonya tried to smile, but her fat lip wouldn't let her.

Dina retreated into the bushes and eased the gate shut behind her. She had to get back to Renfroe's house before he realized she was gone.

She glanced up into the treetops overhead, but she didn't see any cats. She raced away with her heart in her mouth. Now she had to find a way to contact the Children without anyone finding out.

Chapter 11

Dina darted down the path, past the kitchen door, and approached the door in the wall that led into Renfroe's garden. She had to get back inside before the cats returned. She still couldn't be sure they didn't see her talking to Sonya.

She put out her hand to take hold of the door latch when someone grabbed her and towed her into the nearby undergrowth. Dina gasped when she found herself facing Fan again.

"You have to help me, Dina!" Fan whimpered. "I don't know where else to turn!"

"What's wrong?" Dina asked. "Did something happen after I left Hellion House? I thought you were doing well there."

"Oh, it happened, all right, but it happened weeks ago." Fan tightened her grip on Dina's hands. "I'm pregnant, Dina! I'm pregnant with one of the Children—or maybe more than one! I can't go back to Hellion House! I can't go anywhere! If anyone finds out.....oh, what am I saying? They're bound to find out eventually and then I'm as good as dead."

Dina's tension drained away. "I'm sorry to hear that. Who's the father?"

Fan's face contorted in excruciating anguish. She had to fight to say the word. "Kaido."

Dina had to fight down a wave of nausea. Fan didn't have to say exactly what happened. Dina already knew.

She laid her hand on Fan's shoulder. "I'm so sorry. Don't worry. Kaido's dead."

"That doesn't mean anything!" Fan squealed. "What am I going to do? If anyone finds out, I'll be dead, too."

"Okay," Dina breathed. "Just settle down. I'll help you."

"Really?!" Fan clutched Dina's hand even tighter. "Do you mean it? Really? I'm at the end of my rope. I don't know what else to do."

"Of course I'll help you. Do you think I'd turn you away after everything you've done for me?"

"W....what are you going to do? What *can* you do?"

"I did this before, remember? We can do it again. We just need to be careful. Wait here. I'll be right back."

Dina left Fan in the bushes and slipped into the garden. Her mind raced on her way to the house. She had to get Fan out of the city no matter what.

Dina owed Fan too much to abandon her at a time like this. Dina would have done the same thing for any pregnant mother, but she owed Fan even more.

Dina went into the house. Belinda was in the kitchen.

Dina made another tour of the house. Renfroe still wasn't back. She didn't know how long he'd be gone. It might take some time before she found a way to sneak Fan out.

Then Dina would have to leave for at least a day or two to take Fan to the jungle. That would be risky with the Children around, but she'd have to risk it.

She returned to the garden and snuck Fan inside the wall. If any factors saw this, she might have to kill them to stop them from interfering.

She braced herself to do just that and led Fan through the garden to the courtyard outside Renfroe's and Dina's bedroom.

Dina pulled open the door, guided Fan through the bedroom, and installed Fan in the little room where Dina had hidden Tania.

"Stay here," Dina whispered. "Don't make a sound. I'm not sure when I'll be able to get you out, but I'll do it as soon as I can."

"Thank you so much," Fan breathed. "I don't know how to thank you."

"You already did. You thanked me by saving the Auroras and helping me take care of my Children. I'm the one who's thanking you by doing this. Now stay here. I don't know when I'll be able to come and see you. Just stay where you are and know that I'm working on it as fast as I can."

Dina saw Fan about to thank her again, so Dina let herself out of the room and went back to the fountain to wait for Renfroe to come back.

He didn't return until sundown. She'd finished eating her evening meal long before he jumped over the garden wall.

He stalked through the garden flowerbeds and she saw right away that he was still angry and resentful toward the whole world.

He sat down next to her, but he didn't try to get close to her. "I only came to see you so you wouldn't think I was angry at you," he growled. "I'm going out again in a few minutes. I just wanted to see you first. I'm sorry, Dina. I'm not very good company right now."

"I understand." She put out her hand to touch his face, but he turned it away to stop her.

She let her hand drop. "I'm sorry," she murmured.

"I'm the one who's sorry," he rumbled. "You're trying to be kind to me, but I'm not in the mood. I'm not in the mood for anything right now. I just need to be alone."

"I understand. I'm sorry this happened to you."

"Not as sorry as I am. I'll see you later."

He stormed off the way he came, hopped onto the wall, and sprang down on the other side without looking back.

She let out a shaky breath. She couldn't decide which was worse—Renfroe avoiding her or knowing she was going to run out on him again the instant he turned his back on her.

She consoled herself by telling herself that she couldn't have made it better for him by telling him the truth. She couldn't let Fan down. That was the bottom line.

Renfroe got into this trouble by protecting Children—and her—or trying to. If she told him the truth, he might even have encouraged her to help Fan.

She'd often wondered if he knew about Tania and the Auroras hiding in the other room. He could hear and smell everything in his house. He must have at least sensed it if he didn't already know.

He didn't enter the house this time, so he couldn't know about Fan. He might find out once he did enter it.

She had to work fast, take Fan to the jungle, and make it back here before he returned. He wanted her here waiting for him. She owed him that much.

She sat on the bench by the fountain while the light went out of the sky. She listened with all her attention to the sounds of Belinda working in the kitchen. Belinda stayed awake for hours.

Dina realized after four hours of waiting that her sitting by the fountain would seem too out of the ordinary. It would draw attention to herself, so she went to the bedroom the way she normally would.

She didn't lie down, though. She didn't want to risk falling asleep. She sat on the edge of the bed clamping her hands between her knees to stop herself from shaking.

This would be the one time she was the least prepared to escape from Prideland. She had no food, no supplies, and no real plan at all.

At least she had some weapons and the will to use them. She had one other asset in her favor—the Children. She just had to get Fan to the Children and they would take Fan from there. Dina didn't have to take Fan all the way to one of the cantons. That would take too long.

She snuck out of her bedroom four hours later and listened. No more sound came from the kitchen.

She dashed along the corridor and into the spare bedroom. Fan sat on the divan looking petrified. "Come on," Dina whispered. "We don't have any time to spare."

She grabbed Fan's hand and pulled her back into the garden, back to the door in the wall, and out into the streets.

"I can't believe I'm doing this!" Fan whimpered. "I've never done anything illegal before! What if we get caught?"

"If we get caught, you better be prepared to fight back," Dina replied. "Be prepared to fight for your life and your Children's lives. You're doing this to keep yourself and your Children alive. Just remember that. If you want them to die, you can stay here and turn them over to the Hellions. If you go out there, you're betting your own life to give them a chance to grow up. Do you understand that?"

Fan nodded silently in the darkness. The starlight shone on her huge, wide eyes.

Dina turned away. She couldn't wait any longer.

She raced through the streets and out onto the road. She kept watch for the sentinel cats, but they didn't show themselves.

She couldn't figure out why until she made it to a crossroads at the very edge of the city. Some of the Hellions, a few leopards, and ten pumas patrolled the roads.

"Now what do we do?" Fan whispered.

"Now we improvise." Dina retreated into the bushes, backtracked through some neighborhoods, and then snuck through four different gardens.

The last garden opened into the fields between the city and the villages beyond. "We're going to have to be careful," she whispered. "The roads might not be safe to use at all."

"Then what do we do instead?"

"We toughen up and make the best of it. Come on."

Dina strode out into the open field. The darkness hid the two women and they were far enough away to prevent any cats from hearing or smelling them.

Hiking over the fields took a lot longer than walking on the road, but at least no one stopped the two women. They made it as far as the village before the sun rose.

Dina squinted at the village in the distance. She still didn't risk going near it to get back onto the road, so she kept going. She didn't cut sideways to meet up with the road until noon.

By then, she and Fan had drawn level with the outer fringe of jungle. Fan paused to look back. "I can't believe I left my whole family behind!" Her voice quavered with misery. "They'll never know what happened to me."

"Your children are all old enough to take care of themselves," Dina replied. "Your husband never would have understood why you had to run away."

"The Auroras.....the Children I delivered to you....they were his Children." Fan choked on the words. "He would have let them die for the Pride's sake."

Dina rested her hand on Fan's shoulder. "You did the right thing—both times. Your Children are lucky to have you. Do you remember how many times you used to tell me that? Now it's your turn. These Children have a chance because you're giving them one. You can't take that away from them."

Fan nodded down at her hands. "I keep thinking about Tania. I don't want to be like her. I'll do whatever it takes as long as I don't turn out like her."

"No, you're nothing like her. Come on. We don't have far to go and then you'll be inside the canton walls."

Dina turned around....and froze as a cat slipped out of the undergrowth in front of her. Her hand flew to her pocket before she recognized him. It was Osiris.

Chapter 12

Osiris halted in the middle of the path that would lead Fan and Dina into the jungle. "What are you doing here?" Dina demanded. "How did you find us?"

"I hear all kinds of things." He flared his nostrils at both of them. "I was surprised you returned to Renfroe, but I knew you wouldn't be able to submit to the Pride for long—if at all."

"If you came out here to stop us or to take us back, you better be ready to fight me again. This woman is pregnant. I won't let you stop me from taking her to safety. You wanted your Children to grow up. She wants the same thing."

"I didn't come here to stop you. I came to give you this....and a warning."

He stuck his head into the bushes and tugged out a bundle wrapped in a piece of colored fabric. Dina couldn't imagine how he got it this far out of the city because the whole package weighed more than he did.

He pried the knot open with his teeth and nudged back the fabric to reveal a collection of axes and knives. "A party of larger cats is coming this way as we speak," he murmured. "They'll overtake you. You'll need to fight them if you expect to get away from them."

Dina blinked down at the weapons and then up at him. "You came out here to tell me that?"

"That.....and to ask you about my Children. I couldn't do that with Renfroe hovering over you night and day."

Dina opened and closed her mouth a few times trying to understand what he just said. "What do you want to know about your Children? I can't tell you where they are or what they're planning....."

"I don't want to know about that. I want to know how they are—who they are—what they're like." He hesitated. "Did you raise them yourself?"

"Of course. You gave them to me to raise. I took that very seriously."

"So who are they? What are their names?"

"They're…..Emerald, Calliope, Keith, Dexter, and Brock. They….." She found herself suddenly bursting into a grin when she remembered. "They look like you. They have your tortoise-shell fur patterns. Emerald is more green. Dexter is brownish. Brock is dark grey." She laughed in spite of herself. "They're good people—the best."

"I'm sure they are," he murmured. "I'm pleased to hear it." He glanced into the bushes. "I suppose they're involved in the war, aren't they?"

"Yes, they are. All the Children are. There are no Children who aren't involved in the war."

"Of course not. How could they not be? Thank you for telling me." He wrinkled his nose behind her and then tiptoed a little closer to the undergrowth. "They're coming. You should prepare yourselves."

"Wait!" she called after him. "Would you like to meet them? Would you like to meet your Children?"

"I better not," he replied. "Doing that would put them in danger and I don't want that. Take your friend away while you can."

He vanished into the bushes and Dina squatted down by the bundle of weapons.

"That was Senator Osiris!" Fan husked.

"I know who he is," Dina muttered.

"You raised his Children?"

"You knew that," Dina replied. "You were there when I brought them to the canton."

"I never thought……" Fan trailed off.

Dina picked up two axes and handed them to Fan. "You better take these." Dina turned around and surveyed the road. She hadn't seen any cats out there before, but she saw them coming now. "Get ready to stand and fight."

Dina pulled her knife and sickle out of her pockets, but she changed her mind and exchanged the knife for another axe. She would be able to do more damage with that.

Fifteen large cats advanced along the road getting bigger as they got nearer. Three lions, two tigers, half a dozen pumas, and four jaguars trotted up the road.

"They aren't messing around, are they?" Fan croaked. "I guess we tried."

Dina raised her weapons. "We're going to do more than try. Get ready."

"I'm no good at this!" Fan choked. "I've never fought a cat before."

"Then now's your chance to practice on them. Just concentrate on taking out as many of them as you can. Don't worry about killing them. Just injure them. That will make them stop fighting."

"You know so much more about it than I do." Fan's voice cracked again. "I don't know if I can do this."

"You better do it," Dina snapped. "I risked a lot to bring you out here. Don't you dare leave me to fight them alone."

Fan nodded rapidly. "Of course not. I would never do that."

"Come on," Dina urged. "Toughen up and do what has to be done. You're a mother and your Children are counting on you to protect them."

Fan faced out onto the road and her feature's hardened. "Tania. I don't want to be Tania."

"You're damn right you don't."

Dina didn't turn around or speak to Fan again. Dina had to concentrate on the cats. She braced herself to bring these cats down any way she could.

The cats came within visual range and locked their eyes on the two women standing there armed and ready. Three jaguars broke into a dead run and the rest of their party picked up speed to join in.

Dina flexed her knees for the first assault. One of those jaguars would launch at her any second now.

She rehearsed exactly how she would defend herself. Taking out the first jaguar would be easy. The others would be the hard ones.

She put Fan out of her mind. What Fan did wouldn't make any difference to Dina. She just had to fight these cats and let the chips fall where they may.

The jaguars broke into a dead run and bounded the rest of the way up the road to her position. One of them broke away and took the lead. He arched his back, lengthened his stride, and coiled his legs under him to launch at her.

He sailed through the air and she crouched under him counting down the seconds until he landed on top of her.

At the last moment before he struck, she lunged forward, ducked underneath him, and hacked her sickle down the length of his belly.

His body soared over her head and then all the rest of the cats attacked at the same time.

She shot to her feet to confront the other cats. They surrounded her and Fan. Dina raised her weapons to strike, and in that split second, six Children dropped from the treetops directly over her head.

They landed on the cats, slammed the cats to the ground, and another brutal fight broke out all around Dina's ankles. Cats and Children collided with her legs as the combatants tumbled over each other trying to kill each other.

As usual, the Children's sudden surprise attack reduced the cats' numbers by half in the first few seconds. The Children launched from their victims, closed with the remaining cats, and ended the fight before it even got started.

Aries picked himself up off one of the dead pumas, ran his wrist across his mouth to wipe away the blood, and gave Dina a hellish grin. "You haven't lost your nerve, Dina."

"Who the hell is this?" Amir snapped and jutted his chin at Fan.

"This is the woman who smuggled all of you Auroras out of Prideland." Dina pulled Fan forward. "She's the one who helped me raise you when you were babies. Now she's pregnant with one of the Children. She needs to get to the cantons. Can you take her?"

"Why can't you take her yourself?" Abdullah asked. "Don't tell me you're going back to the city, Dina. Adrian will be furious when he finds out."

"I have to go back, but I got you some information. Tell Adrian that the Pride is planning to boobytrap the roads with explosives. If you ever approach the city to invade it, the Pride will blow up the roads with you on them. I'm sure Adrian will know what to do with that information."

Aries raised his eyebrows. "You found that out? From whom?"

"There are helpers in the city who want to help the Children's war. Tell Adrian that. Tell him there's a whole movement of helpers who are arming to fight on the Children's side if he ever decides to invade the city. Tell him these helpers want to know when he plans to come so they can support him. They've asked me to communicate between them and the Children so these people can be as helpful to your cause as possible. He doesn't have to share his plans with them or me. I'm sure he would be worried about one of them leaking the information to the cats or the information falling into the wrong hands. We all understand that. He just needs to know these people are waiting to hear from him. They'll do whatever he wants them to do either to get ready for a strike like that or to help him once it starts. If he doesn't share his plans with them and he does invade the city, they'll just come out to fight for him then."

"That's incredible!" Amir murmured. "We never knew anyone in the city supported us."

"They do......and tell him.....when you see him.....tell him that I'll keep doing whatever I can for your cause from inside the city. He might not believe that, but maybe this information will convince him that I'm still on your side."

"We'll tell him, Dina." Abdullah waved Fan forward. "Come with us. We'll take you the to canton."

Dina turned to Fan. "Go with them. They'll take care of you. You'll be safe with them."

Fan's lips trembled. "Thank you."

"Stop it. These are the Children whose lives you saved." Dina squeezed Fan's hands and then, in a sudden burst of impulse, kissed her on the cheek. "Be safe and be happy. I'll see you soon."

Chapter 13

Dina's heart contracted watching Fan disappear into the jungle with the Auroras. Dina was really starting to wish she could go with them, but the prospect of getting more useful information to aid the Children's cause made her turn back.

She gathered the bundle of weapons Osiris had brought her, slung it over her back, and returned to the fields. She hiked back across country at a distance from the road where no one would be able to see her.

She didn't make it back to the city outskirts until dark. She really hoped Renfroe hadn't returned to find her gone.

Thinking about him made her walk faster. She could travel much more quickly without Fan, but Dina still regretted parting from one of her few friends in this city. Staying here would lose some of its luster, now that Dina couldn't visit Fan at Hellion House anymore.

Dina snuck into the city's outlying neighborhoods, hurried through the streets, and this time, she did see the sentinel cats on the prowl. She took out her sickle and prepared to defend herself, but she hid behind corners and obstacles well enough to avoid the cats.

She entered the dark quiet neighborhoods and made it almost as far as Amaryllis's house before she heard rustling in the treetops overhead.

That sound set her nerves on fire. She almost stopped walking to look up and then broke into a run. She had to get back to Renfroe's house and fast.

She turned at the next intersection still running her fastest when something hit her in the ankles. She had half a second to realize she was falling before she slammed down on the ground with some kind of rope twisted around her lower legs.

Her sickle flew out of her hand, and in seconds, the factors burst out of the bushes and enveloped her. One of them kicked her in the head and another struck a stick across her back.

She cowered under her arms, but they attacked too fast from every possible direction. They landed blows all over her until something very fast and very powerful bowled between them.

A hurtling missile hit one of the factors across the knees, brought him to the ground, and Dina stared in shocked amazement as Adrian brought Harmon Farley down right in front of her.

Adrian exploded from one man to another, struck, slashed his claws, and slaughtered two of them before he went to work on the others.

She didn't see what he did to them. He was still shredding the third one when the other three staggered away and vanished into the dark leaving trails of blood behind them.

He sank his teeth into the third one's throat and tore it out before he looked up. He squatted over his last victim's body with blood running down his chin. He bared his bloody fangs into the darkness and snarled before he realized the rest of the factors were already gone.

He jerked around and glared at Dina before he came back to himself and stood up straight. He ran his face across his shoulder and smeared blood on his fur. Wiping his face did nothing to make him look less deadly.

He strode over to Dina and cut the rope with his claws. "You should be more careful, Dina," he growled. "You shouldn't be out on the streets at this time of night."

"Me!" she exclaimed. "What are you doing in the city? I thought you'd be a hundred miles out in the jungle."

"Maybe I should be," he muttered and pulled her to her feet. "I came to study this place to see about possibly invading it."

She stared at him and then it clicked. He wouldn't see the Auroras before she saw him. He wouldn't get their intelligence soon enough.

She quickly repeated everything she'd told them about what Amaryllis was planning and the messages the subversive helpers wanted to send him.

"Hmmm," he murmured. "That is interesting. That puts a different spin on it, doesn't it?"

"Do you think you might invade this city?" she asked.

"I might, but as you say, I couldn't tell you or them when I plan to do it. The wrong person might find out." He cocked his head to study her. "Thank you for telling me, Dina."

"I don't expect you to change your opinion of me, but I still support your cause. I still want to prove myself to you."

"Now isn't the time to have that conversation. Come on. I'll take you home."

He led her away into the dark. They left the three dead factors lying on the pavement. Adrian didn't ask where she needed to go. He hardly looked where he was going when he walked back to Renfroe's house.

"Why are you out of the house this late at night, anyway?" he asked on the way.

"The woman who smuggled the Auroras out of Prideland—she's pregnant with one of the Children. She came to me and asked me to help her get out. I took her as far as the jungle before the Auroras found us. They're taking her to the canton."

He gazed off into the dark. "That's good. She must be one of the good ones."

"She is. She would have helped me if she'd stayed here. I'm sorry she's gone."

"She isn't gone if she's pregnant with one of the Children—or several of them. We need all the Children we can get."

She studied him in the darkness. She wanted to ask him so many questions, but one burned its way to the forefront of her mind. How did he find her? How did he just happen to materialize out of the darkness just when he needed her most?

He said he came here to check out the city for potential invasion, but that didn't explain how he wound up in exactly the right place at the right time to save her from the factors. Was he watching her, too?

Her heart flipped at the thought. He still cared. He hadn't written her off completely.

She made up her mind then and there to throw herself into this campaign with everything she had. She would prove herself—to him, to Iona, and to all the Children. She would make them understand that she still loved them and supported them.

She would have liked to touch Adrian and show him some affection, but now wasn't the time for that, either.

He led her back to the door in the garden wall, eased it open, and they both stepped inside. They stopped on the grass under the trees and turned to face each other.

The faint light shone on his fur and she marveled again how similar he looked to Renfroe. She suffered another pang of longing to touch Adrian and show him how much she loved him, but he wouldn't appreciate that. None of the Children did.

"Good night, Dina," he murmured. "Thank you again for telling me. It means a great deal that you would help us."

"If there's any way I can pass information back and forth between you and the helpers, you only have to tell me. I'll do anything I can to....."

A deep growl startled both of them from the undergrowth. Adrian spun around and the fur stood up on his neck when Renfroe stalked out of the shadows.

"Who's there?" he boomed. "If you came here to threaten my helper....." He emerged from the trees and froze in place when he saw who it was. "You!!" he snarled.

"Adrian was just bringing me home," Dina blurted out. "He just saved me from the factors."

"Is that so?" Renfroe paced a few yards closer and growled even lower in his chest. "You're taking your life in your hands coming into this city, my boy."

"You're the one who's taking your life in your hands," Adrian snarled back. "I'll be keeping an eye on Dina. If you or anyone else threatens her, I'll be the one to pay them back."

"I am not threatening her, boy!" Renfroe barked. "I'm protecting her."

"You—protecting *her?!*" Adrian countered. "You're the biggest threat to her. She wouldn't be in danger at all if not for you. She would be out in the jungle with us and she would be safe."

"Is that what you think?" Renfroe began, but Adrian cut him off.

"That's twice in less than twelve hours the Children have saved her life—not you. Where were you when she needed you?"

"She was only in danger because she tried to help the Children," Renfroe fired back. "Open your eyes. She's done nothing but try to help you since she came back here. She hardly cares for me at all."

"That's none of your concern whether she's helping us or not," Adrian fired back. "I warn you. If you or anyone else threatens her, you won't last ten seconds against me."

He didn't wait around for Renfroe to answer. Adrian shot off the ground into the trees. The branches thrashed for a second and then he disappeared into the distance.

Renfroe waited until the noise died and then he stormed off to the house without looking back.

Dina hurried after him. "How can you say I don't care for you at all? Do you know what it cost me to come back here? My own Children don't trust me anymore because I came back to you."

"You had three years alone with them, Dina," he growled over his shoulder. "That is more than I will ever have."

"Doesn't it mean anything to you at all that I came back? Don't you care at all that I'm here and that I'm with you?"

"Of course I care, but you've done nothing but throw it in my face that you didn't come back for me."

"Of course I came back for you. Why else would I come back?"

"To help the Children. To make it up to them somehow by gleaning information about the Pride and passing it to them. You've made it clear you only came back because your man died. You've spent every waking hour subverting the Pride to help the Children. You've broken every rule and used my protection to destroy the Pride and the understanding between us and the helpers."

"That isn't fair!" she countered. "The Pride destroyed the understanding by trying to kill the Children. You know that as well as I do and you can't expect me to betray my own Children. I didn't come back here to sell them out and help the Pride destroy them."

"I would never ask that, Dina....."

"Yet you're asking—or at least suggesting—that I stop helping them—which amounts to the same thing. You said yourself that no one can avoid taking sides in the war. If I didn't help them, I would be helping the Pride and vice versa. What I don't understand is how you can have gone as far as you have to help them and you still won't commit yourself to going all the way. You could do more than anyone to help the Children. You could actually help them win this war."

"I couldn't do that. I'm a cat. I belong to the Pride. I would be betraying my own kind if I helped the Children win."

"Will you wake up?!" she yelled back. "The cats are the ones who attacked you. The cats are the ones you said would kill you next time. They've already turned against you. You aren't protecting anyone. They've already betrayed you and they say you've betrayed them. You're already on the other side. When are you going to realize that?"

He made a low rumble in his throat that was half growl and half snarl. "You are right about that, but subverting the understanding is a step too far. I couldn't do that."

"There is no understanding!" she fired back. "The understanding is history. The number of helpers in this city who want to back the Children is growing by the day. You can't stop what's coming. The Pride will never rule this planet again. The Pride doesn't rule the planet now. The understanding between the humans and the cats is over. It's just a matter of certain cats waking up and facing the uncomfortable fact."

He entered the parlor and sat down in front of the blazing fire. Belinda must have left it burning for him.

He turned around and fixed Dina with a piercing glare. She expected him to launch into another argument, but instead, he lowered his voice to an even deeper rumble. "You are right, Dina."

"They're your Children," she insisted. "You're in this mess because you saved their lives. How can you turn your backs on them? How can you not want them to live freely—which means winning this war? If they lose, they'll all die. If the Children win, they won't go on a wholesale slaughter to annihilate every cat on the planet. The Children just want to live. That should tell you everything you need to know about who should win and who shouldn't."

She stopped long enough to inhale a long shuddering breath. She had to keep herself under control.

"I learned a long time ago that, as their mother, I had to do everything possible to protect them," she went on. "I learned that anyone who threatened them or stood in the way of them growing up freely would become my enemy, no matter who does it. I owed the Children that much and I still feel that way now. They're my Children and I'll do everything in my power to help them. I don't care what it takes and I don't care who stands against me. If you aren't comfortable with that, then I don't belong here. I came back to you. I kept my promise. I can leave just as easily if you insist that I stop helping them. I did not come back here to help them. I didn't even know that I *could* help them until all these helpers started approaching me about it. I came back for you. I came back to honor my promise and because I care about you. I admire you for what you've done for the Children. You've taken so many risks and you still are taking them. I can never forget that and I'm grateful to you for that. You're....you're a hero."

"Adrian doesn't appear to share your opinion," he growled.

"He doesn't know you the way I do."

He sighed, turned away, and flopped down in front of the flames. "There is nothing I could do to help the Children's cause, Dina," he growled over his shoulder. "None of the other cats will even talk to me about the Children or the war and the Children would never accept me, either. I am caught in a no-man's-land between both sides. There is no side that I can be on anymore."

She eased up behind him and squatted down to put her hand on his shoulder. "You can be on my side."

"Not if Adrian has anything to say about it," he muttered. "You are right about him. He is as determined and aggressive as you said."

"Are you still proud of him?" she asked.

"More than ever," he murmured. "I only wish I could make him understand that."

Chapter 14

Dina woke up alone again the next morning. How many days had passed? She couldn't keep track of them all.

She wandered out to the portico and froze in horror when she saw Buck limping toward the side door in the wall. Blood seeped through his shirt and his face had been ripped to shreds by claws.

He hugged one broken arm against his ribs and barely put his weight on his left leg. He cast one forsaken glance over his shoulder, made eye contact with Dina once, and then let himself out through the door and shut it behind him.

Dina gulped down a lump in her throat. Adrian did that. He killed three factors and would have killed the other three if they'd stuck around long enough. He did that because they threatened her.

There was nothing more to see here, so she turned away, but right then, Belinda came out of the kitchen. Dina couldn't help but cry out in horror when she saw Belinda's face slashed with three deep gashes.

They cut down her face from her forehead, across her nose and cheek, as far as the opposite corner of her jaw. She was also limping and blood soaked through the sleeve of her tunic.

"Belinda!" Dina gasped. "What.....?"

Dina almost asked what happened, but she could see perfectly well what happened. No cat would have done this—not to a helper. The cats left all that to the factors and the factors didn't slash a person with what could only be claw marks.

Belinda's features trembled with misery, but before she could say anything, Renfroe strutted in from the garden. He came out of the trees near his sandbox, crossed the courtyard, and entered through the portico.

He stopped next to Dina and stared with all his intensity at Belinda. "What happened to your face, Belinda?"

She choked once, lowered her eyes to the floor, and whimpered in a tiny voice, "I...got visited.....by the Children....."

Dina gasped again, but Renfroe interrupted. "The Children—visited you? When? Did they come *here?*"

Belinda nodded down at her shoes. "They came last night. There were three of them—all black with black eyes. Even their skin was black. They said that, if I threatened Dina or did anything to interfere with her, they would come back and kill me. They visited Buck, too."

Renfroe's head snapped around to stare at Dina when Belinda mentioned three Black Children. Dina shivered when she thought about them visiting Belinda, but Dina still felt certain that it was Adrian who did all that damage to Buck.

Renfroe pulled himself together. "You look terrible, but there's nothing we can do about that. You all have a festival to attend at Hellion House in a few hours. You better finish your work, Belinda, and clean yourself up as best you can before it's time to go. Come out into the courtyard, Dina. I want to talk to you."

Belinda went back to the kitchen and Dina followed him outside. She shuddered again when she sat down on the bench by the fountain.

"Did you know about this, Dina?" he demanded. "Did you send the Children to attack Belinda?"

"No!" she insisted. "I didn't even know they were in the city. I was as surprised as you were when Adrian showed up last night. I had no idea any of the others were here—and I never told any of the Children about Buck and Belinda."

"These three Children that Belinda says visited her—are they Khalid's sons?"

She looked away and nodded. "I swear I didn't know they were here. I wondered when Adrian showed up last night if he was keeping me under surveillance. Maybe they all are. I don't know."

"Then there's nothing we can do about it," Renfroe muttered. "The Children are already in the city. They're already exerting their authority over the helpers. It's over. The war is over."

"You know that isn't true. Adrian said he came here to study the city to decide if he wants to invade."

"*Does* he want to invade?"

Now it was Dina's turn to snort. "Are you kidding me? He would never tell me if he did. He keeps his own counsel. He'll make his own decision about what he does, and when he makes it, he won't share it with me. He'll just do it."

"If the Children are here, then we're all in serious trouble."

She didn't tell him again that they were in serious trouble already. The Children showing up and visiting people in the middle of the night didn't bode well at all.

Renfroe sighed again. "You better get your breakfast, Dina. It will be time for you and Belinda to go to the festival soon."

She grasped that lifeline and left to return to the kitchen. She didn't want to talk about the Children or Adrian or the Black or the war or anything else.

She realized the minute she walked into the kitchen that she wouldn't get out of it that easily. She had to sit down at the table across from Buck and Belinda while all three of them ate in silence.

Both Buck and Belinda kept their eyes down. Dina tried to do the same thing, but she found her gaze migrating back to their faces, especially Buck's.

Adrian had slashed Buck's face in multiple directions and made a tic-tac-toe of lines that completely disfigured Buck's features. He would wear those scars for the rest of his life.

How many other people in this city did the Black visit last night? She hated to think about it.

She got her answer when she and Belinda rolled up the Hellion House and joined the crowd in the stands. A tide of conversation surrounded the two women and everyone talked about nothing but the Children.

"I saw a white one on the roof of the Senate building yesterday," one man murmured. "He was just squatting there on the corner of the building looking down at everyone on the ground."

"I saw an orange one at the market two days ago," a woman added. "He looked like a Manx...but he also looked like a person. It was spooky."

"What are they doing here?" a different man asked. "The factors say the Pride is holding the Children outside the city, but that obviously isn't true. If they can get inside the city, they can just as easily invade."

"Maybe they're already invading and this is the way they're doing it," the first man suggested. "Maybe they plan to invade by ones and twos until they build up an overwhelming force inside the city. Then they'll attack and wipe out everyone."

"I don't believe they will wipe out everyone," the woman countered. "I don't think they want to wipe out anyone. The Pride went after the Children first. The Pride killed thousands of Children when they were just babies. The Children are only fighting this war to defend themselves."

"You could get visited even for saying that," the second man warned.

"Well, it's true," the woman snapped. "I was there when five of the younger Hellions entered my benefactor's home and killed a litter of Children a few minutes after they were born. These same Hellions talked about how they'd been going from house to house to eliminate all the Children as soon as anyone gave birth to them. If any mother even spoke up to defend her Children, the Hellions reduced her, too. I don't care what anyone says. I'll keep telling the truth no matter what they do to me."

"The Children have never killed any humans unless the Pride sends helpers out to fight the Children in support of the Pride," the first man added. "If the Children wanted to kill us, they would have done it by now. The Pride wouldn't be able to stop them."

Similar conversations raced back and forth through the stands. Dina and Belinda sat in silence and didn't get involved in any of these discussions, but Dina couldn't help hearing about them.

It sure sounded like the Pride couldn't stop their helpers from talking, either—not anymore. Those days were over.

The anxious tension didn't dissipate when the factors climbed onto the platform to address the helpers. Gasps of horror broke out of the crowd when Buck limped up the steps and everyone saw the condition he was in.

Of the ten factors in attendance, the Children had visited six of them. Three of them had never been on the platform before. They must be here to replace the three that Adrian killed last night.

Two of the injured factors had broken legs. Harmon Farley carried his arm in a sling and all of them sported deep scratches, bruises, and bloody injuries to their limbs and bodies.

"What the hell is going on?!" a man bellowed out of the crowd. "You told us the Pride was keeping the Children out of the city, but we've all seen them right here in the streets!"

Farley hobbled to the front of the platform and raised his one good arm. "Just quiet down and let's get this festival started. Our good friend Solomon Krob is going to tell us about the time he let his friend convince him to turn his back on the understanding...."

"Answer the question!!" another man blurted out from the other side of the stands. "How can the Pride protect us from the Children when you can't even protect yourselves?!"

"We heard the Pride wants to recruit another group of helpers to fight in the war," a third man called out. "If we help the Pride, the Children will kill us all."

"The Children are right here in the city," a woman added. "They obviously aren't afraid of the cats at all."

"The Children must be afraid," Farley countered. "The Children are in hiding. They don't dare to show themselves."

"They sure dared to show themselves to you, didn't they?" a fourth man yelled back.

Right then, Sonya shot to her feet somewhere in the stands. Everyone could see her bruised face, but she didn't hold back at all. Her voice rang through the building for all to hear.

"I have a story for you! When we rode in the wagon that brought me to be a helper in this city, we saw two battles between the Children and the cats. The Children won both of those battles, and in the second one, fifty cats attacked twenty Children in the fields outside the city. The Children were walking along minding their own business when the cats attacked and the Children slaughtered all those cats in seconds."

Gasps and excited talk broke out in the crowd. All the helpers turned to each other and started discussing the story in rapid bursts of speculation.

"Quiet down!" Farley yelled over the noise. "We're here to have a festival—not debate what to do about the Children! That's for the Pride to decide. We just have to trust the cats to deal with the Children."

Everyone ignored him and kept right on talking until another man called out, "Why don't you tell us how you got those scratches on your face, Farley? Why don't you explain to us how all the factors got hurt in one night?"

"Factors don't leave scratches like that and I bet you boys wouldn't visit yourselves," another man boomed. "Cats don't visit people, so it had to be the Children."

"Tell the truth!" another woman yelled out.

Farley raised his hand again, but too many people kept interjecting from all sides of the building. He couldn't make himself heard.

Two more factors stepped forward, but their tattered faces only confirmed what everyone already knew. Everyone could see exactly what happened to these men.

The noise kept rising until a dozen Hellion males strode into the gymnasium. They came through the side door and a hush fell instantly over the crowd.

This was the first Dina had ever heard of any cat attending a festival. Renfroe had been very specific that the festivals were only for helpers.

The Hellions strode into the gymnasium and glared at all the helpers. Anyone still standing instantly sat down and all talk died.

"Now, if you're all finished debating what doesn't concern you," Farley went on, "we can get on with our festival and hear our first account. Solomon—if you would...."

He waved one of the new men forward. This was one of the men with his leg in a splint. He used crutches to lurch his way to the front.

Farley and the others gave him encouraging nods. This man had obviously never spoken at a festival in his life. "Um....." he began. "Well....it happened like this....."

At that instant, ten Children charged through the side door and attacked the Hellions in plain view of everyone. Dina sat rooted to the spot and watched Adrian, the Black, Link's nephews, and the four Manx boys fall on the Hellions in snarling, spitting fury.

Dina couldn't move a muscle. The scuffle escalated and Rex smashed his opponent into the platform. It jolted and the other man with a broken leg fell over.

That triggered the whole crowd. People screamed and bolted for the door. They trampled and fell over each other.

Cairo and Kaiser both toppled their lions too close to the exit and all the helpers surged away shrieking in terror. Adrian and one big lion smashed into the platform again and one of its legs buckled.

It tilted violently to one side and all the factors slid off onto the floor right into the middle of the battle. That set off the crowd again and another wave of bodies charged the exit.

This time, the helpers' terror overcame all their reluctance and they forced their way outside. The Children and the lions kept grappling and slashing on the floor.

Belinda grabbed Dina's arm and hauled her to her feet. "Come on!" Belinda hollered. "We gotta get out of here!"

Chapter 15

Dina had been so stunned that she and Belinda were some of the last people to get out of Hellion House. They ran outside into a scene of mass chaos unlike anything Dina could possibly imagine.

Hundreds of Children mobbed the streets fighting cats coming out of every building. Dina didn't recognize any of these Children. She wouldn't have been able to recognize them anyway. They were all fighting with too many cats on every street corner.

The battle spilled over into the neighborhoods and helpers kept blundering into danger from cats and Children alike.

The Children trounced the cats at every turn, but more and more cats kept coming out of nowhere to join in and help their friends.

Dina held onto Belinda and raced around a corner, only to pull back when they almost got enveloped by five lynxes ganging up on two small Children with silver-grey fur.

The whole knot of flying teeth and claws rolled past Dina and Belinda, smashed into the nearest wall, and broke apart with three lynxes attacking one Child and the other two lynxes taking on the other Child.

Belinda screamed in horror and would have run straight into the path of a jaguar getting torn to shreds by another tiger-like Child with white-grey fur and brown stripes.

Dina yanked Belinda out of the way and they took off down the middle of the street. They avoided all other scuffles for two blocks before a surge of helpers thundered around another corner and nearly mowed the two women down.

The helpers carried shovels, pitchforks, kitchen knives, and other household weapons. They bellowed in fury, rushed into the battle, and set to work attacking the Children to help defend the cats.

Belinda kept on running through the crowd trying to get behind the helpers, but at that moment, Dina spotted Naia, Rome, Egypt, and Dexter in the crowd.

The helpers charged the four Children and a man with a pitchfork raised his weapon to impale Naia.

Dina tore out of Belinda's hold, plunged back into the battle, and drew her weapons from inside her tunic. She shouldered four helpers out of the way, but she didn't get there fast enough.

The mob of helpers overran the four Children and five of them cornered Naia. They knocked her against a wall, dragged her to the ground, and the man stabbed down with his pitchfork.

She yanked out of the way in time to save her own life, but the fork pierced her leg and she screamed out in pain.

Dina exploded into the crowd, brought down her sickle on the man's neck, sprang on top of Naia, and straddled her to face the helpers.

They swarmed her just as fast and Dina struck out with her weapons. She didn't care anymore who or what she hit. She lashed out at any of them, smashed their weapons away, and her blades struck flesh.

She brought down another two, but more and more helpers came out of nowhere to surround her. It took her another second to realize that this new surge of helpers was attacking the first wave. The subversive helpers stormed up the street clearing everyone away from the Children.

Dina brandished her weapons in all directions, but the helpers who'd just been attacking her had to turn away to defend themselves against the subversives.

The battle shifted and everyone got swept up the street moving back toward Hellion House. Dina didn't see any other Children she recognized and none of them paid attention to her or Naia.

Dina finally dared to lower her weapons and squat down to examine Naia. She huddled against a building clutching her leg. She'd pulled the pitchfork out and blood bubbled from the wound.

"We gotta get you out of here!" Dina stammered. "We have to stop the bleeding, too."

She glanced around for something to bandage Naia's leg and settled on the helper who stabbed Naia in the first place.

Dina used her knife to cut his tunic into strips, plastered a wad of fabric against the entrance and exit wounds, and tied them tightly with another strip around Naia's thigh.

She roared in pain when Dina knotted it. "We have to get you somewhere safe." Dina glanced up the street. The battle kept surging back and forth. It came dangerously close to overwhelming Dina and Naia again.

"I don't think....I can walk....Dina....." Naia panted.

"Don't worry. I'll help you. I'll carry you if I have to." Dina put her weapons in her pockets and helped pull Naia to her feet. "Lean on me. You're going to make it. Come on."

She pulled Naia's arm over her shoulder and Naia hobbled up the street while Dina supported her weight.

They made it as far as the corner when Dina spotted Tom ahead. He stood in the middle of the street waving his arms in both directions while another crowd of helpers fled from the war zone.

"Keep moving!" he called. "Keep moving! Don't stop! Don't look at the battle or you might slow us all down! Keep moving!"

He glanced behind him and caught sight of Dina half-carrying Naia out of danger. Dina pulled Naia into a side street and Tom turned back to what he was doing.

Dina made sure to steer far around where he was directing the helpers to go, but a second later, another surge of hostilities poured out of the city streets behind her.

Helpers battled helpers with every weapon they could lay their hands on. Cats and Children roared, bellowed, and snarled in deadly combat that left bodies scattered all over the street.

Five clusters of cats versus Children nearly collided with Dina and Naia. One of these clusters broke apart right in front of the two women and a panther involved turned on them.

Dina let go of Naia to pull her weapons out of her pocket, but the man who'd been fighting the panther attacked at that moment and the two combatants hurtled away up the street.

Dina grabbed Naia and stumbled into another street, but more scenes of combat threatened to overwhelm the two women at every turn. Dina couldn't even see where to go to get away from the conflict.

In desperation, she dove into a random doorway somewhere. It led into a dim hallway with another door at the far end and a stairway off to one side leading to the second story.

She lowered Naia onto the stairs. "We'll just have to wait here until the battle ends. We can't go out there now."

"Thank you, Dina," Naia whispered. "I thought I was dead."

"Adrian is out there somewhere. We'll find him and he'll take you back to the jungle. You'll be safe there." Naia looked so miserable that Dina sat down on the step next to her. "Don't you wish we had some Vaga sap right about now?"

Naia made a face and pulled a tiny wooden box out of her pocket. "Something tells me this won't work for what's wrong with me."

"It's better than nothing. Do you want to do it now? As soon as things quiet down, I can take you back to Renfroe's house. We can do it there if you want to."

"I guess we could do it now." Naia's eyes sliced toward the door.

Neither woman could see what was going on out there. They didn't need to see it. They could hear all the sounds of growling, tearing, and screaming in the distance.

"I don't know how we'll ever find Adrian in this," Naia choked.

She sounded so forlorn that Dina couldn't stand it. She took the box and opened it. It was full of Vaga sap.

"You're right that it won't heal the damage on the inside, but at least it will stop the wound from bleeding." Dina put the box on the step and started untying the bandage. "This might hurt."

"It already does," Naia whispered.

Dina tried not to hear how scared Naia sounded. The Children always seemed so tough, but that might have been because Dina was used to dealing with the boys—and Iona.

Emerald, Calliope, Egypt, and India were all strong and determined, too, but Dina had never dealt with them when they were alone and injured.

Naia didn't make a sound when Dina smeared the sap onto the entrance and exit wounds and then rebandaged Naia's thigh. Dina handed her the box back. "Good thinking bringing it with you."

"I thought I would have to use it on everybody else," Naia murmured. "Maybe I shouldn't have come for this battle."

"Of course you should have!" Dina exclaimed. "I'm sure you aren't the only Child to get hurt. I'm sure Children much bigger and stronger than you are getting injured out there all the time."

Naia looked up and her features twisted in another pang of misery. "Thank you so much for saving me, Dina. We were wrong to doubt you."

Dina sighed. "Maybe you weren't. Maybe I did still think I owed the Pride something and that's why I came back. I don't know. I guess Adrian and Iona weren't as wrong about me as I thought they were."

"Do you regret coming back?" Naia asked. "You could come home to the jungle with us now. You don't have to stay here."

"I could, but I don't regret coming here. I've been able to help the Children from here—at least, I think I have been able to. Maybe Adrian is so far ahead of me that my information doesn't mean anything to him."

"But your intentions do. I'm certain he sees that."

Dina found herself smiling at.....her daughter-in-law. This young woman was Adrian's wife. "I'm really glad he has you. I'm really glad you two have each other. I couldn't ask for him to marry a nicer girl. You two really were made for each other—and Iona and Karim, too. I'm happy for all of you."

Naia lowered her eyes and smiled in a way that would have been blushing if she didn't have fur all over her cheeks. "Thank you. That means so much coming from you."

Dina put her arm around Naia's shoulders and squeezed, but only once and she let go immediately. She didn't want to overstep the moment.

They fell silent to listen to the battle. The noise didn't die down. The stairway in which Dina and Naia hid got darker as the day wore away and the battle still raged.

"Stay here," Dina murmured to Naia. "I'm going to go outside and see what's happening. If I see a way to get out of the city, we'll go."

"Be careful, Dina," Naia urged.

"I will." Dina pulled out her weapons. "Just stay hidden. I don't want you getting hurt again."

She strode to the entrance and looked out. The battle still raged all over the place with just as many cats, Children, and helpers battling everywhere.

She almost retreated when three tigers toppled out of nowhere and slammed into the sidewalk in front of Dina's doorway. She had a split second to see the man from Moonlight canton—the one she'd fought with when Link died.

The tigers smothered him and all dove for him at once. She lunged for them, hacked her sickle into the back of one of their necks, and when the second one turned to see who was attacking them, she nailed her knife into his eye.

The man reared off the ground, tackled the third tiger onto his back, and tore the cat's neck out in a split second.

The man picked himself up and scowled at her like he was trying to put together where he knew her from. "Thanks," he muttered, but a second later, a lion rocketed out of nowhere and collided with him.

They hit the pavement and Dina rushed up behind them to finish off the lion, too, but at that moment, a tidal wave of helpers erupted around the nearest corner.

So many helpers battled so many other helpers that she couldn't tell who belonged to which side. She had to spring back inside the doorway as they surged past her. The crowd swallowed both the lion and the man until nothing but helpers remained.

Dina retreated back to the stairway and sat down next to Naia. "No good?" Naia asked.

Dina shook her head. "We'll just have to wait for nightfall."

Chapter 16

Dina limped the last painful block to Renfroe's house and stumbled up the path toward the garden door. No way could she take Naia into the kitchen.

Dina halted under the trees and leaned Naia against the wall while they both caught their breath. "This is it," Dina panted. "I'll take you inside and you can rest there until we find a way to get you back to the jungle."

"Are you sure it's safe here?" Naia glanced around. "This is a cat's house."

"I've hidden a few different people here. It will work out. Don't worry. I'll make sure you get out of here in one piece."

Naia snorted. "I'm not in one piece now."

"No, but you will be. We might get lucky and Adrian will come here looking for you. Maybe someone saw me helping you and they'll tell him you're with me."

"I sure hope you're right," Naia murmured.

Dina took a deep breath and pulled Naia away from the wall. "Come on. Just a little farther and you can lie down for the night."

She supported Naia through the door and into the shadowy garden. Lamplight shone from the windows and through the portico, but Dina didn't see Renfroe anywhere. Was he home?

She and Naia made their way under the trees toward the courtyard outside Dina's and Renfroe's bedroom. Dina planned to take Naia through there to the little spare room the way she'd hidden Fan in there.

They made it as far as the courtyard wall when Naia tripped over something on the ground. Her one good leg buckled and her weight pulled out of Dina's arms.

Naia collapsed on the ground and she gave a small growl of pain. "Aargh!"

"It's okay," Dina whispered. "We're almost there."

Just then, another voice cracked out of the darkness. "Who's there?"

Dina spun around, grabbed her weapons, and moved in to block Naia from Buck who stepped out of the shadows. "Keep away from her, Buck. I swear I'll kill you if you try anything."

His eyes darted down to Naia who scrambled backward, pushed herself off the courtyard wall, and hefted herself to her feet. She couldn't move, though. She had to stay leaning against the wall to avoid falling over.

"You shouldn't have brought one of *them* here," he growled in a deadly undertone. "You put all of us in danger by doing this."

"She got hurt in the battle and she needs help." Dina jabbed her knife at him. "Now back off. I won't tell you again."

"What's going on?" Belinda called from the portico. "Is someone out there?"

"It's me, Belinda," Dina told her. "I had to hide from the battle and I just got back."

"She brought one of those freaks with her," Buck snarled. "She's harboring one of the Children."

"That's right. I am," Dina fired back. "And there's nothing you can do about it. Go crawl back into whatever hole you crawled out of because the factors don't have the power to enforce any rule in this city anymore. I'll come and go as I please and help whoever I please. If you interfere, I'll kill you myself."

Belinda came over and stared at Dina holding Buck at knife point. Then Belinda gasped when she saw Naia. "You brought none of *them* here?! How could you do this, Dina?"

"I could and I did," Dina snapped. "Go back inside, Belinda. This has nothing to do with you."

"Nothing to do with me!" Belinda exclaimed. "You could get us all killed for this!"

"Killed by whom? The cats?" Dina countered. "The cats can't do anything to anyone. They can't even protect themselves."

Just when Dina thought the situation couldn't get any worse, Renfroe hopped over the garden wall and padded into the lamplight. "Oh, you're finally back, Dina. I was wondering where you.....What is *that?*"

"She's one of the Children as you can see," Dina explained. "She got hurt in the battle. I'm keeping her here until we can contact Adrian to take her home to the jungle."

"This is a terrible idea, Dina....."

"The terrible idea would have been to leave her to die in the middle of the battle," Dina fired back. "I raised this girl from infancy. If you send her away, I'm going with her. I would love to see anyone try to stop me from helping her. The factors don't have the power to punish anyone in this city anymore and the cats are running scared. I'm not hiding anymore. I'm helping this girl no matter what any of you say."

"This is still my house, Dina," Renfroe replied. "I think I might still have something to say about what happens here."

"Fine. You have something to say about it. I'm taking her inside. We're going to clean up her leg and then she's going to rest in my old room until I figure out how to contact Adrian to come and get her."

She turned around and pulled Naia's arm over her shoulders again. Dina changed her mind and led Naia toward the portico. It was closer and now Dina didn't need to hide any of this from anyone.

She made it halfway there when the trees thrashed overhead and Adrian and the Black plunged out of the branches. They landed on the grass beyond the courtyard.

"Hand over Naia now or we'll make you all bleed," Adrian snarled.

"Dina was helping me," Naia explained, but he didn't wait to hear anything else.

He darted forward, snatched her away from Dina, and pulled Naia over to his side. She stumbled on her bad leg, but he caught her, and just as quickly, passed her behind him to Kenji.

Kenji grabbed her, rocketed away into the branches, and vanished taking Naia with him.

Dina sighed with relief, but too soon. "There's no reason to get hostile," Renfroe rumbled. "We were trying to help the girl...."

"*You* weren't trying to help anyone," Adrian fired back. "You're a killer. You'll forgive me if I don't want my wife anywhere near you."

Renfroe froze and his eyes glittered with hidden fire. "Your wife?!"

"Keep away from her," Adrian snarled. "If I see you anywhere near her, I'll kill you."

Renfroe took a step forward. "Be reasonable. She got injured in the battle. Dina brought the girl here...."

Adrian attacked in a blur, struck Renfroe hard enough to send him rolling, cuffed him across the cheek, and laid open three parallel gashes under Renfroe's eye.

Adrian rolled out of range. Buck stepped forward, but he stopped when Karim moved in and planted himself between Buck and Adrian.

Renfroe scrambled to his feet, bared his teeth, and snarled at Adrian, but Adrian only snarled back. Renfroe paced back and forth growling in pain and fury, but he didn't retaliate. He couldn't. Adrian was stronger and faster.

"I told you to keep away from my wife," Adrian growled one last time. "I won't warn you again."

He launched himself into the branches and vanished. Kaiser and Karim waited a second longer just to make their presence felt and then they took off into the dark canopy, too. The branches swayed once and then dead silence fell over the courtyard.

Renfroe paced back and forth a few more times and Dina wilted in relief. It was over.

At least Naia was back with the Children. Adrian and the Black would take her to safety. Dina didn't have to worry about smuggling an injured Child out of town.

Smuggling Tania and Fan out of town had been easy compared to how the same project would have gone with Naia.

Dina finally turned to Buck and Belinda. "The party's over. You two can go back to bed. There's nothing more any of us can do tonight."

Buck and Belinda stared at her in stupefied shock. Neither of them moved until Renfroe barked. "You heard her! Get out of here! Don't stand there with your mouths open. Go!"

Belinda took off back to the kitchen. Dina expected to hear Belinda banging around in there for hours the way she usually did, but not tonight. Belinda vanished without a sound.

Buck limped away into the garden. Dina didn't know where Buck slept or where he spent his time. She was really starting to hope she got out of this city without ever finding out.

Renfroe grumbled to himself a few more times and strode into the parlor where he sat down by the fire. Dina got another bowl of water and a rag.

He didn't snap or complain when she cleaned the cuts on his face. "You wanted to meet him," she murmured. "Now you know what he's like."

"That girl....he called her his wife," Renfroe muttered.

"She's Tom's and Elyse's daughter." His head snapped around. "No one knows. Elyse hid it from Tom. She came to see me in the canton, gave birth, and left her Children with me. He doesn't know he has any Children."

"I pity him," Renfroe growled. "Even having Children who hate you is better than not knowing they exist."

"She's a sweet girl," Dina went on. "They love each other very much."

"I can see that. He's extremely protective of her."

She set the bowl aside. "Do you want to go to bed?"

"I suppose we might as well."

They went off to their bedroom. Tonight did not go the way Dina planned. She'd been prepared to hide Naia in this house—for days, if necessary. She should have known Adrian would never let that happen.

Dina and Renfroe stretched out on the bed, but they both just lay there thinking about the events of the day.

"Where were you just now?" she asked. "Were you out in the middle of the battle?"

"I avoided it, fortunately."

"Are the Children still out there fighting?"

"The Children aren't," he replied. "They've retreated out of the city. The helpers are still skirmishing with each other and a few cats are out there trying to put down the unrest. Don't ask me why they bother."

"What do you mean?"

"No one can stop the Children now and all of Prideland is in turmoil over their rebellion. If they can strike like this without us even knowing they were in the city, then there's nothing we can do to stop them."

"People at the festival said they saw Children in the city these last few days. Didn't the Pride think to do anything then?"

"You and I saw Children in the city," he countered. "Did you think it meant they were preparing to invade and attack? I know you didn't because I asked you if Adrian was planning to invade and attack and you said you didn't know. We thought they were isolated Children investigating us." He groaned and turned his head away. "He's a master tactician."

"He learned from the best," Dina murmured.

"What does that mean?"

"Nothing. What can we do about it?"

"We can't do anything about it and it's too late to try. Oh, I just remembered. I'm supposed to tell you that the Senate has called you to appear before them tomorrow."

She whipped around fast. "They what?"

"They want you to answer questions about the Children's war against us and hear what you say about negotiating peace."

"You mean negotiate surrender?" she countered. "That's what negotiating peace now would be. The Pride would be admitting defeat by offering any negotiation now."

"Call it what you want. They want to talk to you and hear what you have to say. I don't have anything to do with this. I'm merely delivering the message from Osiris."

"So Osiris sent the message? Not any other cats?"

"He may be Chairman of the Senate by now for all I know. He was the one who told me to tell you."

"At least he isn't completely unreasonable about the Children."

"That's the problem," he rumbled. "Only the reasonable cats will be there to hear you tomorrow. The rest will boycott the meeting in protest. They think we shouldn't negotiate at all. Maybe they think we should keep fighting to the last kitten. How should I know?"

"Wow," she breathed. "That's bad."

"Tomorrow's hearing will be a charade," he grumbled. "It's a showpiece to make it look like the Senate is still relevant and can still make decisions about anything when they can't. If Adrian had stuck around any longer tonight, I would have told him that he's already won the war. He can dictate any terms he wishes and enforce them. No one can stand up to him."

"Maybe I should go tell him that."

"He still has to deal with the hostile cats," Renfroe went on. "They'll continue to make trouble until the bitter end. He may have his hands full eliminating them—and that's what it will take—eliminating them all down to the last cat." He heaved another sigh. "I don't suppose he'll have any difficulty doing that. I don't suppose there is anything of which he isn't capable."

Chapter 17

Dina smoothed down her tunic, took a deep breath, and stepped out of the house. She had to appear before the Senate—something only one other human being had ever done before in all of Prideland history.

Renfroe paced by her side on their way down the street. The tension between them threatened to snap her last nerve, but things got worse when they made it as far as the city streets.

Turmoil continued to erupt all over the place with helpers shoving, yelling at each other, and even getting into fights.

She didn't see any cats outside. If Renfroe hadn't been with her, someone might have mistaken this for a normal human city—all except for the dead cats littering the streets.

The Elite Battalion went through every street collecting the dead—all the human and feline dead. She didn't see any dead Children. Did the Children take their dead with them as before?

She would never know that, either, but she didn't imagine them leaving their comrades behind to be thrown into the river like trash.

Renfroe halted across the street from the Senate building. "You'll go around to the side entrance, Dina. You remember the way, I'm sure."

She rolled her eyes to Heaven. "Isn't it time we dispensed with all that nonsense? It's a little late for any of us to be observing all these absurd formalities."

"I don't make the rules, Dina," he growled. "You'll be addressing the Senate in a few minutes. You can take up your grievances with them."

He stalked off toward the building's main entrance steps. Dina fought the urge to march straight through the front door.

Who did the Senate think it was, anyway—ordering anyone to use the side entrance? The senators really must be deluding themselves if they thought they had any authority left in this city after yesterday.

She didn't do that, though. If the senators were right—which they weren't—then negotiating peace with the Children would be the quickest way to end hostilities with the least loss of life on both sides.

How far had the Senate gone toward realizing exactly what negotiating peace meant? Did they even realize how disastrously they'd already lost?

Going inside and talking to them was the only way to find out. She skirted the building, but when she got within a block of the side entrance, a group of helpers accosted her.

One woman jabbed her finger in Dina's face. "You're responsible for this! You brought the Children down on us!"

"I didn't do anything....." Dina began.

Another man shook his fist in her face. "We should visit you right now—or reduce you. That's the best you deserve."

A different man smacked the guy's hand down. "Don't you dare threaten her! We should all join with the Children and eliminate the cats. They've ruled us with an iron paw for centuries. We could all be free if we fought together instead of against each other."

Dina tried to squirm out from in front of them, but they backed her against the wall. "I'm not involved in this. I don't know anything....."

The woman who first threatened her turned to the second man. "Don't you have any understanding with the Pride? You should be ashamed of yourself for calling for open rebellion. The Pride is the best thing that ever happened to us....."

"Don't give me that line of nonsense!" the man fired back. "We all just said that to stop the factors from visiting us. We don't have to say it anymore. There never was an understanding between us and the Pride—except that we were slaves to the cats. We aren't anymore. We're free. The Children freed us. Now we can help them remove the cats entirely."

A dozen people chimed in and voices broke out on all sides. Dina couldn't tell if they agreed with him or if they were arguing with him.

Arms shot back and forth with more people pointing, shaking their fists at each other, and gesticulating in all directions. So many people got involved that they almost crushed Dina under another surge of bodies.

She did her best to elbow her way out from under them, but before she could make it six inches, one man threw a punch and flattened the guy who'd been calling for everyone to join the Children.

He went down under everyone's feet, and in a split second, the whole crowd exploded in a massive hand-to-hand brawl.

Someone threw another punch at Dina's head. She ducked and the fist smashed into the wall behind her.

Once she got down in that position, a million legs separated her from freedom. A wall of flying fists, elbows, and makeshift weapons flew in all directions above her head. She didn't dare to stand up, so she crawled between their legs trying to find her way out.

So many people packed together that they couldn't kick. They surged from one direction to another, but everyone forgot about her in their effort to attack each other. She had no idea which way to go, so she just kept crawling.

She eventually burst out of the mayhem on a sidewalk down the street from the Senate building. Helpers from all over charged for the brawl to join in. She had to hurry another block away before she got clear enough to double back.

The brawl blocked her path to the side door. Oh, what the hell. She threw caution to the wind, went around to the front, and walked up the front steps. So there.

She grinned to herself, but once she got inside, she found her way to the lower floor and entered the Senate chamber from the side.

Renfroe sat on the floor in the aisle beneath the stage. Fifty other cats occupied the seats.

Renfroe gave her a hard look, but he came forward to sit down on the floor next to her when she took her place in front of the Senate.

Twenty cats sat on the stage, including Osiris, Elyse, and a handful of lions from the Hellion family.

"Thank you for coming to see us, Dina," Osiris began.

"Thank you for having me," she replied. "I apologize for being late. There was some unrest outside. I got caught in it and had to find an alternate way to get into the building."

"That's quite all right," he went on. "As you know, we would like to ask you a few questions about the Children and this war they're waging against us."

"I'll tell you anything I can, but I don't know anything about the Children's plans. Yesterday's attack was as much a surprise to me as it was to everyone else. The Children don't share their plans with me."

"Isn't your son their leader?" one of the lions interrupted.

"Yes, he is, but he's completely independent. He doesn't share his plans with anyone except those closest to him. He certainly doesn't share them with me."

"He's coordinated simultaneous strikes all over Prideland," Osiris went on. "Did you know that? He infiltrated every other city in Prideland and carried out this assault on all our cities simultaneously."

Dina's jaw dropped. "He did?"

"You didn't know?" the same lion demanded. "I find that impossible to believe."

"How could I know when I've been living here and he's in the jungle?"

"You've been in contact with him," a jaguar pointed out.

Dina did her best not to snort in his face. "Adrian doesn't trust me. He thinks I betrayed the Children's cause by coming back to the city to be Renfroe's helper. Adrian protected me from the factor's assault. He didn't tell me anything about his plans. He certainly never told me about this attack. I thought he was the only Child in the city until I went to the festival and heard from the other helpers that they'd seen other Children in the city before yesterday."

"I don't believe you," the jaguar snapped. "I believe you incited this rebellion among the helpers to turn them against us."

"The helpers in this city were planning to join the Children's cause long before I came back. The cats of the Pride are the ones who created this problem by slaughtering the Children when they were defenseless babies. The Children fought back to defend themselves as soon as they were old enough to do so. The Children's war only released a long history of resistance and rebellion that has been simmering under the surface for years. It was only a matter of time before the Pride met with an enemy stronger than any cat. Now the helpers are using this moment to break out and finally regain their freedom. If you called me here to soothe your egos by telling you something different, you're out of your minds."

"We didn't call you here to do any such thing," Osiris replied. "We called you here to intercede between us and the Children. We want to bring peace to Prideland. You can communicate our intentions to the Children."

"How exactly do you plan to bring peace to Prideland?" she asked. "If the Children stop hostilities, what will you do? You can't claim that you'll let the Children live in peace. You've already destroyed any credibility you had in that regard. Does the Pride make any guarantee at all that no cat will ever attack any Children again? You can't make that assurance. Renfroe told me that the Senate doesn't speak for all cats and no cat has the authority to tell any other cat what to do."

A few cats on the platform fidgeted and exchanged glances. "That is true," Osiris replied. "We would still appreciate opening a dialogue with the Children along these lines."

"That's what I'm telling you," she countered. "You can't open a dialogue with them unless you have something to offer—something they want. The only thing you could possibly offer them is an ironclad guarantee of total peace and you can't offer that."

"But you can convince your son to accept our proposal," the lion suggested.

"What proposal?" she asked. "I have no authority with Adrian—or with any other Children. They're adults with minds of their own. Me being their mother doesn't mean anything."

"*Their* mother?" the lion asked. "Do you have more than one Child in their ranks?"

She waved that away. "In a manner of speaking. I have several adopted Children in Adrian's immediate entourage. They're the ones organizing this war."

"Then you're our best chance to get them to listen to us," Osiris suggested. "You can communicate with them...."

"And offer them what, exactly? What are you offering in exchange for the end of hostilities? You aren't exactly in the most advantageous position here."

"We would only like you to contact your son and open the line of communication," Osiris repeated. "That is all we're prepared to do at this time."

She puffed out her cheeks. It wasn't much. In fact, it was nothing at all, but she stopped short of telling them just how little it was. "All right. I'll inform them of your intentions. I can't promise it will come to anything, but I'll at least let them know you asked."

"Thank you, Dina," Osiris replied. "We appreciate you coming to see us. You may go."

Chapter 18

Dina squeaked open the side door and peeked outside. The street outside the Senate building was empty except for a few more bodies lying on the pavement.

She didn't see any people fighting, so she slipped outside. She met up with Renfroe on the same sidewalk across the street.

"That went better than I expected," Renfroe remarked.

"How can you say that?" she countered. "It was a disaster."

"Disaster? I've seen Senate hearings that ended in fatalities. That one was remarkably civil."

"It was a complete waste of time. Why should I communicate the Senate's intentions to the Children when the Senate has nothing to offer? You've said it yourself. The Pride is in no position to dictate anything to anyone."

"If Adrian is half the man I think he is, he'll understand this overture for what it is," Renfroe growled. "The simple fact that the Senate is making overtures to peace proves what a powerful position Adrian is in."

"All the more reason why he shouldn't negotiate. He would be stupid to relax his hold on the power he's fought to win. He has the Pride on the ropes, and as soon as I make this proposal, he'll know it if he doesn't already. He'll realize he has the whole war to win and absolutely nothing to lose."

"Precisely," Renfroe replied. "He'll continue to press his advantage—probably until the Senate sees sense and offers unconditional surrender instead of just communication."

"The Senate might offer surrender, but the rest of the Pride won't. The Senate is toothless. It's worse than toothless. It's a relic of the past. The other hostile cats will keep fighting until the end—which means the war will keep going on and on and on."

"I suppose you're right," he muttered. "Come along, Dina. I'll walk you home."

"Aren't I supposed to be going out to the jungle? The Senate just told me to go find Adrian and deliver their message."

"You mean—you want to go now?" He stopped walking and turned around to stare at her. "Isn't that a little sudden?"

"When am I supposed to go—three days from now?"

"I wasn't thinking three days. I was thinking tomorrow."

"It's the middle of the morning," she pointed out. "I understood that they wanted me to go immediately."

He sighed and started walking again. "I suppose so. I don't trust you to go alone. I'll escort you."

"You can't go out to the jungle," she told him. "The Children would kill you."

"I won't go to the jungle, but I fear for your safety—both in the city and out of it. I'll walk you as far as the village."

"Thank you," she exclaimed. "You're very kind."

He snorted under his breath. "Self-serving is more accurate."

She rested her hand on his back the way she used to. "Thank you for coming with me to the hearing."

"You conducted yourself so much better than Tom did. I was proud of you."

She smiled down at him. "There are still a few good cats left."

"I'm glad you think so. I only wish this negotiation would come to something other than more conflict."

"The Pride will never go back to the way it was before," she told him. "You realize that, don't you? The understanding is dead."

"Perhaps there's a way to salvage it. Perhaps the agreement the Pride can reach with the Children will be that those people who wish to stay as helpers to the Pride can do so. Those who do not wish it will be free to leave without reprisal."

"You know that would never work," she countered. "The Pride, the helpers, the subsidiaries, and everyone else have been telling themselves and each other for years that the understanding was completely voluntary. That's what 'understanding' means. It means both parties agree and understand what they're agreeing to."

"Then what is the difference between what I just said and an agreement that is completely voluntary? How would you change it if it was up to you?"

"I'm not sure it can be changed to make it completely voluntary. Maybe it might work if you removed the threat of violence from the whole scenario. The cats wouldn't be able to hunt slags or attack anyone they please or give anyone the House of Man and the factors wouldn't be able to threaten anyone with getting visited if they speak against the Pride. They wouldn't be able to hold classes and the festivals would be totally voluntary...."

"You're right. That would never work," he grumbled. "It is a shame. Things seemed to work so well before."

"They worked well for the cats and for anyone who wanted this life. It didn't work so well for those that wanted something else."

"Hmmm. You might be right."

They continued to the edge of the city. Skirmishes kept breaking out on all sides and Renfroe had to steer Dina far out of their way to avoid getting caught in them.

Cats patrolled the city streets now. Renfroe walking at Dina's side no longer put her mind at ease the way it used to. If multiple cats attacked at once, he wouldn't be able to stop them from killing both him and her.

They didn't attack. They didn't even confront him about why they were out walking at a time like this. Nearly every other cat in the city stayed behind walls to keep out of the conflict.

Renfroe took the main road out of the city.

"I heard Amaryllis wants to mine the road with explosives," Dina told Renfroe. "Whoever is helping her must not have done it yet."

"I didn't hear that, but my information isn't exactly complete," he muttered. "How would they do that?"

"I don't know. I can't fathom how cats would be able to do that or even where they would get explosives on such a primitive planet. They must have human help."

"I don't see them being able to do it now," he replied. "The Pride is in such disarray. I don't see anyone on our side mounting any kind of defense. I can't imagine what defense that could mount. The Children have sewn up the whole battlefield nicely."

A crack of thunder in the distance made Dina stiffen. She and Renfroe advanced onto the open road where large cats patrolled up and down in plain view of anyone passing.

A few subsidiary wagons entered the city. The cats stopped them to search the contents and question the drivers.

Dina and Renfroe passed most of these people before a lion Dina had never seen before approached them and stopped Renfroe. "The city is under lockdown," the lion told him. "No one goes in or out without permission."

"Permission from whom?" Renfroe fired back. "Every cat is free to move where he pleases without interference from anyone."

"Not anymore," the lion replied. "Where are you going and what are you doing out here? The roads aren't safe."

"My helper is here on Senate business. She's under orders from the Senate to go out as far as the village. I'm escorting her for her protection."

The lion sniffed at Dina and turned away. "Deliver her to her destination and get off the roads as quickly as possible. The Children are still at large. We don't know if or when they'll attack again. No one is safe, especially not big cats. The Children seem to favor them as targets."

The lion stalked off and Renfroe headed back down the road. He brooded for a while and then growled under his breath. "Prideland is finished if our own cats are prisoners in our own city."

"They must be really scared," Dina remarked.

He snorted. "They're petrified. I've never seen them like this."

"Who do you suppose gave the order to stop cats from traveling?"

"The hostile cats must have set up a shadow government—or army—or whatever you want to call it. They're making decisions behind the Senate's back. It means they no longer recognize the Senate's authority to make decisions. That's another sign that we're all doomed."

"I'll have to tell Adrian about this," she told him. "I won't be able to keep this to myself."

"Of course you must tell him. Our only hope is for him to end the conflict quickly and decisively, and for that, he'll need all the relevant information."

She angled her head sideways to study him. "You really should be on their side. Why do you hold yourself back from helping them the way you know you want to?"

"We've discussed this already, Dina. I couldn't possibly give the Children the help you're suggesting that I give. What would I do—attack my own kind and wage war against the Pride? That's preposterous. I'm helping the Children in every other way possible already. If you don't see that, I fail to see what more I could possibly do. If you see something I could do, I'm sure you'll tell me."

She sighed and rested her hand on his back again. "You're right."

Thunder interrupted their conversation again. Heavy dark storm clouds roiled in the sky overhead. They cast the countryside into twilight even in the middle of the day.

The tension kept mounting as the day wore on and Renfroe and Dina drew closer to the village. Gangs of subsidiaries took over the patrols, but they didn't stop Renfroe to question him. They wouldn't dare.

He walked her through the village. Dina checked every face, but she didn't see any of the Mathus family around—or any factors she recognized. Were they all dead? Did the Children finish off them, too?

She stopped next to the last house. "You should go back. It isn't safe for you out here. I'll go one alone."

Renfroe eyed the jungle in the distance. "I don't like you going without some protection."

"The Children are out there. They'll protect me and they'll kill you. You can't go any further."

"I don't like it," he growled.

"I don't, either, but that lion was right. You can't go any further. I won't be able to get near the Children as long as you're around."

"Will you come back to my house after this?" he asked. "Will you decide to stay out here with the Children?"

"I don't know what will happen. I'll have to come back to deliver Adrian's response to the Senate, but I can't make any promises about what will happen after that. Everything is so chaotic right now. The whole future is uncertain."

He sighed. "Of course it is." He rubbed the side of his head against her leg. "Be careful, Dina. I hate to think of something happening to you."

"You, too." She rested her hand on his head one last time. "I hate to say it, but I think you might be in more danger than I am."

"I'm afraid you're right about that, too. I don't like to leave you, but I see that I must. I hope I will see you safe at home very soon." He nodded toward the road leading to the jungle. "You better go."

She nodded and turned away. She didn't turn back for another mile, and when she checked behind her, he was gone.

Chapter 19

Dina picked up her pace when she saw the jungle getting closer. It throbbed with so many hidden possibilities and brought back so many memories.

Her pulse quickened when the canopy closed over her head. She had to find the Children.

She headed for Moonlight canton. She might not find any Children she knew there, but she would find somebody. Even one Child would be able to tell her where to find Adrian.

The beaten path turned into a narrow, winding, treacherous route through rougher country. She covered five miles before she heard the branches crashing overhead.

She looked up expecting to see Children in the canopy. She froze and then snatched her weapons when she saw cats up there.

They raced back and forth through the treetops. They moved so fast that she expected them to pass her by.

She pushed forward down the path and made it another hundred yards before a panther dropped from the canopy and landed right in front of her.

He dipped his eyes to her tunic and then to the weapons in her hands. "No helper should be out in the jungle these days. What are you doing here?"

She opened her mouth to answer, but she stopped when she heard more branches beating overhead. She didn't dare to take her eyes off the panther to see what was happening.

Without warning, a massive jaguar plummeted from the treetops and landed right on top of her. He flattened her and sent her sprawling.

She rolled onto her back, but he snarled in her face, hooked her tunic with his claws, propelled her onto her stomach, and pinned her under his weight.

"I know you," he hissed in her ear. "I know this helper."

She roared in fear and frustration and tried to arch back to hit him with her sickle. He lunged for her just as fast and clamped his jaws around the back of her neck.

"Keep still," the panther told her. "Who is she, Kuseka? I don't recognize her."

The jaguar had to take his mouth off her to answer, and the instant he did, she struck. She couldn't hit him by swinging her arms to the sides, so she took a page from Iona's book and went for his legs.

She whipped her sickle backward and landed a brutal crunch on his hind leg at the hock joint. He roared out and lunged for her again, and this time, she let go of all restraint. She was back in a deadly conflict against cats who could kill her easily.

She flung herself onto her side. She couldn't turn all the way onto her back, but she didn't need to.

She lashed out one more time and her sickle thumped into his side. He staggered off and four more cats moved in.

She didn't have time to get off the ground, but staying like this turned out to be the best position. They could only come at her from one direction. She didn't have to protect her back.

The panther got to her first and then two pumas pounced on her. A tiger showed up a few seconds later, but he couldn't get near her with so many other cats already on top of her.

The panther tried to get hold of her throat, but the pumas interfered by trying to do the same thing at the same time. She took advantage of their confusion and stabbed one of the pumas in the chest.

He saw in time to dodge sideways and her knife hit him in the shoulder. The wound didn't slow him down. She had to find a way to cripple or incapacitate these cats.

Even if she did incapacitate one or two of them, the others would take care of her. The tiger stood off to one side watching and waiting for his turn. She couldn't fight them all.

She struck out with her sickle, but the cats avoided it and the second puma hooked his claws into her clothes to hold her down.

Out of nowhere, something else dropped from the treetops and a mob of Children plummeted out of nowhere. Three Children went after each cat and tore them off her. Another two Children landed on top of the tiger completely unawares.

She lay flat on the ground watching the Children jerk the cats away and then the Children tore the cats apart with merciless precision. She didn't see who the Children were until the last two finished off the tiger.

One big man got his jaws around the tiger's throat, but he couldn't finish the job. The man fell onto his back with the tiger's weight on top of him. The man held the tiger there until the second man pounced and crushed the tiger's spine at the base of his skull.

The second man straightened up and spat on the ground. "Die, you bastard," he snarled and then dragged the tiger's body off his friend. The second man pulled his comrade to his feet.

The second man cast a nonchalant glance at the other Children still scrapping with their target cats. These two Children did nothing to help their friends.

He walked over and looked down at Dina. It was the same man from Moonlight canton—the man whose life she'd saved twice before. He cocked his head to one side. "You again! What are you doing out here?"

She gasped for breath. "I....I need to see Adrian.....It's important."

He frowned at her. "You're his mother, aren't you?"

"Yeah!" she panted. "I am."

"Why are you dressed as a helper?" his companion asked. "Are you in disguise or something?"

"She must be," the man from Moonlight canton replied and held out his hand to pull her to her feet. "I know where Adrian is. I'll take you to his camp."

The other Children got to their feet and left the cats dead on the ground. The Children rejoined into a group. Dina didn't recognize any of them.

"Who's this?" one tall man with dark brown fur asked.

"She needs to find Adrian." The man from Moonlight canton turned back to her. "We keep meeting like this and I don't even know you're name."

"It's Dina." She had to stop herself from holding out her hand. "What's yours?"

"Zair," he replied. "Follow me. I'll show you where to go."

"Hold it." One of the others stepped in front of him and stopped him. "She's a helper. She could be working for the other side."

"She saved my life during the battle in the city," Zair replied. "She fought with us on the road, too. She's the Children's ally. If you don't want to take her there, I'll go alone and you can continue with your patrol. Come with me, Dina."

He set off hiking up the path. The other Children watched her walk between them to follow him and then they fell in line behind her.

They walked upright like people even though it slowed them down so much. One or two of their party kept shooting away into the branches to patrol the area before they returned and rejoined the single-file line moving through the jungle.

Zair led the way back to Moonlight canton where he rendezvoused with Cain and Jackal. Zair left Dina standing off to one side while he talked to his leaders.

Then Zair split away and took Dina off alone. "The others are all busy with their next campaign. Scouts and messengers are flying back and forth all over the country. Adrian might be too busy to talk to you. I just want to warn you."

"I understand he's busy. I know he coordinated attacks in every city in Prideland."

"I don't know his plans," Zair added. "He doesn't share them with anyone until he's ready to move."

"I know," she replied.

He headed deeper into the jungle. Night fell long before they got anywhere near Adrian's camp. Dina and Zair kept walking long past midnight before she spotted bonfires in the distance.

Adrian hadn't camped in any of his previous locations. He'd selected an enormous clearing at the base of another ravine many miles from any of his previous camps.

This must have been a semi-permanent location for the Children's army. They'd constructed more houses and turned the camp into a little city like the gorge camp.

Dozens of Children came and went from the camp even at this late hour. Bonfires burned all over the place and lamplight shone from almost every house.

A buzz of activity and voices filled the camp. It looked, felt, and sounded the same as if this had been the middle of the day.

Zair led Dina to another awning attached to one of the houses. Dina couldn't even see Adrian. Too many Children packed under the awning. They were all big, burly, powerfully built men who dwarfed him behind their bulk.

She heard him talking behind all of them. "Once you secure that angle of approach, send a party south to take this road here and this road here. That will stop anyone from bringing in reinforcements from either side. After that, we'll go for the east side and encircle the whole city."

Laughter broke out among the men listening to him. Someone asked Adrian a question and he went on with his explanation to answer it.

Dina didn't understand what they were talking about or which roads he meant. His orders didn't mean anything to her.

That group left and Zair moved forward to tell Adrian that Dina was here to see him, but just then, a different group of Children showed up and cut in front of Zair to block his way.

These Children were all small, slight, delicately built, and almost childlike in their appearance and manner. They gathered around Adrian and he started giving them a tactical lecture, too.

He bent over his table of maps. "I want you to infiltrate through the underground basement the way I told you yesterday. From the basement, you'll be able to sneak into the aqueduct here....Then you can spread out and attack over the wall. That will give you enough cover to stop anyone from seeing you."

The Children giggled and whispered amongst themselves. He finished his explanation and sent them on their way before Zair finally found an opening to get near Adrian.

Zair murmured in Adrian's ear. Adrian shot a glance over his shoulder at Dina and went back to work on his maps. He muttered something to Zair and Zair strode back over to Dina.

"He says you can deliver your message, but make it quick," Zair told her. "He has nonstop briefings all night."

"Is it....is it always like this?" She glanced around the camp. She didn't see anyone sleeping or even sitting down.

"He's been working like this since the war started," Zair murmured. "He hardly ever sleeps."

Dina took a deep breath. She probably wouldn't get another chance to talk to Adrian—about anything.

She strode under the awning, but just then another group of Children arrived. The four Manx brothers turned up with another twenty Children Dina didn't know.

"Dina!" Riggs exclaimed. "How did you get here?"

"It's a long story." She turned back to Adrian. "The Senate asked me to give you a message. They want to open negotiations for peace."

"What are they offering?" he asked over his shoulder without looking up from his maps.

"That's the problem. They aren't prepared to offer anything. They just want to open the lines of communication.....but I also have to tell you that there's a group of hostile cats that has thrown over the Senate's authority and is calling the shots behind the Senate's back. These hostile cats are organizing their own defense—and offense, too, I guess, though I didn't see that. These hostile cats are patrolling the roads and stopping cats from moving freely without any authority from the Senate. We think....I mean, it looks like these hostile cats are planning to continue the war no matter what the Senate does. The hostile cats don't agree with the Senate making overtures of peace toward the Children. The hostile cats want to keep fighting until the bitter end....so if you open a dialogue with the Senate, it might not mean anything."

He froze over his maps while he listened to her blurt all of this out. He held himself stiff and didn't react, but at least he listened.

"Is that all?" he asked when she finished. He still didn't look up.

"I told the Senate you wouldn't accept their proposal without some concession on their part, but they didn't listen. They don't want to admit....well, anything. They aren't prepared to admit what a precarious position they're in."

"Thank you for delivering their message." He finally looked up and made eye contact with her. "And thank you for telling me the other part. It's late. Zair can show you a house where you can spend the night and then he can escort you back to Prideland in the morning."

She didn't take that as the dismissal it was. "The Senate doesn't have the power to enforce anything anymore. The whole structure of Prideland society has completely broken down. A bunch of cats attacked me earlier today even though I was on Senate business. The cats are scared of you and everyone knows it. More helpers are calling for everyone to side with the Children in your favor. They're speaking openly about rebelling against the Pride. No one has to worry about reprisals or retribution anymore."

Before she could say anything else and before Adrian could reply, another group of Children approached the awning.

She knew all these Children. Kaiser, Kenji, Duke and Darius, Aries, Aurelio, Emerald, Calliope, Riyadh, Israel, Leroy, Devon, Egypt, and India halted under the awning with the other Children.

Egypt lit up in a huge grin. "Dina! You're here!"

She beamed at them all and then her smile slipped. "Where's Iona....and Karim? Did something happen to them?"

"Nothing happened to them," Adrian interrupted and he actually straightened up, turned away his maps, and addressed the crowd. "You've all been out too long. Go relax for a while and we'll debrief after sunrise."

"Are you staying for a while, Dina?" Kenji asked.

"I don't know how long I'll be staying. It just depends on if Adrian has any message to send back to the Senate." She turned around to face him. "Where is she? Where's Iona? Isn't she taking part in the war?"

"You mean you didn't know?" Emerald asked.

"I told you to go take it easy for a while," Adrian snapped. "Go on. Get out of here. I'll deal with Dina."

Kaiser opened his mouth to say something, but Adrian cut him off with a death glare. The Children slipped out from under the awning one after the other and separated to different parts of the camp.

Dina's alarm spiked off the charts. "What are you not telling me about Iona?" she demanded. "Did something happen to her? Did she fall in the battle? Just tell me the truth."

"Nothing is wrong with Iona." He bent over his maps again. "She's been sick lately, but she's fine now."

"Sick?!" Dina practically shrieked. "She's sick! Why didn't you tell me?! This is the first major illness any of the Children have had! It could be serious. How could you keep this from me?"

"You're helper to a cat in the city," he snapped over his shoulder. "You aren't part of what happens to the Children."

"Don't you dare pull that crap on me! She's my daughter—and I raised all these Children as their mother! What happens to the Children affects me just as much as it does you. Now tell me what's wrong with her. I'm a biologist. I might be able to do something about it."

"You don't need to do anything about it," he muttered under his breath. "The Children take care of their own. We don't need your help."

"If you don't tell me, I'll go through every house in this camp until I find her. I'll make your life a living hell. She's my daughter, and if something is wrong with her, I'm going to find out about it." She fought herself under control, took a deep breath, and did her best to steady her voice, but it didn't work. "I know Iona and I aren't on the best of terms, but if anything happens to her......" She choked. "Please, Adrian. Just let me see her one time."

He stood up and faced her. She expected him to give her another cutting rebuff, but he finally flared his nostrils and sighed. "All right. Follow me."

Chapter 20

Adrian set off through the camp without looking back to make sure Dina followed him. She hurried to catch up and he stopped outside one of the crude houses.

Lamplight streamed through the door when he ducked inside. Dina entered behind him and her stomach twisted in knots when she saw Iona lying in a nest of blankets on the floor.

She lay on her side with her eyes closed. Her features had sunken since Dina saw her daughter last. Iona had lost her luster and she looked frail and hollow lying there with the blanket across her pale shoulders.

Karim sat next to her leaning against the wall. He passed his hand across her cheek and forehead again and again to stroke her fur. She didn't open her eyes or respond to his touch.

Karim looked up at Adrian and then Karim's hand froze on Iona's cheek when he saw Dina enter the house. The tension in Karim's hand finally made Iona open her eyes and her gaunt face hardened into a mask of pure hatred when she saw her mother. "What are you doing here?" Iona snarled.

"I heard you were sick and I wanted to see you." Dina stepped into the room and squatted down by the bed, but she didn't dare to touch her daughter. "I want to help you if I can."

Iona shut her eyes. "You can't help me. There's nothing wrong with me. Leave me alone. You shouldn't have come."

"I had to," Dina croaked. "You're my daughter and I love you even if we don't agree on everything—or anything. Just let me help you."

"Go away," Iona growled again without opening her eyes. "I don't want you here and I don't need your help."

"I still care about you even though you would all prefer to pretend that I don't," Dina countered. "I've been trying to help you all this time. You can ask anybody."

No one answered for a minute. That silence hung heavy over the room and then Karim murmured low under his breath. "Iona is pregnant, Dina. No one can do anything until she gives birth."

Dina's jaw dropped. "Pregnant!"

"She's the first one," Adrian added from behind Dina's back. "We don't know how normal it is for her to get this sick and we don't know what will happen if any of the others get pregnant."

Dina spun around to stare at him and then at Karim and Iona. Karim went back to stroking his hand across Iona's face. She didn't open her eyes again.

Dina's mind staggered. Iona—pregnant! It was happening. The Children could reproduce—or at least gestate. If they actually could reproduce and raise their own Children....

The situation in Prideland would explode when word got out. The whole disaster of this war would become even more untenable than it already was.

The silence pounding in her ears told her all too plainly that the Children understood the massive ramifications of this as well as anyone. They understood it better than anyone else.

They'd been asking her since they were old enough to think straight if they'd be able to mate and have their own children. Now it was finally happening.

Another giant brick of agony dropped into Dina's stomach when she stared down at Iona's hollow cheeks and shaded eyes. Her daughter. Iona was pregnant with Dina's grandchild...or maybe more than one.

Dina gulped down all the adrenaline pumping through her veins. This wasn't about her.

She squatted down next to Iona's bed, but again, Dina made sure not to touch her daughter. "Let me help you. Let me be here for you. I'll do whatever it takes. Don't let the past come between us—not now."

Iona didn't open her eyes. "I might be able to forgive you if you can find a way for my children to survive to adulthood."

"I will. I swear it." Dina stood up, but she couldn't leave the house—not yet. She faced Adrian and then Karim. "I will find a way. I give you my word on that. I'm going back to the city, but not for Renfroe or to help the cats or even to make peace between the cats and the Children. I don't care about any of that. I left Prideland to build a world where the Children could grow up in safety and I'll do the same for the next generation. That's the only reason I'm going."

"How will you do that?" Karim asked. "The cats will never give in."

"I don't know how I'll do it, but I have to find a way."

None of the others answered and Dina felt her words fall on deaf ears. They didn't believe her and why should they? She had no power to build anything.

Adrian turned away and held the door open for her to leave the house. She didn't want to go, but she really couldn't do anything about this. They were right about that part at least. No one could help Iona. She just had to go through it and see what happened.

Dina stopped in the darkness outside. "We never talked about this....." she stammered, "but it isn't outside the normal range for human women to get this sick when they get pregnant. It isn't a sign that there's anything wrong with the pregnancy or the baby. In fact, some people think that, the sicker a woman gets, the more likely she'll be to give birth to a healthy baby."

Adrian cocked his head to one side and studied her, but she couldn't read his expression. "Thank you for telling me."

She only nodded. "Tell Karim. If you need anything from me, you know where to find me."

He waved her away. "Zair will show you where to go to spend the night and he'll take you back to the city in the morning."

He walked off and Zair appeared out of the darkness. Dina didn't think about where he came from and whether he'd been standing here waiting for her while she'd been inside Karim's and Iona's house.

Zair led her through the dark village, showed her into an empty house, and gave her three blankets to make herself comfortable, but she couldn't sleep.

Iona was pregnant—which meant other Children could get pregnant. Naia could be pregnant from Adrian—or she could get that way. Dina cradled her head in her hand trying to grasp all this.

Having their own children would make the Children even more ferocious and determined to win this war. It would make them deadlier, more ruthless, and even less willing to negotiate than they already were.

How long had this been going on? Dina hadn't seen Iona since their disastrous parting at Riverbend canton. Had Iona been pregnant then? Had Naia been pregnant during the battle and when Dina took her to Renfroe's house?

How much should Dina tell....well, anybody? Should she tell the Senate....or Renfroe?

She might have been able to convince herself to tell him because he was Iona's father, but telling anyone would put Iona and the other Children in danger.

If Dina told a living soul about this, the Pride would become even more hysterical than ever to wipe the Children off the planet. No wonder the Children had been so reluctant to tell her.

Dina understood now why Iona was worried for her children's safety. The Pride would never stand this. They would hunt the Children to the ends of eternity.

The Children might have to do the unthinkable and completely obliterate every cat on the planet just to make sure none of them came after the Children again.

Adrian must have thought of all of this long ago. He would have been the first person to find out about Iona's pregnancy apart from Iona and Karim.

Adrian must have been planning this all along. He must have thought the whole matter through and foreseen every possible outcome far in advance. He was too shrewd not to.

Dina was still sitting on the blankets when the sky lightened outside. She spotted Zair walking past. He probably hadn't slept, either.

She went outside. "I'm ready to leave whenever you are," she told him.

He nodded and headed back through the camp in the direction he'd first brought her here. They passed the awning next to Adrian's house.

He stood under it pointing to his maps and giving orders to bands of Children. He glanced up and his eyes met Dina's.

She immediately turned away and walked off to follow Zair. She didn't want Adrian to think she was eavesdropping on his plans.

She and Zair entered the jungle and began the long, hard trek back to Prideland. Dina had no shortage of things to think about on her way there.

She could think of a lot of ways to ensure that her Children and grandchildren grew up in a safe world without the constant threat of cat attacks.

Her own Children had grown up that way. She understood why Iona didn't want her own children to live with that threat hanging over their heads.

The only scenarios Dina could think of involved wiping out all the cats. She could poison their water supply or something similar.

If she was going to go as far as that, she might as well let the Children do the job by violence. It amounted to the same thing.

She didn't see any end to this war. The Pride and the Children had started off on such a hostile footing that they would probably never make peace. They would never trust each other.

The Children's victory only confirmed that the cats would always feel threatened by the Children, too. The cats would always know that another force on this planet could wipe them at any time.

The Children's very existence posed a threat to the cats' existence and vice versa. That was the fundamental problem. The two races couldn't coexist on the same planet without one or the other trying to kill each other—or one group fearing that the other would kill them first.

She and Zair didn't make it back to the road until sundown on the third day. Renfroe wasn't here to escort her back into the city. Running the gauntlet of patrolling cats and combative helpers would be a challenge.

"You can go on from here," Zair told her. "Adrian told me not to take you any further than this."

"Thank you. I really appreciate you coming with me this far." She smiled up at him. "Good luck."

"You, too. If I can repay my debt to you, I will."

He leapt into the trees and set off at high speed into the trackless wilderness behind her. He would probably make it back to Adrian's camp in a few hours at the most.

Chapter 21

Dina faced the fringe of trees separating her from the road. She didn't see any cats or subsidiaries there, but she would meet them as soon as she tried to approach the city.

She surveyed the fields. She could go around that way and get into the city by another route. That would be safer than taking the road.

She strode forward to leave the shelter of the jungle when another cat dropped out of the branches and landed in front of her. Osiris twitched his whiskers at her.

"I've been waiting for you to come back, but I had to wait for that man to leave before I showed myself. I'll escort you back into the city."

"Thank you so much." She took a few more steps to join him. "I was just planning how to get around the patrols—all of them. I suppose the cats are still stopping everyone who comes in or goes out."

"More than ever. It appears another shadow group of cats is making decisions behind the Senate's back."

"Renfroe and I were speculating about whether the Senate realized that."

"We realize it," he replied. "Were you right about your son refusing to accept our offer to negotiate?"

"He didn't refuse it. He outright ignored it. He thanked me for delivering the message. That's all he said."

Osiris snorted. "Your son is a formidable character."

"You have no idea," she muttered.

"Well, we better go. It will be dark soon. Come along."

He strutted out onto the road and she followed him into the open. She spotted subsidiaries patrolling around the village, but that was all she could see from this distance.

He advanced in front of her. The cats had always gone wherever they pleased in this world, but not anymore.

He made it ten feet away from her when three Children burst out of a ditch by the side of the road. They shot across Dina's path, slammed into Osiris, and bowled him off his feet.

The Children's sudden attack sent Osiris rolling. He tumbled one way and the three Children tumbled the other way.

They vaulted to their feet to spring on him one more time and Dina saw who the Children were. Dina would have recognized those tortoise-shell fur patterns anywhere. They were Dexter, Brock, and Keith—Osiris's own sons.

She charged between them so they couldn't get near him. "Leave him alone!" She got in front of the three Children just in time to stop them, but they ran into her instead. "Leave him alone! He was trying to help me! Back off, Dexter!"

She shoved him away and they woke up to the fact that she was defending a cat against them.

Osiris rolled onto his feet, twisted around, and hissed at his sons. "He's your father!" Dina bellowed. "He was trying to help me! He was trying to protect me!"

Brock bared his teeth right back at Osiris. "You keep away from her!" Brock snarled. "Go back to the city where you came from!"

"Leave him alone!" Dina snapped again. "He was planning to escort me back to the city to get me through the patrols."

"You don't accept help from one of *them.*" Dexter dodged around her and charged Osiris.

Dexter outsized Osiris by a mile. Dexter was the size of a fully-grown human man. He couldn't have ripped Osiris in half, but Osiris sprang out of the way, plunged into the long grass by the ditch, and vanished.

"What are you doing?!" Dina roared. "Now I have to walk all the way out into the countryside to get back to the city! I told you he was trying to help me! You can't just go attacking any cat in the world just because you want to! There are some good cats in Prideland."

"There is no such thing," Brock growled.

"Well, *you* can't get me back into the city!" she fired back. "Now I have to go alone!"

"You should be thanking us," Dexter countered. "He could have led you into danger."

"Will you open your ears and listen to me?!" she bellowed. "He risked his life to save yours by bringing you to me! He's the reason you survived to grow up at all. It cost him a lot to take that risk and he's been trying to help me ever since. He warned me when I was in danger leaving the city and he came here to help me tonight! I would have been better off with him than I would be alone. Do you get that now?"

"All cats are our enemies," Brock told her. "If we see him near you again, we'll kill him."

She gasped in exasperation, but the three of them were already launching into the jungle and racing away.

They left her standing there with nothing to do but hike all the way out into the fields the way she planned.

She had to hike for hours to get far enough away so no one would see her turn toward the city. Then she had another long walk to get to the city's farthest edge before she made her way into the outer neighborhoods. She didn't get there before sunrise on the fourth day.

She cursed the Children and herself and Prideland and everyone else on the way. Everyone involved in this conflict seemed determined to be as unreasonable as possible toward everyone else.

Why couldn't everyone on this planet just tolerate each other and let each other live their lives in peace?

It all started with the Pride. The cats were the ones who didn't tolerate anyone who stepped out of line.

Their intolerance filtered down from there to their helpers and subsidiaries. The rest was history.

Osiris was too small and insignificant a cat to make any difference in the Children's lives. He might be a senator, but in reality, was just a house cat. He couldn't fight anyone.

She had to travel through the entire city to get back to Renfroe's neighborhood. She passed the market just as the first subsidiaries pulled in with their wagons.

At least the city sounded peaceful now. She didn't see anyone fighting in the streets. Everyone in the market appeared to get along and she didn't hear anyone talking about revolting against the Pride or siding with the Children.

She didn't stick around long enough to listen if they did. She turned away to leave, but when she rounded the next corner, she nearly collided with Tom coming the other way. He must have been heading for the market.

He froze when he saw her and then his eyes hardened. "What are you doing, Dina?" he snapped. "Why are you out of your house at this hour? You're already in enough trouble for supporting the Children.....and then I saw you helping one of them during the battle. Don't you know you could get reduced for that?"

Her patience evaporated in a split second. "Is that all you have to say to me after everything that's happened? After all we've been through on this planet, the best you can do is to tell me to behave myself? You really are a fallen man, Tom. I thought you were better than that. I guess I never really knew you before, but I do now."

She walked past him to continue her journey, but he grabbed her arm to stop her. "You're the one who keeps making our lives harder than they have to be by acting so rebellious here. How can you take sides against the Pride? How can you even think about supporting the Children after everything the Pride has done for us? I really don't understand you at all. If you had to get involved in the war, you should have supported the helpers in defending the Pride, not helping the Children."

She spun around and got right in his face. "That girl you saw me helping during the battle is your own daughter! Can I make it any clearer to you than that? You have four Children, Tom—and that girl you saw me helping is married to my son!"

His face went blank and all color drained from his cheeks. "You're lying!"

"I left Prideland for the third time so I could raise my Children in the jungle! Elyse came to me in the cantons and told me she was pregnant from you and she wanted your Children to grow up, but she didn't want you to know about it. She gave birth right there in my house and left her Children—your Children—for me to raise. You have two sons and two daughters. You never knew, did you? That's because Elyse hid it from you. She's hidden everything from you. She's manipulated you from day one. She manipulated you into thinking she was helping our mission when she was really undermining it to keep you here. Renfroe was the one who got you in front of the Senate, not Elyse. Renfroe was the one who tried to convince the Senate to accept our embassy from the Coalition while Elyse was arguing against it behind your back. She played you, Tom. When are you gonna realize that?"

He stared in stunned shock, but he didn't see her. He stared through her at something behind her head. He blinked extra slowly.

She cringed when she saw him like this. She didn't mean for him to find out like this, but she couldn't take it back now.

She forced herself to lower her voice. "I'm sorry, but I had to tell you one way or the other. We could have gotten off the planet and made it back to the *Savannah*, but she tricked you to keep you docile so she could control you. They all do it. That's the way they've kept control over this planet for generations."

He blinked again. He didn't even hear her.

"Listen….just think about it. We could really use your help—and the Children could really use your help. They need all the help they can get—especially from helpers. I'm not saying you have to do anything….."

He blinked at her again, jerked once in a violent spasm of nervous agitation, and turned on his heel before he walked off down the street.

Dina watched him go with those words hanging on her lips. She wanted to say so much more to him, but he couldn't hear it right now. He might not ever be able to hear it.

At least he knew now. At least she didn't deceive him the way everyone else on this planet had been doing since the very beginning.

She couldn't even begin to pity him for that. No one had deceived Tom more than he'd deceived himself. Waking up from that was bound to be painful and he'd betrayed her too many times for her to try to make it easier for him.

She set off on her way back to Renfroe's house. She really needed to catch up on sleep. She just hoped and prayed another disaster didn't strike. Her nerves couldn't take any more of this.

She entered the quiet neighborhood. The conflict didn't intrude here.

Everyone in the city seemed to be feeling the same emotional exhaustion with the war. Even the tree lizards and insects sounded quieter. Maybe everyone had had enough of it and they were all ready to just go back to living their lives. She could only hope.

Chapter 22

Dina didn't want to deal with potentially meeting Belinda in the kitchen, so Dina went around to the door in the garden wall. She planned as usual to use the courtyard entrance to the bedroom so she could slip into the house unseen.

She approached the door when Osiris stepped out of the undergrowth. A gash on his face oozed blood into his fur.

He'd always been one of the most dignified cats she'd ever met. Most cats of the Pride carried the scars of battles old and new, but he didn't. He didn't lower himself to getting into fights like a common mongrel.

That cut on his face gave him a dangerous look. He didn't look like a senator anymore, but then again, he wasn't one. No one was.

"Are you all right?" she asked. "I'm sorry about the way the Children behaved."

"You don't need to apologize for them. They have every reason to hate me. They have every reason to hate all of us. We created them and we caused this war."

"They have every reason to admire and respect you," she pointed out. "They just don't know."

He gazed off into the undergrowth. "I wish I could believe that, but they will never admire or respect me. Why should they when I never supported them—my own Children?"

"But you did. You have. You are," she insisted. "You've helped me ever since you brought them to me."

"I took them to you. I didn't support them. I never spoke on their behalf the way Renfroe did. I never stood my ground to defend my own Children. I would have for any other kittens of mine, but not them. I was too much of a coward. I've always been a coward and hidden behind words."

She didn't know what to say. She didn't consider him a coward. He was just too small to throw his weight around with the bigger cats. He couldn't exactly enforce his will if he wanted to.

He turned around to face her. "Not anymore. I've decided to fully commit myself. I want to fight the war on the Children's side. I don't know what I'll do or how to do it. I was hoping you might be able to tell me."

"You.....want to fight.....on the Children's side?" She had to stop herself from laughing. He was so small and insignificant. He was just a cat like one she might see in someone's home. "How will you do that?"

"That's what I'm asking you. Speaking out won't make any difference. It's too late for words, but I want to help them in any way I can. I want to help the people fighting on the Children's side."

"That's going to be tricky when those same people consider you their enemy," she remarked.

"I realize that, but maybe you can help me out in that respect. I know a great deal about the Pride—more than Renfroe, I dare say. I've been in the Senate while he's been on the sidelines. I could give you information....."

"Do you know what the hostile cats are planning? Do you know how they're planning to either engage with the Children or defend themselves the next time the Children launch one of these assaults?"

"I can't tell you that, unfortunately. I only know of a few hostile cats and they wouldn't share that information with me."

"That's the kind of information the Children need," she told him. "If you can't find out, maybe you could think about swinging your own helpers to the Children's side. You could inform them that you want them to fight for the Children....and you could arm your helpers to defend the Children when they come."

He took a long time to answer. He finally sighed. "I can see that even I am not mentally prepared to carry out my own decision. After my sons attacked me on the road yesterday, I determined to make it up to them by throwing my reservations aside and joining my efforts to their cause—not in a cowardly backdoor way, but outright and with no holds barred. Now I see that I didn't completely think it through."

"Are you changing your mind?" she asked.

"No, no—not at all. I just didn't think it through as far as arming my helpers and turning them to the Children's side, too. I didn't grasp that making such a decision would come to that, but it naturally would, wouldn't it? I'm either with the Children or I'm not. As long as I still have helpers who are loyal to the Pride, then I'm not with the Children, am I?" He sighed again. "It is difficult."

"You're doing the right thing," she insisted. "You're doing the things that would make your sons admire and respect you if they knew."

"Yes, of course I must do it for them." He shook himself out of his trance and faced her. "Thank you, Dina. I needed that."

"Thank you," she exclaimed. "Let me know if you hear any useful information....and I'll let you know if I think of any way you can help the Children's cause."

"I'm grateful. I hope I will see you soon with some intelligence that your son can use in his campaigns."

He trotted off into the bushes. Dina drew in a shaky breath and pushed her way into the garden. She really hoped she didn't meet anybody—not anybody.

She needed to sit somewhere in silence and just think. Everything was happening too fast with one blow falling after the other.

She snuck into the courtyard, opened the sliding glass doors, and walked in to find Renfroe stretched out on the bed. "When did you get back?" he rumbled.

"Just now," she replied and shut the door behind her. "I had to go far out of my way into the fields to avoid the patrols on the road."

He sighed and put his head down on the bedspread. "I feared something might have happened to you. You've been gone so long."

She sat down on the bed next to him, kicked off her shoes, and finally started to let herself relax. "It's pandemonium out there."

"What happened?" he asked.

She gave him a recap of all the events from when he left her in the village, but she left out the part about Iona being pregnant. She had to take that secret to her grave.

"So Adrian didn't accept the Senate's offer," Renfroe muttered at the end. "I didn't think he would. They won't be pleased when they find out."

"I already told Osiris. He already knows."

His head swung up. "When did you tell him that?"

"I saw him outside earlier. I don't think he was expecting much of a response from Adrian, either. Osiris wasn't surprised at all when he heard."

Renfroe relaxed back on the mattress. "That spares me the effort of telling the Senate, then. I wasn't looking forward to that."

She ran her hand down his lustrous coat. "I'm sorry it took me so long to get back. I didn't mean to make you worry."

"Did you see Iona in the camp?" he asked.

Dina looked away. "Yes, I saw her."

"Is she doing well?"

"She's fine," Dina murmured. "She isn't taking part in the war. She's staying behind."

"Why is she staying behind? You said she was as warlike as the others."

"She is. I don't know why she's staying out of it. I didn't get a chance to ask her. She doesn't talk to me."

"I'm sure you two will reconcile your relationship one way or the other. There must be a way for you two to come to an understanding with each other."

She didn't comment on his use of that phrase. She ran her hand down his shoulder. He still carried the fresh score marks of the other cats' attack. "Can I ask you a question?"

"Of course. Ask me anything."

"What I mean is—can I ask you something related to helping the Children? Answering this question would be considered subversive, and if anyone found out I'm asking, we could both find ourselves in hot water if you get what I mean. I wouldn't want you to compromise yourself or put yourself in jeopardy any more than you already have—but if you tell me, it will help me help the Children. It will help me help the Children against the Pride. If you aren't comfortable with that, then I won't ask."

He raised his head and pierced her with his hardest look. "I am prepared for that, Dina. You may ask me anything. If it helps the Children against the Pride, then that's just as well for all concerned."

"Okay, thank you. I was going to ask....do you know a helper named Kubri James....or Angulo Duala? Do you know where I can find them?"

"Oh, I see." He put his head down on his paws. "You want to contact the subversive helpers."

"I'll understand if you don't want to tell me."

"I thought you were already in touch with them."

"They stopped me on the street when I first came back from the jungle," she explained. "I don't know how to contact them."

"Kubri James is helper to the Kadi family of pumas that live along the river. Their patriarch is Diamond Kadi and I believe Kubri James is particularly attached to Familiar Kadi, the oldest son and heir apparent. Angulo Duala is helper to an ancient Maltese by the name of Kama Uki. She's so old and blind that I don't think she even knows there is a war going on. Her house is just down the block from the market. It's a giant white marble building with close to two hundred helpers living in it."

"Thank you so much for telling me," she replied. "I'm really grateful."

"I won't ask why you're going to see them. I'm quite certain Adrian doesn't trust any human being with his plans, not even the ones where humans might be able to help him."

"You're right. He doesn't."

He cocked his head to study her. He looked exactly like Adrian when he gave her that look. "You look tired, Dina. You should lie down and rest."

"You're right. I am tired."

She stretched out on the bed. He adjusted his position to lie down next to her.

She put her arm over his shoulder, but he turned his face away.

"What's wrong?" she asked. "Are you angry with me for staying out so long?"

"No, I'm not angry with you about anything."

"What's wrong, then?" She passed her hand over the rough fur on the side of his cheek. "Why won't you even look at me?"

"I can't look at you....because I want you and I can't have you. Nothing has been the same since you came back. Nothing can ever go back to the way it was between us before and I don't want it to be any other way."

Her hand stopped moving. "Are you saying.....?"

"I waited for you for so long.....and then you gave yourself to me......and now circumstances conspire to take you away from me again. The Children draw a greater obligation from you than I do."

"But....it isn't their fault we don't have a sexual relationship anymore."

"It isn't that. Any children or kittens would naturally draw a greater obligation from you than I do. I don't resent that. I just......want you. I resent that I can't have you."

"Things have been going so well between us these last few days," she remarked. "Isn't that enough?"

"No, it isn't." He growled under his breath and turned his head away again. "The understanding we had before is gone and we will never get it back. I know that now."

He kept his eyes shut and his head turned, even when she went back to stroking the side of his face. She watched him for a long time, but he didn't move or respond.

She felt closer to him now than she ever had. She got along with him better now than she ever did before—probably because this was the first time she ever spent with him when she really did it of her own free choice.

No one made her come back from the jungle. She did it knowing exactly what their relationship would be like.

She understood him. She understood the Pride and her place in it. She knew what she could get away with and what she couldn't. She understood all the rules and everything expected of her.

That wasn't the understanding the Pride wanted her to come to, though. The Pride didn't want her to choose this life of her own free choice. That wasn't the point.

The Pride wanted her to understand that she didn't have a choice. The only understanding Renfroe wanted with her was that she belonged to him to do whatever he wished with her whenever he wished to do it.

A pang of sympathy stabbed her in the heart when she looked at him and touched him. He created this bedroom so they could be together as a couple. That would never happen again.

Either the cats would win or the Children would win. Dina wouldn't be able to stay in Prideland if the Pride won and killed the Children.

She wouldn't be able to stay here if the Children won, either. The Children's total victory would mean freedom for all human beings. Then her relationship with Renfroe would be irrevocably changed if it survived at all.

Chapter 23

"I'm going out this morning, Dina dear," Renfroe told her at breakfast the next morning. "I suppose you want to go out, too."

Dina hesitated a split second before she answered. They sat at the fountain as usual.

Belinda moved around in the house just a few yards away. She might have been able to overhear Dina's and Renfroe's conversation if he mentioned where she was going.

"Yes, I was thinking of going out if that's all right with you," she replied.

"You've made it clear that you don't take my decision on whether you should go out," he growled. "Just be careful if you do go."

"Is it dangerous out there?" she asked. "Are the helpers still fighting among themselves?"

"No, they aren't fighting and it isn't dangerous—not overtly. I mean don't do anything that could put you in danger. The same forces are still at work in this city, including the forces that know what you're planning to do and which side you're on."

She distracted herself by putting another mouthful of food in her mouth so she wouldn't have to look at him. "I understand. I'll be careful."

"I certainly hope so," he grumbled. "You never do as I say anymore—if you ever did."

She didn't look up. So that was another aspect of their relationship that would never go back to the way it was before.

She never truly submitted to him the way another helper might have, but she'd somehow passed beyond even wanting to.

The idea of giving herself to him in that way seemed so far out of reality now. She wouldn't have been capable of it even if she'd tried.

She had no intention of trying. She had no intention of stopping her efforts to help the Children's cause. Nothing in the world seemed as important as that.

He finished eating, nuzzled his head into her hand, wished her a good morning, and stalked off through the garden. He didn't mention where he was going.

He'd been unusually tight-lipped about what he'd been doing these last few days. His activities might have been as subversive as her own—or more so. That must be the reason he didn't tell her.

She finished her breakfast, cleaned up her bedroom, and then slipped out through the garden door.

The city didn't sound any different than it did yesterday. She didn't see any helpers fighting or even any helpers doing anything out of the ordinary.

The tension pulsing through everything didn't throb at the same pitch it did before the battle. She didn't see anyone whispering in corners or any cats acting aggressively toward their helpers, but the tenor of society had definitely changed.

Everyone spoke in hushed murmurs as though they didn't want to antagonize the Children into attacking again. The usual noise of activity didn't clash on Dina's ear the way it usually did. Everyone did their work quietly.

Even the vendors in the market conducted their business in an undertone. Cats strolled through the market examining the subsidiaries' contributions, but the cats didn't attack their prey right there in view of everyone.

The cats instructed helpers and subsidiaries to take oxen and other tribute animals away for slaughter somewhere else. Cubs and kittens didn't play around in the market the way they used to. They stayed close to their mothers and left as soon as the adults finished finalizing their business.

Dina hurried away toward the river, but she didn't get that far before she spotted Kubri James, Angulo Duala, and the same two men who'd cornered her before.

The four of them stood together at the edge of a park. They talked openly, but they occupied a spot where no one would be able to overhear them.

They stopped talking and separated as Dina approached them. "You shouldn't be here," Kubri James told her when she drew level with them. "You shouldn't make it so obvious that you're coming to see us. Everyone knows about you. They'll know you're doing something subversive."

"You're making it pretty obvious what you're doing," she replied, "and everyone knows about you, too. Everyone saw you fighting the cats and loyal helpers during the last battle. I don't think any of us have any more secrets from each other in this war."

"What do you want?" Angulo asked. "Why did you come to see us?"

"I just went to visit the Children in the jungle. They're planning something—something big. They're planning another campaign. I don't know what it is or when it will happen, but it's coming. They're planning something even bigger than the last battle."

"How could they plan something bigger than that?" one of the other men asked. "What's bigger than invading the city?"

"I don't know, but they're doing it. Adrian is organizing Children all over the planet. It will be another coordinated strike and it will be overwhelming. That's all I can tell you. If we're going to participate, we need to start planning and preparing now."

"How can we prepare if we don't know what they're going to do or when they're going to do it?" Angulo asked.

"We know more now than we did last time," she told him. "We know what's coming. We need to arm every subversive helper and hopefully convince a few more. I heard people talking openly about rebelling against the Pride...."

"No one dares to do that now," Kubri James replied. "Not with the hostile cats taking over. They'll kill anyone who speaks openly or gets caught doing anything subversive."

"What do you know about them?"

"They're taking over the city. They're taking over the whole Pride. They say the Senate is impotent and incapable of defending the Pride against its enemies, both internal and external. The hostile cats are the ones patrolling the city now."

She glanced over her shoulder in the direction from which she'd come. "I didn't see any patrols."

"They don't make it as obvious as that. They don't walk around openly threatening anyone. They're more subtle than they were before the Children's war. The cats listen in doorways and gather information from loyal helpers. The hostile cats know who's subversive, who fought for the Children before, and who's planning what. The hostile cats know everything."

"What can they do about it?" she asked.

"They catch the person alone and reduce them," Angulo replied. "The hostile cats don't make a public spectacle out of it. They just reduce the person when no one else is looking and make the person disappear."

"It sounds to me like they're afraid to do it in public," she countered. "What you're describing isn't any different from what the Pride did before the Children's war. The cats are just doing it in secret now because they don't dare to do it in full view of everyone."

Kubri James shook his head. "They're doing it to make everyone tremble in fear. They want to intimidate everyone because no one knows which cats are doing it and which ones aren't. No one knows who to trust anymore."

"I disagree," Dina replied. "If they wanted to intimidate anyone, they would do it publicly and make a big show of it. They would drag the person into the market to make an example of the person and let everyone know what happens to anyone who speaks against the Pride."

"We can disagree on why they're doing it," Angulo interrupted. "The question is what we're going to do about this campaign. How long will it take your son to get everything in place?"

"I couldn't tell you that because I don't know what he's doing or what he's putting in place. You said you would handle things on this end, so that's what we have to do. Can you arm your people any more than they already are? I don't suppose we can get our hands on anything other than household implements."

"What else is there?" Kubri James asked.

"Amaryllis's helper told me that she and some of her accomplices were planning to lay explosives along the road to trap the Children. If the hostile cats have access to that, we might be able to get our hands on explosives, too."

"What would we do with them if we got them?" the third man asked. "We couldn't blow up the roads. That would help the cats and harm the Children."

"We'll think about it and keep our eyes open for a good target," she replied. "I'm sure all of us working together can come up with a solution, but we need to work fast. We need to have our plan in place before the Children come."

"How will we get in touch with Amaryllis's helper about stealing the explosives?" Kubri James asked.

"I'll contact her," Dina replied. "It might take some time, so the rest of you need to take care of things on your end. Do some sniffing around and find out what we could use the explosives on that would have the most impact."

"We could blow up the Senate building," the third man suggested.

"The Senate is already finished," Angulo countered. "The hostile cats probably want to blow up the Senate building themselves."

"I better go," Dina told them. "I'll get in touch with you later about whatever I find out."

She hurried away without looking back. She couldn't even begin to fathom how she would maneuver Sonya into stealing explosives from Amaryllis. Dina should really have her head examined for even considering putting Sonya in that position.

There had to be a way to turn the tide in the Children's favor. If the hostile cats had an ace up their sleeves, then what better way to defeat them than stealing whatever it was and using it against them?

Even if Sonya couldn't steal the explosives, she might at least know where they were. She'd been living in Amaryllis's house all this time.

Dina trekked across the city, returned to the quiet outer neighborhoods, and observed Amaryllis's house for a long time, but Dina didn't see Sonya anywhere.

Dina even snuck into Amaryllis's garden and saw other helpers working in different places, but Sonya wasn't there.

Dina didn't dare to go any closer to the house, not even to look through the windows, so she retreated and went back to Renfroe's house.

Belinda glared at her when she walked in, but Dina ignored that and went back outside to the courtyard to think. Not knowing Adrian's plans made it difficult to decide how to help him.

He probably didn't need her help anyway, but the subversive helpers did. How could she prepare for the next campaign in a way that the subversive helpers could make the biggest impact?

The most helpful thing would be to eliminate the hostile cats. Eliminating them behind the scenes when no one knew what she was doing would have been even better.

She wouldn't be able to do that when she didn't even know who they were. She knew about Amaryllis. Dina assumed Khalid and the Hellions were involved, too.

The Hellions. Hellion House.

If the subversive helpers were going to blow something up to harm the hostile cats, what better target than Hellion House?

Blow up Hellion House? Was Dina really thinking that?

The factors held their festivals in Hellion House. It was as much a bastion of the Pride as the Senate building. Since the war started, Hellion House was far more a bastion of the Pride than the Senate building.

Hellion House also had hundreds of helpers living and working inside its walls. She wouldn't be able to blow it up with them in there.

On the other hand, if the Children invaded again, all the helpers would leave Hellion House to take part in the battle. Loyal helpers would fight with the Pride and subversive helpers would fight against it. No one would stay behind.

Someone would stay behind, though. The helpers' children, the Hellions' kittens, and all the helpers assigned to take care of them would stay behind.

Dina shook those thoughts out of her head. She didn't have the explosives even to begin to plan something like that. She didn't know what the explosives were or how she would detonate them. She wouldn't be able to plan anything until she found out.

She would just have to lie low until she found a way to contact Sonya, but Dina had no way to find out if Sonya was even still alive. She might have gotten killed in the last battle or Amaryllis might have eliminated Sonya for being subversive—in which case this whole plan would be dead before it even got started.

Chapter 24

Dina sat down by the fountain and shut her eyes in the sunshine. She'd just returned from another quick walk to Amaryllis's house. She'd been going every day for a week and still hadn't seen any sign of Sonya.

Dina had to admit to herself that something must have happened to Sonya. She must have stepped out of line one too many times.

Amaryllis must have caught Sonya doing something subversive. A girl as young as Sonya probably didn't know enough to cover her tracks in a den of enemies like the Manx house.

Dina hadn't gone into town to see the other subversive helpers, either. She'd already told them everything she knew. She didn't want to expose them when she had no new information to give them.

The sun made her sleepy, but when she went back inside to lie down, she met Belinda coming from the bedroom. "Oh, there you are," Belinda began. "I have something for you."

"What is it?" Dina asked.

"I'm sure I don't know," Belinda sniffed. "Another helper left you a package. It's in the kitchen."

"Which helper was it?" Dina asked.

"I don't know her. She's a young thing from Amaryllis's house. She stopped by, dropped the package off, and told me to give it to you. She said it's important."

Dina's heart skipped a beat. So Sonya was still alive and well enough to move around the neighborhood. Maybe Amaryllis was just keeping Sonya inside the house where Dina couldn't see her.

Belinda led the way back to the kitchen and handed over a blanket tied into a large bundle with a length of stout rope.

The bundle weighed a ton and sagged in Dina's arms. She had to use all her strength to carry it back to her room.

She untied it, unfolded the blankets, and stared down at ten red ceramic cylinders printed in hieroglyphs. Those hieroglyphs came from a Coalition language belonging to the Frodian people.

She picked up one of the cylinders and read the lettering. *Nydrix.* Each cylinder weighed five pounds and there were ten cylinders in here. That was fifty pounds of one of the most explosive substances in the whole Coalition.

Where did the Pride get this? Dina didn't have to think too hard to get the answer. She'd long suspected that these cats came from some other Coalition planet.

Someone could have been transporting them on a ship and the ship crashed here. Then the cats evolved into this society.

Other Coalition vessels could have been landing or crashing here for years and no one would have known about it. Dina had been an officer in the Coalition Armada and she didn't hear about Alexander Mathus's shuttle crashing here until Captain Doyle informed her and the landing team about the crash.

One of those ships must have been carrying this Nydrix. Now Dina had the explosives in her possession, but that didn't help her decide what to do with them.

Her mind immediately switched to the one person she knew would be able to tell her what she wanted to know. Tom would know how to detonate these explosives. The question remained—would he help her if it meant supporting the Children?

In the meantime, she had to hide these explosives where no one would find them. She didn't trust Belinda not to search or at least clean the spare bedroom. Belinda didn't usually go in there, but anything was possible.

Dina also didn't want to put the explosives under the mattress here in the bedroom. Hiding her old clothes there didn't mean anything. No one could think anything sub-versive about that.

Hiding the Nydrix anywhere in the garden was also out of the question. Buck might find it there.

The ideal place would have been somewhere underground—and then she had it.

She wrapped up the bundle, tied it up with the rope, and hefted it into both hands. God, it was heavy!

She snuck through the bedroom courtyard, glanced around to make sure Buck wasn't here, and made a mad dash for Renfroe's sandbox.

She'd only been out here a handful of times and never fully inspected the place. She noticed during her brief visits here that he only used the deepest sand in the very center of the sandbox.

He only used it once or twice a day at the most and the Elite Battalion cleaned it out every day, too. Their tracks occupied the middle of the sandbox where they knew he used it.

He always did his business and then covered it up before he left. They never had to look very far before they found it and removed it.

That left the sandbox's outer edges. She dropped the bundle, fell down on her knees, and scrambled to dig a hole at the farthest back corner of the sandbox. Renfroe didn't use this part of the sandbox and at least the sand was clean.

She dug down as far as the bare dirt underneath before she stashed the bundle and covered it over. Then she went through a long, painstaking process of smoothing every trace that she'd ever been here.

That took a lot longer than the actual digging part. She had to remove her own footprints, too, which meant working her way to the edge of the sandbox and erasing the imprints behind her.

She stood on the grass looking at her handiwork. The sandbox looked the same way it did when she came out here. No one would be able to tell.

She raced back to the house, but now she really needed to talk to Tom. How many people did the hostile cats have who knew how to detonate Nydrix? Any helpers who worked with those cylinders would have to be Coalition trained before they would be able to use the explosives.

She left through the door in the garden wall and set off for the city center. She would have to be very careful around Tom.

She would have to find out if he really was sincere about helping the Children. She would have to convince herself that he wasn't just messing around before she told him about the Nydrix or mentioned how to detonate it.

She made it as far as the market and spotted him on the other side of the square. He was talking to a man Dina didn't know, but before she could enter the square to approach him, a scuffle broke out to her left.

The city had been relatively at peace for a week. Now two helpers shoved each other near one of the wagons.

She didn't see what caused the disagreement, but the sight of two helpers fighting seemed to wake all the sleeping ghosts that had been hiding under the surface.

More helpers moved in to separate the parties. Two men approached the combatants from the sides, took hold of their arms, and tried to pull them apart.

The combatants ignored these peacemakers until one of the newcomers took hold of his companion's arm and tried to pull it away from the second man's chest.

The man this peacemaker was trying to restrain spun around and decked his friend right in the face. The peacemaker staggered and two more people rushed over to intervene.

The other combatant took the hint and plastered his opponent in the jaw. The two of them collided in a bare-knuckle assault that sucked the other two peacemakers into the conflict.

In seconds. all five piled in and more people gathered from all over to watch. Onlookers yelled at the combatants on both sides, but there were no sides. All five men fought each other in equal ferocity with no one left out.

Dina retreated, but not before five cats left the market to intervene. The crowd parted to let a jaguar, two large male lions, a tiger, and a black panther come through.

Neither the combatants nor the spectators saw the cats approaching. The five combatants kept hammering each other with kicks and blows while the crowd cheered them on.

The cats nosed their way through the mob to get near the combatants. Dina's instincts told her to get out of here before the situation exploded, but she found herself rooted to the spot.

The cats stopped at the edge of the ring of spectators. Before the cats could say or do anything, two of the men locked together yanking at each other's arms and trying to throw each other.

One of them kicked out and hooked the other's ankle, but the second man held onto his opponent so tightly that they both fell over.

They toppled right in front of the tiger. The two men kept grappling with each other in deadly combat.

The tiger put out his paw and extended his claws to grab the man on top. The tiger didn't have a chance to touch him before the man on the bottom pulled a knife from his waistband, lunged under his opponent's arm, and slashed the tiger across the chest.

The man laid open the tiger's muscles from one shoulder to the other and the tiger gave a fearful roar of pain and rage.

The man on top glanced over at the cat. The man underneath used that moment to throw his opponent and roll to his feet two yards away.

He crouched there brandishing the knife at the tiger. Then the man jerked from right to left to make sure no other cats or helpers came at him.

The tiger dove for him and all the other cats moved in to support him. The man swiped his knife at all five of them, and just as fast, ten more men stepped out of the crowd, pulled homemade weapons from under their clothes, and closed ranks with the man to confront the cats.

Half of the crowd retreated to get out of the danger zone. The other half of the spectators surged forward to square off against each other, but not fast enough.

Two men who'd fallen in line with the first attacker didn't wait for the battle to begin. They rushed the cats and one of the men hacked a shovel at the jaguar.

The cat sprang out of the way and the second man caught an ax blade under the jaguar's chin to split the cat's skull in half.

The other cats yowled in fury, but the helpers only charged them wielding every weapon in the book.

Dina stood watching in slack-jawed shock as the crowd overran the cats, brought them down, and killed all five of them right there on the pavement.

The opposing helpers tried to stop the unfolding chaos, but more cats converged from all sides and so did more helpers from both directions.

Dina glanced over the crowd to the far side of the square. Both Tom and the man he'd been talking to were gone.

She tore herself away and raced off into the streets heading for Renfroe's house, but the noise behind her didn't fade for a long time. It kept escalating as she ran farther away. The peace was over.

Chapter 25

Dina sat on the parlor floor eating her evening meal. Renfroe sat next to her crunching up a tree lizard Belinda had brought him.

They'd been sitting here for over an hour and he hadn't said a word to her since he came home.

She didn't break the silence. She'd never known him to brood like this, but trying to talk to him wouldn't get him to open up. It would just make him mad.

She finished her soup and set the bowl aside. How much longer could this go on? If he decided not to continue their relationship, how much longer would he carry on the charade before he called it quits?

She couldn't even imagine what that would look like. He'd always told her she would have a home here as long as she wanted one.

She didn't ask those questions even of herself. He would tell her if he wanted her to leave, but she didn't expect him to. He would just distance himself from her. He already did distance himself from her.

He startled her out of her thoughts by growling, "I suppose you heard about what happened in the market today."

"I heard," she replied.

"Fights are breaking out all over the city. We had a nice week, but the truce is over. Now helpers are fighting cats in the open." He heaved a tremendous sigh and pushed the remains of his lizard away. "It's the beginning of the end."

She took a chance and laid her hand on his shoulder. "Is there anything we can do?"

"I don't see what anyone can do. Helpers are fighting helpers, and when the cats intervene, the helpers turn on the cats. Then more helpers turn on other helpers for defending the cats and the helpers fight even more. It's a doom spiral."

She hesitated and then blurted out, "Is it the beginning of the end for us, too."

He stared into the flames and didn't acknowledge her touch. "I wish I knew. I wish I could believe that we would continue to live here together even after....whatever is going to happen. I don't dare to believe that, though. Something will happen. Something will break all this the same way the peace broke today. All of this is hanging by the weakest thread. It wouldn't take more than a breath of wind to break that thread and shatter everything."

"Are you talking about us or Prideland?"

"Both," he growled.

She passed her hand down his shoulder. She didn't expect him to respond, but he surprised her by lying down and putting his head in her lap.

He shut his eyes and twitched his ears when she scratched the back of his neck. "I've never had a helper like you, Dina. I have never cared for any helper as I've cared for you."

"I can't tell you how grateful I am that I got you as a benefactor," she murmured back. "I can't imagine how I got so lucky."

"I only wish things could have been different," he muttered under his breath. "I wish so many things, but those are all the wishes of a sentimental old fool. I should have known it was all too good to last."

She didn't ask again if he meant the Prideland was too good to last or their relationship. It was both.

He let her rub, scratch, and stroke his head, but in a minute, he groaned again, got to his feet, and turned away. "Come to bed, Dina. It's getting late."

It wasn't getting late, but she followed him to the bedroom anyway. They both stretched out on top of the bed and he growled when he put his head on the pillow next to her.

He didn't speak again, and after forty-five minutes of silence, she fell asleep.

She woke up in darkness and listened. She sensed something wrong, but she couldn't put her finger on it.

Renfroe raised his head at the same time. "Something's happening."

"I know, but what is it?"

He hopped off the bed and paced over to the doors leading out to the courtyard. That was when she noticed a faint reddish glow in the sky over the treetops.

"What is that?" she asked.

"I must go. If the Children are invading again, I must do something."

"What could you do?"

"I don't know, but I have to do something. I have to at least see what's happening. Stay here. You'll be safer here. Don't go out there for anything."

He trotted to the door, nudged it open, and slipped out into the shadows. She stood at the glass doors leading to the courtyard looking at that ominous glow in the sky.

A second later, she saw him slip through the garden on his way to spring over the wall. He never left through the house anymore.

There was nothing else to see, so she sat down on the bed to wait. She should have gone back to sleep, but the thought that something might be happening out there kept her awake.

She wouldn't be able to do anything, either. She kicked herself for not talking to Tom when she had the chance. She should have gone to Elyse's house and talked to him instead of coming home. Now it was too late.

She paced around the room for a while and then went to get herself a drink of water from the pitcher in the corner, but it was empty.

She carried it down to the kitchen to refill it, but when she pushed the door open, she paused when she heard voices in the kitchen beyond.

She eased the door a little farther open. The fire still blazed on the hearth and gave her a clear view of Buck and Belinda talking to six people standing outside the outer kitchen door.

Dina couldn't see who the strangers were in the shadows, but as soon as they started talking, she recognized their voices.

"We know of fifty helpers who are actively arming to support the Children," one man was saying. It was Penja, Fan's husband from Hellion House. "If we all strike at once, we can kill them in one stroke and weaken the subversive force in the city. They won't be able to fight back."

"Even fifty dead won't weaken the subversives enough," Belinda was saying. "They have too many people."

"It will be enough if we all strike together," a second man replied. "I can get you more names and I can tell you the right time to strike, but we need to work quickly before the Children make their move."

Dina's scalp prickled. The second man was Angulo Duala, the man she'd confided in about the Children's next campaign. He was a traitor—a mole working inside the subversive ranks.

At least he didn't know that Dina had the explosives. No one knew apart from Son ya.....and maybe Belinda. Did she check what was inside that parcel before she gave it to Dina?

"We got another supply of weapons from Khalid," Penja was saying. "We just need to distribute them to the loyal helpers."

"We should do that immediately," Belinda told him. "We don't know when the Children will attack."

"They could be attacking now," Angulo pointed out. "We don't know what's going on over there." He nodded toward the southern sky where the glow was coming from.

"Then it's all the more important that we arm and prepare." Buck stepped forward. "I'll go with you. We can arm them now—before the subversives see what we're doing."

"Just make sure you pass out all the weapons, even if you have to double up," Belinda told him. "It would be better for the people we know are loyal to be doubly armed. Don't leave any weapon without someone to use it. We need to be as prepared as possible."

Buck nodded at her over his shoulder. "I will."

He hobbled through the door and vanished into the night along with the other two men and whoever had been standing behind them in the shadows.

Dina watched and listened with her heart in her mouth. Belinda—she was the one telling the men what to do. She must be one of the loyal helpers' organizers.

She shut the door behind them, turned away, and crossed the kitchen so fast that Dina didn't have time to retreat or to hide the fact that she'd been eavesdropping on their conversation.

Dina started to back off, but Belinda got there too fast. She blasted through the door like she usually did and almost flattened Dina.

Dina sprang away, but it was too late. Belinda stopped dead in the kitchen doorway with her hand still on the door handle. "You!" she hissed. "Listening at keyholes now, are you?"

Dina recovered instantly and straightened up. "You didn't exactly make yourselves inconspicuous. You're helping the Pride. You're organizing and arming the loyal helpers."

"Yes, I am, and if you were the helper Renfroe deserves, you would be doing the same thing instead of running around with subversives." Belinda looked down her nose at Dina. "You arm and organize the subversives. I'll arm and organize the loyal helpers and we'll see who's left when this is all over."

"No one will be left when this is all over, Belinda," Dina countered. "Don't you get that? The Pride doesn't value you or your loyalty. The Pride doesn't value you at all. Your life is forfeit to the cats. It always has been. You've never been more than a piece of meat to them......but you already knew that, didn't you? No one knows better than you do."

"What are you talking about?" Belinda fired back. "The Pride is the best thing that has ever happened to us....."

"I'm talking about your sister, Belinda—your sister Elana. You remember her, don't you? She came to you for help and you got her visited when she was just a girl. You were supposed to look out for her, and instead, you eventually got her killed. That's where your loyalty to the Pride got you."

Belinda's mouth fell open in a silent gasp of horror. "Elana.....dead....."

"Don't tell me you didn't know. She had two children—your niece and nephew—and the Pride killed them, too. Do you have any other relatives? Do you have any family at all? How does it feel to know you killed the only family you will ever have?"

Belinda shut her mouth with a snap, straightened her facial expression, and started to turn away. "What do I care if the cats reduce some slag in the jungle? She deserved it. They all deserve it, just like you'll deserve it when they reduce you."

Dina didn't think about it before she reacted. She saw herself pull her knife, spring across the threshold, and attack Belinda in a whirlwind.

Dina caught Belinda by the hair, yanked Belinda's head back, and Dina pressed her knife to Belinda's throat while she backed Belinda against the wall.

"I can't let you do that, Belinda," Dina whispered in a deadly undertone. "You've done enough damage already. I can't let you warn anyone about what I'm going to do."

Belinda's eyes darted from Dina's face to the kitchen behind Dina's back. Dina glanced around the room and made up her mind in a split second.

She couldn't sit on this information about Angulo Duala working for the Pride. She had to warn someone—preferably someone influential enough to actually do something about it.

She had to warn someone tonight before Renfroe came back. If she walked out that door right now, Belinda would send her people after Dina in an instant. Dina didn't trust Belinda not to try something herself.

It would be risky enough to run the gauntlet of sentinel cats and anyone else who might be out there. Dina would have to be careful, but she had to go. She couldn't keep this to herself even for one more night.

One look at Belinda's jittery eyes told Dina all she needed to know. She couldn't let Belinda warn her own people about what Dina was doing.

Dina tightened her fist in Belinda's hair, dragged the cook into the kitchen, and kicked the door shut. "Get over here." Dina yanked Belinda into the pantry.

"What are you going to do?" Belinda demanded. Her voice didn't shake at all. She wasn't scared.

"I can't let you go, Belinda. Be grateful I don't kill you to shut you up."

"You couldn't kill me! Renfroe would find out. You'd be reduced yourself."

Dina paused for an instant. Renfroe. He had told her to stay here for her own safety.

She didn't quite believe him when he said their relationship was over. They still slept together in that bedroom. They still shared meals and talked about everything with each other that they couldn't share with anyone else.

This moment—this moment when Dina shoved Belinda down on the floor—this moment snapped the last cord binding Dina to Prideland.

She didn't care anymore what Renfroe did or said. She didn't belong to Renfroe or anything else related to Prideland. She did have to come back here and she might even have had to come back for him, but not anymore.

He was right. Whatever might have been between them was over. She couldn't identify when it ended, but it was definitely over now. It would be over for good the minute she stepped out that door.

She grabbed a sack of root vegetables off the shelf and unwound the cord tying the neck of the sack closed. It wouldn't hold Belinda, but it would restrain her until Dina found something stronger.

Belinda took advantage of Dina's activity to try to get off the floor. Dina kicked Belinda back down and pinned her there under her heel to hold her in place.

"You remember what I said," Dina snapped. "I'm leaving you alive, but I don't have to. I'll just as soon kill you if you give me any trouble."

Dina got the cord free and sat on Belinda while Dina bound Belinda's wrists behind her back. Then Dina did the same thing with Belinda's ankles.

"Those are my Children out there, Belinda," Dina growled. "They're the Children I had from Renfroe. You might be willing to sell your own family to the cats, but I won't. Now stay there. If I see you out of this pantry before I leave, I swear to God I'll kill you."

Dina left Belinda there just long enough to run out to Buck's gardening shed. She came back with a full length of rope and tied up Belinda in so many knots that Belinda wouldn't have been able to move to save her own life.

Dina used the extra lengths of the rope to tie Belinda to one of the shelf supports. Even if Belinda managed to get free, all those knots would at least slow her down.

"Be grateful I have a little more compassion than you do," Dina muttered while she worked.

"You won't get away with this!" Belinda fired back. "You'll be reduced as the slag you are! You're a traitor to the Pride."

"I'm proud to be a traitor to the Pride," Dina replied. "I hope they put that on my gravestone—that I gave everything to help the Children overthrow the Pride."

Dina went out into the kitchen and came back with a rag. She tore it in half, stuffed one half into Belinda's mouth, and used the other half to tie it in place.

Dina sat back on her heels and looked down at Belinda one last time. "I want you to think about something while I'm gone, Belinda. I know you're too far gone to care about your sister or anyone else who might have cared about you. You don't care about anyone but yourself, so think about this.

"When this war is over and the Children win and take control of this city, they won't kill any helpers who didn't take up arms against them. All they want is to stop the cats from killing more Children.

"The Children will leave as many people alive as possible. The Children could have leveled this city along with everyone in it, but they chose to invade in a way that wouldn't kill innocent, defenseless civilians. Think about that.

"The cats kill on a whim. They kill loyal helpers every day because that's what cats do. They kill helpers for fun. The cats kill helpers out of boredom. The cats kill simply because they enjoy killing.

"That doesn't make them superior and it doesn't entitle them to our loyalty. You've wasted your life serving the cats, but you don't have to do it anymore. Think about that. Think about what the rest of your life is going to be worth when this war is over and what you'll have left when the Children finish off the Pride for good."

Chapter 26

Dina walked out of the pantry. She had no more time to waste on Belinda.

Dina grabbed her knife and slipped out of the kitchen into the neighborhood. She ran as far as the city streets before she slowed to a walk, but she didn't see a single cat. None of the sentinel cats were abroad. That was strange. Something serious must be wrong.

That glow in the southern sky seemed to be getting brighter—or maybe it just seemed that way because Dina was looking at it from outside the house.

She hurried through the streets and found her way to the river. She didn't know where to find the Kadi house where Kubri James worked.

She followed the river for five blocks before she spotted a group of people gathering in one of the yards. They crowded the side yard between a large white stone house and the neighboring fence.

They didn't make much effort to hide themselves and Dina spotted Kubri James standing closest to the house while he addressed the others.

"How many do we have coming from the west side?" he asked.

"We don't know," another man replied. "Angulo was supposed to find that out and he isn't here."

"Something must have happened to him," Kubri James muttered. "We'll just have to go on with our plans without him. Maybe he'll turn up and tell us later. In the meantime...."

Dina raced over to them, shoved her way between the surrounding helpers, and blurted out in a rush. "Listen to me! Angulo isn't here because he's helping the loyal helpers. They're arming against you right now and Angulo is telling them all the names of all the helpers who've been helping the Children."

Kubri James frowned at her. "You better be damn sure you know what you're saying. Angulo has been my righthand man for weeks. He knows all our plans."

"Then you better change them because I just saw him at Renfroe's house fifteen minutes ago. He was planning with the other loyal helpers and giving them all your names. He's working for the other side. He probably always has been."

A few people standing behind Dina cursed. Kubri James compressed his lips and surveyed the yard, but there was nothing to see there. "We'll just have to adjust. Keep arming the way I told you to. We need everyone armed in case the Children invade again."

"That's exactly what the loyal helpers are doing," Dina told him. "They'll be ready for you."

"That doesn't matter," Kubri James replied. "We're ready. They can bring it on whenever they want to." He pointed out six men. "We'll go clear out the weapons we have stashed in the Hellion House basement. If we do that tonight, the loyal helpers won't have time to take them first."

He pointed out ten men to go with him and sent the others on different errands around the city. The sky lightened with every passing minute, but the glow in the south didn't seem to be getting any brighter. Dawn was coming.

Kubri James gave the last orders to his men and then scowled at Dina. "You better go back to your benefactor's house. I appreciate you coming to tell me about Angulo, but it isn't safe for you out here tonight. Go home."

"Okay," she murmured. "Let me know if I can do anything else."

"You've done enough. Let's go."

The men set off for the center of town. Dina went with them as far as the square. They split away toward Hellion House and she turned back to return to Renfroe's neighborhood.

She paused when she heard a noise coming from the west. It didn't sound like anything she'd ever heard before.

Kubri James and his men were less than a block away and they turned around to listen, too. The sound reminded Dina of a low scratching sound, but it was too faint to be anything dangerous.

The instant she noticed it, a vibration buzzed through the pavement under her feet. She glanced around, but she still didn't see anything that could be making either the sound or the vibration.

A yell from one of Kubri James's men made her spin the other way. Her heart dropped into her shoes as a hundred cats charged out of the shadows, raced around corners, and flooded the city.

More cats poured from every direction and they all charged westward—toward where that sound was coming from.

The scratching sound got louder. She turned to see what the cats were running toward and her world stopped when a colossal tide of Children overran the city. The scratching sound was their claws on the pavement.

Her mouth went dry when she saw just how many Children were rushing toward her in an unbroken sea of bodies. They bounded over every obstacle, covered the ground in an instant, and collided with the cats in a battle to the death.

Dina barely flattened herself against the nearest wall to avoid getting trampled by both sides, but the Children didn't pay any attention to her. They closed with the cats and all the tearing, screaming, roaring sounds of all-out war echoed through the streets.

Her hands flew to her ears to block out that noise, but a second later, one of the Children smashed into the wall right next to her.

He was a short, burly man with black fur flecked with dapple-grey spots. His muscular arms and shoulders strained to the breaking point trying to fight off three young lionesses all mauling him at once.

They roared at him and he bared his teeth and snarled in his effort to hold them at bay. His struggle tore them off the wall, but their combined weight buckled his knees and he slammed down on the ground.

Dina leapt out of position, snatched her weapons from under her tunic, and attacked the lionesses. As usual, they were so busy fighting the man that they didn't see her.

She hacked her sickle across one lioness's neck and stabbed another upward under the jaw before they realized what she was doing. The third lioness turned around to see what was happening and the man attacked in fury.

He grabbed the lioness's head, snapped her neck, and threw the body aside, but neither he nor Dina had time to exchange a single word before another mob of cats came out of nowhere and overwhelmed both of them.

Now Dina knew where the sentinel cats had been. They'd all gone to the southern side of town to check out whatever that reddish glow was. That left the west side of town clear for the Children to invade.

Now all the sentinel cats poured back into the city streets and swarmed the Children. Dina slashed, hacked, chopped, and flung the cats away as fast as her arms could move. She lost sight of the man in the confusion.....and then she spotted Kubri James in the chaos.

He fought with two axes, one in each hand. He chopped flying cats out of the air, swung his axes to knock cats away from the Children, and marauded his way through the square like a madman.

Ten sentinel cats swarmed him from all sides, scrambled up his legs while he was protecting two trapped Children, and the cats vaulted off windowsills and ledges to fly at his head while he couldn't defend himself.

Dina battled her way over to him and tried to clear some space around him, but the sentinel cats only came after her next.

She never dreamed there could be so many of them, but she also never dreamed there could be so many Children. Where did Adrian find them all?

Then she remembered. Whatever he was doing, he would be doing the same thing all over Prideland. He must have rallied a lot more than five thousand Children. He might have sent five thousand to this city alone. He might even have sent more.

She didn't have time to think about that because the cats responded in equal numbers. Every size, shape, breed, and variety of cat came out to counter the Children's assault. Dina couldn't even tell who was winning.

She worked her hardest to clear enough cats just to give herself room to stand on the sidewalk. More cats flew at her head from all sides.

She spun from one direction to another chopping them out of the air, using her knife to slash them off her legs, and battle her way backward to the nearest wall.

She planned to take a stand against it so the cats couldn't get behind her. Kubri James and another helper who'd been with him at the Kadi house had the same idea.

The three of them inched backward toward the building behind them. They made it within four feet of the brick wall before another mob of helpers barreled around a corner to the west.

They plunged into the battle and immediately went to work hacking the cats to pieces. Helpers surrounded every Child and added their efforts to destroy all the cats attacking the Children.

The helpers' assistance sparked a fresh wave of fury from the Children and they attacked even more ferociously. They threw the cats off and charged farther eastward deeper into the city.

The helpers who'd just arrived fell in behind the Children and the whole mob flocked toward the square.

Another wave of helpers swarmed in from the northwest to meet this throng and the two sides collided in a thunderous explosion of weapons, claws, bellows, and screams.

Kubri James spun away from the wall, turned his back to Dina, and brandished his axes at the battle. "Get out of here!" he roared over his shoulder. "Get back to your benefactor's house while you can! I'll cover you!"

She would have preferred to stay and help the Children, but the sheer scale of the battle changed her mind.

She leapt out of position and turned away to make her escape, but at that moment, the battle surged back in her direction. The loyal helpers clashed with the subversives and another army of Children came out of the west to meet the battle from that direction.

The mayhem enveloped Dina again and she had no choice but to stand and fight. She stabbed, slashed, and dismembered cats by the dozen.

Most of them were small sentinel cats. The bigger cats went after the Children and vice versa. She attacked these cats when she could to help the Children, but the Children and the bigger cats ignored the helpers whenever possible.

She couldn't say the same for the helpers. The loyal helpers did everything possible to stop the subversives from interfering in fights between cats and Children.

The problem was that all the helpers wore the same style of clothing. Dina couldn't tell who was loyal or who was subversive unless one of them attacked a cat, Child, or intervened in a fight between cats and Children.

These battles took place all around her and blocked the whole street. She couldn't move. She wouldn't have been able to move anyway with all the sentinel cats flying at her from every side.

She got so busy fighting them that she didn't see three of them until they landed on her head, shoulders, and body. She tore them off, slammed them on the ground, and stabbed to finish them off, only for more cats to envelop her all ripping, biting, and kicking.

She shot to her feet scrambling to tear them off. She staggered a few yards away, grabbed a large male tabby perched on her shoulder, tightened her fist in his fur, and ripped him off.

She got ready to destroy him when the other two rocketed away from her for no reason she could figure out. She seethed in rage, but before she could kill the cat, a knot of two Children and three panthers hurtled at her from across the street.

They were all so busy fighting each other that they didn't see her. They slammed into her and knocked her back against the nearest wall. Her head struck the brick and she passed out.

Chapter 27

Dina peeled herself off the pavement, cradled her aching head, and forced herself to look around. It was broad daylight now.

Smoke and mist floated through the city streets, but that didn't stop her from seeing the bloodbath surrounding her. Dead cats and helpers carpeted the streets, but once again, the Children had taken all their dead and injured with them. She didn't see a single dead Child anywhere.

She couldn't tell which helpers had been fighting for which side. It didn't matter anymore because they were all dead.

A few buildings showed damage to their walls and windows, too, but that paled in comparison to all the dead bodies all over the place.

Cats had been torn to pieces. The dead people were missing body parts or had their organs torn out. Others had hack and chop wounds to their heads, limbs, and bodies.

Dina pried herself off the sidewalk and leaned against the wall to hold herself up. Her knees trembled, but at least she didn't see anyone she knew among the dead.

She kept her hand on the wall so she wouldn't fall over as she limped down the street. Then she remembered, went back, and retrieved both the weapons she'd dropped when she got knocked out.

She was just turning back to continue on her way back to Renfroe's house when the familiar squeak of the Elite Battalion's wheelbarrow stopped her in her tracks.

The Elite Battalion came around the corner with one man pushing the wheelbarrow. It was already fully loaded with bodies.

Another twelve helpers followed them with a man in helper's attire pointing to everyone and then to the bodies. "Load up those wheelbarrows. These men will show you where to take the bodies. Come on. Get to work. We can't live in this city with bodies everywhere."

That one man stood by and supervised while all the other helpers got to work. They piled cats and people one on top of the other with no regard to which side they'd fought on during the battle. The helpers didn't show the cats any special consideration—not more than the helpers.

The Elite Battalion tried to stack two more bodies on top of their load. Arms and legs kept flopping off and two men had to stand on either side of the wheelbarrow to hold everything on.

Dina turned away feeling sick. She didn't want to see this, but before she could move, another crowd of helpers streamed down the street coming from the north. They were all armed and their hard, determined expressions made the other helpers draw back.

Kubri James led the group and he cast flinty glances to the left and the right. He outright glared at the other helpers and he and his people didn't try to help out.

His eyebrows flew up when he saw Dina standing there. "You're alive!" he exclaimed. "I thought you went down during the battle."

Dina rubbed her head. "I guess I did." She frowned at him and then at the people behind him. At least two hundred helpers followed him and they were all armed, stern, and tense. "What are you doing? The battle's over."

"We're leaving this city," he told her. "We're going out to the jungle to fight with the Children. None of us wants to stay here in slavery anymore."

"I don't blame you."

"You've been out there," he went on. "You could show us where to go. We don't know where to find the Children or who to talk to among their leadership. You do. You could come with us. You don't have to stay here."

She hesitated, and in that instant, the same snapping sensation she felt last night happened again. She didn't owe Renfroe anything anymore if she ever did. Their relationship was purely platonic and always would be from now on.

The decision made itself in her mind before she even realized it. "All right," she told him. "I'll go with you, but I need to stop by my benefactor's house first. I need to tell him where I'm going....and I have some things I want to get from there."

"Renfroe is your benefactor, isn't he?" Kubri James asked. "His house is on our way."

He waited and the rest of his people waited for her to inch down the wall. She had to walk slowly at first, but her balance came back in a little while.

She and Kubri James led the crowd filing through the streets. Cats sat in their doorways and windowsills watching the helpers leave the city, but no one interfered.

The helpers waited in the street outside while Dina went in through the kitchen door. She untied Belinda on her way to the main part of the house.

Belinda huffed and puffed and gasped and threatened, but Dina ignored her.

Dina stepped out into the main corridor and spotted Renfroe sitting in the sunshine by the fountain. She advanced through the portico and sat down next to him for the last time.

"I thought you might be dead," he muttered.

"I'm sorry I made you worry," she replied.

"I wasn't worried. I don't hold any claim on you anymore. You're going to do what you want to do. Not even telling you to stay inside for your own safety will make you do as I ask anymore. The understanding between us is truly broken."

She took a deep breath. "I'm going back out to the jungle—for good this time."

He only sighed. "I expected as much."

She considered what to say next. She almost told him she was sorry it didn't work out between them, but she wasn't sorry—about any of it. There just didn't seem to be anything left to say.

She stood up, walked to the bedroom, and changed into the clothes she'd worn from the canton. They melded with her skin. This was her—the real her. She wasn't in disguise anymore.

She tucked her sickle and her knife into her belt. She made no effort at all to hide them. She would never hide them ever again.

She went back out to the courtyard. Renfroe sat in the same place blinking into the sunshine.

"I'm going now," she murmured. "I'll miss you."

She put her arms around his neck and hugged him. He leaned his head against hers, but that was all.

"Thank you, Dina," he rumbled. "Thank you for our children and thank you for honoring your promise by coming back to me. It has been a privilege to know you. I appreciate why you have to leave and I'm grateful that you at least have the courage to do it. We could not live here together any longer and I would not have the fortitude to send you away. I care for you too much."

She hugged him tighter, but she couldn't speak. He was right. He had always cared for her so much more than she ever cared for him.

She kissed him on the cheek and walked back out through the kitchen. Belinda gasped again when she saw Dina's clothes, but Dina ignored that, too. Everything about this house and this city lay behind her.

She said, "Let's go," to Kubri James and the two of them led the way out of the city.

None of the helpers talked on the way. An air of death hung over the city, but more than that, the seriousness of this decision weighed on everyone.

They'd never been free to wander anywhere before—not without their benefactors' permission. None of these people had set foot outside the city before.

Now they were on their way to the jungle—the most forbidden place in Prideland. These people were doing the one thing that had been the most taboo for generations.

The whole company stiffened and many people raised their weapons when they left the city streets for the open road. The hostile cats patrolled the roads and Dina drew her own weapons to confront them.

She braced herself for another battle to get out of the city. The tension in the crowd spiked into the stratosphere, but the cats must have sensed it, too.

They backed off. There weren't enough cats out here to bother this many people anyway. They let the helpers pass, but the helpers still rotated outward as they passed. The helpers didn't take any chances of the cats attacking without warning.

Dina had to admire the helpers' attitude. They really wanted their freedom and they were ready to fight for it.

She couldn't call them helpers anymore. They weren't helpers. They weren't slaves or subsidiaries. They were free people with the fortitude to defend their freedom.

A dozen men turned around and walked backward as the crowd advanced farther into the countryside. These men kept the cats in view at all times until the crowd got to a safe distance.

That funeral hush hung over the crowd as far as the village. No one spoke. Everyone in the crowd held their breath and waited for some other disaster to derail their escape.

"How much farther is it?" Kubri James asked when the crowd passed through the village.

"You can see the edge of the trees ahead," Dina told him. "After that, we have to get to the nearest canton."

"How far is that?"

"Maybe seven or eight miles. We got an early start. We should get there before sundown if we keep moving.....and if we don't encounter any resistance."

"What resistance would we encounter?" he asked. "We're here to help the Children. No one will bother us out here."

"There are cats roaming around in the jungle," she told him. "They attacked me and my friend the last time we came through here." He started to slow down, but she just kept right on walking. "You didn't come here for safety. You won't be safe, not even in the cantons."

His eyes darted from side to side. This was the first time she'd seen him uncertain about anything. "What are they like—the cantons? Are they as bad as the factors say?"

Dina snorted. "You should know better than that. They're really nice and the people living in them are just normal people trying to live their lives. Look at me. I lived in the cantons for years. Do I look like I wallow in the mud and eat worms? Those Children are my Children. Do they look like I let them starve when the bad weather came?"

He pursed his lips and looked away. "Of course not. I always knew the factors were lying about that."

"Of course they did. They lied about everything else. They had to make the cantons and the slags sound as bad as possible so no one would get the crazy idea to leave Prideland."

He let out a puff of air through his flared nostrils. His eyes became even more dangerously watchful. "I'm glad you're here. I was planning to ask you to help us leave the city, and then, when I thought you died in the battle—well, I wasn't looking forward to coming out here alone—or leading a bunch of other people out here. I wouldn't want to find out the factors were telling the truth. I needed someone who had been here before."

"They aren't telling the truth. You'll see."

The group pressed on and hushed whispers and anxious murmurs spread through the crowd as the party approached the tree line.

People slowed and the assembly spread out. No one walked as close together and some trailed behind.

"Keep moving!" Dina called over her shoulder. "We don't have far to go and you'll be sleeping safe behind the canton walls tonight. Keep moving! Don't slow down! Everything will be all right. You're free now! The hard part is over."

No one argued with her or reminded her that they'd all made themselves enemies of the Pride by leaving the city.

The group had to spread out even more when they entered the narrow paths winding through the jungle. Kubri James let Dina go in front.

The rest formed a single-file line snaking through the undergrowth. This journey seemed to take so much longer than all of Dina's previous trips out of the city.

She jumped at the slightest sound and kept glancing up into the trees, but she didn't see anything. She didn't even know what she expected to see— cats or Children.

Chapter 28

The route through the jungle became more treacherous. Kubri James came up behind Dina and murmured in her ear. "Don't you think we should stop for a rest now? We've been walking for hours."

"No, I don't think we should stop now for any reason," she replied over her shoulder. "I don't think we should stop until we get to the canton."

"People are falling behind," he pointed out.

"They need to keep up if they don't want to get stranded out here. Life in the cantons is hard. They need to toughen up. If they want it easy, they should go back to their benefactors."

That shut him up. She made a point not to turn around again to check on the people behind her. They didn't leave Prideland for the easy life. She certainly never promised them that.

They made it another two miles and came to a flat section of the jungle. The trail wound between trees spaced farther apart.

People could walk abreast here, but when she checked on them, she saw that the crowd really had thinned out. Only about half of them had kept up. The others dragged behind. She didn't see if anyone had turned back entirely.

She decided to stop here and give them a pep talk about what the cats would do to anyone who went back. She stopped where she was, but before she could turn around, a dozen Children dropped out of the trees.

The former helpers stiffened in alarm, and within seconds, another fifty Children dropped out of nowhere. They didn't make any noise sneaking up on the party. The Children just materialized there and landed in front of Dina to block the crowd's progress.

Zair, a bunch of other Children from Moonlight canton, the Manx brothers, Osiris's Children, and the Auroras all dropped in front of Dina.

She stiffened, but she didn't draw her weapons. The rest of the former helpers did, though. They sprang forward, aimed their weapons at the Children, and closed ranks to defend themselves.

The Children landed in a semi-circle across the crowd's path. The Children would have surrounded the former helpers if the Children had brought more people.

They could have brought more people. They could have surrounded the crowd completely and wiped out everyone before the former helpers even realized what was happening.

Dina opened her mouth to address her Children when the Black plunged out of the canopy, landed in front of their friends, and then, last of all, Adrian dropped down to confront her.

"What are you doing here?" he demanded. "Why are you bringing a body of armed helpers into the jungle to attack us?"

"We don't want to attack you," Kubri James explained. "We abandoned Prideland to join you. We want to fight with the Children."

"We don't need you," Adrian replied. "You can go back where you came from. We don't need any more human help."

"They can't go back. You know that," Dina interrupted. "All these people took up arms against the Pride to help you during both of your battles in the city. You can't just turn your backs on them. Some of these people even saved your lives."

"We would have won those battles without human help," Adrian countered. "You're a liability to us. If you don't want to go back to Prideland, you can live in the cantons with the other slags. You won't join us. You would only slow us down and that's exactly what we don't need right now."

Dina opened her mouth to argue with him, but he was already shooting off into the branches. The other Children took off just as fast and vanished into the branches.

"Now what are we going to do?" Kubri James asked. "We bet everything on joining the Children."

"We just have to keep going." Dina raised her voice to call over the crowd. "Going back to Prideland is no longer an option for any of us. Going back means death. We have to keep going. We're almost there. We can make our homes in the cantons. We'll be all right. I know this canton and it's really nice. Come on. Follow me. It isn't far."

She turned away one more time. She couldn't wait around to see if they listened to her. Going back to Prideland wasn't an option for her, either. She no longer cared what the others did.

"Are you sure about this?" Kubri James murmured in her ear again.

"More than ever," she replied over her shoulder. "You'll see."

He didn't ask again. He followed her without another word. They hiked for another four hours before she found her way to Moonlight canton.

A rush of emotions and memories gripped her when she spotted the high fence between the trees. The canopy cast the canton in perpetual shade. She'd never seen another canton like it.

This canton would always hold a place of infamy and tragedy in her heart. She would never lay her eyes on this place without thinking about Frank and his family.

"It's really nice!" Kubri James exclaimed. "I never imagined it would be like this."

She found herself smiling at him. "I told you so. Just wait until you see inside."

She picked up her pace, but just then, someone behind her yelled out a warning. Dozens of people turned back and drew their weapons.

Dina and Kubri James did the same thing when they saw Children in the trees. They balanced in the branches and didn't come down to the ground.

Dina strode back through the crowd to see which Children they were. She didn't recognize any of them—except one.

Zair dropped down to the ground and she separated from the crowd to go talk to him. "Is anything wrong?" she asked him. "Do your people have any objection to us coming here?"

"Why would we?" he asked. "Adrian told you to come here."

Dina surveyed the Children behind him. "Are Cain and Jackal still your leaders?"

"Yes, they are, but they're in Adrian's camp now. They're too busy to come home very often."

"Who's in charge here in their place, then?" she asked.

"I am," he replied.

Her head shot up to stare at him. He stood six inches taller and he dwarfed her in size and weight.

She opened her mouth a few times trying to decide what to say to him.

He saved her by speaking first. "You are welcome here, Dina. The Children of Moonlight canton have no grievance against you. If you and these people wish to become the Children's allies, then we are agreeable. We need all the allies we can get."

She burst into a relieved grin. "Thank you. That's what we want. All these people want to help the Children in any way we can. If you want us to fight, just tell us and we're with you."

"That won't be necessary. Adrian told you the truth. He has enough Children to fight the war—too many Children, in fact. He wants to protect the humans by keeping them out of the battles. He didn't exclude you because....well, because it's you."

She smiled at him even more. "Thank you for telling me. I really did think it was me."

"He's been turning away escaped helpers all over Prideland."

Her eyes widened. "Are they all leaving?"

"Not all—just large numbers of them—like these. None of them wants to stay in Prideland while it all goes down in flames. Only the loyal helpers want to do that."

She laughed. "Thank you for welcoming us. It will be good to be neighbors with you and the other Children."

"It is an honor to welcome you, Dina. You are a true friend to the Children."

"It might not mean anything, but you might also remind Cain and Jackal that I once offered them hospitality in my home at Riverbend canton."

"I remember," he replied.

Dina jolted. "You do? You weren't there."

"I stayed outside. You didn't see me. You were too busy taking care of all of Adrian's guests inside—but I remember you. You and your husband were the first humans to show us kindness. We won't forget that."

"Maybe we can change things at this canton." She glanced over her shoulder. A bunch of the residents gathered at the gate to watch her and Zair talking. "Do your parents still live here?"

"No, they don't like living this close to Children. They've retreated to other cantons deeper in the jungle." He shot a critical glance toward the gate. "Those people are the only people living here."

"That's all?!" she exclaimed. "There are only fifteen people over there.'

He nodded. "This canton is all but deserted now. As I said, not many are comfortable living this close to us."

"We'll have to change that. Do you and your people live close to the canton?"

"We camp in the trees about two hundred yards that way." He nodded at the dense canopy to his left. "I wouldn't tell any other human besides you, but our females stay there.....our pregnant females. If you need to find me, you can go over there and call up into the trees. If I'm not there, one of them will send me word that you're looking for me. Just....do me one favor and don't tell these other people that we have pregnant females there. I wouldn't want the wrong person to get any ideas."

"I understand. You can rely on my confidence. I won't tell anyone."

His features softened. "Thank you, Dina. I hope things will change between the Children and this canton."

"I'm certain they will. We better get inside. Thank you again. I'll see you soon."

She backed away and he shot off into the trees to join the other Children.

"What did he say?" Kubri James murmured when she returned to the group.

"Nothing. Everything's all right like I said. He's a friend of mine and the Children are happy about us coming here. We're going to be allies."

Kubri James brightened up. "We are? That's great! Your son seemed so hostile. What will he think about another group of Children making allies with us?"

She stopped in front of the whole group and raised her voice again. "The Children who grew up in this canton have welcomed us as allies. They say that the Children really don't need humans to fight in the war anymore. They're turning humans away for their own protection. Adrian is worried about humans getting hurt in the war and he has enough Children to do his fighting for him. He didn't turn us away because he has anything against us. This canton is short on people and it's the closest to Prideland. We're going to make our homes here and prepare ourselves to hold this canton against any cats or loyal helpers who try to come after us. Come on."

She turned back to the gate. She expected another confrontation with the people already living in this canton, but instead, she came face to face with Fan.

She stepped through the gate and held out her arms to Dina with a huge smile on her face. "Welcome back!" Fan gave her a massive hug. "Look at you! You're back."

"Yeah!" Dina murmured. "These people all just left Prideland. Zair said you had room for us."

Fan's eyebrows shot up. "What did he say to you?"

"He just welcomed us. We know each other—from before. We're friends. He's happy that we're here and that we want to support the Children."

Fan gasped and stared at her. "You....you made peace with him?"

"He's my friend," Dina insisted. "I didn't have to make peace with him. There's nothing wrong with him."

"He's threatened us before," Fan replied.

Dina waved that away. "He and his friends grew up in this canton. Their parents couldn't get used to the Children's ways and drove the Children out into the jungle. These Children have an old mistrust of human beings, but we're going to change that. We're allies."

Fan glanced toward the trees. The Children still watched from the branches. "They camp awfully close."

"They're protecting you. Don't you get that?" Dina turned to the other residents listening. "The Children stay this close to the canton to guard you from cats. You wouldn't be able to live here without the Children's protection. The Pride would have wiped you all out long ago. Now we're going to put all that old hostility aside. These Children are our friends and allies. We have the opportunity to live as free people because the Children gave us that opportunity. We aren't going to squander it by treating them as our enemies." She turned back to Fan. "If you have space, we should get these people inside. Which houses are available?"

Fan pointed out five houses. "Those five are the only ones occupied. You can take all the others."

Dina faced the crowd. "You heard her. People are already living in those five houses. You can divide yourselves between the others."

"Where are *you* going to live, Dina?" Kubri James asked.

"She's staying with me." Fan grabbed Dina's arm to pull her away. "You can come, too, if you want to. We have extra space."

Chapter 29

Dina spent an hour going from house to house in Moonlight canton to make sure all the recently escaped helpers settled in. They had to double up with seven or eight people to a house, but no one minded.

Their voices burst out in excited talk as they explored the upstairs bedrooms, divided themselves up according to families and friendships, and dug into the kitchens.

"You'll need to assign yourselves hunting parties to go out into the jungle to hunt," Dina told them.

"Won't that be dangerous?" one man asked.

"No one said leaving Prideland would be safe," she told him. "You won't have subsidiaries bringing you food in their wagons. The Children understand that you need to hunt for yourselves."

"What about cats?" a different man asked.

"You'll need to be prepared to fight any cats that you meet, but the residents of all these cantons have been hunting in the jungle for years. You can do it, too."

She finally made her way back to Fan's house, climbed the ladder, and found Fan and Kubri James talking in the living room.

Fan sat on the couch nursing five newborn Children all with beautiful, lustrous golden fur. Fan kept them nestled in a leather bag when they weren't nursing.

Dina passed her fingertip down their heads. "They're beautiful. Another generation of Auroras is rising."

"The last generation," Fan remarked. "Things are changing. I wonder what will happen when these Children get too old. Will everything go back to the way it was before?"

Dina turned away. "I guess none of us knows what will happen. Do you have anything to eat in this place? I'm starving."

"Check my bag," Kubri James told her. "I brought some food from the city."

"The other residents are settling in nicely. It will be strange to live in this canton again."

"Did you live here before?" he asked.

"I only stayed here for a few days, but it was one of the happiest times I've ever experienced on this planet. The people were kind, determined, and very giving."

"What happened to them?" he asked.

She rummaged in his bag and found a piece of cheese and some dried fruit. She chewed the cheese and stuck some of the fruit in her mouth to avoid answering, but when she returned to the living room, she discovered both Fan and Kubri James staring at her while they waited for her to answer.

She fiddled with the dried fruit in her hands so she wouldn't have to look at them when she said it. "The Pride hunted them down and killed everyone in the canton—even babies. I was the only one who survived because my benefactor wanted me back."

She glanced around the house. This wasn't Frank's and Elana's old house, but it looked identical. It brought back all the old memories.

"They were going to help me evacuate the cantons. I was going to call in Coalition destroyers to lift everyone off the planet. We were going to get away from Prideland for good.....and then the Pride struck. I guess I should have known a dream like that was too good to come true."

"How were you going to evacuate all the cantons?" Kubri James asked. "There are hundreds of cantons all over Prideland."

"My friend traveled to some of the nearer cantons and they all wanted to evacuate." She had to stop again when she remembered Link.

Link knew Frank. Link was one of the people in other cantons who'd talked to Frank about evacuating. That was Dina's very first conversation with Link. They both knew Frank from his efforts to evacuate the cantons.

She tried to shake the memories out of her head, but they wouldn't go away. They probably never would.

"I guess I just have to get used to remembering all of that," she muttered under her breath. "I've spent a long time doing everything to stop myself from remembering. I'm going to have to learn to live with it if I'm going to stay in this canton."

"You don't have to stay here," Fan pointed out. "You could go to any other canton. We'd love it if you stayed here. Everyone admires you, Dina, but if it's too painful, we'd understand why you had to leave."

"No, I'll stay here. I don't want to run anymore and this canton is the closest to the city. If we needed to go there or help anyone else who left Prideland, this would be the best place to do it."

"I wish I shared your confidence in Zair," Fan went on. "You don't know what he's like. He's been so ruthless toward us. He threatened us for going outside the fence to hunt."

"Maybe he had a good reason for it," Dina pointed out.

"What reason would that be?" Fan asked. "We have to hunt to live. Telling us we can't hunt is the same as telling us to starve to death."

"What did he say?" Dina asked.

"Our hunters headed west to keep away from cats and Children. He and his friends dropped out of the trees, got in our hunters' faces, and threatened them to turn back. Zair said he would kill anyone who went set foot in the jungle."

"Oh, I understand now," Dina replied. "The Children camp in the trees about two hundred yards west of the canton. They're protective of their space and they don't want anyone going over there. Just tell your hunters to go south or north first and then head west. Give the Children's camp a wide berth and we'll all be fine."

Fan frowned. "Are you sure it's just that? Why didn't he say so in the first place?"

"It's like I told you. The people who lived here before forced their Children out to live in the jungle. These Children don't trust people. It's going to take some time for us to overcome that mistrust. Just give the Children their space. They have their reasons for wanting to keep their distance from us the same way we have our reasons for keeping our distance from them."

Fan finished nursing the last baby and put the little one in the bag with the others. "I better put these cherubs to bed. You two make yourselves at home. You know where everything is."

She carried the bag upstairs and left Dina and Kubri James sitting there alone together. "I can't tell you how relieved I am that you came with us," he told her. "This is so much better than I ever imagined—and you being here means we can smooth things over with the Children."

"There's nothing to smooth over. They're just normal people trying to live their lives. That's where people go wrong—by thinking the Children are somehow so different from us that we can't talk to each other."

"You have that relationship with them, but you're the only one."

"I can't be the only one," she countered. "In fact, I know I'm not. Plenty of other people are on the Children's side and have earned their trust." She grimaced. "I haven't earned their trust."

"You've gone a lot further than the rest of us." He crossed the room to get some of the food out of his bag and stopped at the doorway. "The sun is going down. It will be dark soon."

She advanced to his side and looked out over the canton falling deeper in shadow. The trees thrashed two hundred yards to the west.

"The Children are over there," he murmured.

"Be grateful," she told him. "They'll protect us from any cats. Here, help me pull up the ladder."

They pulled it up, laid it on the floor, and he shut the door.

"I guess we might as well turn in for the night," he remarked. "It's been a long day and we have a lot of work to do tomorrow. Good night, Dina. Thank you again. You're a lifesaver."

He climbed the second ladder to the upstairs bedrooms. Dina straightened the living room, but he was right. There was nothing more to do here.

Her mind whirled with everything the new residents would have to do to make this canton function the way it did before. It couldn't function with only fifteen people living here.

She blew out the lamps and climbed up to the last vacant bedroom on the second floor. She sat down on the bed and peered through a tiny window looking out into the shadowy jungle.

The Children were out there. They had pregnant females hidden in the trees—which meant all the Children would be getting pregnant. Iona wasn't the only one.

No wonder Zair was so protective of them. A second generation of Children meant Prideland would never go back to the way it was before.

That must have been the Pride's most cherished hope—that the Children wouldn't be able to reproduce. The Pride must have been hoping and praying the Children would all just grow old and die out as soon as the cats and helpers stopped having sex with each other.

Now everyone had to wait and see if Iona gave birth to healthy babies. Dina had to resist the urge to hover over Iona and check every single one of her biological functions every second of the day.

That would never work for a host of reasons, but even that wouldn't have told Dina what she really wanted to know—what everyone in Prideland most wanted to know.

Could the Children reproduce—and what would they reproduce? What would Iona give birth to—Children, cats, or humans?

Looking out this window brought back all the images from Dina's first visit to this canton. Those residents had an organized structure of hunting parties, teams of people to butcher and distribute the hunters' kills, and a tannery to process skins for all the residents to use.

These escaped helpers had a long way to go before they brought this canton back to that level of organization. Those first residents also had gangs of children running around between the houses.

Thinking about Finlay and Jude made Dina shudder. She shook that off and stretched out on the bed where she could look out the window. The view gave her plenty to think about, but mostly she kept thinking about Frank.

If he'd succeeded and she and Frank had called in the Armada to evacuate the cantons, she wouldn't have been on the planet to take part in this war. She wouldn't have given birth to Adrian and Iona.

The Children would still have arisen, but she wouldn't have been around to witness the aftermath.

Would the Children still have gone to war against the Pride if Adrian hadn't incited them to do it? The Children might all be dead now without his leadership.

Her eyes started to drift closed and she floated into sleep. The same images passed across her eyelids. She saw Armada destroyers hovering in the atmosphere and sinking to land in the fields.

People streamed out of the jungle to board those ships. Thousands of people poured out of the jungle and villages and cantons. They came from all over Prideland to leave the planet.....but those people weren't human. They were Children.

Her eyes snapped open and she stared at the dark trees outside the window. The Children.....evacuating the planet. That was the solution.

The Children and the Pride would never come to any peaceful settlement. She'd known that for weeks. They would never be able to coexist on this planet. They posed too great a threat to each other.

She stiffened in bed. Her eyes darted through the darkness outside, but she saw it all.

The Armada could send destroyers to evacuate this planet, but they wouldn't evacuate the human population. They would evacuate the Children—and anyone else who wanted to go with them.

It was the perfect solution—except for the part about contacting the Coalition to send destroyers to pick everyone up.

There was only one way the Coalition would ever find out that people on this planet needed destroyers to evacuate. Dina herself would have to contact the Coalition—but how?

She didn't have a Pod waiting in the jungle this time. She didn't have anything, but she had to do it. This was the answer to Iona's challenge. This was the only way her children would grow up to adulthood—by leaving the planet.

Dina had left Prideland so her Children would have the chance to grow up away from the threat of annihilation. Iona's children deserved the same chance and they would never get it on this planet.

Dina sank back on the bed and stared at the ceiling, but her mind wouldn't stop racing through all the problems, possibilities, and implications. This plan would be difficult—and risky.

She had to do it. She had to do anything to give her Children the future they deserved—and her grandchildren the future they deserved.

She couldn't risk the possibility that the Pride might win and kill every last Child on the planet.

That's exactly what the Pride would do once they found out the Children could reproduce. The Pride would never tolerate that.

Chapter 30

Dina opened the house door and immediately saw that something was wrong. A group of the former helpers gathered near the canton gate. They arranged their weapons and most of them carried bows and quivers of arrows they'd found in the abandoned houses.

She slid the ladder to the ground, scrambled down, and went over to them. They brightened up when they saw her. "We're sending out our first hunting party," one of the men told her.

"Before you do that, we need to organize the canton's defense." She pointed to the top of the fence. "We need to set up watchtowers and a roster of guards and sentries to keep an eye on the surrounding jungle for any cats who come after us."

"You said the Children are protecting us," another man pointed out.

"They can only do so much and it's our responsibility to protect ourselves." She pointed out the first man. "Go through the canton and assign three watches of armed guards to patrol the fence. Then you can go hunting—but not while the canton is unguarded."

"The people who have been living here didn't have any guards," a third man pointed out.

"And you think it's a good idea to leave the canton completely defenseless?" she countered. "Everyone on the planet wants to kill us. Assign your guards. This is the most important thing right now."

"More important than food?" the second man asked.

"Which do you think would kill you quicker—starvation or an invasion of cats?" She pointed at the fence again. "Assign your guards and then you can go—oh, and don't go near that part of the jungle. Do you see those trees to the west? Stay away from those. You can cut farther south or farther north before you go west, but avoid that spot. That's where the Children camp. They don't want you going near it—and pass the word to the rest of your people to stay away from it, too."

She climbed back up into Fan's house and found a different leather bag hanging from the back of the house door. This bag didn't have any Children in it.

She was just raiding some of the food from Kubri James's bundle when he and Fan both came downstairs. Fan carried the pouch with her Children hanging over her shoulder.

Fan took one look at what Dina was doing. "Where are you going?"

"I'm going back to the city. I need to find someone there."

"You can't go back!" Kubri James exclaimed. "Everyone knows you there! All the cats know who you are. Do you know what they'll do to you if they catch you?"

"They won't catch me and this is more important. I have to go back." She stood up and pointed through the door toward the canton. "I've just told those men to assign sentries and guards to patrol the fence and defend the canton in case of attack. They'll need to split it up into watches so everyone takes their turn."

Fan's jaw dropped. "You're serious! You're really going back!"

"I have to. I have something important I need to do there."

"Let me come with you," Kubri James suggested. "You can't go alone."

"I have to go alone. I'll be able to get in undetected if I go alone." She had to smile at him. "You're more recognized and more wanted than I am. Stay here. You'll need to establish a ruling Council for this canton to make decisions about how you run this place. You two should be on it."

"You can't leave, Dina!" Fan exclaimed. "You just got here."

"I have to. It isn't a question."

Fan's features pinched. "I thought we would be able to spend time together the way we did before. I thought you would be able to help me raise my Children the way I helped you." Her voice trembled. "I was looking forward to that."

Dina leapt forward and hugged her. "I really wish I could, but if this works, it will do your Children a lot more good than me staying here and helping you."

"What are you going to do?" Kubri James asked.

"I don't have time to explain it to you. I have to get back to the city as quickly as possible." Dina threw caution to the wind and hugged him, too. "Take care of this place. Maybe sure you don't slacken on defense. Don't rely on the Children to protect you. I'll come back as soon as I can, but you all need to start taking care of yourselves. This is the reason you left Prideland. I can't do it for you. It's time for you to start doing it."

She turned away and scrambled down the ladder to the ground. She wanted to get out of here and get back to the city. She needed to find Tom. He would know how to contact the Coalition—or if he didn't, he would be the best person to talk to about how to go about it.

She had to quell her anticipation of seeing him again. She had to be careful around him. He might have joined the loyal helpers. If he did, she wouldn't be able to tell him anything. She would have to hide what she was doing and make sure he never found out.

Then what would she do? How would she contact the Coalition without his help? She didn't want to think about that.

She slung her bag over her shoulder. It only contained a few leftover pieces of dried fruit, but at least she would have something to eat on the way to the city.

She would have to get something once she got there. She made up her mind then and there not to go back to Renfroe's house unless she absolutely had to. Going there would only make it harder for both of them and she didn't want to rely on him anymore, either.

The new residents had taken her warning to heart. Four of the men who'd been on the original hunting party now stood guard by the gate. Another five patrolled outside it and three more walked back and forth inside the fence.

She didn't see the rest of the hunting party. They must have already left.

She didn't have time to wait around to see if they obeyed her about staying away from the Children's camp.

Her thoughts already ranged ahead of her as she approached the gate. She would have to use stealth to get back inside the city and then again to get near Elyse's house. Dina would have to choose her moment to approach Tom when no one else was around.

If he did join the loyal helpers, he would be the first to try to capture her—or whatever it was the loyal helpers did to subversives. He would play his hand immediately. That would simplify the process of finding out where he stood.

Her mind was already miles away when a shout snapped her out of her trance. The guards and sentries darted in front of her, raised their bows, and aimed into the trees.

A crowd of Children descended through the branches. They bounded from limb to limb falling fast and stopped fifteen feet above the ground.

Dina spotted Zair and his group moving in from the west. They converged with a different group of Children approaching from the south.

The sentries on duty formed a barricade in front of the gate and threatened the Children. "Don't come any closer!" one of the men yelled. "What do you want?"

One of the Children leapt to a lower branch where everyone could see him. He had thick, glistening golden fur. It was Link's nephew, Riyadh. "We want to see Dina. Send her out to talk to us—alone."

"What do you want with her?" the man demanded.

Dina stepped forward. "Put your weapons down. These are my Children." The men didn't move and she pushed his bow down. "Don't threaten them. Back off. These are your friends."

The sentries didn't lower their weapons, so Dina advanced in front of them, crossed the open ground, and entered the trees.

Riyadh and Zair both sprang down to land in front of her. Aries, Amir, Aurelio, Israel, and Cairo lingered in the branches where they could hear the conversation.

"You have to come with us, Dina," Riyadh murmured under his breath. "We need you to come to Adrian's camp right away. It's important."

"What's happening?" she asked. "Is anything wrong with the war?"

"Nothing is wrong with the war. Iona is giving birth. Adrian sent me to bring you to them right away."

Dina's heart leapt into her mouth. It was happening. "Okay. I'm coming—but I can't travel as quickly as you can."

"My orders are to carry you on my back," Riyadh explained. "We don't have time for you to walk there."

"Um…..okay." Dina thought fast. This would definitely be a first.

"I'd be happy to take her," Zair offered.

Riyadh nodded. "Thank you. Let's go."

Dina glanced over her shoulder. Everyone from the canton stared at her. The sentries still held the Children at arrowpoint. That would have to change, but Dina wouldn't be the one to change it.

Zair moved in front of her and flexed his knees so she could climb onto his back. She latched onto him piggyback. He used one arm to hold her under her seat so she didn't fall off.

She wrapped her arms around his neck and he blasted upward into the canopy at high speed. The rest of the Children launched just as fast, and in a split second, they all rocketed away into the jungle heading south.

Dina couldn't look. Zair scaled massive trees to the very top of the canopy hundreds of feet off the ground.

He sprang from branch to branch in a flying streak. He landed on a branch and launched to the next one without waiting for the first branch to stop bouncing. He barely touched them.

She buried her face in the fur on the back of his neck, held on for dear life, and waited for this trip to be over. She had to be the first human ever to travel this way and she hoped she never traveled this way again.

He plunged through the treetops a long way from their starting point. Dina had no idea how far they'd come.

He plummeted downward and came to rest in the same camp where Dina had seen Iona last time. The same crowd of unknown Children mobbed the place.

They surrounded Adrian's awning in such a mob that she couldn't see him behind all the sturdy Children pressing in to hear what he said. She heard his voice, though. He was giving another briefing.

Riyadh shouldered through the crowd to rejoin Zair and Dina. "This way," he told Dina. "Follow me."

He, Israel, and Cairo plowed a pathway through all the Children to the same house where Dina had seen Iona lying sick in bed. Dina heard screaming coming from inside.

The rest of Dina's Children stood around outside exchanging glances. The Black weren't here, though.

Dina peeked through the door and the sound of Iona roaring in pain and distress set the hair on the back of Dina's neck on end.

She couldn't see Iona lying in bed. Kenji and Kaiser blocked Dina's view. She caught a glimpse of Karim kneeling on the floor. That was all.

Dina pulled the door shut with herself on the outside. Karim would take care of Iona. Dina had no way of knowing if Iona had asked for Adrian to bring Dina here, but Dina knew her own Children. Iona wouldn't appreciate Dina inserting herself right now. Karim would send for Dina if they needed her.

Chapter 31

Dina shuffled her feet outside Iona's and Karim's house. All the other Children were here—just waiting. Their whole future hung on this moment.

The rest of the Children in the camp pretended not to hear Iona screaming. They went about their business as if this wasn't the single most important moment in the entire war.

All Children everywhere would stand or fall on the outcome of whatever happened inside that house. Iona was fighting the entire war single-handedly.

Dina and her Children could only knit their fingers together, glance around at nothing, and shift their weight from side to side. They could express their anxiety, but no one else did. They hid it and barely glanced toward Iona's house.

Darius ran his fingers through the fur on his forehead and puffed out his cheeks in a shaky sigh. "I don't think I can handle this. I gotta get out of here."

He was just about to walk away when Adrian strode over to them. His eyes skipped to Dina and then toward the door. "Any news yet?"

"Nothing," Rome replied.

"She doesn't sound like she's slowing down, does she?" India murmured.

"How long has she been screaming like this?" Dina asked. "How long has she been in labor?"

"She started feeling strange in the middle of the night last night," Adrian replied. "Things picked up this morning, but she didn't start screaming like this until about an hour ago." He cocked his head to study her. "Is that normal?"

Dina shrugged. "You're Children of the Pride. Nothing is normal for you. It would be normal if it happened to a human mother in labor. That's all I can tell you—but the truth is that just about anything is normal for a human mother in labor. Anything is possible. I know it doesn't help, but we're entering uncharted biological territory here. We all are."

He paced back and forth a few times before he stopped in front of her staring at nothing. "This better work," he muttered. "That's all I have to say. If it doesn't work, we're finished."

Almost as if his words made it happen, Iona's screams stopped right at that moment and she burst into sobs behind the door. The whole family stood listening in silence.

Karim kept saying over and over in a shaky voice, "I love you! I love you!"

Iona's sobs twisted Dina's heart. Was Iona crying in grief that her children had been born dead—or not been born at all? Was Iona dying in there?

Everyone present jumped out of their skins when Kenji ripped the door open, cast one glance around, and then nodded at Adrian. "You can come in now."

Kenji held the door open for Adrian to enter. Dina took a chance and walked into the house, too.

Karim sat in the same place leaning his back against the wall. His black, furry hand traced back and forth over Iona's head and face.

She lay on her side on the floor in exactly the same position Dina had seen her last time. Tears glistened on Iona's cheeks, but her face shone with so much radiant happiness that Dina had to choke down a lump in her throat.

The blankets covered Iona from the waist down. Four midnight-black babies nuzzled into her chest on the blanket underneath her.

She gazed down at them with such an angelic smile that Dina had to fight back tears. The biggest of the babies clawed his way to Iona's breast and latched on. She stroked her fingertips over his fur with the same loving caress that Karim used on her.

Adrian's hand flew to his mouth. He pressed his wrist against his lips to stifle a strangled groan of relief and emotion. Kenji and Kaiser stood over the little family and stared down at the newborn Children.

They had the same combination of feline and human characteristics as all other Children. They had human features, tiny claws on their ten fingers and toes, pointed ears, and miniature fangs.

Dina couldn't stop herself from inching closer to the bed and squatting down to stare at them. Her whole being ached to touch them and stroke them and pet them, but these weren't her Children. They already had a mother.

"Thank you for coming," Karim murmured. "We weren't sure if you would."

"Of course I came," Dina husked. "I would have come sooner if I thought you wanted me to." She had to fight back another wave of crushing emotion when she looked down at the babies. These were her grandchildren—the next generation of Children. "They're so beautiful. I'm so happy for you."

"Did you find a way?" Iona's voice quavered, but the old iron crept into her biting tone. She hadn't forgotten. Of course not.

Dina looked up to find her daughter staring at her with brutal intensity. These Children being born didn't change anything between Dina and Iona.

"Yes, I did." Dina stood up and turned around to face the others. "I found a way to end the war—forever."

"What is it?" Adrian had to fight his voice under control, too. "It better be something pretty spectacular. When the Pride finds out about this, they'll come at us with everything they have. They'll have to."

"Yes, they will," Dina replied. "The Pride will never tolerate any Children living on this planet no matter where they are. Even if you went out west into the wilderness, the Pride would never stop hunting for you. The only way to get away from them is to leave the planet."

"How can we do that?" Karim asked. "We don't have any way to leave the planet."

"When I escaped from Prideland the first time, I wound up at Moonlight canton where I met a man who was going to help me evacuate all the slags. His name was Frank Mathus. It started with just him and his family wanting to leave this planet so their children could live away from the Pride. Then word got out. He eventually traveled to the other cantons and they all wanted to evacuate, too. I was going to contact the *Savannah* to come down and get everyone. We made a commitment not to leave anyone behind who wanted to evacuate. Things escalated to the point where one destroyer wouldn't be enough."

"You told us the Pride destroyed Moonlight canton," Kaiser reminded her. "You said the Pride wiped out everyone except you."

"They did. Frank and I were going to go out to the Pod and contact the *Savannah* to call in the Armada to lift all these people off the planet. That's when the Pride attacked and Renfroe took me back to his house. After that, I had to concentrate on getting myself out. I couldn't risk telling anyone else what I was doing."

"How does this help us?" Iona asked. "We don't have any way to contact the Armada."

Dina held up her hands. "I know....but don't you see? This is the answer. We have to find a way to contact the Armada to evacuate all of us off the planet."

"The Coalition will never accept us," Adrian pointed out. "We're freaks of nature. We're oddities."

"They'll have to accept you. You're all the children of Coalition citizens—which means *you're* all Coalition citizens. The Armada is under mandate to provide any and all assistance to Coalition citizens in danger or distress—and we can all agree that this situation qualifies. You can find another place—*we* can find another place—a place where the Children can create their own society—a society that has nothing to do with the Pride."

"How do we contact the Coalition, though?" Karim asked. "We have no technology or equipment—or anything. We have nothing."

"As soon as I leave here, I'm going back to the city to find Tom Sharples," Dina replied. "He's the last member of our team left on this planet—apart from Tania and she doesn't know anything about communications equipment. Tom will be able to help us—if I can convince him to help us."

"What makes you think he'll be willing to help us?" Adrian asked. "You said the rest of your landing team became helpers. He might be as hostile to us as Tania is."

"He might be, but I have to contact him to find out. I told him....." Dina hesitated and glanced at Adrian. "He's the Pygmies' father."

"Why is he still helping the Pride, then?" Karim asked. "He won't even help his own Children. Why would he help the rest of us?"

"He didn't know he had Children. The cat who was the Pygmies' mother hid it from him. I told him the truth the last time I saw him. I'm going back to find him again. I'll find out which side he's on, and if he's loyal to the Pride, I won't tell him our plan and we'll fall back on.....something else."

"What will we fall back on?" Adrian asked. "What else is there?"

"I don't know, but we'll find a way. I'm seeing more and more evidence that other Coalition vessels crashed or landed here in the past. There could be equipment or resources on this planet that we don't know about. Keep your hopes up. We'll find a way, but keep it quiet. I don't want anyone finding out what we're doing."

She turned around and cast one last wistful gaze down at Iona and the four Children on the floor. The oldest boy had finished nursing, curled up next to the fur on Iona's stomach, and fallen asleep while the others took their turn.

"I will get you out," Dina murmured. "You have my word on it. These Children won't grow up in a war zone. I swear it."

She strode out of the house and ran into the rest of the Children standing around. "What's happening, Dina?" Naia asked.

Dina smiled at her. "Everything's all right. Karim and Iona have four Children—all black like their father. They're healthy and Iona is resting. Everything's fine."

A relieved sigh went through the group and then Riggs and Dexter burst out laughing. They clapped each other on the back and Cairo threw back his head and whooped out loud.

The rest of the Children in the camp stopped what they were doing, glanced over, and then the whole camp disintegrated into talk. The Children spread out through the camp passing the news from mouth to mouth. Excited laughter, cheers, and rapid conversation rippled outward from the house.

The Children hugged each other and many wiped away tears. The commotion escalated until Dina couldn't hear a thing over the noise.

She pushed through the crowd and found Zair standing by the awning with Cain, Jackal, and some of the other leaders from Moonlight canton.

"Would you mind taking me back?" she asked Zair. "I need to get as close to the edge of the jungle as possible so I can get back to the city."

"I'll have to clear it with Adrian first, but if he says yes, then I'd be happy to take you," Zair replied. Then he frowned. "Don't you want to go back to Moonlight canton?"

"I want to, but I have to undertake another mission to the city. It's important. It could be the most important mission of the war."

Zair only frowned deeper. "I don't like seeing you go back into danger."

"It will be all right." She waved behind her. "Could you please ask Adrian so we can go? I don't want to wait."

He nodded, but when he took a step to go find Adrian, Zair stopped in his tracks when Adrian came toward them.

"Dina has asked me to take her to the edge of the jungle so she can return to the city," Zair told him. "I was just coming to get your permission to leave the camp."

Adrian didn't seem to hear. He turned to Dina. "I'd like.....I'd like you to stay for a little while, Dina. Don't leave just yet."

"Don't you want me to talk to Tom about this?" she asked.

"Yes....but don't leave yet. At least stay until tomorrow morning."

She opened her mouth to answer....and stopped. It had been just past dawn when she left Moonlight canton. It couldn't be more than the middle of the morning now. Why would he want to delay her for a full twenty-four hours until tomorrow morning?

The Children celebrated all over the camp. Everyone hugged everyone and they gave up all pretense of getting any work down. An atmosphere of celebration broke out all over the place.

"I guess I'm not in any rush to leave," she finally agreed.

"Excellent." He waved behind her. Naia, Nova, Emerald, and Egypt came over to them. "You should be here for this, Dina. Go with the girls. They'll give you anything you need."

The four young women escorted Dina away from Adrian's awning. He reentered the crowd of Children standing around waiting for him. Zair and the men from Moonlight canton returned to their briefing and Dina lost sight of them.

Chapter 32

D ina woke up in a different house, pushed the blankets off her shoulder, and sat up. Children covered the floor all around her. She didn't know any of them.

The celebration over Iona's and Karim's Children's birth had gone on late into the night. Dina didn't understand why Adrian wanted Dina to be here for this. She didn't contribute anything to the celebration. Staying here only delayed her journey to the city.

She stepped over sleeping bodies and froze when she discovered Zair standing outside the door. He shuffled his feet while he chewed a hunk of meat in his left hand. He obviously wasn't doing anything other than waiting.

"Oh, good, you're awake," he exclaimed as soon as she showed up. "Adrian asked me to wait here for you."

"Are we going back to the city now?" she asked. "What can he possibly want me to stay for?"

"He wants you to attend a briefing this morning."

Dina's head snapped around. "He does? Why?"

"I'm sure he'll explain everything to you when you see him. He's been awake all night planning this."

She furrowed her brow at him. "He has? Why? What's going on?"

Zair jerked his thumb over his shoulder. "Follow me and I'll take you to see him. He'll tell you everything."

Dina had no choice but to follow him to Adrian's awning. Unlike every other time she'd seen him here, he wasn't surrounded by a million armed Children all waiting to hear his orders.

Instead, only the Children that Dina had raised, including Karim and his brothers, along with Cain, Jackal, Zair, and a few leaders from other cantons stood around his table.

He wasn't talking to them. They all just stood there waiting—for her.

"What did you want to see me about?" she asked him. "Zair said you wanted to give me a briefing."

"I do. This idea of yours puts a different spin on our plans. I had to adjust things to give you a chance to make it work."

"What do you mean? If it doesn't work, we'll just come up with another way. We'll keep working on it until we accomplish it."

"Unfortunately, I can't accept that," he replied. "I'm sending Iona and all the other pregnant mothers back to the gorge camp for safety. The rest of us are preparing to launch a decisive assault on the cats to end the war before it escalates any further—and before word gets out about Iona giving birth. We need to end this now before the cats get too strong for us."

Dina frowned at him even more deeply. "What are you telling me?"

"I planned to launch this assault the day after tomorrow. I was just about to send word to all the slags in all the cantons to join us. The whole Children's force is waiting for me to give the word. Now that you've proposed this plan, I've decided to delay the assault by one week—one week only. You need to get to the city, contact this officer of yours, and figure out a way to send the signal and get the Armada here in that time. If you fail, I'll launch the assault anyway. We'll raze Prideland to the ground to make sure the Pride doesn't come after us."

"You can't do that!" she exclaimed. "Do you know how many people are still living in the cities?"

"I know that everyone living in the cities is loyal to the Pride," he countered. "They're our enemies. If the Pride finds out that one of our females has given birth to healthy Children that will grow up to fight the cats the same way we have, the Pride will rally all their helpers to come after us, too."

"I know all that, but it's just as wrong for you to wipe out the cats and helpers as it is for them to wipe out the Children."

"We no longer have the option to be merciful. The Pride will find out about this and we need to strike before they gain too much strength for us to overcome them. We'll strike fast and we'll strike hard. We'll kill them all if we have to. We'll find a place on this planet where we can live in peace, even if it means the Children and our allies are the only ones left on this planet."

Dina opened her mouth to argue, but the words died in her throat. He was right.

"You have one week. If you fail to make contact with the Armada—or anyone else—I'm going to launch this assault."

She nodded down at the ground. "I understand. You do what you have to do....and so will I."

"Zair will take you as far as the road. I'm receiving reports of fighting and attacks all over the territory. You'll be taking your life in your hands by going back to the city."

"I'm prepared for that. I'll do whatever it takes to make this work."

He paused and locked his eyes on her. They drilled into her deepest soul the way she remembered. "You can go, then. I really hope you succeed. If this works, it could be the greatest thing that could possibly happen to us."

"I'll make sure it succeeds." She had to gulp down the next words. "I owe you that much."

He touched her arm only once. "Go on, then. Let me know if I can do anything to make it happen. Good luck."

She walked out of the awning and Zair followed her to the edge of the camp. She didn't trust herself to look back at her Children watching and listening to her conversation with Adrian.

He didn't say outright that all their hopes rested on this plan of hers. He didn't say that this mission was as pivotal to the Children's future as Iona giving birth.

She knew it. He knew it. They all knew it. He didn't have to say it out loud.

Her own last words to him meant so much more. She owed them. She had to prove herself to them. She had to show them that she supported them as much now as she ever did.

Zair bent his knees to take her on his back again and zoomed off into the trees the way he did before.

She rested her face against his fur and didn't watch where he took her. She didn't care anymore. She wanted to find Tom as quickly as possible. Adrian's deadline only confirmed the urgency of what she had to do.

This was the Children's one chance at a decent future. It was their one chance to get the Pride out of their lives forever.

This was the chance for which Dina came back to Prideland from the *Savannah*. She didn't realize it then, but this was the way she would finally break the Pride's hold on all these people.

Taking them off the planet would end their slavery. It would ensure that none of these people ever went back to Prideland no matter the circumstances.

The Children would never have to deal with the Pride again, either. All the old prejudices would be gone. The galaxy would belong to the Children to write whatever future they wanted on it.

Zair touched down under the treetops, set Dina's feet on the ground, and his expression changed when he straightened up to face her. "Is there anything I can do for you, Dina?" he asked. "I don't like to see you going into danger alone for our sake."

She smiled at him. "Just keep everyone safe for me. I'm happy to go into danger for you—for all of you. Just take care of everyone—including the people at Moonlight canton. Don't turn away from them just because I'm not there. They still want to be your allies."

He nodded. "I realize that now. If Adrian launches this assault, those people will fight with us."

She grimaced and turned away. "Let's hope it doesn't come to that."

He glanced out onto the planes leading toward Prideland. "I wish I could go with you and help you. My wife is pregnant in the camp in the trees outside Moonlight canton. I would give anything to take her away from all this."

She clasped his arm in one quick squeeze. "It will happen. We'll get them all out. I swear it."

He only nodded. His features pinched with buried emotion. "I don't like to leave you."

"I feel the same way about you. I'll see you soon, and when I do, I hope I can give you good news. Thank you for your help."

She couldn't delay any longer. Putting this off only made it harder.

She stepped out from under the trees, advanced onto the road, and hurried away without looking back.

He might have stood there watching her walk away. She didn't trust herself to look back to find out.

She didn't plan to stay on the road. She'd become too well known in Prideland as Kubri James said. Almost everyone recognized her, especially the cats.

She couldn't count on anyone to help her. She would have to be far more careful than she had been before.

Chapter 33

Dina left the road before she got as far as the village. She snuck through the fields, dodged from one stand of trees to another, and crouched to survey the landscape before she dared to dash to her next hiding place.

She took even more time and evaded detection even more as she drew nearer to the city's outer neighborhood. She avoided all streets and roads, even when she didn't see any patrolling cats.

She stayed away from Renfroe's neighborhood, too. She cut north to the river and followed it. More trees lined the river and offered more hiding places.

She paused when she got closer to the urban areas. The river passed right in front of some of the nicer houses.

Almost all these houses had large gardens like Renfroe's. She could travel unseen if she just stayed off the streets.

She hopped a wall into someone's garden and used the shrubbery to get into the next garden.

She did this a dozen times and eventually made her way to a greenway winding through the neighborhood. She made better progress that way, but she still had to be extra careful that no cats or helpers spotted her.

She finally snuck into a thicket near Elyse's house. She had a big garden, too, but she also had more helpers than most cats. She kept them around for sentimental reasons—not because she needed them to do her yard work.

Dina eased open the gate leading into Elyse's garden, crouched behind the bushes, and pushed the leaves aside to check out the house.

Elyse and four of her helpers strolled down a grassy walkway between the flowerbeds. The Persian flicked her tail while she talked to her helpers about something. Dina couldn't make out the words.

Two of the helpers were men and two were women. They crossed a dozen yards of lawn before one of the men picked up Elyse, hugged her to his chest, and nuzzled his face against hers.

Elyse's high-pitched laughter echoed through the garden. Dina looked away. It sure looked like Elyse had a new favorite helper.

Dina crept sideways behind a hedge to sneak closer to the house. She inched nearer, plastered herself against the wall, and then stole a peek through the window.

She looked into a sunny kitchen with four women helpers working in it. They talked and laughed while they chopped vegetables, washed dishes, and one of them sat on a stool by the door sewing on a piece of clothing.

The picture posed such a contrast to Belinda's kitchen at Renfroe's house. Dina became fascinated by watching the scene until a different male helper entered and distracted her.

This one was young. He couldn't have been more than twenty. One of the women took a tray of food off a shelf, handed it to him, and he carried it out of the room.

Dina slithered down the wall to the next window. It looked in on a bedroom with three helpers folding laundry.

The next window gave Dina a view into the parlor where she'd seen Tom and Elyse together. A dozen helpers sat around on the couches and chairs. They talked to each other in casual tones.

None of them changed their attitude when Elyse entered with her four helpers from outside. They all sat down, too, and Elyse jumped onto a different man's lap.

He started petting her and Dina turned away. Was Tom even here anymore? He might have gone into the city on some errand.

She considered hiding in this garden and waiting for him to come back. He would always come back here when he finished whatever he had to do.

She got ready to sneak back into the bushes when she spotted two more male helpers crossing Elyse's garden. They were both tall, strong, muscular men. Elyse didn't keep anyone around her house who was old, ugly, or infirm.

The two men headed to a different part of the garden and started pruning the trees with a handsaw. They didn't see Dina flattening herself against the house, but seeing them made up Dina's mind for her. She couldn't stay here without someone discovering her.

She crept back to the garden gate, tiptoed through it, and hid under the overhanging tree branches while she made up her mind what to do.

She needed to find another place to spend the night—somewhere no one would find her. Then she had to figure out a way to locate Tom.

She couldn't just walk into Elyse's house and ask to see him. Elyse had already proven herself to be cunning, manipulative, and untrustworthy.

Dina could have used the Pygmies' existence to manipulate Elyse. Dina had taken the Pygmies off Elyse's hands when Elyse asked her to.

Dina could have used that obligation to get Elyse to let her see and talk to Tom alone.

Dina didn't want Elyse to know she was talking to Tom. Dina didn't want anyone to know she was talking to Tom.

If Tom was still loyal to the Pride, he would spill his guts to Elyse anyway. Dina needed to find a way to stop him from doing that.

If he did turn out to still be loyal to the Pride, she needed to be long gone where no one could find her by the time Elyse got the word about what Dina was doing.

Dina sighed and passed her hand across her eyes just from thinking about it. Talking to Tom about contacting the Armada sounded so simple in theory. She should have known it would be a lot more complicated than she realized.

Now she needed to find a place to hide—somewhere the Pride wouldn't look for her.

She returned to the greenway and followed it a long way through the city. It led eastward into parts of the city she'd never seen before.

She started to relax. Maybe no one on this side of the city would be looking for her.

She found a thick patch of trees apart from the path. She sat down under them, opened the bag she'd brought, and took out the last of Kubri James's dried fruit. She would need some way to find food in this city, too.

She could always break into Hellion House in the middle of the night and raid their storeroom. Sneaking into one of these houses and stealing food out of the kitchen would probably be easier.

She jolted out of her thoughts when she heard people coming closer—and then she froze when she heard the squeak of a wheel.

The Elite Battalion strode up the greenway pushing their wheelbarrow. They didn't talk. All the men walked bowed and hunched. They kept their eyes on the ground and didn't look up. They didn't see Dina sitting under the trees.

They carried shovels and rakes and the men didn't wear the usual tunic and pants of helpers. The men of the Elite Battalion wore filthy rags with grime smudged all over their faces.

She kept as still as possible as they drew level with her. She didn't want to attract their attention. She just hoped she'd chosen a spot far enough off the path that they would pass without seeing her at all.

The group moved past her still looking at the ground....and then her jaw dropped when she saw the man in the very rear of the group. He was the tallest man there, but he looked as filthy, tattered, and rundown as the others.

Grease and grime made his hair hang in his eyes. She wouldn't have recognized him at all except for the faint curve of his cheekbone sloping down to his jaw. It was Tom Sharples.

He walked past her without looking up. He didn't look to the left or to the right. He hardly seemed conscious of where he was or what he was doing.

The Elite Battalion passed her position and kept on going. The squeaking sound drifted farther away.

Dina sat riveted to the spot thinking fast. Tom.....How did he wind up with the Elite Battalion? Things must have gone disastrously wrong between him and Elyse.

Dina scrambled to her feet, but she didn't dare to leave the trees—not yet. She waited until the Elite Battalion went into another garden.

They came out ten minutes later, kept going in the same direction, and then turned right into another yard behind a different house.

She hid behind a tree and waited and watched. The group of men kept working their way up the greenway heading in the direction Dina had come to get here.

She followed at a distance and made sure to keep herself hidden so they wouldn't see her. She couldn't stop her heart from racing. She didn't want to get her hopes up before she actually talked to Tom and found out what he was doing and how he felt about.....well, everything.

The Elite Battalion took the rest of the day to work their way up the greenway all the way back to the river. They exited onto the street in front of their power station headquarters at sunset.

The whole group headed for the building. They were going inside for the night.

Dina fought down rising tension as she stepped out onto the sidewalk. She made sure to do it at the moment when the men passed her heading for the building entrance.

She stopped on the sidewalk across the street—right where they could see her. None of the other men noticed anything out of the ordinary about her. They didn't even look at her.

Tom looked up and his eyes hardened when he saw her, but he showed no other sign of recognition.

The next minute, the whole group passed by, went into the building, and the door banged shut.

She heard voices coming from inside. They were talking to each other. That was the first time ever she'd heard any of the Elite Battalion talking to each other or anyone else.

They always remained silent when they worked around the city where other people could see and hear them. They were too low on the social ladder for anyone to talk to them or acknowledge their existence.

She considered hiding again, but a second later, Tom came back outside, glanced right and left, and strode across the street with some of his old energy.

Dina retreated onto the greenway and he followed her around the corner where the trees hid them. "You shouldn't be here, Dina," he murmured. "The whole Pride is looking for you."

"I know that," she breathed. "What the hell happened to you, Tom? What are you doing with the Elite Battalion? You were doing so well with Elyse."

He lowered his eyes to the ground. "You were right, Dina. Everything you said was true. After I saw you, I went home and confronted her about it. She admitted everything. She told me all about......" His voice cracked. He had to swallow to make himself heard. "She told me I have four Children in the jungle."

Dina's stomach dropped. "She did this?! She sent you....*here?*"

He nodded without looking up. "She threw me out. She said she's only kept me for being her favorite pet, and if I wasn't that, I'm useless to her. She had her other helpers tie me up and they threw me.....in *there.*"

"Jesus!" Dina croaked. "That's awful!"

His eyes snapped up to her face. They went hard and mean with hidden fire burning in their haunted depths. "I want to help my Children, Dina. You know them. You know what they need. I'm......I'm sorry.....about everything. I should have listened to you.....and now.....everything we had is gone......because of me......"

She couldn't keep away from him. She rushed him and put her arms around him, but the smell coming from his clothes drove her back.

She stepped away, but she kept her hands on his arms. "Listen to me. I need your help. The Children need your help. We need your help really badly. You're the only one who can help us. That's why I'm here. I know it's dangerous for me to come into the city now, but I had to see you."

"What do you mean? What do you want me to do? I'll do anything to help my Children. Just tell me what they need."

"The Children....." She had to take a deep breath to steady herself. She had to be careful even now about how much she told him. "The Pride has been trying to eliminate the Children ever since they were first born. The Pride considers the Children's very existence a threat. The Senate offered to open negotiations for peace, but the Senate doesn't hold any power over the rest of the Pride. There are plenty of cats who are digging in to continue the war until they completely eliminate the Children. Even withdrawing into the wilderness isn't an option for the Children anymore. It's war or nothing—and if the cats don't stop, the Children will have no other choice but to launch an all-out assault to wipe out the cats—and that includes any helpers left in the city. Do you understand that?"

"I understand," he murmured. "I understand perfectly."

"Then help us," she urged. "I found a way to end the war—decisively—permanently—but we can't do it without you. You're my last and only hope."

"Tell me," he repeated. "Whatever it is, I'm with you."

The spark of determination and fury in his eyes told her all she needed to know. She made a split-second decision and took one more steadying breath. "I have an idea....."

Chapter 34

Dina crouched behind the bushes by the river and watched hundreds of cats of all sizes advance out of the city. Lions, tigers, pumas, panthers, jaguars, and dozens of other cats stalked in ranks ten deep. They left the city streets and entered the fields beyond.

The cats faced off against a matching wave of Children coming from the other direction. They walked upright with their heads up, their shoulders back, their arms linked, and their fierce eyes narrowed at their enemies in the distance.

The dark line of bodies crossed the fields heading for the city. The confrontation could only end one way.

Dina raised her head a few inches and glanced to her left. More shrubs and undergrowth covered the riverbank on this side, but she couldn't go any further without someone seeing her.

She turned to the right hoping to find some opening, but at that moment, a hair-raising shriek startled her into spinning the other way. She never knew if that shriek came from the cats or the Children.

It didn't matter in the end because that sound triggered a chain reaction in both armies. Both sides charged each other.

The Children dove onto all fours and bounded across the ground on their hands and feet. They roared in open challenge and bared their fangs at the cats.

The cats lunged forward and the two sides collided in a tornado of flying claws, slashing teeth, roaring, spitting, snarling, and bellowing.

The pumas' high-pitched screams echoed out of the din. Cats and Children closed body to body tearing each other to pieces. They tumbled across the ground. Children pinned cats to the ground, ripped out their throats, and the cats did the same thing.

Dina huddled lower behind the bushes praying to High Heaven that no one saw her here. She'd hidden in this isolated part of the riverbank for two days and no one had seen her yet. She didn't realize it would become a battle scene.

What had been two orderly armies ranked up in separate crowds now flooded each other. They got so confused that no one could see the edge of one or the other. There was no edge.

The Children penetrated to the very back of the cats' position. Dina couldn't see how far into the Children's ranks the cats penetrated.

Everywhere she looked, cats and Children wrestled with each other, tore each other's flesh, scratched each other's eyes, kicked their claws to gut their enemies, and shredded their skin to draw blood.

The Children had one distinct advantage and they played it to the hilt. They could use their arms and legs in different ways that the cats couldn't match.

One huge black man with glossy black spots buried in his deeper black coat went after the biggest, heaviest tiger he could find. The tiger closed with him and dove his giant mouth straight for the man's face.

The man used his arms to grapple the tiger around the middle, twisted his arms upward to lock the tiger's forelimbs, and wrenched the tiger onto his side. The tiger tried everything to get out of that position, but the man held him down. The tiger couldn't move.

The man flung one leg over the tiger's body, swiveled sideways, and in a lightning move of mind-blowing dexterity, the man locked his legs over the tiger's head. The man held the cat there long enough to swivel around, kick out his foot, and gashed the tiger deep across the underside of the ribs.

The man leapt clear and bolted away into the battle in search of another target. The tiger staggered to his feet and immediately collapsed. Blood poured from his diaphragm. The man had torn it out and hit either the tiger's heart or one of the big blood vessels right underneath.

The tiger blundered upright one last time and then fell flat on his face, never to rise again. The Children pulled similar moves all over the field. They could match the cats in speed, strength, agility, and the Children surpassed the cats by far when it came to ferocity.

The cats couldn't match the Children's arms and legs. Dina spotted another Child not far away from her hiding place. This man couldn't have been more than five feet tall with a slight, wiry build and hardly a scrap of muscle on him.

Short, silver-grey fur covered his whole body and his piercing blue eyes sparkled even from Dina's distant hiding place.

This man went after a jaguar half again bigger than his own size. The man zeroed in on this jaguar when so many other smaller, lighter cats covered the field.

The jaguar misjudged his opponent and flew in with all his weight and strength. The man hurtled for the jaguar just as fast.

At the last second before they collided, the man twisted sideways, caught the jaguar by one forepaw, yanked the jaguar out of the air mid-flight, and slammed the cat sideways onto the ground.

The jaguar bounded up with a gut-turning roar to maul the man, but the man hit him too fast. He pounced on the jaguar's head, seized the cat by one ear, and smashed the cat's head into the ground so hard that he stunned the cat.

The man flew into a blood-fueled rage, pounded the cat's head into the ground four more times, and blood poured from the cat's nose.

The man sprang to his feet, kicked out, and smashed his foot into the cat's head hard enough to squash the skull. The cat's head deformed under the pressure, but the man was already streaking away into the battle searching for some other monster to destroy.

The jaguar lay still on the ground. He wasn't breathing anymore.

Dina gulped and tried to look away again. She really needed to get out of here before....

The minute she thought that, a crash startled her into spinning back to her left. The battle had been isolated on the riverbank and the surrounding fields.

Now, for some reason Dina couldn't begin to fathom, four hundred human helpers charged out of the city near the westbound road. They were all armed with hand tools, kitchen knives, and other household weapons.

They bellowed in fury, rushed onto the field, and closed on the south side to flank the Children. The helpers raised their weapons to aid their cat masters in defeating the Children.

Dina's heart stopped, but the Children responded again with unimaginable ferocity. They abandoned the cats by the hundreds, sprinted across the fields, and charged the helpers instead.

The Children had always made a deliberate effort to avoid killing helpers in the past. The helpers who took part in previous battles fought other helpers—helpers sympathetic to the Children.

Now the Children turned on the loyal helpers with all the deadly power the Children previously reserved for the cats themselves.

The Children shot away from the battlefield so fast that the cats didn't know how to react. They didn't react until it was too late.

A tide of Children swarmed the helpers and cut them down in seconds. Dina didn't see one helper land a single blow on any of the Children.

The Children slashed, tore, and slaughtered too fast, moved on, and disappeared before the helpers knew what hit them.

The helpers toppled in a wave of destruction with the Children rushing through them on a dead course for the city. Nothing stood against them—until they got within a hundred yards of the outer rim of houses.

The cats who had been on the planes recovered from their shock and sprang forward to give chase, but the Children got the jump on them. The Children left the cats in the dust.

Dina stole one more peek to her right. The battle was moving away from her. Now she could sneak through the undergrowth, dash up the riverbank to the power station, and meet up with Tom again.

Another spine-chilling screech made her dive for cover as another wave of cats blasted out of the city. They came from the main road leading to the village.

The cats emerged in the Children's path and the two sides crashed together in another tempest of murderous violence, but the cats didn't stop the Children there.

The Children's momentum carried the cats backward and the battle spilled into the city streets.

More cats and Children tumbled down the riverbank and grappled only a few yards from Dina's hiding place. She couldn't stay here any longer.

She leapt out of hiding. It didn't matter anymore if anyone saw her. Anything was better than getting trapped in the battle.

She burst out of the bushes and took off running with all her might to get farther upriver. The battle kept spilling up the river with more cats leaping over walls, charging down the banks, and closing with Children rushing upriver to meet them.

Children bounded past her and slammed into cats rushing the other way. They snarled and somersaulted over and over each other right next to Dina.

She veered sideways to avoid getting tangled up with an orange-grey woman fighting a puma twice her size. Dina nearly tripped over a panther fighting three tiny Children with glossy mushroom-pink fur.

Dina sprinted for the power station. Tom wouldn't be there at this time of day. He had to go out with the Elite Battalion. He wouldn't come back before sundown or maybe even later.

Dina had to take refuge somewhere. The power station was her only option.

She plunged through a hedge trying to get onto the sidewalk. At least she'd be able to run more easily there, but at the last minute, she tripped over something else.

She thought it might be a branch in the hedge. She sprawled on her face, and out of nowhere, a human hand seized her ankle and hauled her back under the hedge. She stared in wide-eyed shock at Sonya.

"Keep quiet!" Sonya hissed. "Just wait here until they leave."

"What are you doing here?!" Dina whispered. "Do you know how dangerous it is out there?"

"Why do you think I'm hiding? I can't go out there. The loyal helpers are all looking for me."

Dina's jaw dropped. "They are?"

"Of course!" Sonya exclaimed. "They hunt down anyone who speaks in favor of the Children. I've done too many things and said too many things to support the Children's cause. All the helpers know about me now." Sonya frowned at Dina. "Did you get my package?"

"Yes, I got it—but Sonya....." Dina broke off.

Dina had no idea what Sonya had been doing since they last met—apart from stealing explosives from Amaryllis and delivering them to Dina to hide.

Sonya waited for Dina to say something and then squinted through the hedge at the battle raging outside.

The Children fought their way onto the city streets. More helpers rushed out to attack with every household implement known to man.

The Children showed no mercy to anyone who came out to fight them. They slaughtered loyal helpers by the dozen. The cats did their best to stop the carnage, but the cats could barely hold their own, much less protect their helpers.

The cats fought the Children into people's yards. A man with brown dappled fur attacked a leopard and they crashed through a decorative shrub to slam down on the porch of one of the houses.

The man pounced on the leopard and tackled the cat behind the greenery. Vicious snarling noises drifted from out of sight and then the man straightened up with blood all over his face.

He glanced around for someone else to attack, and at that moment, a young male lion rocketed out of nowhere and landed on the man's back.

They yanked each other back and forth for a second and then toppled through the nearest window. The glass shattered and more crashing, banging, and breaking noises echoed from inside the house.

Human screams came through the broken window, too, and a second later, a dozen helpers poured from inside. They ran straight into the chaos and fell to more Children charging from the west.

"We have to get out of here," Dina murmured. "We can't stay here."

"Where should we go?" Sonya asked. "Where *could* we go? This city is a disaster zone."

"I know somewhere, but we would have to run through the battle to get there."

Sonya shrugged. "I guess we have nothing to lose."

"If the Children think we're helpers, they'll attack us, too." Dina cast a critical glance at Sonya's clothes and then her own. "I look like a slag from the jungle. You look like any other helper."

Sonya narrowed her eyes at the battle outside. It didn't ease in the slightest as the minutes dragged on. "The Children are only killing helpers who attack them. If we're running away, the Children might leave us alone."

"Might," Dina repeated and then sighed. "I guess you're right. We have nothing to lose."

"So where are we going?"

Dina pointed up the street toward the power station. "We'll get into the greenway. We can hide there."

"I sure hope you're right. Do you know anywhere we can hide overnight? What about your old benefactor's house? You said he was nice to you."

Dina made a face. "We aren't going there. Besides, his other two helpers are as loyal as they come. If we got caught, we'd be just as dead. Now come on. On the count of three. One......two......three!"

Dina scrambled out from under the hedge, grabbed Sonya by the sleeve, and they sprinted across the street. All the Children were busy fighting cats and other helpers.

Dina and Sonya dodged between bundles of cats and Children and Sonya turned out to be right. If any Children had been free to attack, they left Dina and Sonya to run for it.

Chapter 35

Dina and Sonya skidded into the greenway. Dina slipped on the cool grass and almost fell. Then she took off running as fast as she could. She didn't let go of Sonya's sleeve until they covered five hundred yards of ground.

Dina found the clump of trees where she'd been sitting when she first saw Tom with the Elite Battalion.

The spot was just as deserted now, but the minute she and Sonya drew level with it, another group of helpers came out of a nearby yard, entered the greenway, and saw the two women running away.

"This way!" Dina gasped and pulled Sonya into the trees.

It was too late. The helpers had already seen them, but Dina didn't care. She leapt a wall into someone's garden, barreled through the flowerbeds, through a different gate, and onto another city street.

Sonya staggered up behind her and Dina glanced around. No cats or Children fought here, but she and Sonya weren't out of danger yet. They would never be out of danger as long as they stayed in this city.

Dina raced to the end of the block, passed another three intersections, and would have kept on going if she hadn't spotted another mob of armed helpers heading for the battle.

They glared at Dina in her slag clothes, but the helpers must have had orders to join the battle instead of hunting down rogue slags.

They marched past Dina and Sonya and Dina pulled Sonya away. They took off running for a different part of the neighborhood.

Dina spotted more helpers on different side streets and split off to avoid them. More helpers converged on the battle from all over. She had to burst into someone else's garden to get out of the way.

She swerved around a brick wall, but that led her in front of the house's open front windows. She dashed past the side wall, blundered through the back garden, and jumped another wall before collapsing in the greenway.

Sonya buckled onto the ground next to her. Neither woman said anything for at least five minutes while they both gasped and wheezed to catch their breath.

"Are you....okay?" Dina finally husked.

Sonya nodded. "You?"

"Yeah!" Dina gasped. "How long have you been on the run?"

"Since the last battle," Sonya rasped. "I fought for the Children, so I couldn't go back to Amaryllis's house."

"That was days ago!" Dina exclaimed. "You've been hiding in this city ever since?!"

"I had to. I had nowhere else to go."

"You could have come out to the cantons with us!" Dina countered. "You could have stayed there."

"The cantons!" Sonya exclaimed. "What are you talking about? I couldn't get past the patrol cats."

"Hundreds of helpers abandoned the city. Didn't you know? They left the morning after the battle. I took them out to Moonlight canton myself. The patrol cats didn't dare to mess with that many armed helpers. You could have gone with us." Dina blinked at her. "You really didn't know, did you?"

"I would have gone if I had known." Sonya looked away toward the trees. "I guess that explains why the helpers are so worked up now."

"What do you mean by, 'worked up'?"

"They're just loopy about the Children now. You can't set foot on the street if you say anything about the Children. Even saying anything *against* the Children sparks an insane reaction. People are just out of their minds about the whole situation. Gangs of helpers go around hunting down anyone who might have expressed any sympathy for the Children—and don't even get me started on what happens if someone suggests that the Children might win the war."

Dina sank back against the wall behind her. "Wow. It's so much worse than it was before."

"If all the helpers that once supported the Children are gone now, then that explains why. Only the loyal helpers are still here."

"They're scared," Dina murmured. "They see the Children winning the war."

"So what? Let the Children win."

Dina shook her head. "We can't do that. We have to act fast to make sure the Children don't invade."

"How could we stop them—and haven't they already invaded?" Sonya waved at nothing. "Isn't that what this is?"

Dina snorted. "This is nothing. This is the Children trying to keep the cats occupied so they don't see what the Children are really planning."

Sonya's eyes widened. "What are the Children planning?"

"That's what I'm telling you. They're planning a decisive invasion that will end the war for good."

"But....to end the war for good....the Children would have to get rid of all the cats—and probably all the helpers, too."

"Exactly. That's why we have to stop it. Let's go. We need to get back to the power station before the sun goes down."

Sonya scrambled to her feet and hurried to catch up. "Why do we have to go to the power station? The battle is there. That will put us right next to the battle."

"I know. That's why we have to stop it," Dina replied over her shoulder.

"How can we stop it?" Sonya persisted. "What's at the power station that could stop it?"

Dina halted in the fringe of trees. The battle was starting to surge back toward the river.

The cats and Children still grappled with each other. A few helpers limped away cradling their bloody limbs, but most lay dead on the pavement.

The squeak of a wheel drew Dina's and Sonya's attention to the other end of the street. Sunset was still hours away, but someone must have sent the Elite Battalion to come over here and clean up the place.

A group of ten men pushed their wheelbarrow around a corner, parked it near a pile of dead helpers, and started loading the bodies onto the wheelbarrow.

No other helpers remained to see when the men trundled the bodies to the power station and took them inside the building. No one would see the Elite Battalion tip the dead helpers into the river.

The Elite Battalion did the same thing with the dead cats. The Elite Battalion kept going into and out of the building to remove all the bodies from the area.

"Right there," Dina murmured. "That's what's at the power station that will help us stop the war."

"That's just the Elite Battalion," Sonya pointed out. "They can't do anything."

"Maybe not, but we're about to find out."

Dina and Sonya stayed where they were under the trees. The men worked their way down the street getting closer.

None of them looked up when Dina stepped out of the undergrowth and showed herself on the sidewalk. All ten men kept their heads down.

They gathered another dozen bodies and drew level with her position before they turned their wheelbarrow back toward the building for the last time.

She darted back under the branches and buried herself out of sight. "What are you doing?!" Sonya hissed. "If anyone in this city finds out you're here, you're dead! Do you realize that?"

"None of the Elite Battalion ever talks to anyone. You know that. They won't tell anyone."

"You shouldn't have shown yourself like that! It's too dangerous."

"Keep calm. I had to show myself so Tom would know I'm here."

"Who?" Sonya exclaimed. "Do you know one of those men?"

"You weren't there when your father gave us our first class. Tom was on our landing team. He's an officer in the Coalition Armada—or he was."

Sonya's jaw dropped. "No way!" Then she frowned. "How will he help us stop the Children from invading?"

"That's what I'm about to find out." Dina pulled Sonya deeper into the undergrowth. "We need to hide until nightfall. Then he'll come out of the power station to talk to me. You stay here and stay hidden. I'll talk to him and then come back and get you."

"You are NOT going out there without me!" Sonya countered. "You aren't going out there to talk to him and leaving me here like some little kid. I'm as much a part of this as you are. Besides, whatever he says, I might be able to help you."

Dina stopped herself from arguing. "Fine. You can come—on one condition. You can't tell anyone what he says—or what I say. You have to keep this a secret—from everyone."

Now it was Sonya's turn to snort. "Who would I tell? I'm in hiding from everyone that could possibly use this information against us."

"I shouldn't take you. You could get captured and the helpers could torture you to get the information out of you."

Sonya's face fell. "I didn't think of that. You're right. Maybe I shouldn't go."

Dina shrugged it away. "You can come. I guess it won't make any difference in the end. We only have four more days."

"Four days!" Sonya practically screamed and fought her voice under control.

"The Children plan to invade in four days. If I don't come up with a solution before that, we'll have to run for it to the cantons or we'll get caught in the sweep. We don't want that. We don't want to be anywhere near this city when the Children come."

"No, I sure don't. Let's go."

Dina caught her arm. "Not yet. We have to wait for nightfall."

Dina steered Sonya farther down the greenway. They found an isolated spot completely hidden from the main path. No one would see them here, not even by looking straight at them.

Dina opened the leather bag draped over her shoulder. "Do you want some food? I have some here."

"Okay. Thank you."

Dina studied Sonya while she unwrapped a hunk of sausage and then brought out some more dried fruit.

"You aren't starving to death," Dina remarked. "I hate to ask how you've been feeding yourself since the last battle—I mean, the battle where you ran away from Amaryllis."

"I've been breaking into houses at night and stealing food," Sonya replied without a trace of remorse. "I've even gone back to Amaryllis's house a few times. I know where they store the food and I know all the cooks' schedules. I can get around them more easily than going to another house."

Dina used her knife to cut off a slab of sausage, handed it to Sonya, and then Dina cut another for herself. "You're more resourceful than I gave you credit for. I thought you were an innocent little girl when you first came to this city. I thought the Pride would chew you up and spit you out. I never dreamed you could be as tough as you are."

"And I thought you were soft and weak when you cried during the House of Man. I thought to myself, 'What is she crying for when I'm the one getting hurt?' I didn't understand then, but I do now."

Dina winced. "I'm still ashamed that I stood there and didn't do anything."

"You couldn't have done anything, but you're doing it now."

"I hope so. If this works, you'll be able to leave this planet and none of us will have to deal with any of this again."

Sonya's jaw dropped all over again. "Leave the planet?! You're serious! You mean....." Sonya shut her mouth and all expression drained from her face. "Frank."

Now it was Dina's turn to gasp. "You know about that?"

Sonya nodded down at the food in her hand. "I was hiding behind the corner of the house when he told my mother about his plan to take us back to the Coalition. God, I hated her for turning him down! I wanted to run out and beg him to take me with him. Maybe he will now."

"I'm sorry to tell you this, but Frank is dead," Dina murmured. "He died trying to free all these people from the Pride....but maybe if this plan works, we can make it happen for him."

Sonya spun around again. "You did this? You were the one who got Frank to come and see us about leaving?'

Dina shrugged. "Something like that. I want to talk to this officer about contacting the Armada to evacuate all of us off this planet—and the Children. They're Coalition citizens just like we are."

"But...how would that work? The Children are unknown in the Coalition. They aren't human...or any other known species."

"They're the children of Coalition citizens, which means the Children have all inherited Coalition citizenship, too. Either way, we're going to contact the Armada to come and get us....and we have to do that before the end of the week—before the Children invade. It's the only way to save the other helpers."

"And the cats," Sonya added. "We couldn't let the Children kill all those cats. The cats aren't all bad. There are some nice ones."

Dina smiled at her. "I'm glad you realize that."

They ate in silence for a while. The sun started to go down and Sonya stretched out under the foliage. "What are the Children like?" she asked.

"You've seen what they're like," Dina replied. "Why do you ask that?"

"I mean what are they like when they aren't fighting anybody? What are they like when they're alone with each other in their camps? How do they act toward each other?"

Dina looked away. "They're incredibly caring and loving toward each other. They're as close as it's possible for people to be and maybe even more so. They're very good people and they bond with each other even more than people do. I....I envy them in a way."

Sonya gazed up at the leaves overhead. "I thought so. I didn't think they could be as vicious and deadly with each other."

"They aren't. They're just extremely protective of their own. That's why they fight the way they do. They don't stand anyone threatening them or their loved ones."

"The factors say the Children are wild animals who only care about killing. The factors say the Children will kill anyone, even their own kind."

Dina snorted. "What would the factors know about the Children? The factors have never been around the Children even for a second except in battle."

"That's what I said. That's what got me visited."

Dina spun around and then slumped again. She already knew Sonya had gotten visited for speaking up for the Children. Dina didn't know it was about that.

"The Children appreciate anyone who stands up for them," Dina told her. "They would be grateful and proud of you for defending them."

Sonya burst into a huge grin. "I hope I can meet some of them one day. I admire what they're doing."

"If this works out the way I hope it will, you'll meet plenty of them." Dina put the food away and peered through the undergrowth. "It's getting dark. We should get some rest so we can be ready when night falls."

Chapter 36

Dina snuck through the undergrowth and surveyed the power station across the street. No lamp or candlelight shone from its windows.

"How long do we have to wait for your friend to come out to talk to you?" Sonya whispered in Dina's ear.

"I don't know," Dina whispered back. "It just depends on how soundly the other men sleep. It might take a while."

"I wish he'd hurry up," Sonya hissed. "I'm dying of anticipation."

Dina bit back a grin. Sonya wasn't the only one. Dina had been biting her fingernails for two days to find out what Tom had to say about contacting the Coalition and requesting immediate evacuation.

She and Sonya just had to wait, though. They fidgeted in the bushes where no one could see them. If Tom didn't find an opening to sneak out of the power station, at least the two women wouldn't have to go out into the open again.

After an hour of waiting, Dina was starting to consider sitting down when something clicked over by the power station. A shadowy figure separated from the corner of the building and set off to cross the street.

Dina emerged from the bushes as quietly as she could, but Sonya missed her footing, tripped, and fell over into a pile of dry leaves. She made a big noise and an even bigger one getting herself out of it.

"Try to keep quiet," Dina whispered.

"I am!" Sonya countered and brushed the leaves off herself just as Tom stopped in front of them.

"Who's this?" Tom asked in an undertone.

"She's Sonya Mathus—Alexander Mathus's daughter," Dina replied. "She and her family have been trapped on this planet since their shuttle crashed. She's been helping the Children's cause since she became a helper. We can trust her. I trust her and you can, too."

Tom gave Sonya a hard look and turned to Dina. "How are you? I hope you're staying safe. This city is a bomb waiting to go off."

"I know. Did you find out anything that could help us?"

He shook his head. "I've been all over the city in the last two days and found nothing. The Elite Battalion goes into places no one else can go. I even snuck out at night and went to search in places like the basement under the Senate building and the basement under Hellion House. There's nothing—no equipment or parts of ships or even any ruined parts of ships. I can't find any trace that any other Coalition craft has ever landed or crashed here."

"There has to be," Dina insisted. "Sonya was the one who delivered that Nydrix to me. Where else could the loyalists get it if not from a Coalition vessel?"

"I don't have any explanation for it. I only know I've searched this city as well as anyone can search. There is no communications equipment here—or any other equipment we can use."

"We have to do something," Dina exclaimed. "We can't just give up."

"There is one other option." Tom glanced at Sonya again.

"It's all right," Dina repeated. "You can trust her. She's as wanted by the loyalists as I am."

"I wasn't thinking about that. There is another vessel on this planet with Coalition transmission equipment, but there's no guarantee it will still work and we don't even know where this craft is."

Dina's eyes popped. "There is? Where is it?"

"That's what I just said. We don't know."

"I mean....*what* is it? What vessel are we talking about?"

"The Mathus family's escape shuttle—the one they and their crew used to make an emergency landing on this planet. The shuttle is still out there somewhere."

Dina's hand flew to her head. "Of course! That's what Frank said."

"Who's Frank?" Tom asked.

"He was Alexander Mathus's brother. Frank was on the shuttle when it crashed—but Chancellor Mathus didn't mention him because the chancellor didn't care about saving Frank. He only cared about Alexander—but that's not important. Frank was the one who sent the distress signal when the shuttle crashed—which means the ship's transmission equipment may still be operational."

"We have to find it first." Tom turned to Sonya. "You were there. Do you remember where the shuttle crashed?"

Sonya opened her mouth in stunned shock. "Me?!"

"If you can tell us anything, you could be saving millions of lives, Sonya," Dina insisted. "Do you remember anything?"

"I mean.....I was just a kid then," Sonya stammered. "It was almost five years ago."

"Tell us what you do remember," Tom suggested. "Anything will help."

"Well....um.....I remember being on the shuttle....and we were all scared out of our minds that we were going to crash and die. Alva and Jared both started crying. Frank was working the controls and trying everything to stabilize the craft. He kept sending out mayday calls.....and then we crashed in the jungle."

"What happened after that?" Tom asked.

Sonya shrugged, looked around at anything but him, and knit her fingers in agitation. "Then Frank got us out of the shuttle and we all started walking through the jungle. We walked for hours before came to the village. I remember we were all exhausted and we collapsed on the ground near the circle."

"So you wound up in the same village where you've been living all this time?" Dina shut her eyes and held up her hand. "Don't answer that. I know you were. Just tell me which road you used to enter the village."

"It was the one running south. I remember exactly what the village looked like when we first walked into it. It was the south road."

"Well, that's better than nothing," Tom remarked.

"It doesn't narrow it down, though, does it?" Dina pointed out. "There are thousands of miles of territory south of the village."

"You could ask one of my brothers," Sonya suggested. "Peter and Christian both have really good memories. They might remember something I don't."

"We can't trust them," Dina replied. "Christian is too loyal to your father and Peter is likely to be the same way."

Sonya shrugged. "You're right. They are.....or you could ask my mother. Maybe she knows."

Dina made a face. "You'll forgive me for saying so, but I don't trust her, either. We all could have been gone by now if she'd only listened to Frank when she had the chance."

"What are you talking about?" Tom asked. "What does any of this have to do with Frank?"

"It's a long story," Dina replied. "We have to find that shuttle and retrieve any of its equipment that might still be working."

"If you can bring the transmitter here, I can hook it up to the power station," Tom told her. "This place is the only power source on the planet with the juice to boost the signal far enough away. We would likely have to reach the nearest long-range communications relay station before we got in touch with anyone."

Dina nodded. "And then we would have to wait for them to get here. That could take days. We'll need to work fast before the Children invade." She stretched out her hand to him. "Come with us. You can help us find it. You're the best qualified to salvage the transmitter from the shuttle. You don't have to stay here working with the Elite Battalion."

A sad smile curled the corners of his lips. It was the first time she'd seen him smile since their team first landed here.

"You're as caring as you always were," he murmured. "I would love nothing better than to see my Children. I want them to know I did everything possible to help them, but if this works, we'll only be able to send a transmission if we have someone inside the Elite Battalion who can get access to the power station. I hate being trapped like this, but I have to stay."

She squeezed his arm. She would have liked to hug him again, but she didn't want to do that in front of Sonya. "Thank you—for everything. I don't know what to say."

"Don't say anything. I'm the one who should be thanking you. Helping this mission is the only thing giving my life any purpose or hope. It's the only thing I've done that's worth doing since I got here. I'll always be grateful to you for that. Now you two better get out of sight before someone catches you. Find that transmitter and bring it to me. I'll do the rest."

Sonya backed away into the undergrowth, but Dina lingered. She didn't want to leave without him.

She wanted to save him more than anyone else—maybe even more than her own Children. The Children would always be able to protect themselves.

Prideland had broken Tom Sharples in a way she'd never seen it break anyone. It took his youth, his vitality, his strength, his hope—his very spirit. He was a shell of the man he'd been just three years ago.

Sonya crept back out of hiding and took hold of her sleeve. "Come on, Dina," Sonya whispered. "We have to get out of here."

Tom read Dina's mind. "Go," he whispered. "You can't help me."

She backed away, but she didn't turn around. She didn't want to take her eyes off him in case something happened to him.

She got a very bad feeling that, if she took her eyes off him even for an instant, he would vanish and she wouldn't be able to save him at all.

Sonya tugged her sleeve one more time and the leaves closed in front of Dina's face. She lost sight of him and he disappeared.

She finally turned away and came face to face with Sonya under the thick branches. "Now what do we do?" Sonya whispered.

"We go find that shuttle. Come on. We need to move fast. We have to get out of the city before morning."

Chapter 37

Dina glanced around a corner and immediately retreated when she saw a crowd of helpers coming up the street. She and Sonya had been sneaking through the city ever since they parted from Tom.

Daylight streamed between the buildings and the two women still hadn't made it to the edge of the city yet. Just a few more miles and they would leave this city for the open countryside.

The two women kept encountering problems at every turn. Helpers patrolled every city street in search of anyone breaking the rules. They all carried weapons and this group followed the river headed straight for Dina's and Sonya's hiding place.

Dina dove backward and pulled Sonya away. "Come on!" she hissed. "We can't go that way! We gotta move!"

She didn't wait for Sonya to agree. Dina grabbed Sonya's arm and steered her onto the path leading through the city's back alleys and byways.

Anyone would have seen the two women running away, but Dina didn't care anymore. She and Sonya sprinted down the path winding deeper into the city.

They were going the opposite way from where Dina wanted to go, but anything was better than getting caught by those helpers.

The alley ended in a part of town she didn't recognize. She almost blundered onto the sidewalk in front of more helpers going about their morning business.

She dove out of sight just in time, jumped a wall into someone's backyard, and snatched a helper's tunic off the laundry line.

Dina wriggled into it to hide her jungle clothes. Then she and Sonya could walk out onto the street with everyone else.

They walked fast heading west again. Dina had no idea how far she'd have to go before she got out of this city.

They passed another ten blocks before they ran into another mob of helpers. These people were all armed, too, and they appeared to be holding some kind of pro-Pride demonstration.

More helpers gathered from all over, raised their weapons in the air, and chanted something Dina couldn't understand. All their voices shouting together muddied the words.

Dina pushed Sonya around the nearest corner and the two women skirted the crowd by five blocks before they could set off westward again.

"This is taking too long," Sonya muttered. "There has to be a better way."

"What other way is there?" Dina countered. "We can't exactly take the train."

Sonya burst out laughing, but she stifled it a second later when some more helpers glared at her. That kind of laughter didn't belong in this city.

They made it another five blocks before another platoon of armed helpers marched down the street. These people weren't holding any kind of demonstration. They glared at everyone, even other helpers engaged in household tasks.

The bystanders withdrew from these people and scuttled off the sidewalk to get out of their path. The marchers occupied every inch of space and left no room for anyone else even to stand on the sidewalk.

Dina and Sonya diverted into another side street, but they didn't get away quickly enough. The helpers spotted the two women.

One man at the front of the crowd shot out his hand to point at the two women. "There! Those two—get them!"

"Run!" Dina ordered.

She and Sonya bolted to the end of the street. Sonya swerved to the right and Dina ran left.

Sonya thought better of it and skidded backward to stay with Dina. Dina almost told Sonya to keep going to throw the helpers off their trail, but it was too late. Both women raced south to put more distance between themselves and the oncoming helpers.

Dina skidded from one intersection to another, but everywhere she went, more helpers came out of nowhere to surround her and box her in.

She spun around another corner and almost ran straight into Harmon Farley coming from the other direction. Dina sprang back to get away from him, and at that moment, another group of helpers materialized out of an alley.

They rushed the two women from behind and caught both Dina and Sonya. Dina struggled hard enough to yank her arms free, pulled her sickle from her belt, and hacked out at the men trying to grab her.

Her blade bit into one man's wrist and he reared back bellowing in pain. That sound only spurred Dina to new heights of rage. If the Children could win by sheer ferocity, she could do the same thing.

She spun backward. More helpers moved in to capture her, but she swung her blade hard enough to drive them back. That moment gave her the time she needed to draw her knife.

She whirled in both directions slashing anyone who came near her. Sonya huddled near Dina's back for protection, but Dina already saw that she wouldn't be getting out of here.

Fifty helpers closed in from all sides. She couldn't hope any Children were lurking around this city to bail her out this time.

She swiped her sickle to the left and slashed a man who inched too close. She cut him across the chest, sliced his shirt open, and drew blood from a long gash across his sternum.

He yelled and leapt back, but he didn't leave. None of them did. When she turned to her left, they closed tighter on the right. When she whipped around to drive those people off, another bunch crowded nearer on her left.

She gave another vicious chop with her blade to the left and hit a different man in the neck. He collapsed with the blade still stuck in his vertebrae and all the other helpers took that opportunity to pile in on top of her.

They brought her down in seconds and she fell on top of Sonya. Dina roared in fury, but too many helpers attacked at once. They tackled her and their combined weight pinned her knife hand down where she couldn't use it.

She screamed and thundered at them, but nothing worked. She heard Sonya screaming her name, but Dina couldn't help Sonya now.

Dina eventually gave up struggling and lay still. She couldn't fight this many people.

It took a long time for all the helpers to get off her. Farley kept yelling, "It's all over! You can get off now! Get off! Come on! We can't do anything with all of you lying on top of them."

The weight didn't lighten for at least ten minutes. When it did, the helpers took special pains to disarm Dina before they eased off.

Ten big men still flattened her to the pavement when some unseen person came over and tied Dina's ankles together. She tried to kick the person away, but more helpers restrained her. This was hopeless.

They tied a rope around one of her wrists, too. She didn't see how they did it, but as soon as the last man got off her, the helpers pulled the ropes tight and cinched her up so she couldn't move.

In seconds, they trussed her hand and foot and left her and Sonya lying there on the pavement. The helpers had tied up Sonya, too.

Farley stood over them pointing at everyone and shouting orders. "Get over there and see if you can find any of their friends who might be hanging around."

"We don't have any friends hanging around," Dina snapped. "We're alone."

He kicked her in the leg. "Shut up, slag. Don't give me your filthy lies." He turned back to his people. "All of you get out of the way so we can bring the wagon in."

Dina tried to see what he was talking about, but too many helpers crowded around. They kept their weapons ready—as if she and Sonya could go anywhere.

The project took ages with shifts of helpers leaving and others relieving them to stand guard over the prisoners.

Farley kept ordering some groups to search different parts of the neighborhood, carry information to people and cats somewhere else, and then receiving reports from different helpers about stuff Dina didn't understand.

The situation in this city would have resembled Adrian's camp if the helpers had been better organized.

Dina didn't put much faith in Farley's command experience or expertise. He seemed to be making it up as he went along. Adrian commanded much more attention and his people listened to him much better.

The helpers kept murmuring to each other and making comments on everything Farley said or did, but the helpers never said anything outright to his face to contradict him. They just whispered and muttered behind his back, which was worse.

She saw this again and again, even from women and children helpers standing around watching. Some of the women even shook their heads over his orders.

He didn't notice. He finally strode a few paces away, waved his arms in wild circles, and called, "Everybody out of the way! Everyone back away! Don't leave the prisoners unguarded! Are you stupid? Everyone clear the street."

Helpers walked back and forth trying to obey all his contradictory orders. In the end, even those men guarding Sonya and Dina had to move aside to make room for a wagon to pull up next to the two women.

"Load them up!" Farley ordered. "Put them in the wagon!"

The same guards had to come back, pick up the two women, and heave them into the wagon bed. A different man sat in the seat. Farley climbed up and tried to take the reins from him. "You can get down here. I'll bring the wagon back to you when I'm done."

"No way in hell am I letting you take my wagon and my best ox," the driver snapped back. "I'll drive them myself. I don't trust you as far as I can throw you."

"You stupid slag!" Farley fired back. "Do you know who I am?"

"I don't give a damn who you are and don't you dare call me a slag," the driver countered. "This is my wagon and no one drives this ox but me. You can sit there and shut your mouth or you can get down and get yourself another wagon."

The driver shut his mouth into a firm, determined line and glared at Farley in outright defiance. Farley spluttered and humphed again and again, but the driver didn't move. He didn't give up the reins, either.

Farley finally spun the other way and collapsed into the seat. He chopped his hand toward the street in front of him. "Fine. Just get moving and then get out of here."

The driver slapped his reins on the ox's back and the wagon creaked down the street. Dina couldn't see any of the surrounding helpers over the wagon box's sides. "Where are you taking us?"

"None of your business," Farley snapped over his shoulder. "Our leader will want to make an example out of you and your traitorous friend here."

"Leader?" Dina asked. "What leader? You're helpers. You serve the Pride."

"We still have a leader. He organizes the loyalist movement in this city."

"I thought you were the leader," Dina replied. "You certainly have the biggest mouth."

Farley humphed again and didn't answer. Dina sank into the wagon bed and relaxed as well as she could. She might not be able to get out of here, but at least she would find out who was in charge of this catastrophe.

She didn't know the loyalists had a leader. Who was he? She would satisfy her curiosity if nothing else.

The wagon bumped and rattled and creaked through the streets. That was a long wagon ride—almost as long as Dina's first ride from the village to the city.

Neither she nor Sonya dared to sit up to look around, though. Faceless buildings passed on either side.

The sounds outside the wagon returned to normal. Dina didn't hear any chanting or trooping or fighting or....or anything, really. Everything sounded peaceful for a change—but that was an illusion.

Dina's stomach twisted in knots as one minute passed another. The trip seemed to take hours. Every second she spent in this city brought her closer to Adrian's deadline.

She took the time to strategize. What would Adrian do in this situation? Adrian never would have gotten caught by those helpers in the first place.

He could have outrun them, scaled a building, and made it out of the city in a matter of minutes. He could have left the city last night before anyone knew he was here.

Dina didn't like to think how many hours she'd wasted running, hiding, and avoiding helpers in this city when she should have been searching the jungle south of the village for the Mathus family's shuttle.

That would have been a colossal waste of time, too, because no one knew where it was. What she wouldn't give to have Frank alive right now. He would have known exactly where the shuttle was.

Dina's mind switched back to Darcy, but Dina discarded that idea right away. Dina didn't trust Darcy.

Frank risked a lot to free Darcy and her children. Darcy threw that back in his face.

Dina wouldn't take any unnecessary risks to give Darcy a second chance—or a third chance or a fourth chance or a fifth chance.

Frank had returned to the village more than once to check on Darcy and give her the chance to escape to the cantons. She refused that, too. She was beyond saving as far as Dina was concerned.

The wagon finally stopped in front of a palatial mansion somewhere in a different part of the city. Dina didn't recognize this part of town, either. How was she supposed to get out of it when she had no idea where she was?

"Help me unload the prisoners," Farley told the driver.

"You didn't say anything about that when you said you needed a wagon," the driver countered. "I just drive. I'm not here to lift and carry."

"Don't you care at all about the Pride?" Farley snapped. "These are traitors to the cause. You should be as interested in seeing them punished as we are."

"I do my duty to the Pride," the driver muttered. "No one can say otherwise."

Farley smacked his lips in annoyance. He climbed down. "Stay here," he ordered. "You'll have to wait until I bring some others to unload."

The driver didn't respond. Dina tried to twist around to see who he was. Was he subversive and hiding it behind a veneer of loyalty? Was he deliberately antagonizing Farley to subvert the Pride?

Farley came back soon enough and five men dragged Dina and Sonya out of the wagon bed. The driver stayed in his seat and refused to budge through the whole process.

He didn't respond when Farley told him to get out of here and not to come back. The driver only clucked to his ox and drove off without a word.

The men laid the two women on the pavement in a spacious driveway in front of the mansion. Dina didn't see any other people around—or any cats. The place looked peaceful and inviting—except for the helpers standing guard over her and Sonya.

The men stayed there while Farley left and went into the giant house. He stayed gone for another agonizing wait before he came back and told the men to bring the women inside.

They didn't untie Dina or Sonya to make them walk. The men picked up both women and carried them through a magnificent tiled foyer full of statuary, vases of gorgeous flowers, oil paintings of busts on the walls, and tapestries covering every surface.

Renfroe's house seemed downright rustic compared to this, and as soon as they walked in, helpers crisscrossed the hallways doing every kind of domestic work to maintain this place.

They dusted the furniture, carried laundry back and forth, and they all stopped what they were doing to let the men carry Dina and Sonya past.

None of the helpers showed any sign of alarm that these two women were being carried bound hand and foot through this house. This kind of thing might happen all the time in Prideland now. How would Dina know?

The men passed through another hall and exited into a pavilion attached to the back of the house. It formed a kind of breezeway between the house itself and the huge garden behind it.

Shrubs, hedges, trees, flowerbeds, fountains, terraces, and glasshouses stretched out of sight. Dina couldn't see the other side of the giant garden.

The men put her and Sonya down on the floor in the pavilion. Dina tried to see what they were going to do to her and Sonya here, but she didn't see anything except another group of helpers standing nearby.

They crowded around something she couldn't see. Most of them had their backs to her so she couldn't see what they were doing, either.

Whatever it was must have been important. None of them paid any attention to the two prisoners. Men's voices came from behind the crowd.

This definitely reminded Dina of one of Adrian's briefings. The loyalist helpers' leader must be standing back there telling everyone what to do.

Dina surveyed the garden while she waited for him to get around to dealing with her and Sonya.

It was a very nice garden, but she liked Renfroe's better. It had a smaller, more comfortable feel. This place felt more like a royal estate where a slag like she was wouldn't be allowed to set foot on the grass.

A family of fell deer even grazed on the lawns. They gave the estate an even more regal atmosphere. Maybe the cats who owned this house kept the fell deer around so the cats would have something to hunt when they wanted to.

The voices near her changed and brought her out of her thoughts. "You can go now," one of them said. "Come back and report to me when you find out."

A deeper, adult male voice answered, "Yes, Sir," and all the surrounding helpers backed away.

Dina stared in amazement as the crowd of helpers dispersed, strode into the house, and didn't come back.

They left ten men standing around two young teenage boys at the far end of the pavilion. They couldn't have been more than fifteen and sixteen and the resemblance between them broadcast to the world that they were brothers.

Sonya gasped. "Christian! Peter! What are you doing here?"

The older boy looked down his nose at her. "I should ask you the same thing. You were supposed to come to the city to become a helper to the Pride. Now I find out my own sister is nothing but a traitorous slag."

Chapter 38

Dina and Sonya cowered against a wall and watched Sonya's brothers Christian and Peter Mathus talking to another group of heavy-set male helpers on the far side of the pavilion.

Sonya kept cringing in disgust, looking away, and eventually giving in to curiosity and horror by watching her brothers again.

Dina didn't have the same problem. She studied the two boys, especially Christian.

The very first time he held one of these briefings in front of her, she knew he had to be the leader of the loyalist helper movement. All these helpers kept coming to him for orders and giving him reports on everything.

Peter kept a close position at Christian's shoulder and filled in any additional information Christian needed that the helpers couldn't supply.

Dina would probably never find out how the two Mathus brothers wound up in this city—much less how they managed to take charge of the helpers' movement.

It didn't really matter how it happened. They were here now and neither of them made any effort to hide what they were doing.

"The Children approached the city along the river," one man told Christian. "They would have invaded through the northwestern suburbs, but our forces tried to flank them and the Children pivoted to come at them instead. That's how the Children got into the western neighborhoods."

"I don't care about that," Christian countered. "I only want to know if we're holding them at the western neighborhoods."

"We aren't holding them anywhere," a different man replied. "They can get inside the city whenever they want. They slaughter any helpers who go out against them no matter how well we arm our people."

"Then why aren't the Children inside the city now?" Christian demanded. "Why haven't they invaded if they can do it whenever they want to?"

"No one knows," the first man replied. "They keep pulling back when they get too close. They take their casualties, retreat a few miles out of town, wait for us to withdraw, and then they make another assault to do it all over again."

"That's nonsense," Christian snapped. "I don't believe you. There must be some reason they don't enter the city."

"You can go out there and take a look. You'll see for yourself," the same man replied. "There is no reason they can't enter the city whenever they want."

"The cats will stop them," Christian muttered and bent over a map of the city to study the layout. "The Pride is planning another sweep coming down from the northeast. I'll tell them what's going on. They can time their attack with the Children's next surge. The cats will drive the Children back into the jungle."

Some of the surrounding helpers exchanged glances, but they didn't argue.

Christian gave them further orders and sent a messenger to deliver the news to someone named Kumala.

He finally dismissed everyone else apart from the ten men who'd been standing as his bodyguard to begin with. He waited for everyone else to leave before he turned to face the two women.

He heaved a huge sigh. "Now we can deal with these two."

"We caught them trying to get past the square," Farley informed Christian. "Both of them are known sympathizers of the Children and fought in the previous battles."

Christian wrinkled his nose at Dina. "I know all about *her.*" He turned to his sister. "I expected better from you, Sonya. Now you leave me no choice but to execute you both as public examples of anyone who betrays the Pride."

"Execute!" Sonya gasped. "You're going to execute *me*—your own sister?! Are you insane?"

"My first loyalty is to the Pride. Our parents worked hard to get you a privileged position as a helper. You betrayed that to aid our enemies."

"The Children aren't our enemies," Dina interjected. "They've only been trying to save their own lives from the Pride and hopefully free these people into the bargain. They've welcomed everyone who's left Prideland."

"You keep your mouth shut!" he snarled through locked teeth. "Your influence has poisoned my sister. She never would have turned against the Pride if not for you manipulating her and leading her astray."

"I hate to break it to you, kid," Dina countered, "but it was the Pride itself that turned Sonya against the cats. No one else had to do it for them because they did it all on their own."

He pinched his lips and pretended to ignore her while he focused on his sister. "What happens to you isn't up for debate. The penalty is execution for any helper who betrays the Pride. I would have no choice but to execute you even if you are my sister. All I want to know is if you're prepared to do the right thing before that happens."

"What do you mean by 'doing the right thing'?" Dina asked. "We are doing the right thing by supporting the Children."

He rounded on her with a vicious snarl. "I'm not talking to you! If you don't shut your mouth, I'll send you off to execution right now while I talk to Sonya alone. Don't make me tell you again!"

He fought himself under control and turned back to his sister, but that moment gave Dina a crystal-clear view into his heart and soul. He might be out here telling all these adults what to do, but he was just a kid underneath the surface.

"If you really want to help the Pride and do the right thing," he growled in a shaky undertone, "you'll tell us everything you know about the Children's plans, where they're camping, and why they keep harassing us without invading completely."

Sonya tried to brace herself and glare back at him. "How would I know that if I've been hiding out in the city all this time? I've never even spoken to one of the Children."

"Don't give me that," he chided. "You fought with them in two battles and you got visited for speaking out in their favor before the invasion. You helped the subversive helpers plan this whole uprising. You must know something."

"If you want to know the Children's plans, you should be asking me," Dina cut in again. "I know more about the Children's plans than she does. In fact, I know quite a lot about their plans—and where they camp—and why they're harassing you without invading."

His head whipped around. "Why aren't they, then?"

Dina shrugged and looked away toward the expansive lawns. "I might tell you if you commute our death sentences."

"I can't do that. I already told you. If I showed any lenience to you two, I couldn't keep order with the rest of the helpers. A rule's a rule. It applies to everyone, no matter who they are."

"Then I have no reason to tell you what I know. If you execute us, you'll never find out. You sure won't find out from anyone else—especially not from Sonya. She doesn't know anything. We just met up for the first time yesterday. I've been in the jungle with the Children for three years. I know everything about them."

He gasped in exasperation and spun away to storm across the pavilion. She bit back a secret grin when she saw how annoyed she made him.

She glanced over at Sonya just as Sonya glanced at her. Dina read all the anxiety in those eyes. Sonya was scared out of her wits that her brothers would somehow get the information out of her.

Dina probably shouldn't have let Sonya in on so much of the Children's plans, but it was too late to change that now. Dina only hoped to get both Sonya and herself out of this with their lives.

At least the Pride and the helpers didn't know yet that the Children could reproduce. With luck, Dina would be able to evacuate the population before the Pride found out and the whole catastrophe exploded in everyone's faces.

Sonya gulped and did her best to square her shoulders. "Christian.....?"

"What do you want?" he barked over his shoulder. "If you can't tell me what I want to know, I have no reason to keep you alive."

"Do you remember.....do you remember where the shuttle crashed?" Sonya blurted out.

Dina froze at those words, but no one else noticed. Christian turned around and frowned at her. "What?"

"The shuttle that brought us here—do you remember where it crashed? I remember we entered the village by the southern road, but I don't remember anything else. Do you?"

"What do you want to know that for?" he countered.

She opened her mouth to answer. "I was just wondering because we thought....."

Dina nudged her knee into Sonya's thigh to stop her. Sonya glanced at her and Dina gave her a hard look. She didn't want Christian to get any ideas about the Children's sympathizers going after the shuttle.

Christian scowled at both of them and then waved that away. "I don't remember where it was except that it was south of the village. I remember Frank and Father talking about heading north to find civilization, but I don't remember anything else. I had other things on my mind."

Sonya nodded. "That's how it was for me, too."

"Why do you want to know?" he asked again.

"Do you remember that stuffed bear Jared used to have?" Sonya asked. "He left it on the shuttle when we left to go to the village. Everyone forgot about it after the crash and then we all got so distracted by trying to settle into village life. I was thinking of going back to the shuttle to find the bear for him. He might want it back."

"He's too old for stuff like that and no other children Prideland use toys like that. You better forget it." He turned away. "If you don't have anything useful to tell me, I'm too busy to mess around with this anymore."

"Well, what about you, Peter?" Sonya asked. "What do you remember about the shuttle crash?"

Peter started to answer, but Christian interrupted. "I told you it isn't important. Even if Jared wanted that bear, he can't have it. He isn't a baby anymore and we don't do things like that in Prideland. He's better off without it."

"Shouldn't he be the one to decide that?" Sonya asked.

Christian smacked his lips again, rolled his eyes to Heaven, and waved at Farley. "Bring that wagon back here and take these two slags back to the square for execution. Send out your runners to call all the helpers to watch. Tell them attendance is mandatory."

Chapter 39

Dina and Sonya exchanged glances as the sound of Harmon Farley's footsteps got farther away across the foyer leading deeper into the house.

The sound set Dina's nerves on end. He would bring another wagon to take the two women to the square for execution.

She couldn't get out of this with her hands and feet tied together. She surveyed the pavilion one more time. All of Christian Mathus's bodyguards carried weapons. She wouldn't make it five feet away from any of them.

Hers and Sonya's lives were already forfeit. These bodyguards wouldn't care if they killed the two women here instead of at the square. Christian might regret losing the opportunity to make examples of them, but that was all.

The helpers had taken Dina's weapons away, too. She had no way to cut the ropes binding her wrists and ankles, especially not with everyone standing around watching.

Christian and Peter withdrew to the other end of the pavilion while they waited for the wagon to come back. Dina considered appealing to the driver for help. He seemed at least marginally sympathetic—or at least not as fanatically pro-Pride as everyone else around here.

Christian and Peter kept their voices low so Dina and Sonya wouldn't overhear them. The two boys' behavior posed a stark contrast to the way they acted when the helpers first brought Dina and Sonya here.

Christian practically announced his plans to the two women before. Now he whispered to his brother in an undertone.

Did Christian doubt if he would actually be able to execute the two women? Why else would he hide his conversation from them?

His bodyguards stood in a loose semi-circle between him and the two women as if Dina and Sonya posed some threat to his safety. The whole situation only made him seem weaker and more incongruous as a leader.

Farley didn't come back for a long time. When he did, he came alone. "I'll need some extra men to help carry these two out to the wagon," he informed Christian. "That damn driver won't help."

"Go get Amal and Kashi from the barn," Christian ordered. "Everyone else is busy."

Farley turned to leave a second time. At that moment, Renfroe blasted out of the bushes right next to the pavilion. He appeared so suddenly that Christian's bodyguard didn't even have time to turn around before Renfroe catapulted into them from the side.

He must have been stalking them through Christian's entire conversation with Dina and Sonya. Dina had been in a direct line of sight to the estate grounds ever since the helpers brought her in here.

Renfroe must have sneaked through the bushes one inch at a time to make sure no one saw him. Now he crashed into the bodyguards at the far end of the line and toppled half of them in one pounce.

Two of them shrieked in terror and then one of those shrieks ended in a death gargle when he crushed the man's throat in one bite.

Renfroe rode the whole party to the ground, sprang off to drag down one of the few bodyguards still standing, and tore the man's head off with one massive wrench of his neck.

Dina sat frozen in stunned amazement that he could appear so suddenly and so decisively. Sonya, Christian, and Peter stared at Renfroe in dazed horror as he launched himself from one bodyguard to another.

Farley staggered backward toward the doors to get away. He tripped over one of the vase stands and it hit the floor with a splintering crash.

That sound woke Dina from her shock. She kicked out with her bound feet, hitched herself over to the fallen bodyguards, and pulled one of their knives from its owner's belt.

She had to nearly dislocate her own shoulders to angle the knife and slice the ropes around her wrists, but she finally did it.

She ducked to avoid Renfroe lunging for a different bodyguard. His enraged snarls filled the pavilion as he soared over her head and annihilated one man after another.

She slashed the cords binding her ankles and dove for Sonya. "Come on! We have to get out of here!"

"Stop!" Christian yelled and he sprang forward. He pulled another knife from his belt, but he couldn't get near the two women with Renfroe in the way.

He landed on top of another bodyguard, finished the man off, and looked up at Christian in murderous fury. Blood saturated Renfroe's jaws and splattered his coat.

Dina shivered at the sight of him like this. She'd seen him like this before and she'd always hoped she would never see him like this again.

"Keep away, boy," he snarled under his breath. "Save yourself and your brother before you make a big mistake."

Christian trembled, but he didn't lower his knife. "These are traitors to the Pride! They deserve to die!"

"Deserve?" Renfroe growled. "Everyone dies, boy. 'Deserve' has nothing to do with it. The only question is—would you rather die now or another time? I can accommodate you either way." He swiveled his head ever so slightly to the side. "Take your friend out into the garden, Dina. Follow that path past the rose garden and....."

Dina took hold of Sonya's arm to steer her away, but just then, another group of helpers rushed through the doors from inside the house.

Renfroe reacted impossibly fast, roared in fury, and lunged for them. They couldn't have been expecting to get attacked by a cat—not when these helpers had all been working and fighting so hard to support the Pride.

Dina didn't see what he did to them. Their petrified screams and the tearing sounds of bodies coming apart told her more than she wanted to know.

She pulled Sonya farther away, but Christian took advantage of the mayhem to dart in front of them to block them from leaving.

He waved his knife in their faces. "You aren't going anywhere!"

Dina stiffened to fight him off, but before she could move, Sonya rushed her brother, seized his wrist in both hands, and tackled him onto his back.

They wrestled over the knife. She locked both hands around his wrist and shoved the weapon closer to his face.

He fought back and Dina moved in to help Sonya finish the job. Dina stopped next to them and raised her own knife to stab Christian, but at the last second, Sonya gave his arm an almighty jerk and plunged the knife into his throat.

He choked once and Sonya toppled off him to one side. She rolled onto her feet.

He stayed sprawled there on his back with the knife still lodged in his neck. He choked and spluttered while his blood bubbled around the knife hilt. His eyes darted back and forth searching for something.

Sonya looked up and shot a pointed glare across the pavilion. Peter stood there rooted to the spot with his mouth hanging open. He gaped first at Sonya and then at Christian.

Sonya backed away and Dina leapt to her side to catch up with her. The two women backed onto the lawn and then turned away to run for it.

They dashed past the rose garden, but Dina didn't know where to go. This estate didn't seem to have any end that she could see.

The fell deer scattered before her and vanished into the undergrowth. The trees grew in a thick forest to her left. She could have hidden herself and Sonya in there, but Dina didn't want them to get lost.

They sprinted down the lawn in no particular direction. She would have just kept on running forever, but after a few more minutes, she saw a brick wall in the distance.

She headed for it, but when she and Sonya staggered under the trees, Dina realized the wall was too high for them to scale it.

They both collapsed against it panting hard. Dina took the time to check the tree branches overhead. None of them was low enough for her and Sonya to climb over the wall.

"Are you okay?" Dina gasped. "Are you okay......? Christian....."

"I should have killed Peter, too," Sonya snarled. "I should have killed them both long ago."

"He was your brother...."

"I knew he was loyal to the Pride. I always knew he would become a factor like Father. I should have finished him years ago."

Dina didn't say anything else. "Come on. We have to find a way out of this garden."

She started to make her way down the wall. The trees and bushes concealed the two women from view, and a second later, she found a wooden door leading to the other side.

It led the women into another green alleyway running into a neighborhood full of more vast estates exactly like this one.

Dina headed west. She didn't think about anything other than putting as many miles between herself and Prideland as possible.

The two women made it half a mile before Renfroe caught up with them. He sprang onto the wall surrounding a different estate and leapt down next to Sonya.

She reared back to get away from him. Dina laid her hand on Sonya's arm. "It's all right. He saved our lives."

"Who is your friend, Dina?" he rumbled.

"Her name is Sonya Mathus. Her father is Alexander Mathus, the man our landing team came to this planet to rescue. Sonya was a helper to Amaryllis before the Children invaded. Sonya has been helping the Children's cause ever since she became a helper."

"I see." He sniffed the blood out of his nose and then sneezed. "Well, you can't stay here. Follow me. I'll take you to my house, but I warn you. It won't be safe for you there, either. I'll have to keep you hidden until I find a way to get you both out of the city."

Dina put her arms around his neck. "Thank you so much. I'm so grateful for your help."

"I wouldn't leave you in danger. You should know that by now, which is why we can't stay here." He turned away and padded down the grassy path heading westward. "Follow me. We have a long way to go to get to my house."

Chapter 40

Renfroe pushed his head through the bushes. "The way is clear. Get across the street and hide in the bushes there. I'll go into the garden and make sure no one else is around. Go now!"

Dina pulled Sonya out of their hiding place. The three of them had been sneaking, dodging helper patrols, and diverting their route all the way across town.

Now, the three of them had finally made it to Renfroe's house just as the sun was going down again. That was another day gone. Dina only had three days left before the Children launched their assault.

She hustled across the street, cast furtive glances right and left to make sure no one saw them, and ducked behind another clump of foliage against Renfroe's garden wall.

Dina never planned to come back here. She couldn't decide how she felt about it.

She turned to Sonya as soon as the two women concealed themselves. "Don't tell Renfroe anything about the Children's plans—or our plans," Dina whispered as soon as they got under cover.

Sonya's eyes widened. "You've always spoken so highly of him....and he just saved our lives by attacking those helpers. Isn't he....?"

"He's a cat of the Pride," Dina fired back. "He's always treated me well and he's done more than anyone to help the Children's cause, but don't tell him anything. Anything we told him would only compromise him and put him in more danger. Keep it to yourself."

Sonya started to say, "Okay...." and broke off when Renfroe came toward them.

He crossed the street much more casually, bounded over his own garden wall, and disappeared inside the grounds the way he always did. No one watching would have seen anything unusual in that.

"How long do we have to wait for him?" Sonya whispered.

"If anyone is there, it might take a while." Dina squatted down behind the bushes. "We might as well get comfortable."

She got ready to sit down when the garden door clicked open and Renfroe stuck his head out. "You can come in now. It's deserted."

Dina tiptoed into the garden. "Are Buck and Belinda here?"

"They spend most of their time involved in the helpers' campaign now. They aren't here at this time of day."

He advanced into the sunshine, but Dina held back under the trees. She hesitated to go into the open.

He glanced over his shoulder at her and Sonya, blinked, and turned away. "Stay here, then. I'll bring you some food."

He paced into the house and vanished into the kitchen. Sonya peered from one side of the garden to the other. "I see what you mean. He's nice."

"He's polite, but he's still a cat. Don't underestimate his manner. He's as much a killer as the others."

"Oh, I know! I saw him just now," Sonya breathed, but she fell silent when Renfroe came back.

He carried a cloth bundle in his mouth and set it at Dina's feet. "Eat this. You can sit down over here."

He padded to the base of a nearby tree, flopped onto his stomach, and started an elaborate ritual of cleaning his face with his paw.

Dina sat down next to him and tugged loose the knot on the bundle. "I'm surprised Belinda stays away from the house so much. She never left when I lived here."

"Everything changes," he muttered. "None of the helpers can avoid getting involved now. If they even mention their duties, the other helpers accuse them of betraying the cause."

"I noticed. This city is a tinderbox barely holding together."

"It isn't holding together," he growled. "It's every man for himself now. None of the helper factions agree on what to do or how to do it. They're as much against each other as they are against the Children—and the Children aren't even here yet."

"The cats seemed pretty organized when I saw them. They're out there fighting the Children pretty well."

"Someone is organizing the cats into these armies, but no one knows who is doing it. The helpers certainly don't know. The helpers keep launching their own campaigns against the Children, but these helper campaigns wind up interfering with the cats more than helping them."

"We saw that, too."

Renfroe ran his tongue over his jowls. "You're supposed to be eating, not talking."

"Oh, right." Dina bent over the bundle and laid open its corners. It contained a wheel of cheese, a slab of dried meat, and a pile of dried fruit. "Thank you for this."

"I'll only stay a minute and then I'll have to leave you. I need to find a way to get you out of the city before anyone realizes where you are."

"Will you get into trouble for helping us?" she asked.

"No more trouble than I'm already in. The others will ascribe it to my senile madness over you and it's just as well. I can't fathom why you keep coming back to this city, Dina. You know the danger."

"I keep coming back because I think I can help the Children. I wouldn't come otherwise."

He grumbled under his breath and got to his feet. "Do yourselves a favor and stay hidden. I don't know how long I'll be gone. If you really must go into the house, stay in our old bedroom and keep quiet so Belinda doesn't hear you. I'll come back as soon as I can."

"Thank you again," Dina exclaimed.

"You don't have to keep saying that. I'm helping the Children, too, in my own way."

He turned away and headed back toward the garden wall with the door in it. Dina gathered the bundle of food. "Come on, Sonya. Let's move farther into the back of the garden where no one will see us."

She and Sonya got to their feet, but none of them made it more than a few feet before the garden door opened from the outside. Buck, Belinda, Harmon Farley, and half a dozen other helpers strode in.

Belinda's face turned to a block of solid granite when she saw Dina and Sonya standing there for all to see.

"Traitors!" Farley growled.

Belinda's eyes darted from Dina to Sonya and back to Renfroe. Belinda might not have recognized Sonya, but Belinda couldn't fail to see exactly what was happening here.

Buck's hand moved to an axe hanging from his belt. Two other helpers grabbed their weapons, but Renfroe attacked first.

He launched off the ground and went straight for Farley. "Get out of here, Dina!" Renfroe roared over his shoulder. "Get your friend out of the city now!!"

"Get them!" Belinda shrieked. "Stop those two women!"

"Go!" Dina shoved Sonya away, but the garden presented a death trap they couldn't escape.

Dina towed Sonya toward the only other way out—the house. Dina pulled Sonya through the portico, into the kitchen, and shoved her onto the sidewalk.

They both took off running, but this time, Dina knew exactly where she was and where she should be going.

She didn't follow the streets through the neighborhood heading back to the city. She didn't want to meet any more helper patrols.

She steered Sonya through the neighborhood, down a few more winding avenues flanked by magnificent houses, and the two women finally plunged into the open fields with the city behind them.

Dina staggered on the rough ground. She and Sonya had to slow to a walk.

Dina spotted the village in the distance. She would have liked to go there and steal some weapons, but that would have to wait.

The sun went down and the stars came out, but neither she nor Sonya dared to stop until they made it to the jungle.

Dina collapsed against a tree and her legs buckled under her. "We can't stay here," she panted. "We'll have to keep going until we make it to the canton."

"Do you think Renfroe is all right?" Sonya whispered.

"He can take care of himself a lot better than we can." Dina forced herself to open her eyes and untie the bundle of food. "We'll have something to eat and then move on. We're both exhausted."

She broke the meat and cheese in half and shared it with Sonya, but Sonya only nibbled at hers. "I've never been to the cantons. I don't know if I want to go there."

"Of course you haven't been there," Dina countered. "That's the whole point—to make you too scared to go there. The point is to make you understand that you have nowhere else to go. Don't worry. You'll be safe and comfortable there. There are good people there who will help you and take care of you. Trust me."

"You know so much more about Prideland than I do," Sonya muttered down into her lap.

Dina snorted. "That might not be such a good thing."

Sonya took a bigger bite of her meat. "So what are the cantons like?"

Dina leaned back against a tree and chewed some of the fruit. "They're usually constructed with a high fence made out of logs. The houses are usually built on stilts to make it harder for cats to get inside. The nearest canton is Moonlight canton and it has the highest stilts I've seen so far—probably because it's so close to Prideland. The cats attack that canton the most often—or they did when they were in the habit of attacking cantons—before the Children came, I mean."

"So....is that where you're taking me?"

"For now. I'll leave you there and then go after the shuttle transmitter. If I find it, none of us might be staying on this planet for very much longer." Dina grinned at her. "That would be something, wouldn't it—if we could all go back to the Coalition?"

"Yeah," Sonya murmured. "I never thought I'd ever leave this planet....and now Christian will never leave it."

"Well, we will. You'll see."

"I want to go with you to find the shuttle," Sonya told her. "Let me come with you. I can help you."

"No way," Dina countered. "You're going straight to the canton. You should have been out there days ago. If I'd known you were still somewhere in the city, I would have come to find you so you could have come with us then."

"Then Christian would still be alive and he might have executed you."

"The answer is no. You aren't coming with me. I don't want to see you in danger anymore."

"But won't I be in danger at the canton?" Sonya asked.

Dina groaned. "Now you're just splitting hairs to get your way. Come on. Let's get to the canton. It's bad enough we're going to be walking through the jungle in the dark."

They set off, but Dina didn't hear anything moving in the branches. "It sounds awfully quiet," she murmured. "The Children must all be tied up with the war."

"You know, it would be a lot easier to find the shuttle if we had the cats' noses," Sonya remarked. "Then we could find it by smell."

"I know something even better," Dina replied over her shoulder. "The Children will be able to find it."

"How would you ask them, though?" Sonya countered. "They're always so hostile."

"Toward humans, maybe. They're as eager to get off this planet as we are. They'll help us....if they can. They might be too busy fighting the Pride, though. We'll just have to wait and see."

Dina didn't see or hear a single cat or Child all the way to Moonlight canton. The two women came in sight of the walls in the cool grey dawn light. The canton looked as haunted as it did before.....until Dina saw men patrolling the walls.

"There it is," she murmured to Sonya. "You'll be safe here. I know someone here you can stay with. You can help her raise her Children. Then you'll be able to see firsthand what they're like."

Sonya's expression went through a dozen transformations, but Dina didn't let her hesitate.

The sentries drew their bows when the two women approached the fence. The new residents certainly took their defense seriously now.

Dina got within thirty feet of the walls when she heard the branches thrashing overhead. She looked up and spotted Zair and some of his people moving through the canopy.

He stopped on a thick tree limb, squatted at the crook where it met the trunk, and stared down at her with his haunted dark eyes.

She raised her hand to wave, but he didn't wave back. "Who is that?" Sonya whispered.

"His name is Zair. He's the leader of the Children who live in this part of the jungle. They're allies of Moonlight canton. If you need help, you can ask him. He's a good man."

"He looks so.....so dangerous," Sonya husked.

"These are the people you've been fighting to help," Dina told her. "They're just people like the rest of us. They want to live in peace and protect their loved ones just like we do. Now come on. Zair and his friends are the least of your worries."

She turned back to the fence and the sentries lowered their weapons to let her approach. She smiled at them and opened her mouth to speak when Kubri James climbed down the ladder from Fan's house.

"So you're back!" he exclaimed when he saw her. "We didn't know what happened to you."

"I'm not back. I just brought my young friend here to stay with you. She just escaped from the city. She's a friend to the Children and wants to do everything she can to help their cause. She'll fit right in here. I was thinking she could take my place at Fan's house and help out with the little ones."

Kubri James nodded and scrutinized Sonya. "I think I know you. You were Amaryllis's helper, weren't you?"

"Yeah!" Sonya gasped. "I know you, too! You were the leader of the subversive helpers."

He grinned at her. "Dina is right. You'll fit right in here." He jerked his thumb over his shoulder. "You can go upstairs. Fan is making breakfast now."

Sonya turned to Dina and the girl's features wrenched. "Will I see you again, Dina?"

"Of course." Dina put her arms around Sonya and hugged her. "You were spectacular today. You're going to be an asset to this community. I know it."

"Are you sure I can't go with you?" Sonya's voice broke. "Please?"

"I wouldn't feel right about taking you. You'll be able to help the Children more here." Dina gave her one last hug. "Stay here. I'll see you soon, and when I do, I hope I can give you some good news."

Sonya tore herself away and climbed up the ladder to Fan's house, but not without looking back more than once.

Dina didn't fully relax until Sonya finally vanished inside. "I saw her fighting during the invasion," Kubri James remarked once Sonya disappeared. "She was amazing."

"She believes in this cause," Dina told him. "You won't be disappointed in her."

"I know I won't. Anyone who can fight the way she did is more than welcome with us." He frowned at her. "Are you sure you have to leave?"

"I'm sure. I need to leave right away, but I was wondering if you can spare any weapons. I don't want to go back out there unarmed."

"Of course. Follow me."

He led her to the building the previous residents used as a tannery. The new canton residents had amassed an unbelievable collection of every kind of household tool, weapon, blade, and even a bunch of handmade swords, spears, and other primitive implements to fight....well, anybody.

"Take your pick," Kubri James told her. "What's ours is yours."

"Thank you," she replied and took another sickle and knife like the ones she lost in the city. "This is all I need."

"Take some food with you," he urged.

"I have some here. I'll be fine. I really need to go."

He frowned. "Are you sure? You aren't even going to stick around to see Fan?"

"I'd love to, but I have to go. It's urgent."

He grumbled some more, but in the end, he walked her out to the gate and hugged her. "Take care of yourself."

"I will. I can see that this place is becoming a real canton. Keep up the good work."

"If it is, it's because of you."

She beamed at him and walked off into the jungle. She couldn't wait any longer.

Chapter 41

Dina expected Zair and the other Children to follow her into the jungle, but they didn't. They stayed behind and let her go off southward by herself.

She made her way back to the site of Adrian's previous camp. She planned to ask him for just one scout to help her find the Mathus family's crashed shuttle.

Her blood ran cold when she got near the camp and found it deserted. It was worse than deserted. It had been destroyed.

Charred posts and burned piles of thatching gave mute testimony to where the houses had been. Shattered pots, a few discarded pieces of clothing, and some charred blankets stuck out of the cinders.

Dina gulped down despair on her way through the wreckage, but of course she didn't see any remains of dead Children. The survivors would have taken their casualties back to the gorge camp for burial.

She stopped in the middle of the camp and turned in a circle taking in the whole terrible scene. What could have happened? The cats wouldn't have used fire to destroy this camp.

Did that mean the helpers attacked instead? The Children never had any problem defending themselves against helpers in the past.

The helpers might have surprised the Children, but that made no sense, either. No human could sneak up on the Children.

Adrian kept watch over his camps with dozens of scouts in the branches. He would have been doubly and triply careful after Iona gave birth. Adrian wouldn't make a mistake like this.

She couldn't stay here. She had to put this behind her and keep moving, but she couldn't put it out of her mind.

Which of her Children died in this attack? Were any of them still alive?

Adrian sent Iona and the other pregnant mothers back to the gorge camp for safety, but Karim stayed to fight with his brothers. Did the Black fall in this attack? Did Dina have any Children left alive at all?

She shook her head again to get those thoughts out of her mind. If even one of them was still alive, then this attack made it even more imperative that she find that transmitter, bring in the Armada, and evacuate anyone who might be left to evacuate. Time was running out.

She pushed on through the jungle heading south. She traveled for half the day before exhaustion caught up with her. She'd been going for almost two days straight without sleep.

She sank onto the ground at the base of a tree. She planned to eat something and keep going. She didn't want to waste any more time, but the instant she sat down, she passed out into a deep, black sleep.

She startled awake hours later when something sharp poked her in the shoulder. "Wake up, slag!" someone snarled in a deadly undertone. "Wake up!"

She shot off the ground and nearly jumped out of her skin when she found herself surrounded by Children.

A tall man with burnished copper fur and black spots stood over her jabbing her with the claws on his foot.

The minute she woke up, he pinned his foot against her shoulder to hold her against the tree. He glared in her face and bared his teeth. "You're in our territory, slag! What are you doing here? Did you come to spy on us?"

"No, I....." She floundered to haul herself back to consciousness. She didn't recognize any of these Children and they obviously didn't know who she was.

He wedged his foot harder against her shoulder. "Did you invade our territory to attack us? Tell the truth! What are you doing out here alone and armed like this?"

"We followed you from the burned-out campsite," another man growled. "What were you doing there? How did you know about that place?"

"I'm looking for....." She made one last heroic effort to get her brain working. "I'm looking for Adrian. He's the leader of the Children's army. I need to find him."

"That doesn't explain how you knew about the camp," the first man growled and he lunged for her, seized her by the throat, and forced her head back against the rough bark. "Tell the truth or you won't live to tell another lie."

"I....I visited him there....." she stammered. "He's......"

"Liar!" the man roared and clamped his hand around her neck hard enough to stop her from breathing. "Adrian would never allow any human to visit his camp! You are a spy!"

She spluttered and struggled to form the words, *He's my son,* but no sound came out.

The man didn't understand what she was trying to say. He tore his hand away. "As soon as we find out who you really are, you'll be another dead slag rotting on the jungle floor."

She coughed a few times before she found the breath to speak. "Adrian......took me there.....he's......my son......My daughter.....is Iona......You must know about her.....Adrian.....sent Zair.....to bring me to their camp......so I could visit.....Iona....."

The spotted man spun around and narrowed his eyes at her. "You're lying."

"Iona's husband is Karim. His brothers are Kaiser and Kenji. Adrian's wife is Naia. Her sister is Nova and their brothers are Duke and Darius." She dared to look up at him. "I'm their mother. I raised them in Riverbend canton. You can ask Adrian. Just let me see him. It's....important."

The man shook his head fast and turned away. "Don't listen to her, Stone," one of his men murmured. "This could be a trick."

Dina studied them more closely. "Which canton are you all from? I don't recognize you."

"We are not from any canton!" Stone roared. "Now be quiet before I kill you myself."

He grabbed her arm and muscled her to her feet. Two of his men came forward, snatched her weapons from her, and tied her wrists together.

Before she realized what they were going to do, the second man looped her bound arms around his neck from behind, pulled her legs around his waist to carry her piggyback, and they all shot away into the trees at speed.

She tucked her head into her captor's neck to avoid branches and leaves whipping in her face. These Children traveled as fast as ever, leapt from branch to branch, and plunged down gorges with no thought to how high off the ground they were.

She peeked over her captor's shoulder once and relaxed when she realized that the Children were carrying her farther south. She could only hope they would take her closer to the shuttle.

This part of the jungle was miles away from the village, though—maybe even hundreds of miles away. The Mathus family wouldn't have walked to the village from here.

The Children dropped out of the canopy somewhere, but they didn't descend to the ground. They burst through a curtain of vines and tangled leaves to enter a completely different kind of camp.

Dozens of Children lived in the branches, but they didn't build houses. They'd interwoven the smaller branches, vines, and clumps of foliage to make nests for themselves.

Each nest covered a six-foot circular area with at least one Child lounging in it. Some of the nests were bigger with more than one person relaxing in the springy bed.

The Children who'd captured Dina carried her to the far side of the camp and landed in the branches of a giant tree. A large, muscular man with grey fur squatted on a thick tree limb talking to a dozen other Children perched in the branches around him.

He gave them orders about different parts of the jungle to search, patrol, and keep watch over. He warned his people about other patrols in different places and then assigned half of them to rendezvous with other Children in different parts of the country.

The man carrying Dina landed on a branch and balanced her there while he unhooked her hands from around his neck. He held onto her arms, but he did it gently to steady her and stop her from falling. He didn't yank her around or act at all hostile.

Stone sprang from branch to branch to get closer to his leader, but Stone didn't interrupt the briefing. He squatted on a different branch and waited for his leader to finish.

When the leader finally turned to look up at him, Stone vaulted down to the same branch and whispered in the leader's ear for a few minutes. Stone jerked his thumb over his shoulder in Dina's direction.

The leader's hard, dark-grey eyes snapped to her face and his features turned to granite. This was not good.

The leader nodded at Stone once and bounded from branch to branch to stop in front of Dina. "Who are you? What's this nonsense about you being Adrian's mother?"

"It isn't nonsense. I am his mother. You can ask him if you don't believe me."

"I don't have time to ask him and he doesn't have time to waste on spies like you. You could have made up this whole story to get near him and assassinate him."

"That's ridiculous," she countered. "How could I assassinate him when he's so much faster and stronger than I am? He has better hearing, vision, smell, and reaction time. He could kill me before I saw him coming."

He started to answer back, but she interrupted by glancing around at the other Children watching.

"Why do you find it so hard to believe that I'm his mother? All of you must have one human parent. Adrian and Iona are no different."

"That doesn't mean anything," the leader snapped. "How do you know about Iona anyway?"

Dina sighed heavily. "I already told Stone that. I'm her mother. Adrian sent Riyadh to bring me to their camp so I could visit Iona....." She trailed off.

All these Children must know by now that Iona had given birth to newborn Children. Dina had no reason to hide it from them, but she'd gotten so accustomed to keeping it a secret that she didn't want to say it out loud.

The leader glared at her through narrowed eyes. "No one apart from the Children is supposed to know."

"I'm her mother," Dina insisted. "They asked me to come. You can understand that, can't you?"

"What do you want us to do with her, Grey?" Stone asked in his ear. "I can kill her right now if you want me to. Then we won't have to worry about her causing us problems."

"We can't kill her until we at least check." Grey compressed his lips and waved at the man who'd been carrying Dina. "Bring her with us, Dash, but keep her tied up. We can't let her escape until we find out what she's doing here."

Dash raised Dina's arms to put them around his neck. "I already told you what I'm doing here!" she called over her shoulder. "I need to find Adrian! Just send one of your people to tell him I'm here!"

None of them listened to her. Dash took her on his back again and blasted out of the tree camp in a blur. Grey, Stone, and the others surrounded her in a posse moving through the canopy.

They set off heading south again. Dina gave up all hope of getting anywhere near the shuttle. At this rate, they would carry her so far away from it that she would never find it.

They stopped somewhere in a completely different jungle than the one Dina knew. She didn't recognize any of the tree species and the climate changed to a cooler, more temperate forest than the steamy jungle she was used to.

She also saw species of animals she'd never seen before closer to Prideland. Some kind of creature that looked like a mammal-bird-reptile hybrid bounced from branch to branch and squawked at the Children when they passed.

One of the Children lunged for a flock of these creatures and caught one in his mouth in midflight. The man launched himself past it without missing his stride and munched it down his throat while he continued hurtling through the canopy.

They kept going for so long that Dina gave up on keeping track of how far away from Prideland they might be. If the Children abandoned her here, she wouldn't be able to find her way back.

They didn't bring her any closer to seeing Adrian, either—or anyone else she knew. They would never be able to confirm that she was telling the truth—which meant Grey would probably order Stone to kill her.

They stopped in the canopy somewhere. Dina didn't see anything special about the place. Maybe it wasn't. Maybe the Children just picked some random branches to stop in. Maybe they didn't have any permanent camp at all.

Dash set Dina on a branch, unhooked her arms from his neck, and again made sure she could sit comfortably so she wouldn't fall off.

He made eye contact with her once and then started folding the nearby branches into another nest.

"You stay here," he told her when he finished.

He picked her up and placed her in the center of the circle. Then he climbed in with her, flopped down on the leaves, and curled over on his side.

"What canton did you come from, Dash?" she asked again.

He didn't look at her. "Bridgestone canton."

"I've never heard of that."

"It's to the south—farther south than here." He kept his head turned so he could continue to pretend that he wasn't talking to her. "No one from your part of the jungle has visited it."

She frowned. "You must have traveled far north to get near that burned-out camp."

He didn't answer, and just then, Stone came over with three other Children. They settled down to squat on the nearby branches, but they didn't pay any attention to Dash or Dina.

She decided to press her advantage. "Are you all from Bridgestone canton?"

"Of course we are," Dash muttered under his breath. "We've been together since the beginning. Grey was our leader until we met Adrian."

"What was it like in your canton?" she asked. "Were your parents supportive? I know some of the other parents pushed their Children out into the jungle?"

"Our parents were the best parents they could be," Grey interrupted. "No one will ever say anything against them."

Dina sat back on the branches. The nest bounced under her weight. "That's good. I'm glad we weren't the only ones."

"Who is we?" Stone barked. "The Children in the north say their parents were as bad as Moonlight canton."

"I don't know about that," she replied, "but some of us did everything we could to support the Children. We still do."

Grey humphed and turned away. "You talk a good line. You must have practiced a lot."

"How did you meet up with Adrian?" she asked. "Did you meet him by traveling north?"

"He sent messengers to contact us," Dash replied. "We thought we were the only Children in all of Prideland before he contacted us and asked us to join him."

Dina frowned to herself. "How long ago was that?"

Dash shrugged. "A little over two years ago. He sent a little white boy with fluffy, silky fur and blue eyes with a fleck of black in one of them. No one could believe such a little boy could survive in the jungle, but he could fight like anything. He even beat Case over there."

"Duke!" Dina murmured.

Grey spun around fast. "You know him?!"

"I raised him. I told you that. I know his and his sisters' parents in Prideland. My God, I had no idea Adrian was sending messengers out that far so long ago. He was just a boy himself then."

"He was more than a boy," Dash replied. "He was already a leader. We all saw that."

Dina almost said something else, but another shaking in the branches stopped her. The Bridgestone Children stopped talking and looked up into the canopy as another three Children moved in and dropped into the camp.

Dina shot upright when she saw them. "Cairo!" Her eyes darted to the other two. They were Riggs and Leroy.

Riggs's eyes went cold and mean when he saw her tied up. "What are you doing here, Dina?"

"You know this woman?" Grey demanded.

Riggs turned on him and bared his teeth. "Do you know who this is? This is Adrian's mother."

"She's all of our mother," Cairo interjected. "She's the only mother any of us have."

"Adrian could kill you if he found out you captured her and held her a prisoner like this," Riggs growled.

"It was an honest mistake," Dina interjected. "They were trying to protect Adrian."

"From you?!" Riggs sprang down into the nest, almost trampled Dash, and slashed the rope around Dina's wrists. Then Riggs glared at the Bridgestone Children nearby. "Give her back her weapons. You can't tell me you found her unarmed."

The Bridgestone Children squirmed until Grey signaled to one of his men. The guy came forward and handed Dina the sickle and knife she'd taken from Moonlight canton.

Riggs took hold of Dina's elbow and pulled her to her feet. "You're coming with us, Dina. We'll take you back to Adrian's camp."

"That's where I was trying to go when I met up with these people," she told him.

He shot another death glare at the surrounding Children. "You should have known better. You should have checked with us before you took her so far away from our territory." He stiffened. "Wait a minute. Did you find her in our territory?"

"Don't make a federal case out of this, Riggs," Dina told him. "It was a mistake. Let's just go and forget this ever happened. Don't let this come between you. The Children need to work together and not let things like this cause internal conflict."

"At least let us come with you to explain ourselves to Adrian," Grey interjected. "If he's angry and wants to punish us, at least let us face him and tell him ourselves that we messed up."

Riggs glared at him again and Dina murmured, "Let them come. We need everyone together on this."

Riggs jabbed his forefinger at Grey. "You better not have hurt her or you'll wish it was Adrian punishing you."

"No one hurt me," Dina told him. "Come on. Let's get out of here."

Dash tried to take Dina on his back again, but Leroy shoved Dash out of the way and elbowed over to Dina instead. He picked her up, settled her on his back, and the Children took off through the branches.

Chapter 42

The Children carried Dina back over all the territory the Bridgestone Children had covered to bring Dina this far south. All these delays racked her nerves. Would she ever find the shuttle in time? Every passing day made it seem less and less likely.

The Children carried Dina to a different camp somewhere. It looked exactly the same as the other Children's camps Dina had seen.

She didn't see any female Children, though. Everyone here was male. Dina was the only woman present.

The lack of females made the whole atmosphere much more warlike. She saw plenty of men skinning animals and others eating the raw meat. Seeing them like this made them seem much more feral and savage than Dina had ever seen them before.

The Bridgestone Children landed twenty feet away from an awning attached to one of the houses. Dina couldn't see Adrian over there at all. Too many Children crowded the area.

Riggs, Leroy, and Cairo shoved their way into the crowd and vanished behind the other Children. The Bridgestone Children waited to one side with Dina.

They waited for over two hours. Grey got progressively more nervous, paced up and down, and fidgeted openly.

Stone kept glancing toward the awning and then around at all the other Children. Only Dash acted calm and untroubled by this turn of events.

Groups of armed Children kept pushing their way out of the crowd under the awning. They talked rapidly, organized their comrades into parties, and left the camp heading in different directions.

More Children assembled to take their places. The steady hum of voices coming from all sides prevented Dina from hearing any of Adrian's briefing or even if he was briefing anyone over there.

She and the Bridgestone Children waited another hour before he pushed his way through the crowd, snapped a few parting orders over his shoulder, and strode across the camp toward where Dina and the others waited for him.

Grey and Stone both stepped out of line to meet him. Grey held up one hand. "We had no idea who she was. I swear it—and no one better say we hurt her. We never harmed a hair on her head. If you want to punish someone....."

"I don't care about that," Adrian snapped and turned to Dina. "What did you find out? Is there any chance of contacting anyone?"

"That's what I came to tell you. There's a crashed Coalition shuttle somewhere south of the village, but no one knows where it is. The only transmission equipment we might be able to use is the shuttle's onboard communications system. I need you to assign me someone who can help me track it down."

"And then what?" he countered. "We only have two more days before the assault."

"I know, I know," she exclaimed. "I came as soon as I could, but getting out here has been a nightmare. The only power source strong enough to boost the signal is in the city. As soon as we retrieve the equipment, I have to take it back there to hook it up."

"Are you sure you can access the power source?" Adrian asked. "I don't want to dump any more resources into this if it isn't going to work."

"We won't know if any of this will work until we try it—but wouldn't it be worth it if it does work? I'm only asking for one person, Adrian. Give me someone who won't be any good in the assault—someone small and weak. I don't care. I just need one of the Children to use their nose to find that shuttle. I can't find it on my own. No human can."

"I'll go," Dash volunteered.

"We'll all go," Grey added. "We'll prove to you that we're still loyal to the cause."

"I can't spare you," Adrian countered. "I need all the Bridgestone Children on the southern flank."

Stone frowned and rubbed his chin. "I think I might know where this shuttle is."

Dina grabbed his arm before she thought better of it. "You do?! Where is it?! Could you find it again? Are you sure? Oh, my God! Please say you know where it is."

"I know where there is a crashed shuttle. If it's the same shuttle you're talking about, then I could lead you straight to it. I know exactly where it is."

Dina had to stop herself from jumping up and down. "Oh, thank you so much! You're a hero." She rounded on Adrian. "Please, Adrian! Just give me one more day. Don't waste this chance. This could be the saving of all of us—including all of your Children. None of you want your Children growing up in this disaster."

He glanced at Stone. "Are you sure about this? I need you to take her there, get the equipment, and get back into position in time for the assault. We could all be dead if you leave us exposed on the south side."

"We'll be there," Grey told him. "No doubts. Nothing is more important than the assault."

"We have to travel back south anyway," Dash added. "We could just take her with us."

"You couldn't just take her with you," Adrian pointed out. "She needs to get back to the city to deliver the equipment to her friend at the power station."

"We'll take care of it," Grey told him. "We'll cover the south side of the assault and deliver her and the equipment to the city. Give us a chance to correct the mistake we made. We won't let you down."

Adrian gave him a hard look. "All right. You can do it—but be careful and be ready in time for the assault. I'm counting on you. All our lives are in your hands."

Grey nodded. "Consider it done."

Dash turned his back to Dina and she climbed on. She wrapped her arms around his neck and he held her under her seat with one arm before he shot away.

She happened to open her eyes once before he left the camp behind. Adrian stood on the ground in the same spot watching them out of sight.

Then the branches closed behind her and she lost sight of him. She shut her eyes and didn't watch to see where Dash was taking her.

That trip took even longer. She had no clue how far away he carried her. The Children stopped in the branches again. "The sun is going down," Grey decided. "We'll wait here and go after the shuttle in the morning."

Dina sat down on the branch to wait for Dash to weave another nest. "I sure hope this works."

Stone squatted on another branch nearby. "What do you want to contact the Coalition for? They don't even know we exist."

"That's the problem," she replied. "We want to call in the Armada to evacuate all of us—all the humans and Children on the planet. The cats can have the planet—and any helpers who want to stay behind. The rest of us will be out of here—all your wives and Children—and all the slags and escaped helpers who want to leave. None of us have to do this anymore."

Silence fell over the group. The rest of Grey's subordinates stopped what they were doing to listen.

"Do you really mean it?" Stone murmured. "We could just.....leave?"

Dina smiled at him. "Now aren't you glad you didn't kill me when you first found me?"

He looked away and went back to weaving his branches into a nest. "Are you going to throw that in my face all night?"

"Sorry." She looked away, too, but that only brought her face to face with all the other Bridgestone Children. "I'm really grateful to all of you for your help. If this works, it will be the best thing for all of us."

"None of us wants our Children to grow up like this," Grey replied. "Anything would be better than this."

"You're all Coalition citizens," she told them. "The Coalition has to accept you."

"What about the Children of helpers who've been on this planet for generations?" Dash asked. "How would we prove that we're Coalition citizens?"

"Let's worry about that after we evacuate," Dina told him. "We have to use the transmitter to contact the Armada and we have to do it before Adrian's assault." She turned to Stone. "What do you know about the shuttle?"

"I don't know anything about it. I found it in the jungle, but it was inactive. It's been there ever since."

"How did you find it?" she asked.

"I just stumbled on it once when I went out exploring." He flopped down in his nest, and a few seconds later, Dash finished and did the same thing.

"Who are you sleeping with tonight, Dina?" Dash asked. "You can take your pick of ugly, uglier, and ugliest." He pointed out himself, Grey, and then Stone one after the other.

She laughed. "I think I'll go with ugly." She climbed down into the nest with him. "Thank you for making this."

"Just don't kick in your sleep or I'll have to throw you out." He rolled over and made the branches bounce.

"He says that because *he* kicks," Stone interjected. "You come over and sleep with me if he gets too violent, Dina."

She laughed again and the other Children joined in. The canopy started to go dark. She stretched out on her back and looked up at the stars. "This is so peaceful. I've never slept in a tree nest before. This one is going in my travel diary."

"What's that?" Grey asked.

"It's a book where you record your memories so you can remind yourself later about what you did and experienced."

"Remembering is easier," Stone growled.

"Do you always nest in the branches?" she asked. "Some Children like to live on the ground, but I know the Children of Moonlight canton sleep in the trees, too."

"Everyone is different," Grey replied.

"I guess that's just another thing about the Children that no one knew before you were all born."

"Did you really raise all those Children?" Dash asked.

She sighed. "Twenty-nine of them. We had six others that got killed by cats in their first year. The rest are all out there fighting the war."

"Are they all yours?!" Stone exclaimed. "You must have been busy."

Dina laughed. "No, silly. Only Adrian and Iona are mine. The others are adopted—except for Egypt, India, Riyadh, Jericho, and Cairo. They're the nieces and nephews of......" She paused for a split second before she decided what to say next. "They're my husband's nieces and nephews. We raised all those Children together."

"That's incredible," Dash murmured. "That must have been hard."

"Not as hard as you might think. They became independent so fast. It was all over within a year. Then the Children moved out to the jungle and started taking care of themselves."

"I couldn't raise twenty-nine Children," Stone muttered. "That would drive me crazy."

She laughed again, but her exhaustion was catching up with her again. She drifted off looking up at the stars. "I sure hope the shuttle equipment still works....but we won't know until I take it back to the city."

Chapter 43

Dina woke up when the branches under her bounced. She opened her eyes to find Dash sitting up next to her. "Good morning," she told him. "You didn't kick me once."

"That's because you were so busy kicking me that you didn't notice." Her eyes shot open and he laughed at her. "Don't worry. You were so deep in your coma that you didn't move."

She joined in the joke and sat up, too. The other Children were just starting to stir.

Dash leapt over the side of the nest, vanished into the undergrowth, and came back a few minutes later with a gourd full of water. "Drink this, Dina. We'll go to the shuttle and then find some food."

She guzzled half the water and handed the gourd back to him. "Thank you. Where did you get this?"

"We're in our own territory now. We stash supplies for ourselves at strategic spots so we don't get caught in trouble."

He climbed onto a nearby branch. The other Children clambered out of their nests, stretched in the sunshine, and moved around doing this or that.

The party relaxed for a few minutes before Dash came over to Dina, took her on his back, and the Bridgestone Children set off through the jungle again.

They traveled much more slowly this time. Dina didn't recognize this area, either, but in a little while, they came to a part of the jungle where the trees grew thinner.

She caught glimpses of open fields beyond the fringe of canopy. The Children slowed even more and stopped more than once to survey the surroundings.

"Spread out and see if you can see anything," Grey told his friends. "Get down on the ground, Dash. Get that transmitter out of the shuttle as quickly as you can. You go with them, Stone. If anything goes wrong, pull out, and get into the trees. Leave the shuttle behind."

"You got it," Dash replied and dropped out of the high branches.

He paused on each limb. Dina didn't see anything until he stopped a hundred feet off the ground.

A shiny surface of polished metal shone in the sunshine. It reflected the light from the middle of a dense patch of vines and overgrown branches.

Stone landed on the branch next to Dash and Dina. Stone wrinkled his nose and bared his teeth in a snarl. "This place smells like humans."

"Humans landed in this shuttle," Dina pointed out. "They must have left a scent trace."

"It never smelled like this before." He sniffed and made a disgusted face. "It smells like helpers."

Dina spun around. "It does? What would helpers be doing out here?"

"I don't like it," he growled.

"What's the best way to get inside it?" Dash asked. "How does it open?"

"It has a hatch in the back," Dina told him. "I need to get behind it and clear all that vegetation."

"There's a rock face behind it," Stone growled. "You'll be protected there. You get to work opening the hatch. I'll cover you. Just work fast."

Dash sprang forward and vaulted from one branch to another until he got directly above the shuttle. Then he jumped off and plummeted straight through the vines onto the ground.

The ceiling of undergrowth whipped against Dina's sides and he landed under a dome of green. He and Dina stood right behind the crashed shuttle.

Dash spun from right to left and his normally placid expression turned murderous. "Go, Dina! Hurry! They're here!"

"Who?!" she whispered.

"Helpers! Get to work! Now!"

She whirled the other way and attacked the shuttle's rear hatch. She didn't see or hear any helpers, but she trusted these two men. They could hear and smell a lot more than she could.

The hatch mechanism didn't open. The shuttle had no power. She released the locking mechanism, but the lever to lower the hatch didn't unfold.

She had to find a stick and pry the hatch down. She pushed it to the ground and stepped onto it to force it to unfold the rest of the way.

She took one step on board. The shuttle's rear passenger compartment was empty except for a skeleton still buckled into its safety harness in one of the seats. Another skeleton occupied the pilot's seat up front.

She advanced to the cockpit and examined the controls. They seemed to be perfectly intact.

A wall of greenery blocked the front window. She couldn't see anything out there, so she knelt down and opened the access panel near the pilot's knees.

She saw right away what the problem was. A branch had skewered the shuttle's underside, impaled the power packs, and shut down all power to every one of the shuttle's systems.

If the power packs had been intact and charged up, she could have sent the signal from here, but the ship had been on this planet for more than four years. The power packs would have been useless either way.

The communications system seemed to be undamaged. That explained how Frank had been able to send the distress call right before the crash.

She fingered the wires running from the power packs to the communications transmitter. She didn't know enough about electronics to understand how to hook this up to the power station. She needed Tom for that.

She traced the wires back to the power packs trying to decide how to disconnect it without damaging anything. Right then, a screech from outside set her hair on end.

She jolted upright and spun around, but she didn't see anything but the rock face behind her. Dash wasn't there anymore.

She charged back to the hatch in time to see him locked in a battle against five helpers. Vicious snarls, screams, and tearing noises echoed through the jungle from farther away.

"Get that transmitter, Dina!!" Dash roared. "Do it now!"

She staggered back on board the shuttle, but when she made it to the cockpit, something slammed the ship from the side.

She pitched into the wall, bounced off, and lunged for the toolbox. More smashes, crashes, and the sounds of fighting threatened to snap her last nerve.

She tore open the toolbox and laid it on the floor next to the panel. She had to stop her hands from shaking when she snipped the wires connecting the transmitter to the ship's systems.

She only hoped she did it in a way that Tom would be able to work with. If worse came to the worst, he might be able to wire it up to the power station some other way.

Another blood-curdling scream shattered the last of her reserve. She dove for the transmitter, but it took all her strength to lift it out of place.

She set it on the floor, but before she could even examine it to see if it had been destroyed, too, Dash sprinted on board.

He bounded to the cockpit. "Come on!" he yelled and grabbed her.

She barely had time to gather the transmitter in both arms before he scooped her up and took off with her. He plunged through the hatch and Dina's heart dropped when she saw the Bridgestone Children locked in an epic battle against dozens of helpers.

Dash cleared the hatch and launched into the branches taking Dina with him. He didn't stop there. He kept springing from branch to branch and tree to tree covering the miles in massive bounds.

He clamped one arm around Dina's waist and held her tightly as he climbed to the highest canopy. Even then, he didn't stop. He kept racing farther and farther away.

He stopped miles from the shuttle and crouched in the crook of some small branches where the highest leaves gave a view of the sky.

"We'll be safe here for now, Dina," he panted.

"What happened?" she asked at last. "How did they sneak up on you? All of you should have seen them coming a long way off."

"They ambushed the shuttle," he growled. "They hid themselves around the site. They were waiting for us."

"How could they be? No one knew we were coming after this transmitter."

"Someone knew," he muttered. "I don't know who, but the helpers found out from someone."

She didn't know what to say, so she didn't say anything. She looked down at the transmitter in her hands.

It took all the strength of both her arms to hold it. She wouldn't be able to defend herself as long as she had it. She couldn't even hold onto the branch.

Dash read her mind and carried her to a different tree where he made a nest for her. She put the transmitter on the leaves next to her.

"Is it any good?" he asked.

"We won't know until we hook it up to a power source."

"Then all of this could have been for nothing." He glared into the distance and bared his teeth. "If I find out who did this, I'll make them suffer."

She studied the transmitter more closely. "How long do you want to wait here? I should take this back to the city as soon as I can."

"Not yet," he muttered. "The others are still down there."

She looked up. "Do you want to go back for them?"

"Not yet," he growled again. "Just wait a little while. Grey and Stone will tell us what to do."

She didn't ask how they would do that when they weren't here, but she couldn't leave on her own.

She studied the transmitter while she waited, but once again, she didn't know enough to tell anything about it.

She was just about to give up when Dash snarled under his breath. She looked up again. "What is it?"

"Do you hear that?" he muttered.

"I don't hear anything."

"Come on!" he grabbed her, shoved the transmitter into her hands, and took off with her through the trees.

"You're heading back toward the shuttle!" she shrieked, but he ignored her.

He plunged out of the canopy at terminal velocity....and then she heard it. A high-pitched scream of fear and pain echoed through the jungle coming from the ground.

Dash landed in a clearing where the other Bridgestone Children stood around five helpers lying crouched against a tree to one side. All the helpers were bleeding and three had broken arms or legs.

"We told you everything we know!" one man bellowed. "We can't tell you anything else."

"You're a liar as well as a coward," Grey snarled and waved to Stone.

Stone squatted down next to the man, gripped his claws around the man's broken leg, and squeezed.

The man screamed out in excruciating pain, but he couldn't get away. Stone tightened his grip more and more until his claws punctured the man's thigh.

"We'll just keep going until you tell us what we want to know!" Grey bellowed over the man's cries. "We can keep doing this all night!"

The man writhed and thrashed in agony. "All right! All right! I'll tell you—but you won't believe me!"

Grey waved to Stone, who retracted his claws, but he didn't stand up or go away.

The helper collapsed against the tree trunk whimpering and sobbing in pain. His friends averted their eyes, but they had to fight their facial features under control in a futile effort to hide their own distress.

"Now I'll ask you one more time," Grey snapped. "Who sent you out here to stake out this shuttle?"

"I.....I don't know his name....." the same helper whimpered. "He's.....in charge of....the loyal helpers....in the city....."

"It can't be Christian Mathus," Dina interjected. "He's dead."

"It's.....his brother......" the helper panted. "He took over.....after his brother's death. He told us....to come and keep watch over.....this place..... and kill anyone who tried to access the ship."

"Why?" Grey demanded. "Why did he want you to keep watch over it?"

"I don't know....."

Stone gripped his claws around the man's leg again, but the man changed his tune immediately.

"All right! He thinks you're going to use the shuttle to attack the city. The younger brother found out that the Children wanted this shuttle for something. He thinks you want to use its weapons systems against us."

Grey spun around to frown at Dina. Then he waved his men aside so the helpers wouldn't overhear him. "Are this vessel's weapons systems still operable?"

"They might be, but the ship is totally without power."

"Could we get them working?" Dash asked. "Could anyone?"

"No, not while the shuttle is on this planet. It would have to go back to the Armada repair yard and get fitted with an entirely new power system. No one on this planet will be able to use the weapons against anyone else."

"Why did he think we could use them?" Grey asked.

"He probably wants to take the shuttle and use the weapons against us instead," Stone pointed out.

"Peter Mathus was just a boy when the shuttle crashed here. He probably doesn't know enough about the power system to understand the damage—and I'm quite sure the Mathus family didn't check the damage before they abandoned the shuttle and went to the village. Frank might have said something about the communications system still working. Maybe Peter took that to mean that all of it was still working."

"We need to eliminate these helpers," Stone decided. "We can't leave any of them alive to report back."

"I agree." Grey swiped his hand at Stone. "Get the job done and then take Case, Dane, Lance, and Junior to hunt down the helpers that got away from us. Make sure none of them make it back to the city alive."

Stone dipped one nod and turned back to the helpers. Dina couldn't watch this. Grey and Stone were right, but knowing that didn't make it any easier.

Grey turned to Dash next. "Take her back north and report to Adrian about this. He'll decide what he wants us to do. Tell him the rest of us are still in position waiting for his word on the assault. Tell him we're ready whenever he says."

Dash didn't say a word. He snatched Dina off the ground and took off into the treetops again.

Chapter 44

Dash and Dina didn't talk when he paused in the highest branches. He left her sitting in the crook of a giant branch while he vanished into the jungle.

He came back ten minutes later carrying an enormous piece of handspun fabric. He laid it on his lap, took the transmitter from her, and wrapped the transmitter in the fabric.

Then he tied the extra lengths of cloth around her body to position the transmitter on her back. It rode in the fabric sling like a backpack.

He didn't ask her permission to handle her like this and she didn't protest. He was the one carrying both of them. If this made it easier for him, who was she to argue?

He positioned her on his back again and he seemed to travel much more comfortably now even though he could only use one arm. He covered the miles in no time and plunged back into Adrian's camp.

Even more Children assembled from all over if that was even possible. The crowd under Adrian's pavilion became even more enthusiastic to cluster around him and hear whatever he was telling them.

Dina sat down right away. She didn't unwrap the transmitter. She leaned against a tree while she waited for Adrian to find her.

She eventually fell asleep, and when she woke up close to sundown, she spotted Dash and Adrian talking a dozen feet away.

They kept their voices low, so she couldn't hear what they said to each other. Dash nodded a lot and Adrian made some wild hand gestures that Dash seemed to understand perfectly.

At the end of the conversation, Adrian clasped him on the shoulder and they shared a moment of deep eye contact before Dash turned away. He glanced over at Dina and his eyes locked on her, too, before he launched into the canopy and vanished out of her life.

She scrambled to her feet to face her son. He sauntered toward her and glanced down at the fabric-wrapped bundle at her heel. "Is that it?"

She rubbed her face trying to wake the rest of the way up. "Yeah. We got it—at great risk. The Bridgestone Children were great. You would have been proud of them."

He pretended not to hear. "What did you think? Do you think the transmitter will work?"

She shrugged. "I didn't see that it was damaged at all. The power system was, but not the transmitter. Tom will be able to tell us more."

"We don't have time for you to report to me about what he says. Just hook it up, send the message, and we'll take it from there."

"It's too late. You're launching the assault tomorrow. Sending the transmission won't change that."

"You don't worry about my plans. Just send the transmission. If the Armada comes for us, we can get off the planet regardless of what happens during the assault."

"Oh, I understand what you mean."

She shuffled her feet waiting for him to dismiss her. She wanted to leave. She wanted to find Tom and send the message right this minute, but some part of her recognized that she couldn't just walk away until Adrian told her to.

"Stay here tonight, Dina," he urged. "I don't want you going back to the city in the middle of the night."

"Going back into the city in the middle of the night will be the safest time," she pointed out. "I mean.....there won't be a safe time for me to go back to the city—not now that everyone knows who I am, but it will be safer if I go at night when no one is around."

"I don't want you to go back at all," he replied. "I would send someone else if I thought anyone else could do this job, but if you have to go, at least stay for tonight." He waved behind him. "Come have dinner with me and Naia."

She froze and stared at him. Did he just say that? Have dinner with him and Naia—like a family?

She shut her mouth and gulped down a lump in her throat. He didn't have to explain what this meant. He really did care about her. All this risk and danger must have finally proved to him that she was really on his side.

She only nodded and mumbled, "I'd like that."

He motioned behind him again, she picked up the transmitter in both arms, and they set out side by side through the camp.

She didn't know which house he was leading her to, so she took a dive and broke the ice herself. "I didn't tell you this before....I didn't tell anyone this before, but a friend of mine gave me some explosives. They're hidden at Renfroe's house. I didn't know what to do with them, but if you need them, I can get them for you. I don't know how to detonate them, but Tom does. I don't know if they'll be any help to you, but I can get them if you want them. I just wanted to let you know...."

She trailed off to stop herself from babbling so much. She didn't know how to talk to her own son.

He didn't look at her. He only murmured under his breath, "Thank you for telling me, Dina."

She couldn't think of anything else to say, so she didn't say anything. He ducked into some random house. Lamplight streamed from inside.

When Dina stumbled in carrying the transmitter, she discovered Naia, Karim, Kaiser, Kenji, Duke, Darius, the four Manx brothers, Link's nephews Riyadh, Jericho, and Cairo, Aries, Abdullah, Amir, and Aurelio sitting in a circle.

Naia was busy roasting a pile of sliced meat over a pot of coals. The rest of them ate their food raw.

Naia looked up and smiled at Dina. Dina gasped at the sight of Naia's sunken cheeks, the dark circles under her eyes, and the dull, patchy look of her fur.

"Oh, my God! You look awful!" Dina exclaimed.

Naia ran her wrist across her nose, sniffed, and gave a dry, tortured cough. "I feel awful," she groaned. "I feel like I'm half-dead."

"Don't worry," Adrian interjected. "She'll be fine in a few weeks."

Dina spun around. "She's.....Oh, that's wonderful! I'm so happy for you!" She gave Naia a quick hug and immediately backed off.

Naia sniffed again and looked down at her work. "It can't come soon enough."

"What are you doing *here?*" Dina asked. "You should have gone back to the gorge camp."

"I tried to send her, but she wouldn't go," Adrian replied. "She insisted on staying."

"You wouldn't eat or sleep if I didn't force you to," Naia countered.

He beamed at her affectionately. "You're right. I wouldn't. Then the whole war would come to a grinding halt."

Dina froze when she saw his expression. She'd never seen him so happy—ever. He never smiled like that—at anyone.

She didn't blame him. He could only smile like that at his pregnant wife. He was going to be a father.

Dina's heart flipped at that thought. How many other Children were giving birth all over the planet right now?

She had to suppress another surge of adrenaline. She had to send that transmission if it was the last thing she ever did in this life. She had to get her Children and grandchildren off this planet—and all the other Children around here.

All these people she kept meeting—all these men fighting this war—they all had wives and Children in danger. Zair's wife might already have given birth.

Some of Dina's Children were older than Iona. They probably became sexually mature before her—which meant they would be giving birth any day now if they hadn't already.

Naia distracted Dina by handing her a plate of cooked meat. She put a piece of it in her mouth and chewed while she thought over everything that had happened in the last few days.

If Stone and his men eliminated all the helpers that Peter sent out to the shuttle, he would hopefully never find out about the transmitter.

He might send out another party to keep the shuttle under surveillance. He would stay focused on stopping anyone from launching the ship to use against the Pride.

With luck, Dina could deliver the transmitter to Tom at the power station without anyone finding out it was there. Dina didn't care if she got caught as long as it happened after he took the transmitter off her hands first.

The other Children talked in low tones about the war, different groups of Children coming and going from different parts of the country, and which directions they would come to approach the city.

None of the Children present mentioned any of their wives giving birth and Dina didn't ask. She ate and talked with the others, but she kept most of the details of her mission and recent experiences to herself.

She let the waves of conversation wash over her like music. She didn't have to ask what this evening meant. She had her family back.

This evening meant that Adrian forgave her. He no longer considered her a slave to the Pride. She'd fulfilled her promise—to him, at least. She'd proven herself to him.

Iona was another story. Dina had no way of knowing if or when she would ever see her daughter or her grandchildren again, but that didn't matter. Only the evacuation mattered.

Once Dina got all the Children off the planet, then she could worry about Iona's opinion of her. Dina didn't expect Iona to change her mind until Dina actually made good on her promise. Dina couldn't expect anything less.

Dina didn't even really care if she herself got stuck on this planet as long as the Children and grandchildren made it off.

She would be able to die satisfied if she knew they were living somewhere else—somewhere they would be free to raise the next generation of Children without the constant threat of death hanging over their heads.

Naia finished cooking Dina's meal, set the pot of coals aside, and immediately curled up with her head on Adrian's lap. He stroked his hand across her cheek and down her head and neck. "Are you hungry?" he asked her. "Do you want to eat anything?"

"I can't," Naia muttered. "I feel sick."

"Come next door to our house," Darius told her. "It's dark and quiet there. You don't have to stay here listening to us talk."

"I don't want to go next door," she growled. "I want to stay here. You don't have to worry about me."

None of the others argued. Adrian kept passing his hand down her cheek and rubbing the fur on her neck. That angelic light shone out of his eyes when he looked down at her.

The love in the room stabbed Dina in the heart. She felt herself getting emotional again when she realized for the thousandth time how caring and close-knit the Children were—all of them.

An unstoppable well of pride overwhelmed her. These were her Children and they were the best people she'd ever met.

She couldn't take credit for that. They did it themselves. They made themselves into the strongest, most determined fighting force she'd ever known.

Yet they were also the most devoted to each other, the most loving, the most protective, and the most cohesive society she'd ever encountered. They deserved the best of everything and they were willing to fight for it.

She put another piece of meat in her mouth and chewed it. It tasted delicious. This moment fulfilled her fondest wishes of spending a quiet evening with her family again.

She couldn't ask to be any better place than this. She made the right choice to help their cause and give them the very best she had to give. She could be satisfied with herself for that, too.

Chapter 45

Riyadh set Dina down at the edge of the trees. "Are you sure this is where you want me to leave you?" He pointed southward. "You could get closer if you used the road."

"I can't take the chance that someone will see me and recognize me. In fact, I'm certain someone would see me and recognize me. I'm going up the river. I'll be all right."

She hitched the transmitter higher on her back. She'd retied Dash's cloth to carry the transmitter in a back sling.

Riyadh squinted into the distance. "I don't like this. I should go with you."

"You would stick out for all the world to see." She squeezed his elbow. "Go back to Adrian. I have to do this alone and I have to do it now. Don't wait for me. I'll see you soon."

She turned away, and before he could stop her, she darted out of the trees, sprinted down the riverbank, and dove into a thicket of bushes near the water's edge.

She didn't know how she would get farther upriver from here, but she couldn't wait around any longer.

She dropped onto all fours and crawled under the bushes as far as she could before the brambles stopped her. She waited there to catch her breath and then stuck her head up so only her eyes showed above the thicket.

She still had more than a mile to go before she made it to the edge of the city. Even hiding in the undergrowth like this would be dangerous.

She spotted helpers patrolling the streets even here. They left nothing to chance, not even in this remote part of the city with hardly anyone in it.

The power station perched on the hill in the distance. Getting near it would have been vastly easier in the middle of the night, but she wouldn't trade last night's experience for anything.

She could do this—now that she knew what she was protecting. She only had to think of that night.

She ducked back under the brambles, veered sideways, and worked her way another mile up the riverbank before she dared to look again.

More helpers strode up and down the river keeping an eye on everything. This was turning out to be a lot more difficult than she realized.

She couldn't run the risk of leaving the bushes now, not with so many helpers around. They could see almost every inch of the riverbank. The only surprise was that they didn't come down to the water's edge and actually hunt in the bushes for fugitive slags.

She stayed where she was to wait until dark. She had no idea when Adrian planned to launch his assault, but her way lay clear before her. She had to do this, assault or no assault.

She stayed hidden all day, but waiting didn't bother her anymore. She resigned herself to the inevitable. What Adrian did was out of her hands.

Darkness eventually fell. The Elite Battalion returned to the power station and went inside. Tom went with them. He didn't know Dina was here with the transmitter.

Most of the helpers went home. Different groups came out to take up the patrols, but not as many. They left wider gaps between groups now.

She snuck out of the bushes under cover of darkness and crawled the rest of the way up the river to the power station.

The helpers searched the street and filed up and down the greenway. She wouldn't be able to hide in there—not the way she did before. She wouldn't be able to signal Tom that she was here and wanted to hand off the transmitter to him.

She couldn't use the street to get to the building, either. She had to stay hidden along the river.

She clambered over the wall. The transmitter's weight nearly pulled her into the water. That would have been just spectacular—if she got the transmitter this far and ruined it by dunking it in the river at the last minute.

She grimaced with the effort, hauled herself over the wall, and circled the building on the river side. She hid behind the barrels near the back door. She didn't know how to contact Tom, but this was the closest she could get to the building without getting caught.

She let herself untie the transmitter and set it on the pavement behind the barrels. If she got caught and had to run away, she would be able to do that more easily without the transmitter strapped to her body.

She stretched the kinks out of her back and settled in for a long wait until morning. Adrian would start the assault tomorrow. What happened after that was anybody's guess.

Maybe she would get lucky and the assault would take longer than anticipated. It had to. The cats would roll out to stop the Children from invading. That just might give her and Tom enough time to send their message.

The Armada wouldn't arrive immediately, though. They might not get here for a week. The war could stretch on that long and probably would.

She was just getting ready to sit down behind the barrels when she heard footsteps inside the building. They were getting closer.

She stiffened and her hand flew to her sickle when the door burst open and a man strode outside. He halted at the edge of the wall, pulled open his pants, and relieved himself into the water.

Dina stared at the back of his head. Was that Tom? She couldn't be sure in the darkness, but she couldn't run the risk that he would go back inside without her finding out.

She stood up. He pulled up his pants, turned around, and she stepped out of hiding. "Tom—it's me—Dina," she whispered.

"Where have you been?!" He rushed her and whispered low. "I've been worried sick about you! The helpers were all saying you'd been executed, but they usually do that publicly where everyone has to attend."

"I had to get the transmitter. It's been a mission all on its own."

"You got it?!" he breathed. "Is it intact?"

"I think so. Maybe you can tell me. I have it here."

She pulled the transmitter out from behind the barrels and lowered it into his arms. He carried it around the building to get a better look. "It still isn't bright enough," he muttered. "I'll have to look at it in daylight."

"Adrian plans to assault the city tomorrow. I don't know when or how or from which directions." She gave him a rueful grin. "Just saying—no pressure or anything."

He chuckled under his breath. "Right. If it is intact, we'll just have to try hooking it up to the power station, but we need to do that when no one else is around."

"That's only during the day."

"Meet me back here at noon tomorrow." He scowled at another patrol of helpers coming up the street. "Will you be able to stay out of the helpers' way until then?"

"I'll figure it out. It will be easier now that I'm not lugging that around with me." She touched his arm. "I'll see you tomorrow."

She slipped back down the wall and hid in the bushes closer to the building. She waited until she heard him go back inside and then she snuck all the way back up to the building.

She didn't tell him that she wouldn't be able to get near the building in daylight. She would already have to be there to meet him.

Telling him that would only worry him. She found a different hiding place behind the building—somewhere neither the Elite Battalion nor the helpers would be able to see her. Now she really could settle down to wait.

She rested her head on her arms and fell asleep. She woke up when the building door slammed. The Elite Battalion's wheelbarrow squeaked away into the distance.

She listened to the helpers talking about which areas they'd patrolled during the night and which directions they thought an invasion would come.

What dopes they were. They didn't know Adrian. When the invasion came, they wouldn't see it coming.

She dozed off again and woke up with a jolt when she heard the building door slam again. No one should have been here at this time of day.

She didn't hear the wheelbarrow wheel squeaking, either. Tom must have found a way to get back here while the rest of the Elite Battalion was still out working in the city.

She crept out of her hiding place and tiptoed to the building door. No sound came from inside. She had to hide when another helper patrol passed by. Then she dashed for the door, pulled it open, and stepped inside.

The weir extended into the building. She stood at the edge of the spillway inside the building. A solid pad of concrete separated the door from the spillway. That was the whole building.

She surveyed the area in confusion. No way could the Elite Battalion be living in here. She didn't even see any blankets. The men would have to sleep on the bare concrete.

She was still standing there trying to figure it out when Tom strode in from somewhere behind her. "Over here, Dina," he told her.

She turned around to find him coming through a different door. Of course the weir couldn't have been the whole building.

He led the way to a hallway behind the spillway. It branched off into three rooms full of wooden bunks. Those rooms actually looked comfortable and inviting.

The last room at the end of the hall contained a bank of electronic equipment that didn't look like it had been used in decades if not centuries. Tom had set the transmitter on a workbench in front of the equipment.

Dina strode down the wall studying the equipment. "Does the power station still work?"

"Oh, it works," he replied. "The Pride doesn't use it. I don't even think they know what it's good for."

"How do you know it still works?" she asked. "It could be old and defunct."

"It works. Watch."

He crossed the room to a breaker switch on the wall and threw it. Electricity flowed into the equipment and all the instruments flickered on.

Dina darted back and forth checking everything. "This is amazing! This station produces enough power to electrify the whole city!"

"It isn't amazing when you think about how these cats got here. There must have been a Coalition colony here—or something similar." He sat down on a stool in front of the workbench and started tinkering with the transmitter.

She watched him over his shoulder. "Can you hook it up?"

"That's what I'm doing. Give me two seconds."

She bit back a grin. "I'm a bundle of nerves!"

"Keep your cool. If this works, it could be weeks before we get a response."

"I don't care as long as someone hears us."

He frowned at the wires in the back and then twisted them together with more wires connected to the equipment.

He fiddled with the transmitter, opened the back panel, and adjusted something internally before he sat back down. "Okay," he breathed. "Here we go."

He switched on the transmitter and read a series of dials on its front panel. Then he flipped on the speaker, lowered his mouth to it, and called, "Mayday, mayday. This is Commander Tom Sharples, formerly of the Armada Destroyer *Savannah*. We are stranded on the planet Daustina in need of immediate evacuation and rescue. I repeat. Mayday, mayday. The former *Savannah* landing party is stranded on the planet Daustina in need of immediate evacuation and rescue. Please respond."

He went back to checking everything and then transmitted the planet's coordinates.

Dina listened in silence and a prickle passed over her scalp at the tone in his voice. He stepped into this so effortlessly. He remembered the coordinates exactly from the landing team's few briefings on the *Savannah*.

He made a few more adjustments to the controls and made one last broadcast. "Mayday, mayday. The population of Coalition citizens on this planet is in distress and on the brink of annihilation from the native predatory species. Please send multiple destroyers to evacuate the population. I repeat. The population of Coalition citizens on this planet is in distress and on the brink of annihilation from the native predatory species. I invoke article 486-37 of the Armada Charter to request immediate military assistance and civilian evacuation. Please respond with all due haste to prevent any further loss of Coalition lives."

He waited, but when he still didn't get a response, he switched it off. "That's all we can do right now."

"How long should we wait for a response?" she asked.

He shrugged. "Who knows? It sounds like we're all going to have our hands full with this assault in the next few days."

She stared down at the transmitter. Her brain didn't want to accept that it really was over—her part of it, at least.

He glanced at her over his shoulder and then turned around. "Are you okay? You did it. You can take it easy now."

"What does that mean? I don't know what to do now."

He burst into one of the rare smiles she'd seen from him lately. He laid his hand on her shoulder. "Maybe you should go back out to the jungle, find a nice, comfortable, safe place, and get some rest. You did your part. You can sit back and let the rest of us take some of the risk for a change."

She heard her voice saying, "Yeah," but her mind didn't understand any of that. She couldn't rest now. She was just getting started. She just didn't know what she was getting started on.

He got off his stool and turned all the way around to face her, but at that moment, they both froze when they heard the squeak of a wheel outside.

Tom's head whipped sideways. "They're coming back! They shouldn't be here right now!"

"Hide the transmitter!" she whispered. "I'll distract them!"

"You can't!" He hissed. "If you get caught, you really will get executed!"

"Just hide that transmitter! Don't worry about me! I don't matter! Do it, Tom!"

She whirled away, raced down the hall, and got back to the weir just as the squeaky wheel stopped right outside the door. She didn't have a moment to lose.

She exploded out of the building, nearly collided with the Elite Battalion, and swerved hard to her right.

She already knew the barrels blocked her path in that direction, but she did it anyway. She plowed into the barrels, fell over, and the whole stack collapsed on top of her.

The maneuver got away from her and worked out better than she ever dared to hope.

The men of the Elite Battalion all yelled in surprise and got the helpers' attention. Three different patrols spun around and started heading up the hill to intercept the fugitive.

Dina floundered to get out from under the barrels, kicked a few of them away, and they started rolling down the hill toward the helper patrols closing in.

The helpers dodged, but not quickly enough. Barrels slammed into some of them and knocked them over.

The Elite Battalion had been so cowed by their circumstances that none of them stepped out of line to try to capture Dina. None of the men moved at all. They'd already gone too far by opening their mouths in public.

She somersaulted out of the stack of barrels, vaulted to her feet, and bolted into the one avenue where she knew she could get away—the greenway.

She raced down it searching for a way out and ran headlong into another helper patrol. She surprised them and they didn't get into position in time to catch her.

She burst through them, flung herself over a wall into someone's garden, charged out onto the street, swerved a few blocks to the south, and kept on going.

She changed her course often enough to leave the helpers behind and eventually blundered into the same neighborhood where Christian Mathus had held her and Sonya as prisoners.

She avoided his estate. It must be his brother's estate by now, but this neighborhood offered an unlimited number of hiding places.

She dashed up the path behind everyone's brick walls and eventually found a tree dangling its branches close enough to the ground for her to scramble up.

She planned to use the tree to get over the wall and hide somewhere in the neighboring estate. As soon as she got into the branches, she remembered the Bridgestone Children and changed her mind.

She scaled higher into the treetops. The trees of this neighborhood didn't grow closely enough together and they didn't have the right kind of branches to weave into nests.

She chose the next best thing, found a comfortable crook between two split trunks, and settled between them to wait.

Chapter 46

Dina startled out of a doze when she heard helpers' voices nearby. She had to steady herself when she found herself perched in the branches of a huge tree.

The helper patrol passed directly underneath her. They could have seen her if they'd only just looked up.

A smooth, male voice snapped her to high alert. "Don't worry. They won't find you."

She spun around and had to look in all directions before she spotted Osiris balanced on another limb not far from her head.

She collapsed back in relief. "You scared me! How did you find me?"

"You are not difficult to find, my dear," he murmured. "You have a very distinctive smell. Any cat can follow your every move through this city."

"Why haven't the others come after me yet, then?"

"They're far too busy with *this* business." He sniffed at the helpers on the ground below them. More patrols kept passing back and forth. "These helpers have become so fanatical that no cats want them around anymore."

"The cats would do better to worry about the Children than what their helpers are doing. These helpers are actually trying to defend the Pride. The Pride will need all the help it can get against the Children."

"I actually came to find you to talk to you about that," he told her. "I wonder how you would feel about making another embassy to the Children's leadership to propose peace. We'd be prepared to incorporate the Children into the Pride with all the benefits, privileges, and advantages of the cats themselves."

Dina's head shot up. "Is this your idea? Are any other cats going along with this—apart from Renfroe, I mean?"

He sat down and blinked at her. Then he gazed off into the treetops. "It's a pipe dream of my own that I could have my Children in my life."

"I'm glad you realize that because the Children will never make peace now. Even if the Pride hadn't blown that long ago, the Children would never incorporate into the Pride. They're far too independent. Rigid social structures are repulsive to their nature. Besides, there are too many cats who still want the Children dead."

"Ah, yes," he murmured. "Is there any way I can help my Children—any way at all?"

"I'm afraid not," she replied. "The war is out of both our hands now."

He murmured again, "Hmmm," and gazed down at the helpers striding back and forth between the estates. They even stopped under Dina's tree to discuss where to go to search for fugitive slags who'd invaded the city.

Dina studied Osiris more closely. She really wished she could do something for him. He didn't ask for anything except to help his Children.

"You know," she began. "I got very lucky when I became Renfroe's helper. I can see that you're a good benefactor, too. It's too bad more benefactors aren't like you."

"I wasn't like this before the Children's war," he murmured. "I was the same as all the others before this. The Children are the only reason I changed my attitude. You and I could never have had a conversation like this if not for the Children's war."

He sighed again and blinked down at the helpers on the ground.

"I've fathered dozens of litters of kittens and seen them grow and raise families of their own—yet my Children are the ones I think about in my dark hours. It's my great regret that they won't be in my life or even know how much they mean to me. Not even you telling them can make up for me not being the father they should have had. Another man filled that role in my place. I will never live down the shame of that." He glanced up at her. "You are the only person in any position to help the Children."

She made a face. "I'm in no position to help any Children, not even my own."

"The best way to help the Children is to help you." He stood up and tiptoed down the branch toward the nearest estate wall. "Follow me and I'll show you a way to get out of the city."

"Wait!" she called after him. "I can't go anywhere. I'm wanted—by everyone. If they catch me, they'll execute me. They've already tried more than once."

"I know that, but I will make sure they don't catch you or execute you. They *will* catch you if you stay in this tree. The cats will find you and they'll tell the helpers where you are. Follow me if you want to get out of this city alive."

She hesitated to leave this tree. It was the best hiding place she'd found so far.

A few more patrols passed and then the greenway fell silent beneath her. She would never find a better time than now to get out of the tree. More helpers might come back at any time.

She scrambled out of the crook between the split trunks. Osiris hopped down onto the estate wall beneath him and waited for her to lower herself onto it, too.

He leapt down onto the soft moss behind the wall. He landed inside the estate behind a thick clump of trees. It hid him and Dina from anyone passing through the grounds beyond.

She crouched on top of the wall watching and listening with every nerve alert. She heard helper voices coming up the greenway again. They would be able to see her from the path.

She didn't have a choice, so she jumped down onto the moss next to Osiris. He moved out of the way and then strutted a few paces into the trees. "Follow me. We must stay out of sight."

She crept behind the trees, but he followed a route to make sure they were never in any danger of being seen. He stayed close to the wall for a while and then advanced into the garden between two towering hedges that formed walls.

Dina kept glancing behind her to make sure no one saw her. Osiris pranced in front of her with his tail held high.

"How do you know so much about this place?" she asked. "Whose estate is this?"

"It's mine." He glanced over his shoulder at her. "This is my house."

Her jaw dropped and she actually stopped walking. "You....live here?"

"Me and my females and some of our kittens.....and quite a few helpers. This way."

He turned at the end of the lane of hedges and stepped under another patch of trees.

The estate ended here and a section of the paved driveway curved around the house to meet up with the kitchen yard.

A wagon sat parked by the door and the young driver walked back and forth between the wagon bed and the kitchen. He carried boxes, crates, and a few barrels inside, came back emptyhanded, and reloaded for another trip.

"Do you see that wagon?" Osiris murmured low. "It's going north after this. The driver lives in one of the northern villages. He comes into town to deliver subscription to the Pride. Then he drives home in the evening."

"How does that help me?" Dina whispered. "Is he sympathetic to the Children's cause?"

"Not at all. If he sees you, he'll turn you over to the helpers, so you must make sure he doesn't see you."

"How do I do that?"

"I'll go inside the house and distract him by calling him to do a job for me. As soon as he's gone, go out there and hide yourself in his load. Once he drives north from the city, you'll be able to get off the wagon somewhere and escape unseen."

She studied the scene more carefully, but she didn't see any flaw in his plan. "Um....okay. I can do that. Thank you."

He walked away from her, slipped into the house, and came back with another piece of cloth tied into a bundle. "Here's some food you can take with you. That should keep you going until you get back to the Children."

She couldn't thank him again and he didn't give her a chance to.

"Take care of my Children, Dina," he murmured. "I know you will. You always have."

He walked away again without waiting for a response. He strolled right out into plain view, entered the house through one of its opulent rear terraces, and vanished from sight.

Dina hunkered behind the trees waiting for her opportunity. How long would this take?

She never expected a cat to help her like this. Her heart overflowed with gratitude that Osiris would give her a chance like this, but he always did care about his Children. He was one of the very few cats to risk his life to save his Children.

She stiffened when she heard his voice calling inside the house. The driver stood at the wagon bed arranging his boxes into another stack.

He left his work, went into the house, and she heard Osiris talking to the young man in there. Now was her chance.

She darted out of hiding, hustled over to the wagon, and climbed on. A tarpaulin lay draped over a bunch of barrels behind the wagon seat. She dove under the tarp, shifted the barrels around to make a hollow big enough to hide herself, and pulled the tarp back into place just as the driver came back.

He spent another hour unloading more stuff, going back and forth to the kitchen, and carrying on a flirtatious conversation with some woman in the kitchen. He took a lot longer than he should have to finish his job.

His ox kept shifting its weight and heaving massive sighs. The driver finally climbed into the seat, got his ox moving, and the wagon rumbled out of the city.

Dina huddled under the tarp in the dark and strained her ears to listen to every sound. She kept her hand on her weapon the entire time, but after an hour of endless squeaking, jostling, bumping, and rumbling, she sank onto the wagon boards to wait.

She waited a long time before the axel sounds changed. She stole a peek out from under the tarp. The wagon was just leaving the city.

She didn't recognize the road except that it led north. She'd never seen this part of Prideland and knew absolutely nothing about it.

She had to wait another several hours before the wagon got far enough out of the city. She couldn't leave the wagon this close to where she might get captured.

The wagon climbed a steep hill, and at the top, she gazed back over the landscape at the city she'd just left.

She knew that city so well. She knew everything that went on there and she could see plain as day that there was no assault going on. No Children invaded from all sides. No escaped slags mobbed the streets.

The city basked peacefully in the evening light. No sounds of mayhem or chaos drifted on the breeze. The few helpers she could see from this distance went back and forth on domestic errands or in the patrols.

She stared at the scene and let the truth sink in. Adrian didn't launch the assault. Did he ever plan to? Did he change his time frame without telling her? Did he do all this to trick her somehow?

The same truth sank deeper into her heart and mind. What Adrian did no longer mattered. She did what she had to do. She and Tom had sent the transmission.

Neither of them could know if anyone received their mayday call. If they did or if they didn't, he and Dina would just have to keep trying until they got a response.

Chapter 47

Dina jumped out of her skin when the wagon stopped suddenly. She'd been thinking about something else when the wagon turned off the road and parked on top of a high hill.

She tightened her grip on her weapon when she heard the driver talking to people. "It's good to see the hunt again," a husky man's voice exclaimed. "It seems like the old way is dying too fast."

"It isn't dying," the driver told him. "We'll get over these troubles and the Pride will be stronger than ever. You'll see."

"I hope you're right," a woman replied. "Nothing seems the same since the Children's war started."

"At least we can still enjoy the hunt," a younger, higher female voice pointed out. "The hunt proves the Pride is still the strongest force on this planet."

"Will you have room for the bodies in your wagon?" the older man asked. "I thought you'd come with an empty wagon bed."

"I'm sure it will be enough," the driver replied. "The hunts never leave too many bodies—not like reducing a whole canton."

"You're right." The older man's voice faded as though he was turning away. "Which cats are coming out? Does anyone know?"

"I heard it was Adiel, Kian, and Adonis....and maybe some of his brothers," the younger woman replied.

"Oh, good," the older woman gloated. "I love watching Adonis hunt! He's so powerful and dangerous!"

"They should come from the head of the valley over there," the older man told them. "Those two hills will box in the slags so they can't get away."

Goosebumps raced down Dina's arms. These people were about to watch the cats hunt slags.

Dina had been so preoccupied with the Children and the war. She didn't think the cats still hunted people. She should have known better.

She had to get off this wagon before the helpers discovered her here. She wedged herself between the barrels.

The wagon bed pointed toward the road—away from where the four helpers gazed down into the valley to watch the hunt. They wouldn't see her get off the wagon and slip away.

She crawled to the edge of the wagon bed and slowly, painstakingly lowered herself to the ground. She made extra sure not to make any noise that could distract the helpers.

She took off running for a clump of trees on the other side of the road, plunged into the shadows, and hid herself with her heart pounding out of her chest.

A cheer drew her attention back to the helpers. They all stood with their backs to her. None of those people would see her now.

The younger woman's long blonde hair bounced up and down when she jumped into the air with excitement. "Look at Adiel go!" she squealed. "He's going to box those slags in! Go, Adiel!"

The driver crushed his knuckles into his mouth. "Oooh! That slag almost got Kian!"

"Those two men are teaming up to fight back!" the old man exclaimed. "The woman is breaking away! She's going to escape. Get her, Adonis! Cut her off! She's making for the river!"

Dina tiptoed sideways through the trees. She took advantage of the helper's excitement to put more distance between herself and them.

She came out on the road two hundred yards around the corner where they couldn't see her. She picked up the pace and started looking around for another place to hide.

Osiris said the driver came from the north. The man had stopped his wagon too far away from the city to take the bodies back there. He must be planning to transport them farther north to another city somewhere else in Prideland.

That meant he would drive past Dina to get there. She would need to conceal herself and then figure out a way to return to her own part of the country.

This was definitely not turning out to be the nice, comfortable, safe place Tom had in mind for her to recover from her strenuous ordeal.

She turned another corner. The road followed a ridge with steep hillsides plunging into the valley to the left. The river snaked along the valley floor and the hills cut this part of the valley off from where the cats were hunting.

Dina started to turn away when a flash of gold made her stop in her tracks. The woman the helpers mentioned had broken through a gap between the hills.

She raced up the river at speed with three pumas on her tail. She ran well, but they closed the gap and caught up with her on a promontory where the river turned around a gravel bar.

She spun around to confront them and her long blonde hair whipped across her face. Dina caught a split-second's glimpse of the woman's face before she turned aside to confront her attackers. It was Tania.

She wore the handsewn clothes of the cantons and carried two short flail-type weapons. Spiked balls twirled from the ends of chains attached to the handle pieces in both her hands.

She crouched there flexing her knees and swinging her flails at the three cats. They circled closer to surround her on all sides.

Dina's eyes darted over the landscape just as three more people charged up the river through the same gap between the hills. All three of them wore canton-style clothing and more cats hounded them every step of the way.

Dina didn't think twice. She ripped her two weapons out of her belt and plunged down the hillside to intercept the cats. She couldn't stand by and watch them hunt these people down.

The three pumas circled tighter around Tania, but she held them off—for now. The other people didn't fare so well. Ten cats overtook them and closed the fleeing people in a dragnet.

Two men turned back to defend the others. Two panthers and two lions split away from the pack to go after those two men while the other cats kept racing over the landscape to bring down the fugitives.

Dina barreled down the hill and through another stand of trees. It separated her from the river and hid her approach just enough to get her to within striking distance of the cats.

She spotted a tiger and a jaguar closing in on a different woman and three young teenage boys. Dina blasted out of the undergrowth, and went for the nearest cat to her, which was the tiger.

He saw her at the last minute, but she surprised him into stopping, crouching, and coiling himself into a compact ball. He flattened his ears and hissed up at her as she raised her sickle to strike.

His own defensive posture worked against him. He could have torn her in half if he'd only answered her assault. She leapt for him, adjusted her first strike, and drove her sickle down into his body.

She aimed for his ribs and the blade thunked into his chest. He reared back with a frightful roar and she struck out with her knife, slashed his throat through the thick ruff of fur, and yanked her sickle out to spring away.

He staggered and she veered hard to run upriver toward Tania. The other cats following the woman and the three boys broke off when they realized another person was coming out of nowhere to help these people.

The pumas surrounding Tania didn't recover as fast. Dina charged one of them from behind and he whipped around to meet her.

Tania struck out and smashed one of her spiked flails down onto his back hard enough to crack his spine. She had no problem fighting cats now.

The other two pumas hesitated and Dina plunged for one of them. Tania went after the other.

The two cats spun right and left trying to counter both women at the same time. That moment of distraction gave Tania and Dina enough time to get close to them.

The two pumas recovered just in time. Both cats dodged away from the women coming at them. Dina's target cat veered left and Tania's target cat spun right.

They crossed paths, and without realizing what they were doing, each cat ran straight into weapons range of the other woman who hadn't been attacking them.

Dina struck out at her target cat and wound up swinging at the other puma instead. Tania did the same thing at the same time.

Dina brought her sickle down with all her strength. She'd been aiming for her target cat's head, but the second puma was running too fast and got farther underneath the blade than she expected.

The blade slammed down into the hollow between his head and his neck and he dropped right there at her feet.

Tania swung her flail down at her target cat's head and hit her mark. She flattened the cat into the gravel and caved its skull in.

The other cats slowed their approach when they saw everyone fighting back. Dina's sudden appearance had given the boys a chance to make a stand, too.

They took out the panther. The woman and two other men teamed up on the jaguar.

The group brought all the cats down in a few minutes until none remained. "Where's Johann?" Tania asked.

"He fell back there." One of the boys jerked his thumb over his shoulder.

Dina followed his gesture and spotted the helpers standing on the hilltop watching. They didn't clap or cheer or jump up and down. They stared down at the people and dead cats in the valley. The hunt wasn't supposed to end like this.

"Let's get out of here before they get any ideas," Tania muttered. "Come on, Dina. You can come with us to our canton. You'll be safe there."

Chapter 48

Dina followed Tania up the river toward the distant hills. The helpers on the hilltop watched Tania's group pass out of sight.

"How far away is your canton?" Dina asked.

"Five miles," Tania replied over her shoulder. "What are you doing this far north? Aren't you living at Riverbend canton anymore?"

"No, I'm not and what I'm doing this far north is a long story—too long to tell."

"We have a five-mile walk," Tania pointed out. "We have all the time in the world."

"Let me put it this way. I got stuck in the city and those helpers' wagon was the only way out of town. I stowed away and rode it here."

"Why did you go back to the city?" Tania asked. "You went to all that trouble to get out of it."

"Like I said, it's a long story. What about you? I heard you were living at Northfall canton."

"That's where we're going now," one of the boys replied from the back.

Dina turned around and surveyed the rest of the group. They hung back to let Dina and Tania talk.

"Thank you so much for your help," the woman exclaimed. "It's so rare for anyone to help another person these days."

"It isn't so rare. Besides, I'm a fugitive myself. We can help each other."

"You fought those cats so well," the same boy remarked. "That was impressive."

Dina found herself smiling at him. "I've had a lot of practice—unfortunately. How often do the cats come out to hunt you?"

"This is the first time in a long time," one of the men replied. "We thought they might have stopped.....what with everything else that's going on."

"The Children were planning to launch an assault today," Dina pointed out and squinted at the sky. "I guess it's too late for that now."

"It's the Children's fault this happened," one of the boys grumbled. "This whole thing is the Children's fault."

Dina spun around to stare at him. "What are you talking about? It's because of the Children that the cats haven't come out to hunt you sooner. The Children are waging war against the Pride."

"The Children are freaks," a different man snarled. "Killing all the Children was the one thing the Pride got right."

Dina actually stopped walking and gaped at them in horrified shock. Then she glanced at Tania. "Did you do this? Did you convince these people to hate the Children?"

"I didn't have to. Any sane person can see that the Children are an aberration. They don't belong on this planet. At least some people still have the sense to see that."

"We killed as many of them as we could, but they were too strong," the woman added. "We barely managed to drive them out."

Dina couldn't even gasp. "You.....what?!"

"We killed all the Children who were too young to fight back," the first man repeated. "We got at least thirty of them, but the others escaped. They set up a camp in the trees outside our canton. We sent out raiding parties to reduce them, but the Children always got away from us. They were too fast."

"You....killed.....your own Children?"

"They aren't our Children," the woman snapped. "They aren't human. They're filth. This planet is better off without them."

"But.....your slags!" Dina blurted out. "The Pride says the same thing about you! Those cats came out to reduce you—to kill you in cold blood. The factors are out there telling everyone that *you're* filth and that the planet is better off without you.....and you have the nerve to turn around and do the same thing to defenseless babies?! Are you all out of your minds?"

"Give it a rest, Dina," Tania cut in. "You always had your head in the clouds about the Children. You would throw your own life away for a bunch of genetic anomalies who never should have been born. The Pride was right to kill as many Children as they could. They had to keep the human and feline bloodlines pure. No one would know which species was which otherwise."

Dina spun around to confront her. "How can you go along with this? You're talking about your own sons!"

"That's exactly what I am talking about," Tania countered. "I never should have let you keep them."

"What is she talking about, Tania?" the woman asked. "You said you didn't have any children."

"I don't," Tania snapped.

"That's a blatant lie, Tania!" Dina fired back and she turned around to face the group. "She has three Children—three boys. Their father is a panther and the boys are all as black as he is. Their names are Karim, Kaiser, and Kenji and they're....."

"Shut up, Dina!" Tania barked.

Dina ignored her. "You all might like to know that Tania came to my benefactor's house begging me to help her when she got pregnant because she was in fear for her life. I risked my life to smuggle her out of Prideland. That's why she's standing here alive and well—because of me! She gave birth to her sons in my house and then left them for me to raise while Tania ran off to Northfall canton so she could pretend they didn't exist."

"Khalid forced himself on me," Tania countered. "I never wanted those Children. I should have reduced them myself the minute they were born."

"He never forced you to do anything. You told me yourself you planned to give yourself to him to gain his favor."

"Is that true, Tania?" the woman asked.

"Your sons are the best men I've ever known," Dina went on. "They're out there fighting cats to save all our lives! That's a hell of a lot more than you cowards are doing! The Children are humanity's only hope for survival on this planet as you've just seen during the hunt."

"If you think that, you're as bad as they are and you deserve to die, too," one of the men growled.

Dina's hand flew to her weapon again. "You bastard! I never should have helped any of you during the hunt. I should have let the cats take you. Then the world really would be a better place. Raising the Children was the greatest privilege of my life. I'm proud to be a mother to all the Children, including the ones that cowards like Tania abandoned on my doorstep. If you really cared about what happens on this planet, you would ally yourselves with the Children."

"Never!" the second man spat. "If any of them come near our territory, we'll hunt them down."

"You wouldn't make allies of the Children even to save your own lives?!" Dina roared. "Have you completely lost your minds?!"

Everyone in the group glared back at her. "You can forget about coming to our canton if you talk like that," the first man growled. "If you aren't prepared to help us against the Children, you can rot and die in the jungle along with them."

"Help *you*—against the Children?! Are you insane?!" Dina fired back. "I would gladly give my life to defend and help the Children against any enemy, even so-called humans."

"You better watch your mouth," the woman snapped. "There are a lot more of us than there are of you."

"You think you can threaten me?!" Dina tightened her grip on her weapon. Her fury erupted. She really wanted to kill these people. "Anyone here who raises a hand against the Children better be prepared for me and a whole lot of other people to fight for the Children with our lives. The Children have saved and freed hundreds of people who are all rallying to the Children's cause. I'm not the only parent who supports and loves their Children more than anything. We would gladly die to protect them."

She swerved away. She couldn't stand to be near these people a second longer. She didn't trust herself not to resort to violence if one of them opened their mouth to her again.

"I'll keep loving, supporting, and defending your sons as my own, Tania," Dina snapped over her shoulder as she walked away. "I won't let anyone hurt them, not even some stranger who is supposed to be their mother. I'm going somewhere where people know how to behave like real human beings because it obviously isn't here. I can get that in any of the Children's camps. I'm more the same species as they are than I am to you."

She stormed off not knowing or caring where she was going. She didn't stop fuming until she strode into another stand of trees across the river.

How dare they! She might have been able to explain Tania's abhorrence for her Children in the aftermath of escaping from Prideland. The Black reminded her of Khalid, but that was almost four years ago. She should have gotten over it by now.

Tania sure found her people. Those idiots! They were the ones who didn't deserve to live if they could kill their own Children when the little ones were too defenseless to protect themselves.

No wonder Adrian told the Black not to come near Northfall canton. He said it would be bad for them and he was dead right.

Dina cringed when she replayed those words in her mind. How could anyone be so stupid? How could anyone be so vicious and unfeeling toward their own Children?

She gulped down despair when she thought of those people killing their own defenseless little ones. She would gladly have raised a hundred Children to spare them that—maybe even a thousand Children. Then at least they would be alive.

She collapsed against a tree, let her head fall against the bark, and shut her eyes. She struggled to breathe in a combined turmoil of rage and anguish.

She had to get back to her own territory—the west country where Adrian was gathering his army. She didn't even know which direction to go to get there.

She swallowed hard and forced herself to open her eyes. She would just have to start working her way southwest. If she ran into any Children along the way, she could ask them which way to go.

Then she remembered the helper's wagon and the road leading south toward the city. It might take longer, but at least she knew which direction to travel.

She could get within sight of the city, skirt it to the west, and sneak away into the jungle. She just had to hope and pray the assault didn't start before she got there.

She pushed herself off the tree—and froze. Kaiser stood directly in front of her and stared at her with his impenetrable black eyes. How long had he been standing there watching her?

"Kaiser!" she exclaimed. "What are you doing here? I thought you were....." She glanced around at nothing. "Aren't you supposed to be involved in the assault?"

"Adrian sent me here," he replied. "He wanted to scout for potential allies among the other cantons. He wanted me to find out if the slags of Northfall canton wanted to join the Children's war."

Dina winced again. "They don't."

"I heard it all, Dina," he murmured. "I heard every word."

She choked down the urge to burst into tears. "I'm sorry you had to hear that—especially from your own mother. Just.....don't judge us too harshly."

"I heard every word you said, too, Dina," he replied. "You have nothing to apologize for. I followed you from the wagon. I saw you save those people—and Tania."

Tears streaked from her eyes no matter how hard she tried to stop them. "I wish all humans were like the Children. I just wish....I just wish Adrian and Iona understood. People like that make me ashamed to be human."

"You have nothing to be ashamed of, Dina. You're the only mother I've ever had. You're the only mother any of us have ever had. I love you as much as if you were my real mother. Tania is nothing but a stranger. You gave us everything a mother could give. My brothers and I owe you our lives a dozen times over. You're the only mother in my heart and the things you just said make me proud to be your son."

She really did break down then. She buried her face in her hands and burst into tears. "I just want to do right by all of you!" she wailed. "I just want to give you all the best life. I don't want anything but for all of you to live in a world where you and the younger generation of Children can grow up. That's all I've ever wanted. I would give anything to keep my promise to you to find a way to make that happen!"

"You are doing that." He took a few steps closer, rested his hand on her shoulder, and then put his arms around her.

She sobbed even harder when she understood how unnatural this kind of affection was for him. He did it for her.

The rift between herself and the Children made that one quick hug mean even more. She thought she'd lost them.

He pushed her back and she fought to get herself under control.

"Come with me, Dina," he murmured. "I'll take you back to Adrian's territory. I heard enough. I don't need to make contact with those people."

Chapter 49

Kaiser descended through the treetops late at night. He landed on the ground in a different Children's camp somewhere. Dina had never been here before, but it looked like all the other Children's camps she'd ever been in—the ones on the ground, that is.

The Children hadn't lit any fires. They walked back and forth in the dark. They could see perfectly well like this.

Kaiser led Dina to a cluster of her own Children who stood off to one side. The Manx brothers, the Auroras, Osiris's Children, and Duke and Darius separated to let Dina enter their group.

"Adrian is out with the patrols," Dexter informed them. "He's checking the position of all the different factions who are preparing to assault the city."

"Why hasn't he launched the assault?" Dina asked. "He said he would do it yesterday."

"Everyone is in position," Rey replied. "He just hasn't given the word yet."

"Is anything wrong?" she asked. "Is there some reason he's delaying?"

"He doesn't explain himself to us," Amir replied. "He has his own reasons for doing things."

"Come to my house, Dina," Darius told her. "We're supposed to keep the camp dark, but I can find you some food and you can lie down for a while."

"If you're supposed to keep the camp dark, then that's more important," she replied. "Don't compromise your safety for me. I'll be all right.....and I have some food here. I forgot I had this."

She squatted down on the ground and started to untie the bundle Osiris had given her. She was still tugging at the knot when a flurry of commotion broke out at the far end of the camp. Voices raced back and forth from group to group.

"He's back!" Riggs murmured. "Adrian is back."

"He's early," Brock remarked. "He shouldn't have come back so soon."

Dina got to her feet, but so many people crowded around Adrian that she decided to stay where she was.

Kaiser crossed the camp and met up with Adrian, Karim, and Kenji approaching from the trees.

Dina watched Kaiser and Adrian murmuring to each other apart from everyone else. Dina looked away when she thought about what Kaiser must be telling him.

Adrian only nodded and walked off in a different direction to give instructions to the rest of his people. Kaiser went with him and rejoined his brothers as Adrian's bodyguard. They didn't come back.

Dina went back to untying her bundle and eating her food. She eventually sat down at the edge of the camp.

She wrapped her arms around her shoulders trying to keep warm. Not being able to light a fire or even a lamp made this camp seem colder than it was. She would have given anything for a blanket right now.

The other Children didn't notice. Their fur kept them warm and they all stayed standing in a state of tense readiness.

They split off in different directions as the night wore on. They formed different groups going off to do different jobs and join different factions for the coming assault.

In the end, only Dina and the Manx remained. Dina cupped her hands and blew into them. The Manx didn't notice. They kept a constant watch on the Children around them.

Dina was just thinking about lying down on the bare, cold ground and going to sleep when Adrian strode over to them with the Black right behind him.

"You four go down to the Broken Fork and join the Moonlight Children in the western flank," he told the Manx. "Tell Cain to wait until they see us make the first move. Tell him not to show himself until he sees us begin the assault. Tell him everything depends on the Moonlight Children staying hidden."

"Do you want us to do anything special when we get into the city?" Riggs asked.

"Yes, I want you to take the Senate building. As soon as you get into the city, I want the four of you to break away and make sure no one else enters the Senate building—no cats, no helpers—not even any other Children. Don't get involved in the assault. Just hold the building against everyone. Make sure it's deserted by the time I get there."

"No problem," Rome replied. "We can do that."

"Go do it, then. Good luck."

Adrian clapped Riggs on the shoulder and pushed the brothers away. Then he looked down at Dina. "What's happening with the transmitter?"

Dina scrambled to her feet so she could face him standing up like everyone else around here. "We sent the first transmission, but we didn't get any response."

"Does that mean the transmitter doesn't work?"

"No, not at all. In fact, I'm certain that it did work. It just takes time for the signal to travel that far."

"How long will it take before we can expect a response?"

"I have no idea. We just have to wait and see. I was planning to go back into the city to check in with Tom about that. I only left it because the Elite Battalion was about to catch us and I had to create a distraction while Tom hid the transmitter."

"I see." He waved to one side. "Take a walk with me."

She tucked her bundle of food back into her shoulder bag and set off at his side. He sauntered through the camp, and for some reason Dina couldn't figure out, none of the other Children crowded around to talk to him. They kept their distance.

"How do you plan to get back inside the city?" he asked after a few minutes of silence. "You said it was dangerous for you before. It will be even more dangerous now."

"I know. There aren't many places I can go where I'll be safe from the helpers—and the cats are even worse. I saw Osiris last time and he told me the cats all recognize my smell now."

"Will you go up the river again?"

"No, there are too many helpers there. It will be worse, now that they've already seen me there. I'll go back to Renfroe's house and hide in his garden. No cats will go there. It's the only place where they'll be least likely to smell me. His helpers hate me more than anyone, but at least they won't be able to smell me."

He didn't look at her. He gazed off into the dark. "I don't like you going near Renfroe's house."

"He saved my life from the helpers the last time I went into the city."

He turned his head farther away and snarled through gritted teeth. "I won't mention him again. I don't want to offend you by calling him the killer that he is."

"I don't blame you for hating him. I've never been completely certain whether he manipulated me from the beginning or if he ever really cared about me."

His head snapped around fast and his eyes glittered in the darkness. "Really? Did you really see through him like that? I thought you were head over heels for him."

She made a face. "He's a cat. Nothing will ever change that. We could never be equals. I don't think he's even capable of relating to any human being that way. None of the cats are capable of it. He told me himself that the soft approach was one of the tools the Pride uses to break down a helper's will to resist. He told me he knew the hard approach wouldn't work on me, so he treated me nicely. I'm sure he came to care for me in the end, but it didn't start out that way. I'm sure he cares for you and Iona, too. He lost his position in the Senate and even became an enemy of the Pride because he spoke out against killing the Children. He's been arguing in the Children's favor since the mutation first happened. Other cats have even attacked him and brutalized him for speaking out. He's the only cat I know of who has done that."

Adrian looked away again. "I didn't know about that."

"I don't expect it to change your opinion of him." She found herself looking away, too, even though he wasn't watching her. "You were right about me—the way I acted around him. He....he has a way of getting in my head. I did go back for him—more than once. I came back from the *Savannah* for him. I didn't do it for anyone else. I....I don't know if I can ever get him completely out of my head."

"I thought you were all in with the Pride," he murmured. "I didn't know you understood them this well."

"Renfroe got annoyed when I told him about Link. Renfroe picked up right away that I never would have gone back to him at all if Link had been alive. I guess....I guess Link's death broke something for me. I needed to see if there was anything left between me and Renfroe—but there isn't now. I care about him and I know he cares about me, but that's all. That's all it can ever be anymore."

"I really hope this plan of yours works out the way you say," he breathed. "A fresh start somewhere away from the Pride will be the best for all of us."

She took a chance and rested her hand on his shoulder. "You're going to be a father soon. It's natural that you would think that way. I'm proud of you. I'm proud of everything you're doing.....and I know Link was proud of you, too. I couldn't ask for any of you to grow up better than you have. You're doing something great here. I only hope I can help you in some way—whatever it is you need me to do."

"I hope I can be the kind of father Link was. He was a good leader and a good protector. He gave his life for his Children and all Children. That's what I call a father."

"I'm sure you will be. You're already doing it with all these Children. You're the leader and protector they need you to be. You will be a good father. I'm certain of it."

Adrian stopped walking in the dark. Dina didn't notice until now that almost all the Children had left the camp. They'd drifted away while Adrian and Dina had been talking.

The Black stood around them listening and waiting for Adrian to finish. Starlight glistened on the dewy leaves overhead.

"I'm proud of you, too, Dina," he murmured even lower. "You've redeemed yourself beyond anything I could ever ask. I didn't think you would, but you've surpassed everything I thought possible. This mission of yours is the only thing giving most of us the hope to go on. If you do this....I could never ask anything more of you. If you do this, you would be the hero of this war, not me. I can't express my gratitude to you for giving us this chance—all of us—especially our Children. We all owe you something—something even bigger than our lives. I don't know how to express exactly what it is you are giving us. It's too big."

She would have liked to hug him, too, but she didn't want to spoil the moment. She squeezed his elbow. "I would do all of this again and more for you—for all of you. It's nothing less than you deserve as my Children. Any risk is the least you deserve." She allowed herself to glance around at the three brothers. "You all deserve that. Now I better go. Every minute seems like wasted time before we can make this happen."

He nodded. "I'll let you go, then. Kaiser will take you to the road. Be careful....and let me know if you need anything."

She opened her mouth to ask him about the assault, but she changed her mind. If he didn't explain himself to his closest friends and associates, he wouldn't explain himself to her.

She got a sense of him as the general in charge of this army. She was nothing but his subordinate. She couldn't expect him to explain his decisions to her.

Chapter 50

Dina stepped onto a low-hanging tree branch so she could peek over Renfroe's garden wall. She'd snuck around the city's western neighborhoods and worked her way here at last.

She had to stop every few blocks to hide from helper patrols. They crisscrossed every inch of the city now, but they couldn't cover every street in every neighborhood.

The patrols concentrated their searches on the main roads, the city center, and the river. She'd made better progress through the outlying neighborhoods.

She scrambled over the wall, dropped down into the garden, and hid behind the bushes while she observed the house. She didn't see or hear anything or anyone except the fountain.

Sun shone on the courtyard. The doors stood open to the portico and the corridor inside. Belinda should have been working in the house right now, but Dina didn't see her. Belinda must have been out with the loyal helpers.

She didn't plan to approach the house, but when she glanced around to find a better, more concealed hiding place, Renfroe strode out through the portico.

He sat down next to the fountain and blinked into the sunshine. He didn't appear to be doing anything other than relaxing there.

She made a decision and stood up from behind the bushes so he could see her. His head swiveled around, his eyes locked on her, and he flared his nostrils.

She initially planned to just stand there and wait for him to come out into the garden to meet her. She didn't want to risk anyone seeing her, but she changed her mind and strode out to the courtyard.

She sat down next to the fountain in her old place. "How are you?"

"I'm as well as can be expected," he rumbled. "I can see you're doing well, too."

"I was wondering if you would mind if I hid here in your garden. I don't want to go near the house in case Buck and Belinda find me, but I need a place to hide in the city and this is the only place I could think of."

"You're welcome here at any time, Dina, and you don't have to worry about Buck and Belinda. They're both gone."

"Gone!" she exclaimed. "What do you mean?"

"Belinda is dead. I killed her."

Dina's jaw dropped. She couldn't even ask.

He looked away and twitched his whiskers at the breeze. "I killed her during that last fight so you could get away. Don't act so shocked. You know I would do anything to help you. Belinda had been causing you nothing but problems since you returned."

She shut her mouth with difficulty and gulped. "Thank you."

"That isn't necessary. You're welcome to stay in the house if you wish."

"What about Buck? Is he....?"

"He fled after the fight. I don't know where he is, but he doesn't come back here anymore. I'm quite sure he knows what would happen if he did."

She looked away across the garden. This garden meant so many things to her.

Now that memory would join the others in all her conflicted feelings about Renfroe. He killed his own helper to save her—again.

She wanted to thank him again, but he obviously didn't want that. "What about you?" she asked. "It must not be safe for you in this city anymore, either."

"It isn't....but then again, it isn't safe for anyone—cat or human. Only a handful of helpers still make a pretense of doing their jobs. The rest are all involved in the war somehow. I suppose it's just as well that we all follow our convictions now. I respect that you're doing it the way you are." He turned to study her. "What brings you back to the city at such great personal risk?"

"I need to see Tom."

Renfroe snorted. "I should have known you would renew your acquaintance with him. I'm only surprised you didn't do it sooner."

"I'm not renewing anything with him. I told him about his Children and he confronted Elyse. She threw him out and sent him to work with the Elite Battalion. The man I knew is long gone. He's helping me with a mission for the Children. That's all."

"Ah," he murmured. "I see."

"You should know better. I would never go back to Tom—not after the way he betrayed me."

"Why couldn't you? You can't hold it against him that he had relations with Elyse when you gave yourself to me."

"That isn't the reason," she muttered.

"What is, then?"

She looked away again, but the words wouldn't stay buried. "I talked to Adrian last night.....about Link.....and you. I guess talking to him brought it all back. Too much water has passed under the bridge. None of us can go back to who they were before."

"No, you're right about that, Dina," he growled. "I've come to the same conclusion myself."

"Whatever happened between me and Tom is in the past now. That time is over. I'm not the person I was when I fell in love with him. My life is the Children now. Maybe I'll feel differently after the war is over, but by then, I'll be a completely different person again. This war is changing everything, including me. I promised Iona that I would find a way for her and all Children to live their lives without the constant threat of annihilation. I can't think about anything else until I fulfill that promise."

"The time has passed for us, too, Dina," he murmured. "I know that now."

She rested her hand on his shoulder. "I know."

He looked away. "How are Adrian and Iona doing? Tell me about them."

"He says.....he still feels that Link is the only father worth having."

"I couldn't be a father to him under the circumstances," Renfroe fired back. "Even he must understand that."

"I know and he does understand it, but Link was there and you weren't. It's no one's fault.....and there are other reasons he hates you. He thinks.....he thinks I'm a slave—or that I was one."

Renfroe snarled under his breath. "Not that again!"

"He's right if you think about it. The relationship between you and me could never be an equal one. It would always be at least partially coercive and manipulative. We never had a relationship of equals. We never could have."

"I admit the understanding between the cats and humans on this planet makes a relationship of that kind impossible between a helper and a benefactor. We had a helper-benefactor relationship within the Pride. If that's what you mean, then the understanding would seem to preclude the possibility of anything happening outside it. The question would always remain whether I was your benefactor or....something else."

"I know you're a good person and I trust you, but that's as far as it ever could have gone between us. I know you did everything you could to protect me and all Children."

"That doesn't change the past and we can't rewrite the past," he growled. "You'll never be my helper again and there's no other possible relationship we can have together." He got to his feet. "You should come inside. We'll spend the night together and you can see Tom in the morning when he comes with the Elite Battalion."

He padded into the house and she walked by his side, but she didn't rest her hand on his back the way she used to. He didn't go to their old bedroom, either.

He went into the parlor. No fire burned in the fireplace. The cold fireplace left the house feeling cold and haunted. The house sounded way too quiet.

He stretched out on the carpet in his old place, but Dina couldn't settle down here. She went into the kitchen. No fire burned in there, either. A layer of dust covered the worktable, the counters, the floor, and all the pots and pans.

Dina collected an armload of firewood from the box by the hearth, took the wood into the parlor, and lit the fire herself. She fed it, brought in another armload of wood, and finally sat down next to Renfroe. "Are you hungry? I can get you something to eat from the kitchen."

"I'm not hungry," he growled. "I hunt for myself these days, but you should help yourself."

"I have enough here." She untied the bundle Osiris had given her.

Renfroe cocked his head at the bundle. "Where did you get that? Did Osiris give it to you?"

"How did you know?"

"I recognize the cloth. It belongs to one of his helpers."

"He helped me get away from the patrols. He wants to help his Children, too. If you need to talk to someone or you need help with anything, you can trust him."

"Hmmm," he growled. "That is good to know."

"He delivered five of his Children to me at the canton," she told him. "I raised them—along with all the others. They won't have anything to do with him, but he wants to help them in any way he can."

"I doubt there is a cat in this city who doesn't have some offspring among the Children," he muttered. "It sounds to me as though more cats wanted to protect the Children than let on. They made a show of wanting to destroy the Children when, behind the scenes, these cat parents were doing everything possible to save the Children from death."

"You're right. My Children are proof of that."

He inclined his head the other way. "How many Children did you raise?"

She burst out laughing. "Twenty-nine altogether."

"That many?! You never said."

"There was Adrian and Iona, four from Tom and Elyse, six from Aurora Helion who were fathered by one of her helpers, three boys from Tania and Khalid, five from Osiris, four from Fallon...."

"Fallon?!" he snapped.

She glanced up from her meal. "You didn't know? Amaryllis brought one of Fallon's helpers to me. The helper was pregnant from Fallon and Amaryllis said she wanted the last of Fallon's young to survive. The helper gave birth to four boys and then took her own life.....and then there were five of Link's nieces and nephews."

"I never imagined," he murmured. "I thought I was the only one."

"The Pride probably wanted you to think that. I'm sure Amaryllis never wanted anyone to know she saved those boys' lives. She wanted everyone to think she hated the Children and would slaughter any Child born—and maybe she did. Maybe she only cared about Fallon's young and no one else's."

"This Pride is doomed to extinction if we keep these secrets from each other like this," he muttered. "I never dreamed the cracks could run this deep."

"Just look at the defense," she pointed out.

"What defense is that?"

"The defense the Pride isn't putting up against the Children," she countered. "The cats are so internally divided on how to organize their own society that they can't even mount an effective defense. That's the Children's true advantage. They're so much more cohesive. They have one definite leader and everyone follows his orders without question. There's no difference of opinion on what they should do or how they should do it."

"You're right," he growled. "We could never fight a force as organized as that."

She glanced around the familiar parlor. She couldn't count the number of nights the two of them had sat here talking just like this.

The hours wiled away into the night. The fire made her sleepy, and after a while, she lay down on the floor, rested her head on his side as a pillow, and fell asleep.

Chapter 51

Dina stared through the parlor window at the garden outside. Renfroe sat by the fountain grooming himself in the sunshine. No one looking at him would see him doing anything he hadn't done every other morning of his adult life.

He looked up when the door in the garden wall opened. The Elite Battalion pushed their wheelbarrow into the garden. None of the men looked at him when they continued down the row of trees to his sandbox in the corner.

He went back to licking his paw and passing it over his face and behind his ears. He kept going while they worked and eventually pushed their wheelbarrow past him on their way out of the garden.

Tom went with them. He didn't look sideways at Renfroe. Dina's stomach twisted in knots watching one man after another slip through the door and disappear outside.

"Wait!" Renfroe's deep voice boomed through the garden.

Five men stood by the door. They looked back and the color drained from all their faces when they realized that a cat was actually talking to them.

No one talked to them. No one acknowledged their existence.

Renfroe got up very slowly and stalked across the courtyard. He halted in front of the Elite Battalion. "You!" he snapped at Tom. "You stay here." Renfroe's eyes darted to the others. "The rest of you can go."

The other men scrambled to get out of the garden in a hurry. The door banged shut with Tom still inside the garden.

He braced himself in front of Renfroe. Poor Tom. He had no idea what this was about.

Dina hustled out of the parlor to the portico, but she slowed when she stepped out into view. Tom's countenance went hard and icy when he saw her.

"Come over here, Tom," Renfroe growled. "Dina wishes to speak to you."

Renfroe paced back to the courtyard and sat down by the fountain. Tom looked back and forth between Dina and Renfroe. Tom had to think about it before he decided to comply and cross the courtyard.

"Are you okay?" he whispered and cast another suspicious glance at Renfroe. "What are you doing here? You shouldn't be here. It isn't safe."

"I had to see you and this is the only place in the city that was safe enough to come. How are you?" She gave him a meaningful look. "How are things?"

"Things are good. You should......" He checked over his shoulder.

Renfroe sat there listening to every word. He kept twitching his ears and inclining his head from one side to the other.

Tom lowered his voice even more, but nothing could stop Renfroe from hearing. "I need you to come back to the power station. It's important."

"I don't know when I'll be able to do that except at night when the rest of the Elite Battalion is there. I can't travel around the city freely during the day."

"It can't be at night," Tom insisted. "It has to be during the day—and even then, I can't guarantee that the Elite Battalion won't come back in the middle of their shift. Things are so chaotic right now. We don't always stay out all day."

Renfroe interrupted. "I can arrange for the Elite Battalion to stay away from the power station during the day. Dina can hide herself near the power station at night, and during the day when the Elite Battalion leaves, I can arrange for you to meet her there alone."

Tom jumped and spun around when Renfroe broke in on their conversation. Tom stiffened to confront Renfroe and then relaxed slightly. "Thank you. I'd really appreciate any help you can give us with this."

Renfroe cocked his head the other way. "I would do anything to help Dina, Tom. You should know that by now."

Tom took a deep breath. "I do know that.....and I know now that you tried to help us when we first landed on this planet. I know you were the one who got me a hearing with the Senate and that you argued for the Pride to incorporate this planet into the Coalition. I didn't know it at the time, but I know now."

"I always wanted my kind to expand our contact with the wider galactic community, Tom," Renfroe rumbled. "Now it will never happen. If meeting Dina at the power station helps you and her, I am happy to do what I can to make it happen."

Tom shut his eyes and lowered his head. "Thank you. I'm grateful—and I'm grateful for all the protection you've given her. She's.....she's special to me....."

"She's special to me, too, Tom. She always has been."

Tom turned around the other way to face Dina. "What time do you want to come?"

She shrugged. "If we do it this way, then I'll have to be there all day. I can do it whenever you get away from the Elite Battalion."

"Let's plan on noon again, then. That worked last time.....as long as the Elite Battalion doesn't come back and surprise us....."

"They won't," Renfroe interrupted from behind.

Tom stiffened again, but he didn't turn around. "Don't take any unnecessary risks," he murmured. "It would be terrible if something happened to you now—after all you've done."

She found herself smiling at him. "I can't even wake up in the morning without taking unnecessary risks. This whole thing is risky, but I have to do it. We're too close to victory."

"All right. I'll just have to trust you. I'll see you tomorrow." He turned around to face Renfroe, murmured, "Thank you," again, and strode out of the garden.

"I won't even ask what you're doing, Dina," Renfroe muttered as soon as Tom shut the garden door behind him.

"Telling you would only put you in more danger—from everyone, including the Children." She sat down by the fountain in the sunshine. "I'm pretty sure everyone will know soon enough anyway. We won't be able to keep it a secret—and we won't want to."

"Is it really that important?"

"Yes, it is," she replied. "More important than you can imagine."

"Then I'll just have to trust you, too." He strode over to her, rested his head in her lap, and shut his eyes when she put her hand on his head. "Will I see you again after this, Dina?"

"I don't know," she husked. "Every time I see you could be the last time."

"I sense you slipping through my fingers," he growled. "You slip farther away from me every time I see you, and yet, the farther away you get, the closer I feel to you."

She bent down and kissed the top of his head. "I feel the same way. These moments are sweeter because I know they won't last."

"I would have kept you locked in this house forever to keep you safe," he murmured. "I would have kept you to myself forever to avoid parting from you. Now I know I can never keep you. You would never stay with me."

Her throat hurt too much to answer. She would have stayed with him forever—under any other circumstances than these.

She never would have met him under any other circumstances. This one tiny possible sliver of reality was the only dimension of existence where the two of them ever would have met.

Their paths wouldn't have crossed if he'd been some random tiger and she'd been some random ship's biologist. He wouldn't have become her benefactor and she wouldn't have become his helper.

They couldn't have related to each other in any other way. Trying to relate to each other in any other way produced this repulsive effect that drove them apart.

Eventually, they would get so far apart that they didn't interact with each other at all.

Chapter 52

Dina slipped out of Renfroe's house into the shadowy garden and set off across the city once again. She had to hide and dodge numerous times to avoid getting caught by helper patrols.

They made it easier by carrying lanterns. The light blinded them from seeing into the shadows.

She snuck from one shadow to another, made her way back to the power station, and hid herself behind the building. She knew all the best hiding places now.

She fell asleep there and woke up when the Elite Battalion went out to work. Tom went with them.

She wasn't the only one keeping her plans to herself. Renfroe didn't tell her how he would arrange for Tom to come back to the power station alone or how Renfroe would distract the Elite Battalion to stop them from finding out what Tom and Dina were doing.

Hours passed one after the other. The sun climbed higher and Tom still didn't come back. Dina might have to use the transmitter alone if he didn't come soon.

She fidgeted in her hiding place and imagined all kinds of nightmare scenarios. The sun climbed to its highest point.

She was just about to give up and go into the building when he came striding down the street. He walked faster than she'd ever seen any of the Elite Battalion walk. He kept his shoulders back and his head up.

He gasped in relief when she stepped out of her hiding place. "Thank God you're here! I thought I'd never get away."

"What happened?" she asked. "Did Renfroe let you go?"

"He made a big show of telling me I was in trouble and to come back here to await punishment. Then he took the rest of the Elite Battalion off somewhere. I didn't see where. We have to work fast. Come on."

He pushed open the door and the two of them returned to the power station control room in the back of the building.

Tom pulled the transmitter from under one of the workbenches. He'd covered it with a piece of cloth to conceal it and protect it from dust.

"Do any of the other men know you have this?" she asked.

"They never come in here. They never look very closely at anything." He set the transmitter on the workbench and started wiring it up. "I received a return transmission with the wavelength modulation readings to dial up the nearest Armada outpost. We can contact them directly."

"That's great!" she exclaimed. "Did they get our last transmission?"

"They got it and apparently they've called in Captain Doyle to brief the rest of the Armada on the situation down here. The *Savannah* is on deployment somewhere else, but everyone knows now."

"They don't know about the Children, though," she pointed out.

"No, they don't and they don't need to know. The Armada doesn't need to know anything except that Coalition citizens are in danger and distress." He sat down on his stool. "Throw the power and let's do this."

She threw the power breaker switch and power flooded the controls. The transmitter came on.

Tom adjusted it again and turned on the microphone. "Mayday, mayday. This is Commander Tom Sharples formerly of the Armada Destroyer *Savannah* broadcasting from the planet Daustina along with Lieutenant Dina Dyer, also of the *Savannah*. Please acknowledge. This is Commander Tom Sharples and Lieutenant Dina Dyer broadcasting from the planet Daustina. Please acknowledge."

The transmitter crackled and then a clear male voice called back. "This is Corporal Francis McFarlane of the Ebror Defense Outpost. We read you clearly, Commander. Your request for immediate evacuation and rescue has been accepted and a fleet of ten destroyers is on its way to rendezvous at your location."

Dina squealed in excitement, grabbed Tom's arm, and nearly wriggled out of her skin. "They're coming! They're on their way!"

Tom lowered his voice to the microphone. He didn't try to stop his voice from trembling. "That is wonderful to hear, Corporal. Thank you so much! Which coordinates should we use to assemble the evacuees?"

"You would know that better than I would, Commander," McFarlane replied. "If you send us the coordinates, we can bring in the destroyers there and lift off your people."

"Stand by one moment, please, Corporal."

"Yes, Sir," McFarlane replied.

Tom glanced up at Dina. "What do you think? Where should we bring them in?"

"The farmland near the village is probably the best place. It's open country with no trees. The destroyers will be able to land there."

"We're going to need a lot of destroyers." He switched the microphone back on. "Can you bring up charts of the planet, Corporal? If you locate our original Pod's landing site, you'll notice some open farmland with a small village west of the city the landing team first made contact with. The farmland is your best option for landing destroyers."

"Yes, Sir, acknowledged. I'm looking at the charts now and I see the place you mean. I'll transmit those coordinates to the destroyers. Just....um.....the brass was waiting to hear from you to find out exactly how many destroyers you'll need."

Tom winced. "I'm really not sure how many people will want to evacuate to be totally honest with you, Corporal. I couldn't even begin to guess. It could be in the thousands—or maybe even more."

"There will be at least ten thousand Children alone," Dina chimed in. "That's not counting slags, subsidiaries, and other helpers who want to leave."

Tom turned the microphone on again. "Let's start with the ten destroyers you have coming, Corporal. We'll lift off as many as they can carry, and if we need more, we'll bring them in, too."

"Yes, Sir," McFarlane replied. "I know the brass plans to send more. These ten are just the nearest ships we can spare at short notice. If you need us to bring in the big guns, you only have to say so."

Tom burst out in excited laughter before he pushed the button again. "Bring them, Corporal. Bring everything you got."

"Yes, Sir. Acknowledged. We'll be there. I'll be monitoring this channel continuously until the liftoff. Contact me tomorrow and I'll be able to give you a more definite ETA for the destroyers to land."

Tom couldn't stop laughing. "Thank you so much, Corporal. You have no idea how good it is to hear your voice."

"We'll get you all out, Sir," McFarlane told him. "The Armada is on its way."

"Thank you, Corporal. Sharples out."

He clicked off the microphone, turned to Dina, and then they both grabbed each other in a huge hug. Dina couldn't contain her glee. She bounced up and down in his arms and nearly knocked him out by slamming her shoulder into his chin.

"This is great!" she crowed. "They're coming! The Armada is coming! I can't believe it! It actually worked!"

He pushed her back and beamed down at her with tears in his eyes. "You did this. Now you better get the hell out of town and pass the word to the Children—and any other people you can contact. Get them ready to assemble in the fields west of the city. I'll stay here and keep in contact with the Armada. I'll get word to you somehow about when we can expect the destroyers to come in."

She gripped his hands and jumped up and down a few more times. She couldn't stop squealing in excitement. This was actually going to work! Tom, Dina, and everyone they cared about were all getting the hell off this planet.

He sat back on his stool grinning at her. He squeezed her hands back just as tight. She'd never seen him so happy. "Go on," he repeated. "Get out of here."

"Thank you so much!" She darted forward and kissed him on the cheek. "I can never repay you for this."

"Cut it out. It was the least I could do."

She wanted to say more and maybe hug him a dozen more times, but he was right. She had a lot to do and not much time to do it.

He followed her to the exit and she peeked out. She didn't see any helpers around. She would never get a better chance to hide herself along the river.

Tom held the door open for her. "If you ever see Renfroe again, thank him for me. We couldn't have done this without him."

"I will. Take care of yourself. We're almost home."

He glanced past her at the street outside and lowered his voice to a murmur. "Don't you think it's ironic? He's the one who made this happen for us and now we're leaving. He's the one cat who wanted to broaden his horizons and make contact with other cultures. Now he'll be stuck on this planet with no way off it or any contact with anyone outside the Pride."

Chapter 53

Dina dashed away from the power station and dove into the bushes by the riverbank. She wouldn't have trusted traveling along the river, but the excitement of getting out of town and delivering the news to the Children overrode everything else.

She hunkered down to wait for another helper patrol to pass. Then she crawled a hundred yards down the river to where it bent toward the farmland beyond.

She stayed where she was and waited two more hours for the sun to sink toward the horizon. She needed to be extra careful not to get captured with this information.

She stole a peek out of her hiding place and watched another patrol pass by. They didn't keep as close an eye on the river as they did before. They paid more attention to the streets.

She remarked again that Adrian still hadn't called the assault. What was he doing? Was he toying with the Pride? How could he be when no one inside the Pride knew he was even preparing this assault?

She suffered another surge of doubt that he'd tricked her into hurrying this whole transmission plan along. Did he even plan to assault the Pride? Was it all a giant ruse?

She pushed those thoughts away. She couldn't start questioning him now.

The patrol passed. The riverbank was clear for her to continue her journey.

She crawled to the edge of the bushes and peeked out at the spot where Riyadh had parted from her last time. A few dozen yards separated her from the jungle. She could get there easily.

The sun was going down again and she still had to find a way to get to the Children's camp. That would take a while without one of them to carry her there.

She considered waiting for dark, but she decided against it. No one was around.

She burst out of her hiding place and bolted across the open ground on a dead run for the jungle. She put her head down. Everything depended on getting under the trees and hiding again.

She got within ten yards of the undergrowth when a colossal weight slammed into her from the side. She hit the ground and a jaguar landed on top of her.

She struggled to get out from under him, but he lunged for her and clamped his jaws around her neck. He could have killed her in an instant if he wanted to.

He roared at her and shoved her down hard on the ground to pin her. His breath seared her skin and she bellowed in terror. She tried to raise her arms to protect herself, but he was too big and too fast.

"Keep still," a gruff voice snapped. "You're dead to us already. Don't make it worse by giving us a reason to kill you."

She froze at those words. She didn't recognize the voice.

The jaguar held her there until she stopped struggling. When he finally let her go, she stole a peek up at him and her stomach plummeted into her shoes. It was Victor.

Khalid paced back and forth a few feet away. "You can't trust this one," he growled. "She'll make another escape attempt."

A large male lion strode over to Dina and nudged her with his nose. "Hmmpth. We need some helpers to tie her up and carry her there."

"What do you want from me?!" she blurted out.

Victor banged his big head into her hard enough to knock her down on the ground. "Be quiet, slag," he snarled. "You've caused enough trouble."

She made the mistake of trying to sit up again. The lion brought his paw down on her chest and pinned her to the ground. "You go, Khalid," he ordered. "Tell them to hurry up."

Dina huddled under his paw. The lion didn't take it away and Victor loomed over her glaring at her in undisguised hatred.

She had no choice but to stay where she was. Her one consoling thought kept repeating in her mind. The Armada was on the way. She just had to survive until the destroyers got here.

She shut her eyes and didn't fight back when Khalid returned with ten helpers. They tied her up again, and just to make sure she couldn't escape, they tied her into a large canvas sack after that.

A bunch of the men carried her all the way back into town. She heard plenty of wagons, people talking, and all the sounds of activity she'd just taken so much trouble to leave behind.

The Armada was on the way. These people couldn't stop the destroyers from coming. Tom would make sure she got off this planet along with all her Children. The Pride was finished.

That thought gave her more comfort than she'd ever felt on this planet. She didn't have to fight these people anymore. She was almost free, and this time, she would never come back.

The air inside the sack dropped ten degrees and the helpers set her down on a cold floor somewhere. Then a door slammed and someone pulled the sack off.

She looked around at a dim basement under a house. Human legs passed back and forth outside a thin window at street level. She was back inside the city, tied up, and a prisoner of these cats.

There were no Children in the city now. No one knew where she was. No one would come to her rescue this time.

Khalid, Victor, and the lion paced around her and scrutinized her lying helpless on the floor. The lion stopped in front of her. "Well, here you are, finally."

"What do you want?!" she demanded. "If you brought me here to kill me, just do it and get it over with. Killing me won't stop the Children from winning this war. You've lost! Do you hear me? The Pride is finished and you can't stop what's about to happen!"

"You're going to tell us everything you know about the Children's plans," Victor growled. "Your son killed my brother....."

"And how many Children did you kill?" she countered. "How many defenseless babies did you kill before these Children escaped? The Children are only defending themselves. You cats wrecked your own society by turning against the Children....."

The lion swiped his paw at her, raked his claws across her shoulder, and sliced open the skin down to the muscle.

She screamed and toppled onto her other side, but she couldn't even stop the bleeding when she had her hands tied behind her back.

"Tell us what you know about your son's plans," the lion boomed. "This is your last chance to save your own life."

"I don't know anything about my son's plans!!" she shrieked between screams of pain. "He doesn't tell anyone his plans—and I wouldn't tell you even if I knew! You're going to kill me anyway! Don't lie about it!"

"She's right, Kojo," Khalid muttered. "She's too much of a slag at heart. She'll never talk."

"If you won't talk, we have no choice, but that doesn't mean we have to kill you quickly," Kojo told her. "Maybe you'll think differently if we soften you up first."

He slashed her with his claws again—across the back this time. She was still writhing in pain and bellowing her lungs out on the ground when Victor pounced on her again.

He clamped his jaws around her face and growled in fury while she twisted and struggled to get free.

He held her down on the floor, and when she fought too hard, he tightened his grip. His fangs pierced her skin and tore at her face.

"Where are the Children camped in the jungle?!!" Kojo barked over the noise.

"I DON'T KNOW!!" she screeched. "THE CHILDREN MOVE AROUND ALL THE TIME!! SOMETIMES THEY NEST IN THE TREES....."

"You're lying," Khalid muttered. "You always lie."

Victor gave one last tight clamp with his teeth and tore away hard enough to tear her face in spots. She lay there screaming and convulsing in pain.

She fought to get herself under control. She had to get out of here. She had to find a way to get her hands and feet free, but that would be impossible with these cats standing over her.

They stood back watching her collapse in a whimpering pile of hopeless despair on the floor. She didn't dare to look up at them.

Blood ran in her eyes from the puncture wounds on her face. Her back and arm screamed in pain and these cats were only getting started. They would kill her, but at least the Armada would evacuate the Children. She didn't care about anything else.

Kojo glared down at her from directly above. "We can keep going like this as long as necessary before you tell us what we want to know. I can call my brothers from Hellion House to tear you apart piece by piece. Is that what you want?"

Her head shot up and she blinked at him through the blood in her eyes. "You're.....you're a Hellion?"

He snorted. "You slags are so stupid. You don't even recognize the cat right in front of you. I've seen you at Hellion House before. I remember the very first time you ever set foot in the place."

She gaped at him putting the puzzle pieces together. She'd first set foot in Hellion House over three years ago. He must have been nothing but a cub then. She could still remember them jumping, wrestling, and playing on the floor.

Without warning, she burst out in hysterical laughter. She couldn't stop it. These cats held no power over her anymore. Nothing they did or said would stop the Armada from coming.

"What is so funny?" Victor took another swipe at her face, but he didn't extend his claws.

His paw smashed her head aside and she sprawled across the floor, but she couldn't stop laughing. Her laughter poured out of her. It would never stop.

"Be quiet!" Kojo roared.

"You're a Hellion!" she shrieked. "You're a Hellion!"

"I already said that," he snapped.

She wrenched herself over on her side so she could look up at him. Blood streamed down her face and trickled from the corner of her mouth. "My son killed Kaido Hellion! Do you hear that?! My son killed Kaido Hellion and he'll kill you, too! Aurora Hellion has Children out there fighting the Pride right now!"

"You lying slag!" Khalid pounced on her, struck her hard enough to knock her backward, and sent her rolling. "Shut your mouth!"

She fell across the floor again, but she wouldn't be quiet—not now. "I raised ten of her Children—ten of them! Ha ha! What do you think of that? My son killed Kaido Hellion—which means there is no cat in the whole Pride who is strong enough to beat him! You cats are dead! The Pride is dead! Everything you knew and cared about is gone! You lost the war, you idiots! You lost the war a long, long time ago the first time you sank your teeth into one of the Children!"

She exploded into another bout of insane laughter. Some shattered part of her brain recognized that she was laughing like this because she already knew she was dead. She was beyond saving.

She just had to throw it in their faces one last time. They would never know until it was too late, but she was the one who defeated them. She was the one who called in the Armada.

She was the one who would take all their helpers away. The Pride would be left behind on this planet with no one to support them, no one to worship them, no one to scratch them behind the ears—because of her.

She might not live long enough to see that and enjoy her victory. She didn't care. She got the last laugh. She was getting it right now—before they killed her.

"She's out of her mind," Victor growled. "Finish her off, Kojo. I want to go hunting."

"Not yet," Kojo replied. "We can still get some information out of her." He stalked over to her and pinned her under his paw. "What do you mean—your son killed Kaido Hellion? Answer me!"

He slashed his paw across her face and laid open her cheek. She screamed again, but he kept striking her again and again with his claws retracted.

His paw clubbed her head aside over and over. He finally let her fall backward on the floor. She landed on top of her bound wrists, but she didn't care anymore.

She wilted in relief when Kojo strode back to Victor and said, "This is a waste of time. Finish her off and let's get out of here."

Kojo kept walking and Khalid joined him on their way to the door. Victor stalked over to Dina, lowered his head between his shoulders, and opened his mouth in a deadly snarl.

She hitched herself onto her side again. "What's the matter, Khalid?" she called after him. "Are you too cowardly to come near me even when I'm tied up? Are you worried you're going to get hurt again? You can't even kill anymore. You're a toothless old woman."

He spun around and growled at her, but he didn't come near her.

Victor snapped at her to be quiet again, but she only laughed. "Untie me and fight me," she called across the basement. "Otherwise everyone will know you're afraid of an unarmed slag—if they don't already know."

Victor lunged for her again, slammed his head into her face, and she reeled back down on the floor with blood pouring out of her nose.

He dove for her throat, but before his teeth could break the skin, a soft female voice interrupted. "Stop, Victor! Don't kill her yet. We need her."

Victor gave another murderous growl and let go. Dina didn't dare to move, much less sit up.

"The Senate is calling her back to another hearing," the same female voice went on. "They won't be happy if you kill her first."

"To hell with the Senate," Kojo snarled. "They have no power anymore."

"You know that isn't true," the female voice countered. "They still command most of the helpers and plenty of cats. You have to at least show her to them and let them see that she's alive. You can kill her after that."

Victor grunted under his breath and finally turned away. "Bring in the helpers to take her. This is taking too long."

He stormed away to leave the basement, and this time, Khalid went with him.

Chapter 54

K ojo Hellion stood guard over Dina while another group of helpers entered the basement. They untied Dina's ankles, but they kept her wrists tied.

The men yanked her to her feet, shook her a few times, and marched her toward a wooden staircase rising to the ground floor of whatever building they were in.

Dina didn't see the female until she got onto the staircase. A tiny hairless cat perched on the step staring down at Dina's pulverized face.

The cat sprang up the steps ahead of Dina. Kojo's heavy tread thumped on the stairs behind them. The helpers had to adjust their position to march Dina upstairs.

They passed through a grand house almost as opulent as Osiris's, but it wasn't his house. They pushed Dina out onto the sidewalk. They were in the middle of the city only a few blocks from the Senate building.

The helpers flanked her on both sides and kept hold of her elbows to make sure she couldn't get away.

More helpers turned around to stare at her as she passed them. Blood saturated her clothes and hair. She felt her face swelling up and blood streamed from the gashes on her cheek.

She didn't care about any of that. Her heart skipped a beat when the helpers took her back to the little door in the Senate building's sidewall.

She hoped and prayed Osiris would be able to get her out of the building after the hearing. She would see him in a few minutes. Then he would realize what was happening.

She couldn't imagine what he'd be able to do against Victor, Khalid, and Kojo Hellion, but at least she was about to go somewhere where she would see some of her allies—or at least one of them.

The helpers stopped her outside the entrance, untied her wrists at the last second, and pushed her through the door. They didn't follow. She staggered into the hallway and stumbled up it toward the Senate chamber. She was alone in here—again.

She crossed the threshold.....and her world came to a screeching halt when she saw the scene inside. Dozens of cats occupied the seats, but Renfroe wasn't here this time.

Osiris wasn't on the stage, either. Neither was Elyse. In fact, Dina didn't recognize a single cat up there.

Every cat present turned around to stare at her as she advanced into the chamber. Their eyes followed her. They could all see her bloody and bruised with Victor's teeth marks embedded in her face.

She did her best to rally her courage. These cats were the only people who could keep her alive.

She took her place and had to turn her back to all those cats to face the Senate.

"We understand from your previous hearing that your son is the leader of the Children's army," a female puma began.

"Yes, he is, but I don't speak for the Children," Dina mumbled. Her lips were already swelling up and going numb. "I don't know their plans and I don't have any authority to negotiate with them or on their behalf."

"The Pride has made numerous overtures of peace to the Children....." the same puma went on.

"Excuse me, but the Pride has never made even one single overture of peace to the Children," Dina interrupted. "The Senate sent me once to open communications with the Children. The Senate has never offered any concession that could be mistaken for an overture of peace and the rest of the Pride certainly never has. The Pride has repeatedly stated that they would fight to the last cat to annihilate the Children."

"Do the Children hold the same position toward the Pride?" a different male lion boomed out in a deep, rumbling voice.

Dina took a deep breath. "The Children feel they have no choice but to take that position. They feel the Pride poses such a grave threat to the Children's existence that the Children have no choice but to mount a decisive assault against the Pride—and possibly annihilate all the cats before the Pride does it to them first. That is the Children's position. They feel they're fighting for their very survival since the Pride has made so many threats against it—and continues to threaten it."

"How agreeable are they to a peace proposal?" the female puma asked.

Dina shrugged. "It's a little late for that, isn't it? The Senate doesn't hold enough authority or influence to stop any cats from attacking the Children. The Children have no reason to make peace. They hold all the power and they have the numbers to back it up. They have thousands of escaped helpers living in cantons who will fight against you. If you really want peace, you should be preparing to surrender. That's the position you're really in. You're all just too delusional to realize it."

Murmurs and grumblings drifted through the cats behind her. The tension in the chamber escalated.

She probably shouldn't have antagonized the Senate, but she didn't care anymore. Why in God's name were they talking about peace now of all times? They couldn't even control their own or defend this city from the Children.

Whatever Adrian's reason for not calling the assault, it was the only reason anyone in this city was still alive. These cats didn't have a clue what was really going on in this war.

"You don't paint a very promising picture," the lion rumbled. "You make it sound as if the hostile cats are correct and that we should be moving to annihilate the Children before they do it to us first. Is that what you'd have us believe?"

Dina squirmed. She didn't know how to answer that—and then it came to her. She'd been keeping the real situation a secret for so long.

Something snapped in her mind. The time had come to play her trump card.

"I have an alternative," she announced.

"What is it?" the puma asked.

"I have a way to evacuate the Children off the planet—entirely. I have a way to remove every last Child from this planet along with all the slags, escaped helpers, and anyone else who wants to leave. We'll all go and only loyal helpers and subsidiaries who want to stay will remain. You won't have a Children problem anymore and the war will be over."

The senators on the stage exchanged whispers. "How is that possible?" the lion asked. "How would you carry out this evacuation?"

"We've made contact with ships that will take us. They're on the way now."

"Then....you plan to evacuate regardless?" the puma asked. "You arranged this evacuation without consulting us?"

"We're in a war, Madame Senator," Dina countered. "We aren't under any obligation share our plans with you or anyone else. Yes, we plan to evacuate regardless. The only question is if the Pride resists and tries to stop us. If you do, we'll fight back and defend ourselves. If you want the evacuation to turn into another massacre, that's up to you, but we're leaving this planet either way.....and you might like to know that the ships that are coming are all heavily armed. They're under a mandate to defend us from any attacker—so you might want to stay behind in the city and let us evacuate peacefully."

Dina paused to catch her breath. Her chest hurt from the tension. She shocked herself with her own nerve, but this hearing was her last chance. She had to convince them now or never.

The senators exchanged a few more whispered snatches of conversation. Dina held her breath waiting for their answer….and then she realized. Whatever they decided didn't matter anymore.

The evacuation would take place. This whole hearing was a giant waste of time.

She just had to get out of this building and make it back to the jungle. She didn't have to talk to these cats at all.

"Very well," the lion finally boomed out. "We will allow this evacuation to proceed."

"You won't be able to stop it," Dina countered.

"We will allow it to proceed peacefully, then," he corrected. "We would be grateful if you would inform any Children who will listen to you to proceed peacefully on their side as well."

"I won't be able to inform the Children of anything if I don't get out of this city alive," she replied. "I came here directly from a basement where three cats were about to kill me—as you can see. If I walk out of this building now, more cats and helpers will threaten my life. If you want me to tell the Children anything, I'll need an escort to take me to the jungle."

"We will assign you an escort," the puma replied. "Thank you for meeting with us."

Dina nodded, but she didn't answer. No one asked her if she wanted to meet with the Senate.

Her tolerance for everything on this planet was rapidly coming to an end. She didn't have to put up with it anymore and she didn't plan to.

Chapter 55

Dina headed down the Senate hall to the side door. The helpers standing guard grabbed her the minute she stepped outside.

They started to haul her away, but just then, the same female puma senator pushed her way through the side door, too.

"This woman is under my protection," the puma told the surrounding helpers. "You can all go back to work now. Follow me, Dina."

Dina didn't ask how this cat knew her name nor did Dina ask the puma's name. Dina didn't want to get acquainted with any more cats ever again as long as she lived.

The puma set off down the street heading west. Dina's face still felt three feet thick. She could only imagine what she looked like. Adrian might not even recognize her.

She followed the puma as far as the market. Dina glanced around trying to see where she could lay her hands on some weapons.

The market distracted her. The usual helpers and subsidiaries stood around talking, trading, and cats strode from wagon to wagon examining everything the subsidiaries had brought to offer.

The market sounded normal now. Everyone conducted their business as if there was no war going on.

The helper patrols didn't interfere with the market, either. In fact, Dina didn't see any patrols at all. Was something changing? The city actually sounded.....peaceful.

Right at that moment, at the very moment when she was thinking how peacefully normal it all seemed, a scream echoed through the streets. It came from behind Dina and she spun backward to protect herself.

More screams and cat roars rang off the nearby walls and a surge of people rushed up the street from four blocks away.

Dina still didn't see right away what the problem was. More and more people rushed down the street all heading the same way. They shoved and pushed each other in their haste to get away from something coming from beyond the crowd.

Dina backed against the nearest wall and turned to the puma to ask what was going on, but the puma wasn't there anymore. She'd vanished.

Dina planned to stay where she was and wait for these people to pass her by, but when they got near her, so many people shoved and jostled in a hysterical frenzy that they knocked her away from the wall.

She floundered in the crowd and finally managed to jump into a doorway out of the main crush of bodies. The door was locked and she landed on the step where she stood six inches above the rest of the crowd.

Her heart stopped when she saw what they were trying to get away from. A solid tide of cats advanced down the street coming from three blocks away.

Dina had never seen this many cats, not even in the Prideland forces that went out to fight the Children.

The cats marched shoulder to shoulder and attacked any helper who got in their way. The cats formed a solid barricade of teeth and claws to stop any helper from getting behind them.

The helpers shrieked and ran. A few tried to get back to the cats, only to fall under the cats' attack.

The cats left a carpet of bodies behind them. More cats broke away from the ranks, streaked into nearby buildings, and drove all the helpers out into the streets.

Screams and roars drifted through the windows. Women ran to join the crowd carrying their children and babies in their arms.

The cats kept advancing and the crowd of fleeing helpers kept swelling as more and more people rushed outside to get away. The cats came within half a block of Dina's position. She couldn't stay here any longer.

She dove into the crowd and all the stampeding bodies swept her away with them. She didn't have to try to follow them. She didn't have a choice.

The crowd carried her to the next intersection. Dozens of people tried to dash away into the side streets only to run into more cats rampaging through the streets.

They pounced on helpers, tore bodies apart, and charged anyone who fell too far behind.

The helpers screamed in terror, turned back, and raced to rejoin the crowd. They squashed Dina under countless bodies. She couldn't move a muscle except to keep on running and pray to High Heaven she didn't fall under all these trampling feet.

Every intersection offered another scene of mayhem, destruction, and cats killing indiscriminately. They attacked helper children, ripped families apart, and invaded every building and house to drive out every helper they could find.

Dina tried to see past the people in front of her. The crowd poured through the streets heading westward. She could see the last buildings flanking the street on both sides. The crowd had almost made it to the road.

More crowds of thousands of helpers streamed from other streets. All those people converged into a massive throng. No one could go back inside the city with all those cats there.

The crowd picked up speed once they got onto the road. Those in front ran ahead and left more room for the helpers behind. Everyone kept on running and the space around Dina cleared.

She made it another mile before she saw more cats driving their helpers down from the north. The hostile cats didn't wait for the Senate's decision. The whole idea of evacuating peacefully went straight down the drain.

Dina tried to see anyone she knew in the crowd, but more and more people packed in behind her. The cats kept advancing in epic numbers. They all joined together in an unbreakable wall to stop anyone from going back to the city.

The first helpers made it as far as the village. The subsidiaries came out to meet them. Dina slowed to a walk. She made the mistake of thinking she was far enough away to avoid the cats if they decided to attack again.

Hundreds of people entered the village, but hundreds or even thousands more followed behind. They filled the village and overflowed it. There was nowhere left to go but the jungle.

Dina turned back one more time and stood up on her tiptoes trying to spot Tom in the crowd. Was he here somewhere or did he stay behind at the power station the way he said he would?

The instant she turned around, the Children launched out of the ditches on both sides of the road. Everyone was too concerned about getting away from the cats to see the Children in time.

The Children rushed the cats in record numbers. Dina couldn't figure out how the Children hid so many in such exposed ground.

The Children swarmed onto the road and locked in another murderous battle against the cats. The Children's attack drove the cats back and the rest of the helpers raced clear to the village.

They ran into another blockade of all the other people standing in the middle of the road. No one could go any further.

All the helpers stopped there and stared at countless Children coming out of nowhere. They seemed to spring from the very soil.

The turmoil of cats and Children battling to the death swayed across the countryside as far as Dina could see. The line of cats stretched all the way north and south from the city where the cats had driven their helpers out.

The Children attacked the whole line. Cats and Children tumbled over each other gnashing their teeth, snarling, and tearing.

The line undulated another mile backward and invaded the city streets. The cats couldn't break through to get near the helpers again.

The noise receded farther away and dozens of voices broke out in the crowd behind Dina.

"What are we going to do?" a woman whimpered. "We have to go back! We have to go back to the Pride!"

"We can't go back," a man exclaimed. "They drove us out. The cats don't want us anymore."

His voice cracked and a few people started crying.

"We have to go back!" another man argued. "We've given everything to the Pride. The cats must know we're loyal."

Dina turned around. All the faces near her wrenched in anguish. All these people had lost the one thing that gave their lives meaning.

"We can't stay here," Dina told those closest to her. "We need to go out to the cantons. We can take refuge there."

"We can't go to the cantons!" a different woman shrieked. "We'll all die there!"

"You won't die," Dina replied. "People have been living there for years—and living very comfortably."

"Forget it," a man snapped. "I'd rather die than go to the cantons."

She was just about to argue with him when the crowd parted. Darcy and Alexander Mathus worked their way through the crowd calling to everyone.

"Come into the village!" Alexander ordered. "We can give you food and blankets. We don't have enough room in all our houses for everyone. We'll take children and babies. The rest of you will have to camp out in the open until the Pride resolves this situation."

"How will the Pride resolve *this?*" another man asked and all eyes turned back to the battle.

"I don't know how the Pride will resolve it, but they will," Alexander snapped. "We can count on the cats to solve whatever the problem is. Now come into the village. You'll be safe here. The Children won't attack you here."

"The Children didn't attack us," one woman told him. "The cats attacked us."

"Never mind," Darcy interrupted. "We'll give you what we have to make you as comfortable as possible. That's all we can do right now."

She and Alexander turned back to lead everyone into the village. The helpers took a few more minutes to follow them, but eventually, all the displaced helpers migrated the rest of the way up the road.

People sat down on doorsteps and in the subsidiaries' yards. The village filled up in no time. Everyone had to sit on the open road just to find space for themselves.

The sound of children crying and more tense conversation bubbled from all directions. Subsidiaries of all ages went through the crowd handing out food and blankets, but Dina didn't see how the village could sustain this crowd.

Helpers surrounded the village in a mob of thousands. The cats had completely emptied the city. Now everyone was out here in the open.

Dina wound her way between them trying to get to the other end of the village. She wanted to take this opportunity to get out to the jungle.

She had to find the Children, but from what she could see, they were all battling the cats through the city streets. Maybe she should stay here.

She tried to avoid the Mathuses, but they either didn't recognize her pulverized face or they pretended not to. They were all too busy anyway.

She got as far as the circle in the middle of the village when she spotted Tom. He shot to his feet in the middle of the southbound road and waved to her. "Dina! Dina over here!"

They couldn't get near each other without stepping on a bunch of people. Everyone complained a lot, but she finally made her way over to him.

"What happened to you?!" Tom hissed. "You look awful!"

Dina snorted. "You should see the other guy."

"You need medical attention," he murmured.

"Forget that," she countered. "How can we check the transmitter if we're both out here?"

"We don't need to check the transmitter. We're here...and all these people are here. We're at the evacuation coordinates."

"But the Children aren't here. I still need to get word to them to bring their......" She stopped herself just in time.

"Their what?" he asked. "The Children are all over there. It won't be too hard to get word to them."

"You don't understand." She shut her eyes and held up her hands. "I can't explain right now, but we need to let them know as soon as possible—before the destroyers get here."

He frowned at her. "Why? What's so important?"

She hesitated to tell him, but then she threw caution to the wind. He would find out soon enough anyway.

She pulled him to the nearest house. It was full of helpers, too, so she drew him around the corner. She wouldn't be able to find a place that was totally private. She just had to bite the bullet and tell him.

"The Children are....having Children, Tom. They can reproduce. My daughter gave birth to four Children of her own and most of the female Children are pregnant. Your daughter is pregnant. It's only a matter of time before she gives birth. No one knows. The Children are reproductively viable. We need to get the pregnant females and their babies off the planet first—before the Pride finds out."

His eyes blazed and he glared down at her. "You're serious."

"I've seen the babies with my own eyes. I was there when my daughter gave birth. We have to get word out to the jungle now—tonight at the latest." Dina glanced over her shoulder toward the city. "I would go back into the city right now if I thought I could get some of the Children to listen to me. This is more important than anything."

He straightened up and shot a furious glare toward the city. "You can't go in there with the battle going on. Neither of us can. We'll just have to wait and hope the destroyers don't land before you tell someone."

"The destroyers might not land until they hear from us," she suggested. "We need someone at the power station to coordinate all of this."

"You leave that to me. You are NOT going back into the city—not now. Just sit tight. The Children have to come back this way to get to the jungle. We'll talk to them then."

She drew in a shaky breath. "All right. I just hate waiting."

"The Children can move a lot faster than you can," he pointed out. "Waiting here to tell them in person will be quicker than you walking out there on foot."

Chapter 56

Dina shifted her weight on the step of one of the village houses. She didn't even know whose house it was. It wasn't the Mathuses' or any of the other factors' houses that she and the landing team had stayed in during their first nightmarish visit here.

Tom sat next to her. Helpers surrounded them on all sides. None of them tried to talk to either Tom or Dina.

She didn't want to talk to anyone. She wanted to see the Children and no one else.

The hours of waiting racked her nerves. She couldn't keep this information to herself a second longer, but she still had to wait.

She glanced right toward the city, but the Children didn't come back. Were they still in there fighting the cats?

The view to the left didn't offer any hope, either. The wall of jungle blocked her from seeing any Children in that direction.

The sun was already going down. All these helpers would have to spend the night on the road.

Tom didn't tell her to stop squirming. He didn't squirm, but she did catch him keeping a sharp eye on the road in both directions.

The same carpet of helpers covered the road and spilled all around the village. No one had moved for hours. How much longer could this go on?

The subsidiaries kept migrating back and forth through the crowd, returning to their houses, and coming back out with food and other supplies.

Darcy, Alexander, and their younger children worked tirelessly to take care of all the displaced helpers, but Dina couldn't bring herself to feel anything but contempt for them.

They would be the first to kill her if they found out the part she'd played in their son's death. Dina never doubted that for a second.

None of them acknowledged her, not even when they walked by right in front of her.

Tom didn't remind her again how awful she looked. Her face weighed a ton and one of her eyelids drooped. It blocked her vision and she couldn't close her mouth properly, but she just had to put up with it.

The wounds on her arm and back hurt, too, but her agitation over the impending evacuation took her mind off her injuries. She'd be on an Armada destroyer in a few hours. She could worry about her recovery then.

Tom startled her out of her thoughts by murmuring in her ear. "Here they come."

Her head shot up and she followed his gaze toward the city. A giant throng of Children advanced up the road coming toward the village.

They walked upright with one man in front. Dina sprang to her feet, but all the other helpers slowed her down from meeting up with the Children.

A wave of terror went through the helpers at the Children's approach. The helpers scrambled to their feet, too, and they surged backward to get away from the Children who'd just saved all their lives.

Tom and Dina elbowed through the crowd. Plenty of people shoved and stepped on Dina, but she eventually burst through onto a bare patch of road between the helpers and the Children.

She raced up to Adrian, but he didn't stop walking. "Listen to me, Adrian!" she blurted out. "The Armada is coming in right now! They're sending destroyers to evacuate all of us! You have to get word out to the gorge camp to get all the pregnant wives and newborn babies up here into this stretch of farmland so we can evacuate them first! Do you understand? You need to send word out there now—tonight!"

He stopped in his tracks and scowled down at her. "How soon are they coming in?"

"We don't know," Tom interjected. "We have to get back to the transmitter and communicate with the destroyer captains to give them clearance to land. I was supposed to hear from them tomorrow to find out their ETA. They could be in orbit right now for all we know."

Adrian turned sideways and dipped a single nod at Leroy who stood behind Adrian's shoulder. Leroy, his brothers Devon and Franco, and three other Children from Moonlight canton shot forward, sprang onto their hands and feet, and bounded away toward the jungle. They vanished in a second.

Adrian turned back to Dina. That's when he noticed the helpers in turmoil behind her. They fell over themselves trying to retreat from the Children, but no one could move with so many people blocking the road.

Armed men moved to the front and pushed women and children behind them toward the houses. The armed helpers formed ranks across the road to confront the Children.

Adrian frowned. "What's wrong with them?"

"They're loyal helpers," Dina explained. "They probably think you're going to kill them."

"We just saved them from the cats," he countered. "Why would we kill them now?"

She waved that away. "They're out of their minds. They still want to help the Pride."

His hard eyes snapped to her face. "We can't keep them here. They would see our Children and try to attack them, too."

"Why don't we evacuate these people, too?" she suggested. "We don't have to leave them behind."

"I'm warning you. If one of them threatens our young, we'll kill every last one of them."

"Don't do that. Give them a chance."

He clenched his teeth. "Aren't you supposed to be going into the city to check the transmitter?"

"Don't do anything to these people, Adrian," she insisted. "They're victims of the Pride just like we are."

He snorted. "That is exactly what they aren't."

She would have argued the point, but he walked past her. She watched him and realized that he was heading for another throng of armed people coming out of the jungle.

All those people wore canton-style clothing and she recognized dozens of people in the mob. Troy Engle, Kubri James, Sonya Mathus, Fan Tiko, and hundreds of others advanced to join the Children.

They halted in front of Adrian and his voice drifted on the wind as he called orders to all of them. He pointed in different directions and assigned all the canton residents to defend different parts of the landscape.

"We better go while we have the chance," Tom murmured. "We can't do anything more out here tonight."

She tore herself away and summoned all her resolve to turn her back on the crowd. She would have rather stayed here, but she absolutely refused to let Tom go back into the city alone.

She'd seen this through to the end. This transmission would be the final act to end the war. She had to do this.

She picked up her pace and they left the village behind. Tom touched her elbow. "Let's cut over to the river. We can get closer to the power station that way."

She didn't argue. They struck out across the fields and made it to the river by sunrise.

She had to pull Tom behind the bushes. He wasn't used to this and his size made him harder to hide.

"We need to stay out of sight," she whispered. "The cats will be a lot harder to avoid than helper patrols."

"The cats aren't looking for us," he pointed out. "They're too busy fighting the Children."

"They aren't looking for *you*. They all know me—and my scent. If anything happens, you get to the transmitter and call in the destroyers. Tell the captains to come down and land even if they don't hear from us again. Tell them to be ready to defend the evacuees with guns blazing."

"Nothing is going to happen. I won't let it."

She made a face, but she didn't contradict. The closer they got to this evacuation, the more doubts crept into her head. What if something did happen? What if some other disaster snatched this chance from her at the last second?

"I don't see any cats," Tom remarked. "Let's get to the power station and get this done."

"Not seeing cats doesn't mean anything. We need to be careful."

"There's careful and there's just wasting time. What are we waiting for if the cats aren't here?"

She surveyed the riverbank ahead. She really wished now that she'd brought a weapon or three.

"All right," she decided. "Let's go—but be careful."

They snuck out of the bushes. Tom swerved onto the riverbank where no more shrubbery would slow him down.

Dina wanted to pull him back, but he was already sprinting up the riverbank getting closer to the power station.

She raced after him, but he turned out to be right. No cats came out to pounce on them.

He burst into the power station. It was completely empty. None of the Elite Battalion was here anymore.

He charged down the hall to the back room and pulled out the transmitter. "Turn on the power."

She shot the breaker. Power flooded the equipment and lit up all the readings.

He adjusted the wavelengths and flicked on the microphone. "This is Commander Tom Sharples transmitting from the planet Daustina to the Ebror Defense Outpost. Come in, Ebror."

He waited, but no one answered. He frowned at the transmitter, adjusted it a few more times, and tried again.

"Ebror Defense Outpost, this is Commander Tom Sharples of the Armada Destroyer Savannah transmitting from Daustina. Please acknowledge."

Nothing.

Dina held her breath listening for the voice that didn't come.

Tom attacked the transmitter again, made a few more adjustments, and his voice tensed when he leaned in a third time. "Ebror Defense Outpost, this is Commander Tom Sharples transmitting from the planet Daustina. Please acknowledge and advise on rescue destroyers' ETA for immediate evacuation. The population is waiting at the rendezvous point and we don't know if we'll be able to transmit again. Please relay a message to all destroyer captains to land and begin the evacuation without waiting for further clearance. Please inform all destroyer captains of the immediate need to defend the population from attack. I repeat, please inform all destroyer captains of the immediate need to defend the population from attack."

He let his finger off the button, slumped onto his stool, and stared in defeat at the unresponsive transmitter.

The voice cracked out of the transmitter and startled Tom and Dina into jumping out of their skins. "My apologies, Commander," Corporal McFarlane replied. "We've received your transmission and I'm relaying your information to the destroyer captains."

Tom attacked the transmitter. "Thank you, Corporal. Any word on the destroyers' ETA?"

"Stand by, Sir. I'll find out."

Tom shot Dina a sidelong glance. His eyes glittered with excitement. It was happening.

McFarlane came back on the line. "The first destroyers are entering orbit now, Sir. They should be with you shortly."

Tom burst out in excited laughter. "Thank you, Corporal."

"Sir, the destroyer captains are asking to be advised what class of weaponry the enemy is using. The captains want to prepare their troops to be ready to face the enemy."

Tom laughed harder, but he stopped himself when he reopened the channel from his end. "They're cats, Corporal. I think the Armada troops can handle it with the weapons they have."

McFarlane hesitated. "Sir? I don't understand."

"They're cats, Corporal—lions, tigers, panthers—that kind of thing. The population is unarmed. That's why we're in distress."

McFarlane cleared his throat. "Yes, Sir. I'll pass that on to the destroyer captains."

Tom leaned back on his stool laughing behind his hand. "I wish I could be there when the captains find out. The Armada has definitely never faced an enemy force like this before."

"We better get back out there," Dina replied. "The destroyer captains will want to meet Armada officers to organize the...."

A crash startled both of them into spinning around. Dina froze when she heard barrels toppling outside the power station.

Tom stood up and stormed down the hall toward the entrance. He walked right out onto the weir into a crowd of cats pouring through the door.

Three tigers swiveled to face him and he rushed them. "Get out of the building, Dina!" he roared over his shoulder.

"Tom!!" she yelled, but it was too late.

He lunged for the nearest two tigers. One of them reared onto its hind feet to confront him, bared its teeth, and roared back at him.

Dina stood rooted to the spot watching Tom close with the tiger. He slammed into it and strapped his arms around the cat's chest.

He might have been able to fight a cat that big when the landing team left the *Savannah*. Tom had lost a lot of his strength since coming to this planet and the cat took him down easily.

They both toppled onto the pavement and all the other cats surrounded him. "TOM!!" Dina screamed and rushed forward to try to help him, but she only had her bare hands to fight these cats.

"Get out, Dina!!" he bellowed. "Get over the weir!"

She glanced toward the weir. The spillway flowed under the far wall to join up with the river outside. More cats crowded through the door to get inside the power station. They would take her down, too, if she stayed here a second longer.

She saw in an instant why Tom attacked the cats the way he did. All the cats went after him instead of coming after her. The commotion left one clear path between the hall and the weir.

"GO, DINA!!" he thundered. "GET MY CHILDREN OFF THIS PLANET!!"

Those words shocked her out of her trance. Some of the pumas and panthers were already losing interest in Tom's fight against the tiger. The cats turned toward her instead.

She rocketed to the weir and didn't hesitate an instant. She plunged headfirst into the water and kicked out for spillway.

She bobbed up for air right next to the wall and caught one glimpse of Tom going down under a pile of cats. Three pumas and a panther stood on the weir looking down at her.

She swallowed every emotion she ever had about Tom Sharples, dove underwater, and plunged under the wall. The current caught her and spat her out into the river.

She came up thirty feet from the building. Sunshine flooded the shadowy landscape. The cats who'd been patrolling the street dashed uphill toward the power station.

The screech, roar, and crash of fighting came from inside the building. Tom was still in there with fifty cats or maybe more. He would never leave the power station now.

She paddled another hundred yards downriver. The current carried her away, but it also took her farther away from the Children. If she stayed in the river, it would take her all the way to the jungle.

She swam with the current until she decided she'd gone far enough. Then she stroked for shore, hauled herself onto the bank, and clambered up into outlying city streets.

She didn't see any cats this far from the city, but she couldn't take that chance. She set off southward at a jog trying to get back to the road.

She made it another mile before a boom resounded through the atmosphere. She looked up to see the big, rounded sides of an Armada destroyer descending through the clouds.

She took a deep breath and took off running as fast as she could. She had to get back to the village to help the Children evacuate.

She swerved around a corner and ran into another blockade of cats coming up the street toward her. They were coming from the west. They must have come from the road, too, which meant these were the cats who'd been fighting against the Children.

She skidded backward and bolted deeper into the city only to run into another bunch of cats closing from the north. Blood stained their jaws. Were these the cats that just killed Tom?

They broke into a run to bring her down. She staggered away and almost tripped over a tiger coming up behind her. She screamed once and dodged out of the way before she recognized Renfroe.

He plunged past her. "Go, Dina! Get out of the city!"

She spun around to see what he was doing....and changed her mind when she saw all those cats closing in.

He planted himself in the middle of the street to stop them from getting near her. Another tiger lunged for him.

They both yowled in fury and collided. Dina couldn't watch this. She couldn't stand by and let all these people she cared about go down to protect her.

She whirled away and took off as fast as she could. Cats streaked past Renfroe and the other tiger. The cats didn't pay any attention to Renfroe's sacrifice.

She couldn't squander the chance he'd given her. She bolted through the streets dodging from one intersection to another. She raced through the neighborhoods and finally stumbled onto the road.

She screamed again when Renfroe plunged out from behind a house, bowled three panthers aside before they pounced on her, and got into another fight of clashing teeth and claws while she made her last sprint for the village.

Chapter 57

Dina burst out of the city and skidded to a halt. The ranks of cats stood between her and the village. She couldn't get through by the road.

An equally massive army of Children and people confronted the cats on the village side. Only Dina stood behind the cats where the city ended.

The destroyer descended to the fields behind the village, but no one on the ground saw it. They didn't see three more destroyers sinking through the clouds at the same time.

The helpers packed the village and didn't leave it. Armed jungle people from the cantons stood shoulder to shoulder with the Children's.

The sound of cats fighting each other made Dina glance behind her again. A mob of them surrounded Renfroe. He whirled from one side to the other slashing everywhere with his fangs.

Some of those cats tried to dive past him to get to Dina, but he attacked them and drove them back to keep them away from her. She had to keep going as long as he gave her cover.

She had nowhere left to go. Cats flooded the landscape as far as the eye could see. She couldn't see the end of them, but the Children's force was even bigger.

She caught one glimpse of Adrian at the very center of the Children's ranks. He narrowed his eyes at the cats, bared his fangs, let out a thunderous roar, and the whole line charged.

The cats plunged forward at the same time and Dina sprinted away to the south. She couldn't think of anything except to get around the battle before it swept backward and caught up with her.

She blundered into the fields. The rough ground made her stagger again. Her legs and chest hurt from running so much, but she didn't dare to stop.

The noise of battle stabbed into her brain. Cats and Children screeched, roared, slashed, and slaughtered each other by the hundreds. People raced through the mayhem attacking cats and getting attacked by them in turn.

Four of the cats who'd been chasing Dina through the streets overtook her. A leopard rocketed through the air from the side and landed on her shoulders, only to get tackled by a small, yellow Child no taller than her chin.

He slammed the leopard to the ground and they rolled away toward the city. The battle swept past her and the combatants surrounded her on all sides.

Another puma lunged for her out of nowhere. She spun toward it to meet the attack, but at that moment, Renfroe catapulted from her other side, caught the puma in midair, and brought it to the ground.

He crunched his jaws on the back of the puma's neck and sprang off. He landed in front of Dina, whipped backward, and faced outward toward the battle. "Get behind me, Dina! Get to safety!"

She didn't have time to move before Adrian collided with Renfroe from the side, attacked Renfroe in fury, and they somersaulted away from her.

Adrian kicked out with his feet, slammed Renfroe in the chest, and sent him rolling farther away while Adrian sprang into a crouch to confront him. "Get back with the other evacuees, Dina!" he ordered.

Renfroe gave a vicious snarl and spun around to confront him. "You attack me?! I was trying to protect her, you fool!"

Adrian bared his teeth at Renfroe. "I told you to keep away from her. Come near her again and I'll kill you."

Renfroe flattened his ears and hissed, but the battle surged at that moment. A confused jumble of cats, Children, and helpers flooded between them. Renfroe had to back away.

Adrian backed up, too, and barked one more time, "Get the evacuees to the ship, Dina! Get everyone on board! We'll cover you!"

She tried to see Renfroe in the mayhem, but she couldn't distinguish him from every other tiger on the field.

She turned away one last time, but she had to stumble around for a few minutes before she oriented herself well enough to get out of the battle line.

Adrian kept backing up and shredding anyone who came near her. She spotted the village ahead and picked up her pace.

She broke through the edge of the chaos. The village lay ahead of her with all the helpers still staring at the battle in shocked horror.

Beyond the village, another massive assembly of Children advanced across the fields heading for the ship. Dina recognized Iona, Naia, Nova, Egypt, and all the other mothers who'd retreated to the gorge camp to avoid this war.

Iona carried a leather bag over one shoulder. She clutched it against her body to protect it with her arms. More new mothers carrying their newborn Children in similar pouches.

Dina broke into a run, but before she could get out of the battle line, another surge of noise made her look back over her shoulder.

More people rushed into the mayhem from the north. They all wore canton-style clothes, too, and Tania led the charge swinging her spiked flails at the Children.

They had to break off fighting the cats to confront the flanking assault, but before the Children had a chance to defend themselves, dozens of cats burst out of the battle and attacked Tania's people instead.

Tania's people joined the fight on the cats' side, but the cats turned on these people with even more vicious fury than the cats attacked their own helpers. Dozens of people fell in the first wave of assault.

The Black raced out of the mayhem and Kaiser tackled Tania to the ground. Kenji and Karim dove between them to stop any cats from coming near her.

She exploded in a frenzy, kicked and thrashed to break Kaiser's grip, and struggled her hardest to get away from him. "Get off me!!" she shrieked. "Get your hands off me!!"

He snatched her off the ground, strapped his arms around her body so she couldn't hit him, and wrestled her off the field toward the village. Cats dove to intervene, but Kenji and Karim drove them back.

The two brothers guarded Kaiser as he hauled his mother toward the village even as she fought to get away from him. "Get away from me!!" she bellowed. "Don't touch me!!"

He ignored her and physically carried her toward the ship.

More Children withdrew from the battle, retreated as far as the village, and swiveled to guard the mothers. The cats launched assault after assault, but they couldn't break the Children's line.

Dina raced behind them and rushed Iona just as Armada troops advanced from the first ship's hold. The other two ships were just setting down.

"Get on board the ship!" Dina herded them backward toward the ship's hold. "All of you get on board! Hurry!"

Iona and the other mothers glanced behind them. "We can't go over there with those armed soldiers in the way," Iona countered.

"Follow me!" Dina yelled. "Come on! It will be all right!"

She ran toward the soldiers. They shouldered their weapons and she raised her arms above her head.

"I'm Lieutenant Dyer of the Armada Destroyer *Savannah!*" she bellowed. "I'm the one who called you to evacuate these people! I'm organizing this evacuation! These women and their Children are boarding your vessel! I'm Lieutenant Dyer! I'm an Armada officer and these are the people you came here to evacuate!" She spotted the lieutenant in charge of the troops. "These women are boarding your ship! They need to evacuate immediately!"

He nodded. "Yes, Ma'am. Go ahead. Get your people on board."

Dina waved to Iona and the other mothers. "Come on! Get on board! Everybody get on board! Come on, Iona! Show the others the way! Go straight up that ramp! It's all right!"

The mothers still hesitated until the troops passed them on the way to the battlefield. Iona finally set off for the ramp and Dina waved the other mothers forward.

The mothers passed her and she found herself pushing them to make them go faster. More and more Children streamed out of the jungle and crossed the fields to converge on the landing destroyers.

Kaiser burst out of the mayhem dragging Tania kicking and screaming toward the ship. She kept trying to yank herself out of his arms yelling, "Leave me alone! Let me go!"

His brothers flanked him. They never left him unguarded for a second.

The troops marched across the fields closing on the battle. They didn't understand who everyone was, so the lieutenant and his men waved the displaced helpers and subsidiaries toward the destroyers, too.

"Everybody get on board!" the lieutenant ordered. "Everybody move! Get on board the ship!"

The helpers and subsidiaries squirmed and then obeyed him. They streamed across the fields and joined the throng of Children already climbing the ramp.

More and more people disappeared inside. The troops moved out onto the battlefield where a hundred Children still grappled with cats all over the place.

The Children separated from the battle one after another, cuffed the cats away, and retreated behind the troops.

Adrian stayed there until the very end. He blasted from one cat to another tearing them apart, breaking bones, ripping out throats, and sending them running for the city.

He didn't stop until he came to a huge lion who spun around to confront him. It was Kojo Hellion.

Adrian charged him and they both went flying. A few other nearby cats paused in their battles against the Children to see if Kojo needed help.

He did. Adrian slammed him down on the ground and used his arms to wrestle Kojo onto his back.

More cats stopped what they were doing and the troops moved into position with the last Children behind them.

Adrian didn't notice. He lunged for Kojo's throat, but Kojo's strength saved him at the last minute.

He twisted onto his other side and kicked out to hook Adrian. Adrian dodged in the nick of time, dove over Kojo's body, and tried one more time to force Kojo onto his back.

Kojo overcompensated by contorting onto his stomach, but that must have been what Adrian wanted him to do all along.

Kojo landed on his back and hunched low to protect his throat and underside. Adrian pounced on him, slammed Kojo's face into the dirt, pushed Kojo's mane aside, and crunched his jaws on the back of Kojo's neck.

Dina couldn't hear the crack from this distance, but that one bite sent a shockwave through the cats. They all stopped fighting, and when the troops kept moving forward, the cats backed away toward the city.

Adrian remained standing alone in the middle of the battlefield. He didn't see all the armed troops behind him.

Dina's last glimpse of Prideland was of thousands of cats perched on walls, windowsills, and rooftops all over the city. They all looked down at Adrian standing defiant and protecting everyone while they evacuated the planet.

He threw back his head and roared at the cats. He didn't need the troops to win this battle or the war. He'd won a long time ago.

The troops drew level with him and he finally turned away, dropped onto his hands, and bounded across the fields to catch up with the crowd.

Iona appeared at Dina's elbow and tugged her sleeve. "Come on, Dina," Iona murmured. "Come on board."

She pulled Dina backward. Dina had to turn around to climb the ramp.

As soon as she got inside, so many Children and people packed the ship's hold that she lost sight of the city, the cats, and everything else.

Bodies crushed against her. Adrian fought his way over to her and Iona. The Black, the Manx brothers, the Pygmies, and the Auroras surrounded them and then the whole ship boomed as the ramp slammed shut with all of them inside.

People screamed and fell against each other as the destroyer rocketed into orbit. The vibration of engine noise shook the hull and everyone held onto each other for support.

The noise didn't stop. It kept going on and on and on as the ship kept climbing.....and then dead silence descended over the hold when the ship left the atmosphere and started floating through space.

Dina glanced around. Everyone was here—except for the people who weren't. Tom was gone....and so were a lot of other people who should have survived to start a new life somewhere else.

Tania stood against the opposite wall with a bunch of her people from Northfall canton. She didn't come near her sons even after they saved her life.

Karim put his arm around Iona's shoulders and touched the bag still locked in her arms. "Is everyone all right?"

She opened the pouch, looked inside, and a beautiful smile spread across her lips. "Everyone is fine." Her head fell on his shoulder and she shut her eyes with a deep sigh of relief. "It's over. We're free."

The End.

Sign Up Once--Get all Theo Mann's free books including brand new releases

Sign Up Once--Get all Theo Mann's free books including brand new releases

Humanity on the brink of annihilation.

A mysterious package, a corrupt officer, and a conspiracy that goes all the way to the top? What could possibly go wrong?

When a routine mission goes horribly wrong, Warrant Officer Ewing Archer and a handful of faithful friends get trapped in a battle to save the last survivors of Earth.

The human race has abandoned the ecological disaster of Earth. Now all that remains is a network of interconnected ships, stations, and satellites surrounding the planet.

But when war breaks out, Archer becomes a firebrand that could destroy it all....or save it.

Sign up at www.theomann.com to read it for free

About Theo Mann

I write 70 books per year—and yes, before you ask, all these books are my original creative work. Nothing written under my name is AI-generated or ghostwritten because I write better than AI and any ghostwriter out there.

People don't read fiction for entertainment or to escape from reality. People read fiction to see their humanity reflected in another person's character and story.

This is my promise to you. When you read my books, you'll see your own humanity reflected in the characters and stories. I take this commitment to my readers very seriously. My books are an intimate form of communication between us. I would never disrespect my readers by turning that over to a machine or another writer. This is my bond between me and you as my reader.

I write 20,000 words per day as my daily work output. If anyone with a public platform would like to challenge me to prove this in a controlled environment, feel free to contact me on this website's contact page.

I worked as a professional ghostwriter for fifteen years. Now I'm on a mission to set a Guinness World Record by writing 700 books over the next ten years and 1400 books over the next twenty years, all originally written by me. See my website for the full book list.

I'm also the author of *Proof for the Existence of God* and the *Crimes Against Fiction* blog. You can find all my nonfiction work at www.crimes-against-fiction.com.

If you have a story idea, or if you would like me to explore a series in more depth, or if you'd like me to explore a character by writing a spinoff series about that character or world, leave me a message on my website's contact page. I answer all reader emails, so ask me anything, tell me what you liked and didn't like, and let me know where you'd like your favorite series to go. I would love to hear your ideas and find out what you'd like to read next.

Find out more at www.theomann.com.

Also by Theo Mann (so far)

www.ingramcontent.com/pod-product-compliance
Lightning Source LLC
Chambersburg PA
CBHW070207310726
48976CB00001B/248